THE SENSATION OF HIS LIPS
WAS EXQUISITE . . .

. . . It awakened such tingling and heated
sensitivity that Lettie's lips parted in surprise. He
took instant advantage, deepening his exploration.
He spread his hand at her waist, drawing her closer
against him so that she was molded to his long
length. He blazed a trail of kisses along the curve of
her cheek to the turn of her jaw. His warm breath
wafted over the gentle curves of her breasts pushed
up by her corset before he pressed his lips to the
valley between them.

She was lost in the fascination of the sensations he
aroused. Joined together, male and female, they
moved in passionate wonder to the ageless and wild
rhythm. It transformed them for a single bright and
blinding moment, fusing their spirits for that brief
time, giving them ineffable grandeur . . .

Southern Rapture

Jennifer Blake

FAWCETT COLUMBINE • NEW YORK

Southern Rapture

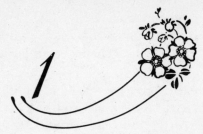

*T*he baying of the bloodhounds on a warm trail was faint at first. It grew louder as the dogs neared the house, becoming a deep and clamorous howling with an undertone of such doleful menace that it chilled the blood. Mingled with it was the thin ring of shouts and the pounding of hoofbeats.

Letitia Margaret Mason looked up from the letter she was writing as her attention was caught by the sounds. An expression of amazement followed by disgust and distress rose in her wine-brown eyes. No doubt the dogs were being followed by men in white sheets, men intent on riding down some poor black man running pell-mell and terror-stricken through the warm summer night. She had been told that Louisiana was a place of violence and danger just now, while it was undergoing the chastening process of reconstruction. She had not expected to have evidence of it the first evening of her arrival.

She had also been warned that the state was no place for a woman traveling alone, particularly a Northern woman. She might well be subjected to insult and ostracism, it was said, if not worse. The protective attitude of Southern gentlemen toward ladies might not extend to females from above the Mason-Dixon line, certainly not to those who were headstrong and argumentative.

Her elder sister, and especially her sister's husband, had been astonished, even aghast, at Letitia's need to journey to the South. They had considered it madness enough when she had insisted on getting a teacher's certificate after the war, since there was no financial need for it. This new start of hers was beyond anything. It was her mother who had supported her. "Leave Lettie alone," she had told them. "She's only doing what she must."

Lettie had begun to think the tales and warnings greatly exaggerated. She had received nothing but courtesy and kindness during the long trip by train and stage here to Natchitoches. Inquiring about accommodations of the stationmaster on her arrival, she had been told about the large, square-columned, two-storied house called Splendora that was three miles out of town, where she was now settled. The man had even commandeered a seat in a wagon for her from a farmer going in that direction.

It seemed that only that morning the lady of the house, Mrs. Emily Tyler, had decided to take in a boarder. The older woman, who was plump and kindly, with graying hair and snapping blue eyes, had accepted Lettie at once. She had been so afraid, she had declared, that she would have to give houseroom to a swearing, tobacco-spitting carpetbagger! Lettie must tell her if anything was wrong— she had never been a landlady before. But she had decided that money must be obtained somehow or the house that had been in disrepair since halfway through the War for Southern Independence was just going to fall down around their ears, those of herself and her nephew. She did hope that Lettie liked her front bedchamber. She must make herself at home, use the veranda and hall sitting room as she liked, and if she needed anything or if there was anything lacking for her comfort, she must not hesitate to say so.

So warm had been Aunt Em's welcome, so natural her chatter, that within five minutes Lettie had been made to feel that she was an invited guest, "company," instead of a boarder. The older woman had insisted on being called

Aunt Em, since she was known that way to one and all, and Letitia had quickly become Lettie. Though used to more formality on first acquaintance, Lettie hadn't had the heart to repulse so friendly an overture. She had been pleasantly relaxed in her new surroundings, until she heard the hounds.

The sound of the bloodhounds came closer. They seemed to be on the road that ran before the house. The need to see what was happening brought Lettie to her feet. She glanced down at herself. She had already dressed for bed in a nightgown of pink cotton flannel and had taken down her hair so that it fell in a mass of golden-brown waves down her back. The nightgown, with a high neck and long sleeves, was heavy for the climate, so heavy and warm that Lettie had not been able to bear the thought of putting on her dressing gown. Still, as totally covered as she was, the risk of being seen in her present state of dishabille was not one she cared to take; her Puritan ancestors would rise up as a body from their graves to condemn such wanton disregard for decency. The problem was easily solved, however. Leaning toward the lamp on the table at which she had been sitting, she cupped her hand at the top of the chimney and blew out the flame.

Lettie moved swiftly toward the open window. It was a jib window that gave onto the long veranda that fronted the upper floor of the house. By unlatching and opening the small jib doors that formed the sill, then pushing the sash up as far as it would go, one could step through the opening as if it were a door. Brushing aside the muslin curtains, Lettie ventured out onto the dark canvas matting that covered the floor. The darkness of the night was a good cover for her. She moved to the railing and leaned over it.

There was an excellent view across the picket-fence-enclosed front yard of Splendora to the road stretching in either direction. The dogs had already passed the house and could just be seen—long, lean shapes in the darkness—loping away down the road to the left. Almost directly in front of the house was the troop of horsemen, two of them carrying pine-pitch torches that flared with the wind of their passage, the sparks flying back over their shoulders. In that orange glow could be seen, not the white of bed sheets, but the dark blue of uniforms. The men following the dogs were soldiers of the Union army, the occupation troops of the area. They thundered by with their faces forward, intent on their quarry, though there was no sign of who that might be.

Lettie stared in perplexity after the soldiers. After all the things that had been said before and during the war about the cruelty of hunting down human beings with bloodhounds, after the way it had been condemned in the papers, after the speeches against it at abolitionist meetings where the Southerners who practiced it were categorized as monsters, it seemed impossible that bloodhounds would be used for any such purpose by Union troops. It seemed unlikely that their quarry was of the black race. If he was white, however, the use of the dogs must be deliberate, a taste of their own medicine for the people of the area, or else there was hypocrisy involved. Both explanations were equally disturbing.

The noise of the pursuit died away. Silence returned, a silence with an undertone of the whirring of peeper frogs, crickets, and katydids. The night was balmy, with a soft, silken feel to the air. The moon had not yet risen. The stars shone bright, so close they looked as if she could gather a handful in a single sweeping grasp. The shadows under the trees were dense, gently moving in the breeze that meandered here and there. The night wind wafted across the veranda, and on its breath came, now faint, now strong, the rich lemony smell of the magnolias that starred the great dark-leaved tree on her left, just beyond the veranda.

By degrees, Lettie relaxed once more, lulled by the warmth and fragrance and caressing softness of the air. The soldiers forgotten, she stared around her at the Southern night, feeling it about her like an enveloping and seductive aura. It was entrancing, enticing, with a promise of hidden joys tinged with danger. Lettie felt the rise inside her, totally unbidden, of a slow, sweet yearning.

It was not a sensation she could acknowledge with comfort. Turning sharply, she moved back inside her bedchamber. She closed the small jib doors and straightened the muslin curtains, though she left the window open for air. She hesitated for a moment, thinking of her unfinished letter to her mother. It would wait until morning; her brain was too drugged with weariness and unaccustomed nighttime warmth to concentrate. She turned toward the bulking shadow of the tester bed, which was turned down for her comfort.

There came the scrape of a footstep outside on the veranda. It was a quiet sound, not furtive but not quite forthright. Lettie turned with quick alarm racing along her veins. A man's shadow loomed at the window, a black shape against the pale glow of starlight. In a single swift movement, he put his leg over the sill of the open window, batted aside the curtain, and eased into the room.

Lettie drew in her breath with a strangled sound. In an instant, the man was upon her, clamping his hand on her mouth and catching her against him in a grip so tight that she felt her ribs bend. There was a flash of fiery pain where her hipbone struck the holstered gun at his belt, then she was pressed to him, molded against his hard length.

Shock and surprise and something more vibrated between them. The man felt the slender, yet well-rounded form in his arms, smelled the warm female scent of her—both things he had not experienced in some time. His first thought was for who she might be; his second and most virulent was for what in the name of living hell she was doing there in that room, at that hour.

"Keep quiet," he said, his voice a whisper that had a rough edge to it, yet was soft in its menace. "Don't make a sound, and I'll let you go."

Lettie, her throat aching with her trapped scream and her heart a pulsing knot in her chest, managed to nod. By slow degrees the pressure on her mouth lessened. She forced herself to remain still, though she was aware with every particle of her being of her breasts pressing against the intruder's hard chest and her thighs brushing the muscled lengths of his legs, of the vital strength and height of him. She was a woman of average size, even perhaps a little taller than average, and yet she felt overwhelmed in a way she had never known before by the sheer force of will she sensed in the man who held her.

It affected her like the scrape of a fingernail on a slate. The instant she felt his hold relax, the moment his hand left her lips, she twisted from him with a cry of outrage bursting from her.

She was whirled back against his hard body. He captured her mouth with his, stifling her outcry. She struggled, writhing, pushing at him, trying to turn her head away. His grasp was firm, inescapable. He brought his hand up and tangled his fingers in the thick silk of her long hair, holding her head immobile as he plundered the sweetness of her lips. His kiss was burning, implacable, and yet seemed to hold a trace of reluctant curiosity. The hard pressure grew less. She felt the brush of a mustache as his lips, warm and smooth and sure, moved on hers, soothing, savoring. He tasted the full, gently molded curves, awakening their sensitivity, testing the smooth, resilient surface of them, from one delicate corner to the other.

Lettie's movement slowed, then stilled. She felt disoriented, light-headed with the sudden leap of sensation along her veins. There crept in upon her a strange, primeval languor that seemed to promise an answer to her earlier yearning. She swayed, wanting, needing to move closer to the man who held her, though she fought the urge, tried to repress it. Desire and revulsion warred inside her, beating up into her brain until she shuddered with reaction, trembling uncontrollably.

The man released her with a quiet imprecation. There was a moment when the only sound was their breathing. Abruptly, he caught her arm and pulled her toward the table that had served as her writing desk, pressing her down into the chair beside it. Before she could gather herself to protest or even to make a sound, he had removed some kind of scarf from his neck and was tying it over her mouth. She reached up to catch his arms, half rising. He grasped her wrists, pulled them down behind her as he forced her back into the chair, then fastened them to its back with lengths of grass rope that he took from his pockets. A moment more and he was kneeling in front of her to wrap the twisted rope about her ankles and tie them to the front rung of the chair.

Lettie tried to speak, to call him a dog, a sneak thief, an unprincipled ruffian. The words were muffled, though the intent was in her voice.

The man laughed, a low sound of real mirth that sent a strange quiver along her nerves. He rose to lean over her. Though she drew back as far as she could, he brushed a swift kiss across her forehead while one hand rested in a feather-light caress on her breast. Lettie stiffened with a sound of protest. He gave another soft chuckle, then straightened, backing away. His footsteps whispered on the Turkey carpet, there was a flickering shadow at the window, and then he was gone.

For an instant Lettie went limp with relief, then pure rage stirred inside her, rising in a rush to her head. She felt hot all over, and tears sprang into her eyes. The nerve of the man, the sheer, unadulterated gall! She had never been treated in such a way in her life. Never! How dare he mock her as well as attack her and truss her up like a sheep ready for slaughter. Who was he? Who *was* he?

So great was her fury that it took little effort to rock her chair against the table so that it butted the wall, then tip it forward again and again to make a regular thudding noise.

Everyone was sound asleep. No one was going to come. She was going to have to sit in this chair until morning, or later if no one thought to look for her when she failed to appear for breakfast. The ropes chafed her skin, rubbing it raw as she moved, but they were securely knotted. There was little hope of freeing herself without help.

A faint light shone into the room, coming from the crack under her bedchamber door. The glimmering brightness grew and there came the shuffling sound of footsteps. A soft knock sounded on the door. "Lettie? Are you all right?"

Lettie banged the table harder, making indignant noises around her gag. The door opened and Aunt Em put her head around it.

"Good gracious!" she exclaimed, her eyes widening. "Oh, my stars!"

She bustled into the room with her dressing gown of limp batiste flapping around her, the faded ribbons of her nightcap fluttering and the gray braids of her hair swinging on either side of her face. She set the oil lamp she carried down on the table, then began to work with energy to unknot the scarf around Lettie's mouth.

"What happened, child? Who did this to you? I just can't believe it. That such a thing could take place in this house with me not two doors away makes me so mad I could spit."

The gag fell away. Lettie answered the older woman as best she could while Aunt Em worked at the knots that held her hands.

"Came through the window? Well, I never! You must have been scared half out of your wits. Oh, dear, I may have to get a knife—no, it's a slip knot. Right thoughtful of him." Lettie's hands were freed. Aunt Em moved around in front of her and plumped down on her knees to untie Lettie's feet.

"That's not the word I would use," Lettie said with some asperity. "The man was vile, utterly base. He meant to rob you, I'm sure."

"He wouldn't have got much. But whatever he intended, you seem to have changed his mind, and for that I'm grateful." The older woman loosened the last rope and looked up, her mouth opened to speak. She made no sound, however, but sat gaping as she stared at the front of Lettie's pink nightgown.

Lettie, rubbing her chafed wrists, looked down. There was an object clinging to the cotton flannel just over the soft and rounded peak of her right breast. Fragile-looking, a light tan-gold in color, it appeared to be the empty shell of some insect. It clung by its desiccated claws, which were still intact. It was quite whole except for the split down its back where the insect had emerged. Thrust into that split so that it came out the bottom was a tiny tapering spike that was polished to a shining black.

"What is it?" she asked as she detached the shell, turning it this way and that in the lamplight.

"A locust shell and a thorn."

The blood drained from Lettie's face. She dropped the

shell to the table as if it had been a scorpion. A locust and a thorn, left attached to her where the man who had entered the room had touched her last. They were symbols of the man known simply as the Thorn, the vicious murderer who had killed her brother, the man she had come South to find.

The name rose unbidden to her lips, a soft whisper.

"It must have been him the hounds were after," Aunt Em said in agreement.

"Yes." Somehow, Lettie had not connected the man with the pursuit by the Union troops and their bloodhounds. It seemed obvious now. He had given his pursuers the slip by some trick and doubled back, looking for a place to hide. He must have thought he had found it until he discovered her. She had been close, so close to him. He had held her, kissed her. She raised the back of her hand to her lips, wiping them in sudden disgust.

"He might have killed me," she said in strained tones, "or—or worse."

"Oh, no, my dear! Never think such a thing!"

"But I've heard such stories!"

Aunt Em shook her head. "I don't know what you've heard, or where such things get started for that matter, but the Thorn has done as much good as harm around here. I can't believe he would hurt a woman."

"You can't know that," Lettie protested. "The soldiers were after him. That must mean something."

"Humph. Probably means their officers needed something to keep them busy."

A quiet knock fell on the bedchamber door that Aunt Em had left standing ajar as she entered. Two people appeared in the opening, a man and a young boy. Lettie, her nerves still disordered, looked up quickly as the man spoke.

"What is it, Aunt Em? What's wrong?"

The older woman swung around. She caught hold of the table and pulled herself upright, puffing a little. Instead of answering the question put to her, she said, "Ranny, what are you doing up? This is no place for you. Run along now, there's a good boy."

The man stepped into the room. He was tall and broad and so very handsome, in the fashion of the sword-wielding archangels depicted by the old masters in their religious paintings, that he was beautiful. He was perhaps in his late twenties or early thirties; his forehead was broad and his golden-brown brows straight and thick above heavily lashed blue eyes. His nose was strong and straight, and in one cheek was a slight hollow that looked as if it might crease into a dimple when he smiled. His jaw was square and his chin firm, and his mouth had the chiseled molding and wide curves that spoke of strength and of strong desires held in sure control. His hair was soft and blond, shining with sun streaks, and combed back from his face in soft waves that at his left temple almost covered his single blemish, the jagged mark of an old scar that was silvery-gray against the bronze of his skin. The clothes he wore were old and faded: a pair of butternut gray pants and a soft blue chambray shirt with the sleeves rolled to the elbows.

Lettie got to her feet and moved in haste to where her dressing gown lay across the foot of the bed. As she leaned to pick it up, she was acutely aware of the way the heavy material of her nightgown swayed against her, outlining her waist and hip. Grasping the dressing gown to her chest, she swung around with it in front of her as a covering. She held her chin high, but there was the heat of a flush across her cheekbones and an odd trembling in her hands that could only be reaction from the incident just past.

"I heard a noise," the man called Ranny said to Aunt Em before repeating his first question. "What's wrong?"

"This lady had a fright, a visit from the Thorn if you must know."

Ranny looked at Lettie. "The Thorn? But why?"

"No reason," Aunt Em said, "just a mistake."

"People say he's a bad man. Did he hurt you?" Ranny's candid gaze was still on Lettie's face.

"No, not exactly," she answered, lowering her lashes, looking away.

"Your arms are red."

"It will go away soon. I'm fine."

"I'm glad." The blond man turned to his aunt. "Who is she?"

Aunt Em made a sharp sound with her tongue. "This is Miss Lettie Mason, Ranny. Lettie, my nephew, Ransom Tyler."

The man inclined his head, surveying Lettie once more. To his aunt he said, "Why is she here?"

"Really, your manners, Ranny! She's staying with us, our first boarder. You will meet her at breakfast, but just now she doesn't want to see you or anyone else. Go back to bed." Aunt Em's words, for all their astringency, had a coaxing undertone.

"Yes, ma'am. She's a pretty lady."

Aunt Em looked beyond her nephew to the young Negro boy who was his companion. "Lionel, please?"

The boy, perhaps twelve years old, with tightly curled black hair and huge brown eyes in a triangular face, stepped forward. He moved to the side of the handsome man and reached to catch his square, well-formed hand, holding it in his two smaller ones. "Come on, Mast' Ranny."

Ransom paid no attention. He stared at the young woman in front of him, inspecting the shimmering mass of her hair; the creamy perfection of her skin; the regularity of her features in the oval of her face; the rich, almost pagan, brown of her eyes with their sherry-wine tint around the pupils. Her form, even hidden by her enveloping night-gown, was magnificent, the slim proportions perfect. Her every movment held grace and confidence.

There was only one flaw. She lacked warmth. Her mouth, though beautifully formed, was pinched at the corners like that of a confirmed spinster, and her expression held reserve overlaid with suspicion. And yet there was in the depths of her dark eyes a hint of banked fires, almost, but not quite, smothered. She was, in fact, altogether intriguing. It was a good thing he had kissed her before he had seen her, otherwise he might not have dared.

Lionel tugged at his hand. "Mast' Ranny, come on, you making the lady blush."

Ranny looked down at the boy. He smiled. "I mustn't do that, must I?" He permitted himself to be led away. He paused at the door. "Good night," he said.

Without waiting for an answer, the two of them, the blond man and the black boy, stepped into the dark hallway of Splendora and moved out of sight, their footsteps slowly receding.

"Oh, dear," Aunt Em said, "I'm so sorry. I should have told you about Ranny, but I never expected— I thought there would be plenty of time to explain in the morning. He had one of his headaches this evening. He doesn't see company, doesn't do much of anything except lie in a dark room until they are over."

"When you mentioned a nephew earlier, I somehow expected a small boy." Lettie made a valiant attempt to gather her self-possession enough to clarify the matter.

Aunt Em sobered. "Ah, well, you weren't so far wrong, but Ranny is the owner of Splendora, the house and land, everything. I just look after it for him."

Lettie returned the gaze of the older woman, saying with some delicacy, "I presume that's because—because he can't look after it himself."

"He's like a child, the way he was when he was eleven or twelve. It just breaks my heart still, after all this time, but there it is."

"I see."

The older woman squared her shoulders. "He's a dear, sweet boy, wouldn't harm a fly, but I'll understand if you feel you can't stay here in his house, especially after your scare tonight. If you want to leave, I'll see that you have a ride into town in the morning. Your money will be returned, of course."

Lettie had certainly felt the impulse to flee, but with human perversity, the instant the means to do it was offered to her, she became determined to stay. Though the man Ranny was disturbing, she was not afraid of him. And if the Thorn had appeared at the house once, he might do so again. Her voice firm, she said, "I wouldn't think of leaving."

"I knew it!" Aunt Em exclaimed in satisfaction, her face beaming. "I knew you had gumption the minute I saw you."

Lettie smiled in return, a movement of her mouth that altered its curves, touching her face with classic and breathtaking beauty. "Thank you, but perhaps it would be as well if I knew a little more about—about the situation here."

"You mean about Ranny. There's not much to tell, really." The older woman sat down rather heavily in the chair Lettie had vacated. "You saw the scar on the side of his head? He was wounded in the war like so many others. He was an artillery officer, Confederate, of course." The older woman sent her a quick glance, half-apologetic, half-defiant. "There was a skirmish during the last months of the war. One of the big guns exploded and a piece of the barrel cracked his skull."

"It's a wonder he wasn't killed."

Aunt Em nodded. "His men left him for dead, but he was found by a Union patrol and treated in a field hospital. He was unconscious for weeks and would have died most likely if it hadn't been for Bradley, his body servant from childhood who had been with him all through the war. Bradley went with him when he was transferred to a hospital near Washington. When peace came, he brought him home."

"And your nephew was . . . like he is now?"

"No, not then. He had come to his senses in Washington, Bradley said, and was nearly normal, except he couldn't remember a lot of things. But the trip home was too much. He had terrible headaches all the long way. Somewhere in Mississippi he just passed out. By the time he reached Splendora, he was nearly gone. He stayed unconscious, perfectly senseless, for the best part of six months. When he finally woke up that time, he was—was the way you saw him."

"It must have been distressing. He is, if I may say so, such a nice-looking man."

"Oh, but you should have seen him before the war, when he was full of his devilment, always laughing and carrying on, always pulling a joke or off on some wild rampage. The house was full in those days, boys and girls coming and going, a party every Saturday night, the boys—young men actually—acting like fools, the girls setting their caps all innocent-like for Ransom while he never noticed. They all used to dance and sing, to play charades and get up amateur theatricals—why, there are still three trunks in the attic full of outlandish getups they used to wear. I filled 'em up with popcorn, cookies, and candy, and enjoyed it all as much as any."

"The boy Lionel, is it really necessary for him to lead your nephew about?"

"Not exactly. Lionel is Bradley's boy, raised by his grandmother, Mama Tass, our cook here at Splendora for thirty years. Not only Lionel's father, but his grandfather and great-grandfather had served the Tyler men in the past. The boy was always around, even after Bradley left us to go looking for his freedom. Ranny, in the early days when he was convalescing, used to forget sometimes where he was, what he was doing, and Lionel got in the habit of leading him back to the house, helping him dress and undress, taking care of him. The boy's a big help to me."

"I'm sure," Lettie murmured.

Aunt Em got to her feet. "Well, is there anything I can get for you? A glass of warm milk or maybe some of my blackberry cordial? I wish I could offer you something a bit stronger, but it's been years since we had spirits in the house. Such things are higher than a cat's back, I do swear."

When Lettie declined, Aunt Em offered to make up another room for her or even to let her sleep in her own bedchamber if Lettie was reluctant to remain where she was. Lettie thanked her for her thoughtfulness but finally convinced the older woman that she was not going to lie awake starting at shadows for the rest of the night.

Later, when Aunt Em had gone, taking away the lamp, Lettie lay wide-eyed in the middle of the great tester bed. She was not certain she should have been quite so intrepid. The curtains at the window shifted like pale ghosts in the night air that sighed through the opening. The house creaked and popped, while outside could be heard now and then the soft rustling of some night creature prowling among the shrubs and perennials of Aunt Em's door-yard garden. Lettie thought of getting up and closing the window, but the night was too warm for that. Besides, she was loath to go near it. She did not really think that the Thorn was lurking outside, waiting to grab her again, but her rational thought processes and instincts seemed to be at odds.

She had never felt so helpless in her life as she had in that moment when the Thorn had held her. She had never been kissed like that, so thoroughly, yet with such vital enjoyment. It was not an experience she wished to repeat.

In truth, with the exception of the chaste salutes on her forehead of her father when she was a child, she had only been kissed by one other man. Her fiancé, Charles Smallwood, had swept her into a dark corner once or twice, and had even driven her out into the country one spring day with just such caresses on his mind. Those caresses had never been particularly pleasant. His lips had been hard and puckered and his excitement so great that he had bruised her mouth and left her feeling mussed and indignant instead of . . .

Lettie turned her head sharply on the pillow, flinging her arm up to cover her eyes. Charles was dead, killed at Manassas. Her brother Henry was dead also, dead and buried here in the South where he had been sent as an officer of the Union troops to enforce Reconstruction. That her womanly senses could have been stirred by the man who had shot Henry in the head as he knelt to drink at a wilderness spring filled her with shame and distress. She had never lied to herself, however, and she would not deny that she had sensed the rise of some unholy desire. If she had felt that way when Charles had kissed her, she might have succumbed to his pleas to be wed before he went to war, might have submitted to the frenzied need for physical union that he had pressed upon her.

Instead, she had been cool and sane and sensible. When he had broken down and cried, begging for her affection, she had retreated into hauteur, assuming an air of superior wisdom that now made her wince to remember. That coolness had been possible because she had been so little moved by her fiancé's touch. Strange, but she could not think now why she had ever agreed to marry him. Except that she had been seventeen and Charles had looked so very mature in his uniform, and all her friends had been getting engaged or married.

The curtains billowed at the window and she turned her head toward the faint movement. The Thorn. She could not believe he had been there in her room. It was almost as if she had imagined the whole thing, had conjured him up out of her intense need to bring her brother's killer to justice. She tried to think of what he had looked like but could form no real picture. He had been big and had a mustache, and she had the impression that he was dark, though the room had been so dim she could not be certain. What she remembered best was the quietness with which he had moved, his strength and lightning reflexes, and the feel of his body that was as lean and tough as cured leather.

At least she knew she had come to the right area, the right place. If she believed in fate, she might think that she had been led to Aunt Em and Splendora.

Aunt Em was a dear, so warm and concerned. She did not fit Lettie's conception of a Southern lady, someone pampered and protected, used to being waited on hand and foot, insulated from life's daily problems. The way of life that had supported such women was gone, of course, had been swept away when the war began nine years ago. So many men had died; in her trip South it had seemed that most of the women in every town she passed through were dressed in black. There must be many who, like Aunt Em, were learning to cope with their changed circumstances, to make the best of what was left to them.

Aunt Em not only had a house to keep up and provision to make for herself, but she had the care of her nephew. What a tragedy it was that he had been so incapacitated by his injury. To look at him, one would never guess. There was intelligence and sensitivity in the molding of his smooth-shaven, golden-tan features and a sense of fathomless depths in his eyes. She had felt drawn to him, aware of him, to an astonishing degree. It was most peculiar.

It was also confusing. There had never been a great deal of warmth or overt affection in her family. Composure under all circumstances was greatly admired, displays of emotion frowned upon. They all liked and respected one another, and she and Henry had been close, but she had grown up believing that the nature she had inherited from her parents was cool. It was strange then that she had been so affected by two different men on the same night. Perhaps it was something about being in Louisiana. Some claimed that the damp heat of such Southern climes seeped into the blood and inflamed the senses, that it advanced the passionate responses so that women matured young, coming into early bloom like flowers forced in a glasshouse.

It really was quite warm. If the gesture were not so unthinkable, so entirely abandoned, she would like to strip off her heavy nightgown and throw it on the floor to lie naked on the high mattress of the bed.

What if she did that and the Thorn returned? Dear heaven, there was no way of saying what might happen to her!

She was being ridiculous. There had been nothing in her response to either the man known as the Thorn or Ransom Tyler that was not easily explained by the upheaval of the incident that had occurred and the strangeness of her situation here among people unknown to her, combined with her extreme fatigue from the three-day journey here.

Reaching back under her neck, Lettie dragged the thick silken swath of her hair from under her shoulders and spread it to one side over the pillow for coolness. She pushed up the long sleeves of her nightgown and undid two of the three buttons that fastened it at the neck. For long moments she lay still with her eyes closed and her hands at her sides. A faint breeze drifted in at the window, touching her face. It brought with it the sweet scent of magnolias and some other fragrance that she thought might be honeysuckle.

Lettie frowned and wrenched herself over on her side, drawing her feet up. The minutes ticked past, became an hour, two. Somewhere in the house a clock struck the hour, the faint chiming spreading in the stillness. Lettie's lashes quivered on her cheeks. She sighed. Slowly she reached down with one hand and caught a flannel fold of her nightgown. She drew it up a few inches, exposing her ankles to the coolness of the air. A few inches more, and her knees were bare. Higher still. Lovely. But the weight and heat around her chest was unbearable. Minutes passed. The clock chimed the half hour.

Lettie sat up. With a quick, almost furtive movement, she drew off the nightgown. Carefully, she turned it right side out, feeling for the seams in the darkness. She smoothed it and then placed it beside her, ready to be donned at a moment's notice. She lay back down on the smooth linen sheet and slowly stretched full length. She brushed her hair from under her neck once more and closed her eyes. She sighed in relief, a soft, voluptuous sound. She slept.

Breakfast at Splendora was an informal meal taken as hunger and time of rising indicated. Because there was, as Aunt Em put it, no rhyme or reason to when she and her nephew ate, they often sat down in the morning at the table in the outdoor kitchen to save time and trouble. Lettie could do the same, or she could step out to the kitchen and tell the cook what she wanted and Mama Tass would serve her in the dining room, whichever she preferred.

To reach the kitchen, it was necessary to go along the long hall that divided the house, and was used as a summer sitting room, to the double doors that opened onto the back veranda. One then crossed this veranda and descended the flight of stairs that led down to the ground. A path with velvet-green moss growing between bricks set in a herringbone pattern and a knot garden of herbs on either side connected the house to a small brick building that housed the kitchen and laundry. This separate kitchen kept the heat of cooking from the main house as well as the smells, smoke, and danger of fires.

As Lettie made her way along the path in the golden sunlight of morning, a calico cat came to meet her, winding itself about her skirts. The warm air was laden with the smells of bacon frying, coffee brewing, and something being baked in the oven. There was also a resinous tang lingering in the area, and from not far away could be heard the rattling whacks of someone chopping wood.

At the door of the kitchen, Lettie paused to peer inside.

A large black woman with a white kerchief wrapped around her head and a starched apron over a faded blue dress moved back and forth between a cast-iron stove, a brick oven, and a heavy wooden table with a scarred top that had been scrubbed so hard and so often that the wood was white. To one side was a huge, smoke-blackened open fireplace with spits and racks in it that looked as if it might still be pressed into use when the stove was crowded, though for now it held only ashes. On another wall was a dish cabinet with open shelves displaying great serving platters and bowls and tureens and enough china and glassware to serve an army of guests.

The black woman turned. "Don't you come in my kitchen!"

Lettie blinked and retreated a step. "Excuse me."

"Lord, miss, you oughta know I didn't mean you! I'm talkin' to that cat. That rapscallion tries to sneak in a dozen times a day, though I've chased him out with my brush broom till I'm plumb wore to a frazzle."

"I hope I'm not too late for breakfast?"

"No, ma'am. The biscuits are 'bout ready to come out of the oven now and the gravy's near made. You eating in the kitchen with Mast' Ranny?"

"I . . . Yes, if you don't mind." The courtesy and the decision were instinctive.

"Mind? Why should I mind?"

Lettie clapped her hands at the cat, shooing it away before stepping inside the door. "Is there anything I can do?"

The cook, who must be the Mama Tass that her hostess had spoken of, sent her a glance of frowning surprise. "Why, no, ma'am, you're paying company."

Lettie shook her head with a smile. "I don't like being idle while other people are working."

Mama Tass, holding a spoon poised in the air in one hand, looked Lettie up and down with a frown on her round face. "You talk funny. You ain't one of them radical Republican abolitionists?"

"No," Lettie said warily. She had never approved of slavery in any form, but this didn't seem like a good time to say so.

"Good. I don't hold with them folks, coming around here and making trouble. But if you really want to be a help, you can step around to the woodpile back of here and tell Mast' Ranny breakfast is nigh ready."

Lettie, feeling a little as if an honor had been conferred upon her, and at the same time that she had made a lucky escape, did as she was told.

Ransom Tyler was splitting wood for the stove. He stood the rounds of oak on end on the chopping block and, with a single mighty stroke of the ax, clove them apart. Again and again, he lifted the gleaming blade of the ax and brought it down. He had removed his chambray shirt and cast it to one side. With each powerful stroke, the muscles of his back and shoulders bunched and stretched under the sun-bronzed skin. As he leaned to prop the wood for the next cut, his trousers clung to the hard length of his thighs and the tight curve of his hips, outlining the muscles that gathered and lengthened there. The stack of wood in manageable sticks was growing, while beside it lay a pile of pine kindling that had been splintered from a large stump rich with resin.

Lettie had come to a stop in a swirl of skirts at the corner of the kitchen when she saw that the man called Ranny was half-naked. Uncertain whether to retreat or to ignore his state, she did neither. She stood watching the way the sun caught golden gleams in the fine hair that fell over his forehead, the way the sheen of perspiration on his skin highlighted the sculpted bands of muscle that wrapped his upper body and glistened in the fine triangle of golden hair on his chest and along the ridged hardness of his arms.

There was something fascinating about the ease with which he worked, the precision of his movements, the concentration he brought to his task and the grace with which his body performed it. It affected Lettie strangely, causing a drawing, knotting sensation in the lower part of her abdomen. It was impossible to believe, watching him, that his mind was damaged, that there might be some danger in allowing him to wield the lethal tool in his hands.

Ransom was aware of Letitia Mason from the moment she rounded the end of the kitchen. What she wanted he could not imagine, but she looked so flustered at the sight of him and so proper in her gray morning dress with the buttons fastened right up to the standing collar at her throat and a cameo brooch as a reinforcement for them that he bided his time, waiting to find out. It was no hardship. She was very pleasant to look at, with a pink flush from the heat across her cheekbones, her hair in a thick, gleaming coronet of braids around her head, and her breasts straining against the material of her bodice as she breathed. Her presence at Splendora looked to be a major impediment to his activities, but there might be compensations.

Lettie half expected the owner of Splendora to look up and acknowledge her; she would have sworn that he knew she was there. As time passed and he gave no sign of it, she grew uncomfortably aware that she was staring. To go away without speaking seemed suddenly priggish, if not an act of unkindness. She cleared her throat. What to call him? If she must err, let it at least be on the side of good manners.

"Mr. Tyler?"

He straightened and gave her a slow smile, inclining his head in a nod that was like a small, gallant bow. "Morning, ma'am."

"I've been sent to say that your breakfast is ready."

"So am I," he said, and set the ax aside. Without haste, he brushed the wood chips from his shoulders and reached for his shirt, which was draped over a log. He suppressed a grin as she turned away while he shrugged into it. Teasing her was unfair, perhaps, but very nearly irresistible; she was that prim. He banished amusement from his face with an effort and knelt to gather a load of stove wood in his arms. Rising in a single smooth movement with the burden, he made a brief gesture to indicate that she must precede him.

Lettie led the way, though she was acutely conscious of the man behind her. She searched her mind for something to say. "It's a lovely morning, but warm already."

"Yes, ma'am."

The words were solemn enough, but their very solemnity gave them the faintest of mocking edges. Lettie turned her head quickly to stare at Ranny. He gazed back at her, his eyes clear, the expression in them guileless. Perhaps he had meant only that he was much hotter than she after his exertions at the woodpile?

Ransom let his breath out in soundless relief as Letitia Mason looked forward once more. She was a sharp lady. He was going to have to step more carefully around her than he had suspected.

Breakfast was on the table. The biscuits were as light and fluffy as clouds, the gravy rich, the bacon in crisp brown curls. Mama Tass had fried three eggs for Ranny and offered to cook as many of them, yard fresh from their own hens, for Lettie as she wanted, any way she wanted. One, scrambled, was all that Lettie could face, though it was deliciously creamy and perfectly done, almost like a small omelet.

As the cook stood at the workbench washing dishes, she spoke to Ranny about various tasks that needed doing about the place. His answers, couched in short, simple sentences, were intelligible enough. Some of the jobs seemed rather menial to Lettie, such as taking the kitchen scraps to the hog pen. He made no complaint, however, and she assumed the request was not unusual.

Mama Tass moved to the door to throw out her dishwater, then stepped outside for a moment. A small silence fell. As it stretched without the return of the cook, Lettie said, "Where is your aunt this morning?"

Ranny glanced up, then looked down at his plate. "She's gone visiting."

"Oh?" The questioning inflection was deliberate. It was not that Lettie was curious about the movements of her landlady, but simply that she wanted to hear Ransom Tyler talk.

"She went to Elm Grove. Walked. They have the summer sickness there. She took them some chicken broth."

"I see. That was kind of her."

The big man across the table from Lettie gave her a level look that made her suddenly feel that her comment had been as inane as it sounded in her own ears. She went on in some haste. "Elm Grove, is that a place, a town?"

"A house. My Uncle Samuel's house. Just down the road."

"I see. And the boy Lionel? Where is he?"

Ranny smiled and the slashing crease that was not quite a dimple appeared in his cheek. "Lionel's asleep. If he gets up early, Mama Tass finds jobs for him."

"I thought he was supposed to—that is, I thought his job was being your companion?" Surely if this man was as backward as Aunt Em had indicated, he might not realize what she had started to say, but a flush mounted to Lettie's cheeks regardless.

Ransom, watching the color rise under her clear skin and wondering if it was sensitivity that caused it or annoyance with his supposed slowness, almost forgot to answer. "Sometimes."

Lettie pushed her plate back. After a moment she said, "Could you tell me what would be the best way to get into town?"

"There's a horse and buggy."

"Do you think your aunt would mind if I used it? I would be glad to pay."

"She won't mind," he said with a smile. "I could drive you."

"I can drive myself, but I would be glad to pay for the use of the buggy."

"No need to pay. And it would be nice to drive you. My pleasure."

There was exquisite courtesy in his words, a briefly caught echo of what he must once have been. Lettie, acknowledging both, chewed the inside of her bottom lip. She did not know if it was possible for him to do what he suggested and his aunt was not there for her to ask. Certainly it took more strength than knowledge to drive a horse and buggy, but there were rules of the road and some responsibility was required to follow them.

"I won't overturn you. I promise." Ranny waited.

It appeared he considered the prospect a treat. There were several things Lettie needed to do in town, a few small purchases she needed to make, but her main object was to discover the whereabouts of the headquarters of the Federal occupation troops and begin her inquiry into her brother's death. It could wait a little while, however, at least until her landlady returned. She summoned a smile. "Perhaps later."

Mama Tass came back inside carrying a handful of young green onions from the knot garden. Their pungent smell filled the kitchen as she began to clean them. Watching the black woman's swift, sure, movements as she stripped the outer leaves and cut off the roots, Lettie wondered if they were for some strange Southern breakfast dish or if the cook was already preparing the next meal.

The black woman was not as intent on her work as she appeared, for the moment Ransom Tyler put down his coffee cup, she glanced over her shoulder. "If you through, Mast' Ranny, why don't you show the young lady around the place? She'll be wantin' to know where everything is, and I bet she'd like to see Miss Emily's flowers."

"There's no need, really," Lettie protested. "I'm sure Mr. Tyler has other things to do."

But the owner of Splendora was already on his feet and moving to draw out her chair as she rose. "I like this job better. And you can call me Ranny, if you want."

There seemed to be little choice. She would see Splendora. Her tone dry, she said, "Thank you, Ranny."

Splendora was built in the style known as a planter's cottage. It was not actually two stories tall but rather had one main floor that was built on top of a so-called raised basement, a brick-walled storage area constructed above the ground due to the high water table in the area. Its hipped roof was pierced by three dormer windows that gave light into an enormous open room in the attic, a room that before the war had been used for everything from dancing in wintertime to sleeping space for visitors. The upper and lower verandas on both front and back shaded the house from the sun, helping to keep the summer heat at bay. The columns of the lower verandas were of brick to match the basement walls. Those on the upper verandas were of heart cypress cut four-square, in keeping with the cypress planking of the house.

The front entrance was reached by a wide set of high, railed steps that led up to the veranda, also edged with railing, at the level of the main rooms. Through the heavy, double front doors surrounded by side lights and a transom was the great hallway. There were six large rooms opening from it. To the left at the front was the parlor, a room furnished in rosewood and frayed brocatelle that remained in perpetual gloom from closed shutters to prevent further deterioration of the furnishings. Beyond the parlor was a dining room filled with heavy mahogany pieces while behind that, with access to the back veranda through jib windows, was the bedchamber where Ranny slept. Across the hall was Aunt Em's room. Next to it, in the middle of the right side, was an empty chamber, and after that was the room Lettie had been given, which opened onto the front veranda.

The so-called raised basement, the lower floor, also had a central hall. Leading from it were a variety of storerooms and also the room where Mama Tass had slept for years as a trusted house servant, though she now had a cabin of her own. Only Lionel used it at present, in order to be close if Ranny needed him during the night.

There was a drive of rust-colored sand dotted with potholes that led from the road to the front of the house, then curved around it to the left in order to reach the stables and carriage house. Farther along that drive was a blacksmith shop and a few other outbuildings, with a double row of what had been slave cabins stretching beyond them.

The ravages of war, and of some nine years of neglect, were everywhere. The whitewash of the house had faded, leaving it the soft silver-gray of weathered wood that gave it a look of decay. The split-rail fences that had closed off the fields were gone, burned as firewood by the troops of two armies. The iron tools from the blacksmith shop had been confiscated, along with the mules, most of the horses, and as many of the chickens, ducks, beef cattle, and hogs that could be caught. A cotton barn still lay in blackened rubble where it had been burned by the Confederates to keep the white gold from falling into the hands of the enemy. Fields close to the house had been planted and were showing the tender green of rows of new cotton, but others farther away lay fallow, taken over by sweet gum and pine saplings, by choking weeds and wild morning-glory vines. Smoke rose from four or five of the slave cabins where Negro sharecroppers lived, but most had sagging porches, missing doors and steps, and were festooned with the twining vines of honeysuckle and Virginia creeper.

One of the fences around the house had been replaced. It was the picket fence that protected Aunt Em's flowers from her chickens and also the livestock. Cows and rooting hogs were beginning to be replenished but were allowed to range free throughout the countryside, living off the land for lack of other feed. Inside that barrier, the yard was bare of grass and the sandy soil raked into geometric patterns. But clustered around the edges and on either side of the front flight of steps were beds of sweet william, verbena, daisies, and blue salvia, along with rows of irises and jonquils that were no longer in bloom. There were sweet olive shrubs in the corners, plus glossy camellias, snowball viburnums, spireas, and monthly roses. There was a running rose with rampant canes decked with glossy green foliage growing beside the front gate. Its pale pink blooms tumbled in profusion over the arbor that arched above it, giving off such a sweet scent in the morning sunlight that it drugged the senses.

Ranny came to a halt at the rose arbor. Lettie stopped beside him and closed her eyes, breathing deep of the incredible fragrance. It was so quiet that she could hear the humming of the bees among the flowers and the soft rustle of a breeze through the glistening rose leaves.

How very peaceful it was here compared to the town she had left with its wheeled traffic and cursing drivers and shouts of street vendors. It was difficult to think of death and vengeance, difficult to remember that this pleasant land had been torn by war and was still being made hideous by nighttime violence. And yet she must.

There was a small snapping sound near her shoulder. Lettie opened her eyes to see Ranny breaking a delicate pink rosebud from an arching cane. His face absorbed, he removed the lower leaves, dropping them to the ground, and with a callused thumb flicked off the thorns one by one. He stood holding the bloom for a moment, then, inclining his head in a slight bow, presented the tight, half-open flower to her.

"For you, Miss Lettie."

"Why?" There was suspicion in her tone. She was not used to gifts from men. The offer of the rose and the use of her name, even with the title of respect, gave her a disturbing sense of unwanted intimacy.

"It looks like you."

She searched his face, her senses alert to some faint undercurrent of meaning. Finally, she said, "With or without the thorns?"

"What?"

There had been sincerity in his gesture and a cavalier's grace. It was ungracious of her to question the token so carefully prepared for her. Nor could she refuse it without offending him. Lettie accepted the rose, lifting it to inhale the scent even as she watched for some indication of the reason it had been given to her. But if there was one beyond the impulse of the moment or some half-remembered fragment of the art of flirtation, it was not apparent.

Ransom Tyler was a good guide, explaining in brief, uncomplicated phrases the uses of the rooms and buildings he pointed out, answering her questions promptly if in scant detail. He knew the house and grounds well, which was not surprising since Splendora was his home. She wondered if he managed to communicate as easily when he was away from it.

There was something about this child-man that caught at her imagination. She could not seem to stop looking at him, at the sheer masculine beauty of his face and body. There was such confidence in his bearing, such pride, a holdover from other days, no doubt, though now and then there was a wariness in his manner and a flash of uncertainty in his eyes that was painful to see. His voice was deep and soft, and the slow smiles that creased his cheeks gave her an odd feeling in her chest. The knowledge that she found him so interesting should have made her feel foolish, and would have, if she had not realized that it was because he posed a study in the ability to learn, or rather the loss of that mental process. As a teacher, it was only natural that her curiosity should be aroused.

"Do you read, Ranny—I mean, since your head injury?"

"A little."

"But you recognize letters and words?"

He gave a short nod.

"You can write?"

A shadow crossed his face. He repeated, "A little."

"Would you like to be able to do more?"

"No."

"But why?"

"I can't!"

"You might be able to do more than you think."

"Don't mock me." His voice was flat as he swung away from her.

Lettie put out her hand to catch his arm. "I'm not, truly. I would like to help."

Ransom went still as he turned his head to look down at the firm oval of her face and the steady light in her eyes. A sudden shiver ran through him so that he had to tense his muscles against it. It had been a long time since a woman had looked at him with anything more than embarrassment or pity. "You couldn't," he said, his voice low.

"I could try."

Lettie felt the tension in his arm under her fingers. It was amazing, but she had a nearly uncontrollable urge to reach up and brush back the soft wave of hair that fell forward over the scar at his temple, to explore that old injury with her fingertips almost as if she expected her touch to heal him. She subdued the impulse, but she could not seem to withdraw her gaze from his. The seconds ticked slowly past. A bee droned around him. A cream-colored butterfly fluttered by.

Above them a rose shattered. The petals fell, whispering down to land on Ranny's broad shoulders where they lay soft and delicate on the rough blue chambray of his shirt. One settled on Lettie's hand as she held his arm, and she felt its sun-warmed caress like a benediction.

"Hey, there, you two! What are you up to?"

Lettie jumped, startled at the call. It was Aunt Em. The older woman was coming along the road toward them with a sunbonnet shading her face and an empty basket swinging on her arm.

Aunt Em's question, it appeared, was completely rhetorical. She did not wait for an answer but, as she reached them, inquired after Lettie's comfort during the night, asked if she had eaten breakfast, and, with brisk concern that robbed the query of any sign of prying, wanted to know if she had made plans for the day. Told of the proposed trip into town, she seemed to have no reservations about permitting Ranny to drive Lettie there. There were one or two errands he could run for her while Lettie was busy; she was in need of a paper of pins and her copy of *Demorests Illustrated Monthly* should be at the post office. The gardening articles in it were good this time, or so she had heard. The Yankee editors didn't know much about Southern gardens—they were mighty set on tulips and peonies, two flowers that faded away in the heat—but there was some mention of cannas that she wanted to see.

By the time Ranny had hitched up the buggy, Lettie had pinned on a small, ribbon-trimmed straw hat that tilted forward over her braided hair, put on her gloves, found her parasol, and was waiting on the steps. They set out down the drive in the direction of Natchitoches.

Before his death, Lettie's brother Henry had been an excellent correspondent. He had had a quick mind and a keen interest in the place to which he had been assigned. He had found the countryside pleasant and the history that dated back to French colonial days intriguing. He had often spoken of buying land and setting up as a planter himself when his enlistment was over. From his letters, Lettie had gleaned much information about the area where he had been killed.

Splendora was located some three or four miles north of the town of Natchitoches, near what had been another small town called Grand Ecore. Grand Ecore, a thriving port on the bank of the Red River, had been burned by the Union troops under General Banks during the ill-fated Red River campaign in the spring of 1864. Natchitoches, of less importance for shipping, had been spared.

The word *Natchitoches*, according to Henry, was generally accepted to mean "chinquapin eaters" and was the name applied to the Indian tribe that had once claimed the area. The settlement was actually the oldest in the Louisiana Purchase territory, older than New Orleans by some four years. It had been established as a military outpost in 1714 to hold the western boundary of the colony of Louisiana against the encroachment of Spain. At that time, it had been located on the Red River. But early in the present century, the Red had begun to alter its course to a more northward loop. The water level had gradually fallen in the thirty-odd-mile bend where Natchitoches was located until it became obvious that the stretch was little more than a branching tributary that became known as the Cane River.

The old town itself was a picturesque place where French and Spanish influence was obvious in the plastered walls, the wide verandas that shaded the houses, the wrought-iron decoration, and the air of shuttered privacy that clung to many of the houses. The homes were shaded by huge old oaks and there were many cool gardens half hidden behind them. It was not uncommon to hear French spoken on the streets or to find newspapers, books, or advertising placards in that language.

The main street, paved with brick and facing the waterway that had once been its life's blood, was called Front Street. Here the names of the merchants with their foreign ring reflected the town's heritage. Many of the emporiums were two-storied, with projecting balconies that provided a resting place and view of the river to the apartments above and shelter from sun and rain to pedestrians below. Under that protection ladies strolled, always in pairs as propriety demanded. They were dressed in voluminous skirts ornamented with the small bustles decreed by fashion, usually in the black or gray or purple of mourning, and wore gloves on their hands and veils to protect their complexions from the sun. Gentlemen moved about their business, some soberly clad and grave of face, some wearing bright plaid shooting coats and brighter waistcoats. A few trailed clouds of smoke from the cheroots clamped between their teeth. There was one elderly man who caught Lettie's attention. He was white-headed, with a flowing white beard, and he walked with the pride and dignity of a man of means, yet his coat was shabby and his shirt collar frayed. And on his face was a look of such despair that it wrenched at the heart.

Ragged children, black and white together, ran here and there. They leaped over the groups of black men sitting or lying in the sun, laughing and talking on the street corners, and dodged around the portly figure of a nun hurrying down the street with her rosary clacking at her waist. Negresses walked along with baskets balanced on their heads, calling out to each other with bright smiles in their brown faces or singing to hawk their wares of berry pies or sausages in biscuits, knots of herbs, bouquets of flowers, or bags of spices.

Beyond the buildings, rising among the treetops, was the tower of the cathedral of the Natchitoches diocese, the Church of St. Mary. Its bell was tolling as Lettie and Ransom drove through town, a mellow yet doleful sound. It signified a funeral, that of a free man of color who was a planter from Isle Brevelle farther down the river, or so Ranny said. He was being buried in consecrated ground apparently, though he had killed himself in grief over the accumulated tragedies of his life: the death of two sons in the war and the loss of his fortune, on top of the more recent loss of his house and lands, property as extensive as any white man's, for taxes. Lettie would have liked to question Ranny more closely about the matter, but there was no time. They drew up then before a dry goods store and he got down to hand her from the buggy.

Lettie's purchases and Aunt Em's errands did not take long. They might have been completed more quickly if she and Ranny had not been detained in the post office while the man behind the grille entertained what was apparently a trio of his cronies with the tale of an incident that had occurred that morning.

"I swear, if it wasn't the dangest thing you ever saw in

your life! There was that carpetbag tax collector, O'Connor, the most money-grabbin' scoundrel in the state—and that's saying something nowadays—tied up to a lamp post on Front Street in his underdrawers. He was dancing a jig, trying to hide his two hundred and fifty pounds of pork fat behind the post and get rid of the sign around his neck at the same time."

"Sign? What kind of sign?" The question was asked by one of the listeners, a bearded, slow-talking man with the hard hands of a farmer and dirt embedded in the cracked leather of his shoes.

"Just a piece of paper with one word on it: *Oink!* Lord, but ain't that Thorn something?"

The men had lowered their voices at the sight of a woman and Lettie had moved away, turning her back on them, pretending an interest in a yellowed and fly-speck-covered advertisement for ladies' hats in the window. At mention of the Thorn, her attention abruptly sharpened.

"How d'you know it was the Thorn?" another of the men questioned.

"Who else would it be?" The narrator of the tale searched around under his counter, pulled out a periodical and a handful of letters, and slapped them down on the counter in front of Ranny without looking at him. "Besides, he left his calling card, a locust and a thorn, and he was spotted just out of town by a bluebelly. Seems the mighty Union army spent half the night chasing 'im up one side of Red River and down the other."

"Robbed O'Connor, did he?"

"I should say! The cream of it is, the army was so set on catching Thorn and puttin' an end to his fine career that they didn't know till this morning about the robbery. They never saw the tax collector at all. It was the doc found him, coming home from delivering a baby before daylight."

There was a general round of guffaws. The farmer, a grin showing through his beard, shook his head. "Lord, just think of the mosquitoes. Wonder why O'Connor didn't yell out?"

"Hoped he'd get free without anybody seeing him, I'd say."

"Serves 'im right. Tried to hold me up, O'Connor did, last time he came around. Wanted to take my prize sow 'cause my tax bill was a day past due. Told him to step down and take 'er—'course I had my double-barrel shotgun in my hand at the time. The money for 'er never would've showed up on the record, that's sure."

"Reckon the money the Thorn took will maybe turn up again at the next tax sale."

"Widow Clements's place goes up for auction in two days' time. What'll you bet she comes up with the exact price it takes to buy it back?"

"It'll be one of them miracles, dang me if it won't."

The postmaster directed a shot of tobacco juice at a spittoon in the corner. "There's some figure this here Thorn's worked a miracle too many, such as interrupting the hanging party last Friday night and taking off Black Toby. The boys were a bit put out."

The conversation came to an abrupt halt. Lettie, glancing over her shoulder, saw the men eyeing each other with grim and suspicious faces. The exchange was obscure, though she thought it might refer to the activities of the night riders, the sheet-wearing citizens known in the state as the Knights of the White Camellia. They were the men most apt to be involved in what the men chose to call a hanging party.

Ranny, with Aunt Em's mail in his hand, moved to touch Lettie's elbow. "Ready?"

Lettie moved beside him as they left the post office, though there was a frown of concentration between her eyes as she went. Ranny helped her into the buggy and walked around to his own side. Climbing in, he set the vehicle in motion. They had not gone more than a few feet when Lettie turned to him.

"You heard what they said about the tax collector, Mr. O'Connor?"

"Yes, ma'am."

"What do you think?"

"Think?"

"About what was done to him."

"I don't know."

Ransom realized that he should have foreseen her questions. He might have hustled her out of the post office if he had. Instead, it had seemed a good opportunity to expose her to a different view of the Thorn from the one she apparently held, judging from the comment he had overheard the night before. There was nothing he was going to add to it, however, even if he could.

"You must know!" she insisted. "The man was attacked and publicly humiliated. I realize—that is, I've heard that taxes are high and the men who collect them sometimes less than fair, but did Mr. O'Connor deserve what was done to him?"

"What," he asked, "does humil—humil—that word mean?"

Lettie looked at him, meeting his clear gaze for a moment before turning her head away. She was expecting too much. She had forgotten. The man beside her had his limitations and she must not press him. Strange, how badly she had wanted to know what he thought.

Her voice low, she said, "I'm sorry, Ranny. It isn't important. Shall we go to the Freedmen's Bureau now?"

The Freedmen's Bureau had been established to aid the Negroes in adjusting to freedom and to their newly acquired rights. It had been charged that the bureau had instead become a substitute master, encouraging the former slaves to depend on the government and guiding them toward support of the radical Republican party and its aims. It was true that a great many promises had been made, such as the pledge of forty acres and a mule for every Negro male. Where the promise had originated could not be said, but it was equally true that it had raised expectations that could not be met. The bureau, with many of its offices filled by former Union soldiers who intended to settle in the South, was, in general, conscientious. Its greatest contribution, most agreed, was likely to be in the education of the Negroes.

Lettie's appearance at the bureau office was greeted with enthusiasm. She had written ahead and was expected. Unfortunately, she was told, it would be a month, maybe more, before she could begin work. This was the planting season and there would be few students who could be spared from work until after the crops were laid by—that was to say, until the final plowing of the seedlings as summer advanced. In the meantime, she must be patient. They would let her know when her services would be required.

From the Freedmen's Bureau, Lettie asked to be taken to army headquarters. The building, formerly a private home, was very like Splendora in style, with the same raised basement and wide verandas. Ranny, his expression stolid, handed her down outside and prepared to wait.

The officer in command of the Natchitoches district was Colonel Thomas Ward. A tall man with a soldier's bearing, he was perhaps a little over thirty and attractive in an upright military fashion. His hair, worn long and curling in the back, was walnut-brown, and there was a touch of red in his brown cavalry mustache. His green eyes were red-rimmed with fatigue at the moment, as if he had been up most of the night before. He stood as Lettie entered and his greeting was cordial enough before he invited her to be seated in the chair across from his desk.

"Miss Mason, how may the United States Army, and I, be of service to you?"

Lettie had prepared what she was going to say with care. Unfortunately, she could not quite remember just now how she had meant to open the subject. She moistened her lips, suddenly doubtful for the first time of the wisdom of her quest. "I—I believe you knew my brother, Henry. You wrote my mother a letter of condolence."

"Yes, indeed, a fine officer, your brother. I take it you are here about his death?"

"Yes," Lettie said in relief, and plunged into a recital of why it was so important to her to discover his killer and what she intended to do in the coming weeks, including her teaching commitment with the Freedmen's Bureau. The colonel heard her out, only giving a slight nod now and then, though his gaze touched in turn the shape of her lips as she spoke, the curves of her breasts, and the narrow turn of her waist.

"You are aware," he said when she was silent at last, "that the army has already conducted its own investigation?"

"So I understand. It doesn't appear to have been conclusive."

"There was simply no evidence. It pains me to have only discouragement to offer you, Miss Mason, but I doubt that you will be able to find anything sufficient at this date to show who your brother's killer may be, much less hang him."

"I know it won't be easy. I thought I might start by looking at the place where he was shot, this woodland spring, if you can direct me to it?"

He frowned, touching a forefinger to his mustache as

he leaned back in his chair. "The site is some distance away and in rather wild country, not the kind of spot you would want to visit on a picnic outing."

"Indeed?" Lettie's tone was cool. It always amazed her how ready men were to jump to the conclusion that all women were foolish about distances.

The colonel smiled. "I realize that may sound odd, considering that you have just made a journey halfway across this country, but what you may not realize is that the area is the stamping ground, so to speak, not only of the man you seek, our local Robin Hood, the Thorn, but also of a collection of other unsavory characters. These desperadoes are, many of them, former Confederate guerrilla fighters or else the deserters of the Confederate army known around here as jayhawkers. We are beginning to believe the organization may be of some size, rather like a band of the kind of outlaws that are epidemic in the Southwest. One thing we do know about them for certain is that they can be completely ruthless."

She paid scant attention to his last words, seizing on the phrase that caught her interest. "Robin Hood? A strange name surely for such a vile criminal!"

"That's what the locals are calling the man, though for myself, being in something of the same position as the Sheriff of Nottingham, I find the comparison less than apt."

"I should think so," she said, relaxing a little in appreciation of his wry humor.

"At least you know something of the man, and so are aware of the danger. I can't say that he would harm a woman, but then neither can I say that he would not. We have had so many descriptions of him, with hair and eye colors every shade of the rainbow, and such a list of crimes laid at his door supposedly perpetrated on the same night and miles apart, that it seems he may be capable of anything."

There was more than a trace of bitterness in the colonel's words. The tone as much as what he had said reminded Lettie that there was something he should know. "I understand you were out last night on the trail of this man. Well, I saw him."

Leaning forward in her chair, she explained the incident.

"Extraordinary that he should have stumbled upon you," was the colonel's comment. "I can't say I'm surprised he was in the area. We've lost him there before. Seems he uses a pool of water in the vicinity called Dink's Pond to confuse the dogs."

"But if you know that, surely you could set a trap, wait for him there?"

"It isn't the only such place he uses. There are a dozen holes of water and streams, not to mention two rivers, where he can throw the dogs off the scent. As for setting a trap, he seems to have some kind of abnormal perception about where we will be. Clever bas—" He stopped, coughing. "That is, he's confoundedly clever."

"Clever isn't the word I would have chosen." Lettie scarcely noticed the colonel's momentary embarrassment, in her interest in the object of her long journey South.

The colonel lifted his brows in inquiry.

"I would have said sneaking, overconfident, even conceited," she said with disdain. "Only look at this symbol he leaves behind him."

"Yes, well, I will admit we aren't too happy about it, but he isn't the first to hint that the army and the radical Republicans we are supporting are a plague."

She looked blank, then an exclamation that was half annoyance, half admiration escaped her. "A plague of locusts and a thorn to impale them."

"Exactly so."

"But I had heard the symbol was for something else."

"The renewal of the South, as the locust renews itself? You can hear anything. But you may rest assured, Miss Mason, that we will look into your report, along with all the others."

As he spoke, he waved at a pile of papers of some thickness that lay in front of him. Lettie took the gesture as a hint and got to her feet. "Thank you, Colonel. I won't keep you from your work any longer, though I appreciate the time you have given me. If you will just give me the directions to the spring?"

Colonel Ward stood up as she rose. "I'll have a map drawn up and delivered to you at Splendora."

"Oh, there's no need to go to so much trouble. Just a quick sketch, a few lines to show me the roads will do."

He gave her a warm smile that made his mustache rise at the corners. "No trouble at all, Miss Mason, no trouble at all."

3

Lettie heard the chanting before she reached the buggy. The voices were light and shrill with excitement, and they carried that edge of jubilant cruelty peculiar to the young. "Run, Ranny, run," they chanted. "Run, Ranny, lost your sense; left it hanging on the fence; buy it back for fifteen cents! Run, Ranny, run!"

Ranny had elected to wait beside the buggy where he had wheeled it around into a large patch of shade across the street from army headquarters. Between the wheels, underneath the high vehicle's body, Lettie could see the bare prancing feet and short trousers of a group of boys, while Ranny was backed against the struts of the buggy top. Indignation rose inside her. She picked up her skirts, hurrying forward.

As Lettie skirted the horse that backed nervously at the commotion, straining at the weight that anchored the reins, she saw much what she had expected to see. Ranny stood at bay with his legs set in a firm stance and his face impassive. Around him skipped five or six boys from nine or ten to perhaps thirteen in age. Their faces were wild with glee as they chanted their nonsense rhyme. One, larger than the others and obviously their leader, bobbed up and down in front of the tall blond man, feinting and punching at him. Ranny caught the blows on his forearms but made no attempt to return them.

Lettie had not been a schoolteacher for some three years without learning a thing or two about the handling of half-grown boys. Her eyes snapping with anger, she lifted her voice in sharp authority. "What is the meaning of this? Stop it at once!"

The capering came to an abrupt halt. Except for their leader, the boys turned to look at her, their eyes big. He threw a single glance in her direction, then went on punching.

Lettie marched forward and caught the boy's shoulder. "What is your name, young man? Who is your father?"

The boy, nearly as tall as she, swung on her with his hair falling into his eyes and a scowl on his face. For an instant, she thought he meant to strike her, but in a movement too swift to follow, Ranny's hand shot out and caught the boy's wrist, clamping tight. The boy gave a choked cry. His face turned white and he gave at the knees.

Lettie reached out to put her fingers on Ranny's corded wrist. Her voice quiet, she said, "Let him go."

Ranny obeyed, releasing his grip abruptly, as a dog might release a rat. The boy, considerably subdued, stood rubbing his arm.

Lettie glanced from the culprit to the others. "I think you had all better go home. And take care next time where you find your fun."

They straggled away with many a puzzled or baleful glance over their shoulders. She watched them for a moment, then swung around to Ranny. He did not seem to be hurt in any way. He was so large and so unruffled, in fact, that the way she had rushed to champion him seemed suddenly a little ridiculous. She could meet his gaze for only an instant before turning away. The words stifled, she said, "Shall we go back to Splendora?"

"Yes, ma'am."

Ransom handed her into the buggy, then stood watching with a suspended feeling in his chest while she settled her skirts and straightened her hat of woven straw. He allowed his gaze to rest on the dark brown fans of her lashes that cast their shadows on the creamy skin of her cheeks, on her slender yet capable-looking hands that smoothed her gray skirts, then were clasped in her lap. Who would have guessed that there was so much fire and fury hidden behind that cool, demure front or that it could be aroused for poor Ranny's sake? It intrigued him, and that would not do. That would not do at all.

It was late afternoon when Colonel Thomas Ward brought the map to Lettie. He found her on the front veranda of Splendora taking the evening air and helping to snap beans from Aunt Em's garden for supper. With Lettie was the older woman and Ranny, as well as Aunt Em's niece and great-nephew from down the road at Elm Grove, a young widow named Sally Anne Winston and her small son Peter.

It was Sally Anne's mother, her younger married sister, and her two children who were ill and whom Aunt Em had been visiting that morning. The boy Peter, a solemn and rather thin child of five or six, was not strong, and Aunt Em had invited Sally Anne and him to stay with her for a few days or until the summer sickness was over at their house. The two had arrived perhaps an hour before Colonel Ward had.

Sally Anne was a silver-blond beauty with the translucent skin and calm blue eyes of a China doll. She wore black, as she had explained in her soft voice, for the death of her husband who had been killed at the battle of Mansfield, but most of all because there was little money for anything else. She felt guilty at deserting her mother and the others while they were sick, but there was an old nurse who was taking care of them and she did have Peter to think of. He was all she had, all she was likely to have.

"Fiddlesticks," Aunt Em had answered, and as the nice-looking colonel had tied his horse to the picket fence and ducked under the rose arbor to approach the house, she had introduced him to Sally Anne with a certain smiling emphasis.

It was lost on Sally Anne. The blond widow, shrinking a little from the blue uniform, had acknowledged the colonel politely enough, then retreated into silence. She reserved her smiles for Ranny, who sat on the steps, alternately snapping beans and playing cat's cradle with young Peter and his companion Lionel.

The colonel was not their only visitor. Following close behind him was a gentleman who was rather elegantly dressed in a fawn coat and trousers to match, a cream waistcoat, yellow cravat, and a flat-crowned, wide-brimmed hat. He removed his hat as he greeted the lady of the house, kissing Aunt Em's hand with an air that made the lady bridle and simper at the same time. Turning to Sally Anne, he executed a bow so deep that he swept the canvas of the veranda floor with his hat.

"Miss Sally Anne, how charming you look. I swear every time I see you that you are far too young to be a mother, especially of this hulking boy."

"Don't be ridiculous!" the Southern woman reprimanded him, her tone amused but with a hint of coquettishness. "You know very well—"

"Ah, but knowing and believing are two different things."

The gentleman, who was of medium height, with crisply waving black hair, a small and neatly trimmed mustache, and brown eyes that were as merry as they were dark, turned to Lettie. "And this lady beside you must be the Amazon I heard about in town. The news of her fierceness and her beauty have spread so fast that I had to ride out at once to be presented."

"Lettie," Aunt Em said, "this rascal is Martin Eden, a friend of Ranny's since they were boys together and something of a flirt."

"Aunt Em!" Martin protested, his expression pained.

"A flirt," the older woman insisted.

Lettie was just as happy to be given no chance to reply to the outrageous compliment paid her. What was there to be said, after all? It was some comfort to reflect that nothing, really, was expected.

"What is this about Miss Mason?" Sally Anne asked.

"Yes, indeed?" Aunt Em took up the question. "What kind of things are being said?"

Martin turned to his hostess, his smile charming. "Why, only that the lady singlehandedly routed a group of bullies plaguing Ranny. This was after she had bearded in his den the most cantankerous Federal occupation officer in the state."

"I protest!" the colonel said, though his tone was mild.

"False on both counts, I assure you," Lettie said with some asperity.

Martin swung around to Ranny. "Old friend, I appeal to you. True or false?"

Ranny looked up, a faint smile curving his mouth as his gaze rested on Lettie. "True."

Aunt Em's eyes were large with wonder. "I declare! And last night she scared off the Thorn."

It was a remark that had to be explained to Sally Anne and Martin, though Lettie left the task to Aunt Em. Afterward, however, there were so many questions to be answered concerning her visit to army headquarters that she was forced to explain her brother's death and her intention of exposing his murderer.

"How very brave of you," Sally Anne said. "I would never dare."

Lettie, more than a little uncomfortable at being the center of so much attention, shook her head. "Stubborn is the word, I expect."

"Miss Mason is altogether valiant," Martin Eden said.

"She is to teach for the Freedmen's Bureau also." He turned to her. "I'm covered with chagrin at being away from my post this morning when you came to the office. I have come this afternoon, all jesting aside, to welcome you to Natchitoches and to offer you every aid and comfort in my power to bestow as you take up your new job."

"You are with the Freedmen's Bureau?" She could not keep the surprise from her voice. Other than former Union soldiers, the men most likely to be with the bureau were those with ties to the abolitionists of the prewar years. Martin Eden, with his gallantry and soft drawl, did not appear to fit either category. It was possible, of course, that he had been and was now a Unionist sympathizer. There had been many in the South.

The attention of those on the veranda was at that moment, thankfully, diverted by a new arrival. He came cantering up in a whirlwind of dust and slid from his horse with more speed than style. He let the gate with its chain and anchor-weight closure clang shut behind him and moved up the path, beating dust from his clothes as he walked. Bounding up the steps, he clapped Ranny on the shoulder with an affectionate greeting and a handshake, ruffled young Peter's hair, pretended to pull Lionel's nose, and swooped down upon Aunt Em to give her a hug.

It was easy to see, from the cries and smiles of greeting, that here was a general favorite. His name was Johnny Reeden. His hair, of a bright copper-red, curled with exuberance over his head. His skin was freckled, his eyes hazel, and his smile infectious. He was a little tongue-tied while speaking to Sally Anne, but when he turned to Martin, he buffeted him on the shoulder with the familiarity of long acquaintance.

"Martin, you old scalawag, as dapper as always. How do you manage never to look wrinkled? Tell me the secret, I really need to know."

Martin Eden smiled, but it appeared to be an effort. "I'd let you in on it, but I doubt it would help. And I've asked you before not to call me by that name."

"I've never cared to be called carrot-top, either, but that doesn't change the color of my hair," Johnny said with a droll grimace.

Scalawag. That was the word that Eden had found objectionable. It was the term given to Southerners who cooperated with the Republican Reconstruction administration. They were considered in most cases to be joined with the carpetbaggers to despoil the prostrate Confederacy. It seemed a shame that a man would have to bear with such a slur simply because his convictions ran counter to those of his neighbors.

"It's been a long time," Martin said with deliberation, "since I said such a thing to your face."

"Would you prefer that I called you a scalawag behind your back?"

"I would prefer you didn't use the term to me at all!"

Before Johnny could answer, Aunt Em spoke. "Now, now, none of that at my house. I've had enough fighting to last me all my days, and I'd think the two of you would, too."

There was a small, uncomfortable silence. Lettie broke it. "You fought in the late war, Mr. Eden?"

"We all did; Johnny, Ransom, and I." The tightness of his face relaxed as he answered. "We were in the same company starting out but were separated toward the end."

"A Confederate company?"

"Of course."

"And yet now—"

"Now I work with the Yankees. And here you are among the enemy, Miss Mason. Strange how things work out, isn't it?"

"She's been fighting, too," Johnny said, "or so they say. What's this about you routing the multitudes?"

Once more Lettie was the center of attention as she repeated the tale of the events of the morning. It was a position she was growing to relish less and less.

Only Ranny did not participate in the interrogation, though she knew from the way he watched them that he followed it with little difficulty. Except for his docility, his polite obedience to authority, his failure to understand large words or complicated questions, there was not a great deal to show that he was less than normal. She did not know what she had expected when his aunt had said he had the mentality of a twelve-year-old. Boys of that age were far from deficient in understanding; one had only to look at Lionel to prove it.

Ranny had put away the string with which he and the two boys had been playing. Peter took a handful of marbles from his pocket and showed them to Ranny and Lionel, turning the brightly colored glass spheres in his hands. There was a low discussion and then an apparent agreement. As Lettie watched, Ranny set aside his pan of beans and stood up, leading the others down into the yard. There between the flower beds, in the area of sandy dirt scraped free of grass, he drew a circle and the three went down on their knees to play marbles.

It was an odd sight: The handsome blond giant and the boys, one slight and pale, the other stocky and coffee-brown, all kneeling in the dirt, intent upon the marbles they were shooting with a flick of thumb and forefinger. It made Lettie smile, as much with an odd pleasure as with amusement.

Ranny, looking up, caught that small movement of her lips. He ducked his head. A few minutes later, he leaned and spoke to Peter. The boy turned and called, "Mama, come and show me how you can shoot!"

"Oh, no, Peter," Sally Anne called back. "I can't."

"I know you can. You told me Cousin Ranny taught you when you were both little."

"Really, my love, I would rather not."

"Please!"

"Please," Ranny echoed.

Sally Anne rose with the stiffness of reluctance. She put aside her bowl of beans and moved down the steps with her skirts trailing over the wooden treads. "Very well, but you'll be sorry when I lose your precious marbles for you."

Johnny, a grin on his freckled face, pushed away from where he leaned on the railing. "This should be worth seeing."

"Indeed," Colonel Ward agreed, and sauntered down the steps after them. Martin, whistling a little and with his hands in his pockets, followed.

Aunt Em reached for Lettie's bowl. "You may as well go, too. I can see you want to."

Lettie gave her a rather rueful grin. She had never played marbles, but she had often watched the boys when she was small and wished she could handle the smooth balls of glass. Brushing at the spent bean blossoms and stem ends that somehow clung to her skirts, she got to her feet and moved after the others.

In no time at all they were all down on their knees, digging their knuckles into the dirt, chasing marbles in the flower beds, and squabbling over those with their favorite colors and designs. The front of Lettie's skirt where she had knelt on it was hopelessly soiled, but then so was Sally Anne's, to say nothing of the knees of the men's trousers. Peter was totally happy as he ran after the marbles his mother shot as far as the fence or when he solemnly explained the best way to shoot to Lettie. Lionel said little, but the pile of marbles he had gained was bigger than anyone else's. Johnny was not particularly effective, but he kept them laughing with his antics as he practically stood on his head for difficult shots or made such wild plays that they had to duck the bouncing, flying spheres. Lettie, after wincing from the hard, cracking shooting of Martin and Colonel Ward, declared that they should be given a handicap, such as using their left hands. It was when she looked around for Ranny in order to appraise his skill that she realized he had left them.

He had not gone far. He was sitting on the high steps of the house with his chin propped in his cupped hand, watching them. His lips held the suspicious quiver of a smile, his brows had a quizzical lift, and in his eyes was bright hilarity.

It was a joke, a practical joke. Ranny had deliberately used Peter to entice them all down into the yard to scrabble in the dirt like children, like the child they thought him to be. The conviction was so strong that Lettie drew in her breath. Then Ranny met her accusing gaze. The laughter vanished and in its place was disconsolate but resigned pain.

What she had seen, Lettie realized, had been nothing more than a mercurial mood. It might amuse Ranny briefly to watch the adults playing, but he was left out of the game.

Lettie got to her feet and shook the dirt from her skirts. Almost as if drawn, she moved toward the big blond man on the steps. What she meant to say or do, she did not know, but in any case she did not have to decide. At that moment Aunt Em called to them all to come and partake of coffee and Mama Tass's pound cake.

The Union commander did not stay long after the refreshments. When he had taken his leave of his hostess, Lettie thanked him once more for the map he had brought and walked with him to where his horse was tied near the gate in the fence.

During the war, Lettie, like most young women her age, had followed the course of the battles and scanned the lists of casualties for friends and relatives. The reasons for the conflict had been firmly established in her mind: to prevent the division of the United States into two weaker sections and to abolish slavery. With the surrender of the South at Appomattox Courthouse, she had assumed that the objectives for which so many had died had been met and that life could therefore return to normal. The political squabbles that had ensued had lacked importance compared to her grief over the death of first her fiancé and then her brother or to the necessity of making some place for herself teaching. The assassination of Lincoln had been devastating, but afterward she had lost track of events except in a vague kind of way.

That was, until she had set out for the South. As she had listened to people on the train and stagecoach that had brought her, she had tried to piece together just what it was, besides the natural bitterness between former foes, that still divided the country. It appeared to be a contest over power.

The Republican majority in Congress, to prevent what appeared to be a resurgence of Southern Democrats as the defeated Confederates returned home and took up office, had discarded the conciliatory policies of Lincoln and his successor, Andrew Johnson. They had refused to recognize the congressional delegations of the Southern states on the grounds that since these states had seceded from the Union they were now conquered territory. This seemed an odd turn of events in view of the fact that the whole aim of the war was to prevent their secession. Surely, since the North had won, the attempt to secede must be considered unsuccessful? That being so, the South could only be viewed as never having been a separate entity. Not that it mattered in the long run. It was traditionally the right of the victors to lay down the terms of future relations.

The terms of the Republican Congress were simple. In order to be accepted back into the Union, the Southern states had to guarantee the abolition of slavery within their borders by their own laws; further, they had to ratify the Fourteenth Amendment granting Negroes citizenship and the Fifteenth, which gave them the right to vote. Former Confederate officers were denied the privilege of running for public office; men who had served in the Confederate army, along with other white males, were required to take an oath of allegiance, one that contained a request for pardon for their crimes, before regaining their voting privileges. The former slave states would be divided into five military districts, the commanding officers of which would have the power to make an official count of the vote in elections.

The effect of these so-called "Iron Laws," the Reconstruction Acts of 1867, had been to bar the natural leaders of the South from office and to disfranchise many white voters, those who declined on principle to take an oath that would brand them as former criminals. In the most recent election in Louisiana, the radical Republican party had gained an overwhelming majority, securing a legislature in which nearly fifty percent of the state representatives and twenty percent of the senators were Negroes.

Lettie had accepted the situation as a natural outcome of the war without question. In the past few days, however, she had seen too many men like the elderly gentleman on the street that morning and those in the post office, defeated men with hopelessness in their faces, men who clung to odd ideas of justice such as those represented by the night riders or even the Thorn. They bothered her, those men.

The colonel had released the reins of his horse and

gathered them in his hand. He turned to Lettie. "Well, it's been a pleasure to hear a crisp Yankee voice again. I rather like the Southern sound, but I do get homesick sometimes for something more familiar."

Lettie gave a wry nod. "It's rather like being in a foreign country, isn't it? The same, and yet, vastly different. I catch myself watching every word, afraid of offending."

"It isn't hard to do. They are rather touchy."

"I suppose it's natural."

"Yes," the colonel agreed.

"Do you mind— Would it be an imposition to ask you what you think of it all? Of what is happening with Reconstruction and the attempt to better the condition of the Negro, with the men they call the carpetbaggers and the Knights of the White Camellia?"

A smile rose into his green eyes, crinkling the weathered skin around his eyes. "You expect quite a lot."

"There's no one else to ask, no one who might be unbiased. However, if you would rather not say because of your position . . ."

"It isn't that. It's just that it's a complicated problem. Officially, I'm here to keep order and make certain the duly held elections are fair. Personally, I think the thing has gone too far. Of the Negroes I have dealt with, perhaps a third have sufficient education and understanding to vote intelligently and to hold an office. Another third could probably be taught and certainly have the willingness to learn to be good citizens. But the last third are plain thieves and immoral rascals who think that freedom means they are free from work forever."

"I expect the same could be said for most slave races when they are first freed."

He nodded. "Unfortunately, the radical Republicans have been more likely to attract officeholders from the last group than from the first. The rascals are all too ready to accept the inducements offered in the way of bribes and booty, while the educated Negroes—those other than the free men of color—are mainly those who were house and body servants under the old regime and who hold fast to the standards and beliefs of their former masters. The one exception that comes to mind is Tyler's former manservant, Bradley Lincoln. If more like him could be recruited, we might see something."

"You are saying, then, that the present state government is as bad as—as the editorial writers for the New Orleans newspapers claim it is?" She could not keep the shock from her voice.

"It could hardly be worse. Give the Negro the vote, make him a true citizen—that in itself is a worthy ambition. But the way the Republicans are going about it has turned the legislature here into a forum for nothing less than petty vengeance and a form of pillage that, had the Northern armies been guilty of committing it, would have made them liable for hanging to a man. I feel sometimes as if I had defeated a soldier in a fair fight, given him terrible wounds, but that now I'm under orders to hold him down while the vultures feast."

"A harsh indictment, surely, Colonel?"

He shrugged. "If you like."

"You condone the actions of the men who hide under sheets to terrify the countryside?"

"I'll put it this way. It's my job to stop the night riders, but I can't say I'm surprised that they are riding. This so-called Reconstruction is being imposed on a group of men who have had their blood at fever heat for years during the longest and bloodiest war this country has ever seen. The wonder isn't that they are fighting back but that it hasn't turned into another civil war. Make no mistake, if the South ever gets to the point where it can feed itself and have anything left over again, it will. After all, what has it got to lose?"

"Their lives, their homes?"

"We killed them in the thousands before, and the only thing that stopped them was starvation and lack of ammunition. We burned their homes and stripped their fields, and still they fought. It's stupid to grind men like that into the dust. You don't make them humble that way; you turn them into deadly enemies. As for the homes that we left to them, the tax collectors are taking those right and left now."

"Big places like Splendora?" she scoffed.

"What's here? A house and land. Most of the planters like the Tylers, both here and at Elm Grove, are house and land poor. They can't eat them, can't spend them. They could sell a few acres here and there, but nobody wants to buy because they haven't the money to pay the freedmen to work it. Still the legislature increases the taxes every few months until it amounts to near confiscation of property. Where is the money to pay them to come from?"

"Do I detect a note of treason, Colonel?" she asked, her voice light.

"It probably sounds that way," he agreed, his smile grim. "But it's the politicians who make wars, then scuttle for safety while the men like me fight them. And I'll tell you the truth, Miss Mason. Like Aunt Em, I've had enough fighting."

The colonel's words were disturbing, not the least reason being because he had no reason for saying them beyond simple conviction. Lettie was thoughtful as she watched him ride away, then moved back up the path toward the house.

She was climbing the steps when Aunt Em looked up from her pan of snapped beans. She had poured all the different pans of beans into her own large one, finished snapping the crisp green pods into lengths, and was sifting through them for trash.

"Mighty fine-looking man, the colonel," the older woman said.

"Yes," Lettie replied.

Ransom scowled, his gaze on the back of the departing officer as his blue uniform merged with the gathering dusk.

Lettie, when morning came once more, did not intend to be deceitful. She told Aunt Em that she was going to take the buggy and drive to Campti, the small town across the Red River where she was assigned to teach, just to look over the buildings, to gain some idea of the distance she would have to travel each day and the difficulties involved in crossing the river. The conversation took place at breakfast. Ranny looked up from his plate, his gaze searching.

"I could drive you," he suggested, his voice light.

Lettie gave him a quick smile. "It's kind of you to offer, but I don't know how long I'll be."

"I don't mind. I can wait."

"You wouldn't like it, really. Besides, if Aunt Em will trust me with the horse and buggy, I would really rather drive myself. It will be best if I get used to it."

Ranny nodded his understanding with his gaze on his plate. On impulse, Lettie reached out to touch his hand in apology for his disappointment and reassurance. The moment she felt the warmth of his skin, she drew back. It was, she realized, the first time she had ever voluntarily touched a man other than her brother Henry or her father, who had died when she was a child. It was embarrassing, that impulse, and confusing. Her only consolation was that Ranny hardly seemed to notice.

Ransom looked up to give her his most meaningless smile.

He reached for his coffee cup in unconcern, though the place on his wrist where she had touched him burned like a brand.

The problems in getting to and from her assigned post were not insurmountable, but there were problems. In the first place, if she remained in her present lodging, Lettie would have to cross the Red River by ferry twice each day, coming and going. That was in addition to a drive of some few miles on the other side. The Freedmen's Bureau had promised to provide her with a horse and conveyance so that she need not impose on Aunt Em for hers. Still, it might be better if she changed her place of residence.

After looking around the Campti settlement, however, and noting the few small houses left by the Federal troops who had burned it during the Red River campaign, the stretching fields of cotton, and the inhabitants who watched her from behind their curtains but did not approach, she was not certain that was a reasonable option.

The school was much what she had been led to expect. It was a one-room cabin built of logs. The front door had no more than a leather thong for a latch. Inside, the walls were sheeted with rough, unpainted planks of random widths. There was a mud daub fireplace in the end wall that showed traces of the Spanish moss and deer hair used to keep the mud on the framework. The furnishings were just as spare: a few benches, a few books, a desk for the teacher, and a fly-specked picture of President Washington on the wall.

Lettie sat for a few minutes at the desk, trying to picture the students she would teach and the joy they would bring to learning. It wasn't easy. She thought of the neat brick school building she had left, with its cheerful bell, clean, plastered walls, and tight iron stove, and her heart misgave her.

What in the name of heaven was she doing in this place?

Her lips tightened, and she got to her feet. Never mind. It would be all right. She would make it all right.

No one displayed any curiosity about Lettie's brief explorations or seemed to notice when she left the schoolhouse. She climbed up into the buggy seat, then sat holding the reins for long moments.

The spring where her brother was killed was in this direction. The morning was not at all far advanced. Mama Tass had packed a lunch of fried chicken, biscuits, pickles, and chocolate cake, and provided a jug of water. The map the colonel had given Lettie was on the seat beside her since she had been following the route to her post on it. The day was so bright and quietly peaceful that it seemed impossible that there could be any danger attached to driving a bit farther into the countryside. If there was any sign of trouble, any feeling of disturbance of any kind, she could always turn back. She might be a little later than expected returning to Splendora, but her time was her own and she need not account for it to anyone. The idea of going had been in the back of her mind since breakfast, though no formal decision had been made. Until this moment. There was, she told herself, no deceit involved, not really.

The road was scarcely more than a wagon track with landmarks instead of signs to guide her. Its deep ruts and numerous holes were at least evidence that it was well traveled and served to separate it from the many side roads going to small towns, churches, gristmills, sawmills, or farms that led from it, roads that were not drawn on her map.

It was an ancient route, once an Indian trail, that had been used by the troops of the old French fort, St. Jean de la Baptiste de Natchitoches, as they traveled to another settlement on the Ouachita River some ninety miles north, where the town of Monroe was now located. Designated for more than a hundred years as a military highway, it had served the Spanish, the Confederates, and also the United States Army.

Over the route she was following, the Federal payrolls, after coming upriver along the Mississippi and the Red to Natchitoches, were transferred to the troops stationed at Monroe and points east. The officers charged with carrying such payrolls could, and usually did, request an escort for the sake of safety. In the past, however, it had been thought just as well not to call attention to the gold in that manner, that there was as much safety in having a man ride through as if he was no more than a messenger, with the payroll in his saddlebages. That method was satisfactory so long as no one knew what was being carried.

On the day that Lettie's brother was killed, there had been some delay in the forming of the escort that was supposed to ride with him. Henry Mason had not waited but had gone on alone. Either someone had seen him ride out and noticed the fullness and weight of his saddlebags or else there had been a leak of information concerning the payroll movements. The result was that someone had been waiting for Henry at the spring and had shot him dead.

Not just someone, but the Thorn. Henry Mason had been interested in the man's activities, had written to Lettie of some of them. He had been assigned to investigate the Thorn and had seemed puzzled by his deeds, finding as much to admire in many as he did to deplore in a few. Gradually, he had compiled a written portrait of the man, though one he had admitted might be flawed. He had judged him fearless and daring and sometimes fiendishly clever, had conceded to him a woodsman's knowledge of the countryside and the devil's own luck. Moreover, he had discovered in him a puckish sense of humor in the most unlikely of situations, but also the most conscienceless cruelty when the occasion demanded. Alternately intrigued and repelled, Henry had watched the men in the vicinity of Natchitoches whom he thought might fit into the picture he had constructed.

Then he had hit upon a promising lead. He had written to Lettie about it, his excitement as much for penetrating the Thorn's daytime disguise as for the hope of bringing him to book for his crimes. He would not set the name down on paper, he had said, until he was sure, but by the next mail he would tell Lettie the man's identity. Two days after that last letter was posted, he was killed.

It did not take a genius to understand that the Thorn had removed Henry with two motives in mind: the theft of the money and the silencing of a threat.

The sun shone down on Lettie unremittingly. The sand of the road seemed to capture and hold the heat. It made a whispering sound as it fell from the wheels and billowed into a long white cloud behind the buggy. Flies droned, zipping about the lathered horse and around Lettie's face. As the day advanced, there was little shade, even in the stretches of woods, as the shadows retreated nearer to the tree trunks. The air took on a thick, sultry feel that made breathing a chore.

Even with its discomforts, however, Lettie began to enjoy her outing. There were wildflowers growing in profusion along the roadside and between the wheel ruts: yellow daisies, pink and white poppies, puff balls of purple, and white blooms on the long arching stems of blackberries. Now and then she crossed a small bayou or creek on a narrow bridge of logs without railings or else splashed across a shallow ford in a cooling spray of water. More than once she sat in the buggy in the middle of the stream enjoying the shade of the inevitable overhang of trees while the horse drank and blew before trotting on again. Birds called in a multitude of trilling and melodious or rasping and strident noises. Crickets and peeper frogs sang. Startled rabbits bounded away down the road in front of her, and once a deer, a large doe, stood silently watching as she bowled past. Near farms, she sometimes had to pull up until ranging cows, munching the grass in the road, or families of piglets rolling in the dirt of the potholes, deigned to amble out of the way.

The only people she met were two Union officers who saluted as they passed and turned in their saddles to look after her; a man with his wife, five towheaded boys, and two dogs piled in a buckboard on the way to town; and a white-bearded patriarch herding perhaps two dozen rather dirty sheep.

The miles rolled away under the wheels. Lettie did not consider herself a judge of horseflesh, but the animal between the shafts, a chestnut mare, seemed uncommonly fine to her, sweet of temper and instantly responsive to the least pressure on the reins. There was a whip in the socket beside her, but she had no use for it. She felt responsible for returning the mare in good condition since she could guess how much value it must have to Aunt Em.

Lettie felt free. It was odd, but she had never quite had that sensation before. Perhaps it was because she was alone, far from her family and friends, in a strange part of the country. Women were so protected, so hemmed in by restrictions and prohibitions and warnings that they seldom had the opportunity to enjoy this sense of being on their own. From everything she had heard, Southern women were even more hampered in that way than those of her own region, and heaven knew that was bad enough. It was possible that Colonel Ward had become imbued with this sense of masculine alarm over excursions of females and therefore had felt it his duty to warn her away from the spring where her brother was killed. No one else had thought it necessary to persuade her to forgo the journey. Of course, no one else had been told exactly what she meant to do.

Regardless, it was good to be doing something definite at last about looking into Henry's death. She had thought about it and fretted over it for so long that it had seemed as if the day would never come. Not that she expected to discover anything of importance by looking at the spot where he had been killed, but it was a place to start. It would aid her to picture in her mind exactly what had happened, and would therefore enable her to think about it constructively.

Lettie stopped at a farmhouse, a crude dwelling made of logs rather like two cabins built with an open hallway connecting them, a hallway of the kind known as a dogtrot because it was where the dogs always stayed. There were certainly enough of those about the house. They came streaming out in a most alarming fashion when she pulled up in the yard. Their barking brought out the farmer's wife, however, who yelled the dogs to silence while she wiped her hands on her apron.

The woman took a long look at Lettie's serviceable tan poplin carriage costume with its separate bodice trimmed in brown velvet braid and the latest drawn-back-style skirt without hoops, and at her wide-brimmed hat of plaited straw trimmed with daisies centered with brown velvet eyes. She apparently approved of what she saw, for a slow smile of appreciation transformed the suspicion on her face to friendliness.

"Morning. Won't you get down and set a spell?"

"Thank you, but no," Lettie said, though when she saw the woman's obvious disappointment she was sorry she could not be more obliging. "I'm looking for a spring in this part of the country. Perhaps you could help me?"

"A spring? Only one hereabouts is some miles farther along, t'other side of Saline Creek, the one where the Yankee soldier died."

Lettie swallowed on a constriction in her throat. "That will be the one. You're sure I'm on the right road?"

"Sure as sure can be." There was curiosity in the woman's tired eyes, but though she moved closer to the buggy, the better to see and to hear, she asked no questions, a form of backwoods courtesy. "I've a pot of greens on the stove and a nice bread pudding in the oven, if you'd care to partake?"

There was a real warmth in Lettie's smile as she lifted her reins. "It's very kind of you, but I had best be on my way."

The woman gave a slow nod. "You take care of yourself, now," she said with emphasis, and stepped back. She stood watching, with her hand shading her eyes, until Lettie had driven out of sight.

Past the farm, the road wound through virgin timber. The great towering trunks of pines and oaks, ash and black gum and sweet gum seemed to block out the sky, while beneath them was an understory of smaller trees, dogwoods and mulberries among them. Along the sides of the road where there was more sunlight, these were hung with thick vines that trailed from tree to tree and tangled with the bushes and vines growing below to such an extent that the mass appeared impenetrable.

She came upon the landmark for the spring suddenly, an open, cleared area beside the road in a curve. There were signs of several campfires where people had stopped for the night or else paused to boil coffee or to cook using the sweet water available there. The spring was supposed to be the best in the area, a great boon for people traveling the military road, many of them heading west to Texas.

Lettie pulled up the buggy in the shade and got down. She tethered the horse, then took her noon dinner, which was wrapped in a cloth, and walked toward a dim trail through the trees that looked as if it would lead to the spring.

It was cooler under the tall canopy of trees. The path, winding amid the undergrowth and matted with a thick carpet of leaves and pine needles, descended a rather steep slope toward what appeared to be a small stream with moss-grown banks. The air here smelled of wet earth and crumbling, decaying vegetation. Along the meandering water course at the foot of the hillside was a glade of ferns, the soft green color like a promise of Eden. The stream, however, was hardly more than a clear rivulet of water, the overflow from not one but several springs—small, clear pools seeping from the high bank that rose behind them, reflecting like woodland mirrors the green of the leaves that arched over them.

Some effort had been made to render the largest of the seep springs, which lay among the roots of the tall trees, more usable. A big, bottomless barrel of cypress wood had been sunk into it to form a curb to hold back the sandbanks. On the broken branch of the great dogwood that leaned over it was a gourd dipper, which was hung by a leather thong strung through a hole in the handle. A green leaf or two floated on the water; one had an orange and black butterfly perched upon it. Otherwise, the water was pure and unsullied.

Lettie pushed aside the leaves and dipped the cup Mama Tass had given her into the water, drinking deep. Dipping again, she wet her handkerchief and wiped her face and hands, removing the dust of the drive. Then, stepping away a few paces, she spread her dinner among the ferns and sat down to eat.

She was ravenous; in fact, she could not remember when she had been so hungry. It was well past noon, but she had not wanted to stop until she reached her destination. The fresh air and the exhilaration of accomplishing what she had set out to do, with possibly even a bit of the spice of danger, gave her appetite such an edge that she ate as if she expected the bread and chicken and cake to be snatched from her. When every morsel was gone, she licked her fingers, then, with a hasty glance around, wiped them on the checked napkin provided.

Grinning a little at herself, she pulled off her hat and threw it aside, then lay back among the ferns, stretching with clenched fists. A shaft of sunlight striking through the distant cathedral ceiling of leaves overhead glittered in her eyes. She closed them and was aware abruptly of one of those moments that come so seldom and so briefly in a lifetime, a golden moment when her every sense was alive and it was good that it was so. She lay still for long minutes, savoring it.

The sun went behind a cloud and the woods grew dimmer. Lettie felt the irritating tickle of grass against her neck. She wrenched herself up into a sitting position again and reached for her cup. Another drink would be good. The water was so sweet and delicious that it was better than the finest champagne.

Lettie was standing at the curbed spring, sipping the water and looking about her, when she saw the cross. It was a crude thing made of two gnarled and blackened pieces of pine nailed roughly together. It stood on the high ridge that ran behind the spring, on the opposite side of the stream from where she had left the buggy. There was a cleared area around it, as if some attempt had been made to form a suitable resting place for the dead.

Henry's grave. Lettie had known it was somewhere at hand but had not expected it to be quite so close. She had been told of how a young man out looking for strayed cows had seen the buzzards circling the spring and gone to investigate. He had found Henry's body lying almost in the water, as if he had been shot while kneeling to drink. Whoever had killed Henry had taken his identification and his outer clothing and left him to the wild animals, so he had been buried on the spot as an unknown victim of a shooting. It was only later that he was identified as the payroll carrier from Natchitoches.

Lettie put down her cup with care. She caught the front of her skirts and, weaving her way among the great trees and smaller saplings, climbed the slope of the ridge. She did not stop until she reached the cross.

The grave, if ever it had been mounded, was flat and covered with tufts of grass, pine and sweet-gum seedlings, and a scattering of last year's dead leaves. Solitary, silent, it kept watch over the spring and fern-filled glade.

Lettie reached out to touch the crude cross with gentle fingers. She stared down at it through a blinding shimmer of tears, seeing instead Henry as she had seen him last, laughing, excited in his quiet way about his posting to Louisiana. He had given her a hug as she saw him off on the train, a rare show of the deep affection between them, and he had hung out of the train window waving until he was out of sight. He had loved apple cobbler and maple trees, old books and thunderstorms. And now he was dead. Murdered. Left to lie alone in this godforsaken spot.

She heard not a sound. It was a prickling along her spine, a sudden, primitive tightening of the nerves that warned her. She lifted her head, dashing away her tears with a quick, almost furtive brush of her fingers. Alarm burgeoned inside her, coursing along her veins as she turned first one way, then the other, her gaze searching among the trees.

Then she saw him, a man in a rusty black suit standing so still and tall in the shade of a great pine that he almost merged with its trunk. He wore a gun in a belt around his narrow waist and a black hat pulled low over his eyes. His face was shadowed, though the line of his dark mustache could be seen as he pushed away from the tree he was leaning against.

"I didn't kill him," he said.

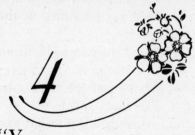

4

"You!"

The Thorn. Lettie would recognize that husky voice anywhere, and though she had only seen his tall form against the starlight, it, too, was familiar.

"Who did you expect, riding out alone like this? Should I be on the watch for the man you are to meet?"

"I'm meeting no one." She allowed the scorn she felt for the question to edge her tone, even as she realized that it might have been better to claim a rendezvous so that he would think she had a male protector near.

"All alone? Don't tell me you weren't warned of what a risk that could be for a woman? Or did you come because of the risk? Maybe I should consider your presence an invitation?"

It was anger that drove him. Ransom acknowledged that truth without surprise. Anger because she was so damnably vulnerable and didn't seem to have the sense to know it, because she was beautiful standing there with the breeze lifting the fine tendrils of hair that curled at her temples and molding her skirts against her, because she was oblivious of the effect she had on men and with which he was waging battle. It would be so easy to take her there among the ferns, so easy to be the kind of man she thought him.

Lettie's eyes narrowed. "An invitation? To what?"

"Why, to a larger portion of the charms I tasted when last we met."

"You must be mad!" The color that swept across her cheekbones was not all caused by anger. "I came to visit the grave of my brother, nothing more!"

"Too bad. It might have enlivened what looks to be an otherwise dull afternoon."

His easy acceptance of her rejection was less than complimentary. A tremor passed through Lettie as the memory of the brush of his mustache and the smoothness of his mouth crossed her mind. Her tone waspish, she said, "You can always dress up and frighten the locals."

"But not you?" The words were dangerously quiet.

"Do I appear frightened?"

"I can't say that you do, which makes you either a good actress or stupid."

"Stupid?" she repeated, her fury so great that she could hardly speak.

"Shall we say lacking in forethought if the more exact word offends you? First, for failing to recognize your danger, and second, for adding to it by throwing down a challenge."

That he was right did not make his strictures any easier to bear. "Are you saying that if I cower before you in terror I will be free from harm, whereas defiance will give you leave to do as you please?"

"In a word, yes."

Disdain curled her lips. "I don't believe it. You will do as you like, regardless."

"Does that mean," he inquired in a tone that was like the slice of a knife, "that you have resigned yourself?"

"Definitely not!"

"It must indicate then that you absolve me of ill intent. I didn't know you thought that well of me."

"I don't! I believe you are capable of anything, anything at all."

"You and half the rest of the world. You have no idea

how flattering it is to be charged with every crime that takes place within a hundred miles, from robbing a drunken senator while dressed in curled wig and satin skirts to molesting a sixty-year-old widow in the guise of a three-hundred-pound mule skinner. Flattering, but hardly helpful."

"I wonder what can have given people the idea it was possible?" she said with mock innocence.

"I wonder why you are still unmarried, with such a beguiling tongue in your head."

She gave him a cold stare. "And then there's the question of why you are still unhanged when you openly show yourself in the light of day."

"Luck and cowardice. I only show myself to unarmed victims."

Was she to be a victim after all? The truth was, she had no idea what he meant to do and, in her present state of mind, did not much care. Her greatest concern, one that was shocking in its virulence, was how best to insult him now.

"Very intelligent," she gibed at him.

He ignored the provocation. "And on the day your brother was killed, he never saw me."

"He was armed, of course."

"Miss Mason, I am telling you as plainly as I can that I had nothing to do with the death of your brother."

She stared at him without the least change of expression. "How it is that you know my name?"

"I have my sources of information."

"I'm sure you do."

"You haven't listened to a word I've said."

"I can't imagine why you should think I would."

"An excess of optimism, I suppose."

Lettie heard the bitterness in his voice and was surprised. She looked away from him, lowering her gaze. This exchange of words over Henry's grave suddenly seemed vulgar. She turned, moving away a few steps. She knew the Thorn followed her, for she heard the dry rustle of the grass under his feet. He did not come close, however. Over her shoulder, she said, "If not you, then who?"

"At a guess, the jayhawkers in this area. They cast a long loop these days."

"And make good scapegoats."

"I suppose you could look at it that way."

She swung on him, her wine-brown eyes blazing. "My brother wrote to me that you were giving the army more trouble than the outlaws and the Knights of the White Camellia combined. He was sure that you were the brains, if not the actual perpetrator, behind the robbery of a post office two months before he died and the deaths of at least three wagonloads of settlers going west with their gold hidden among their belongings. He said that you were half devil and half avenging angel, that you pretended to be such a white knight and actually could have been something fine and good, a force for what was right, but that you had channeled your wits into murder and theft, making a game of it, and that was the worst thing of all."

"I've never pretended to be a knight in armor or any kind of crusader. All I've done, all I'm trying to do, is to see that as few people as possible are hurt while this madness called Reconstruction lasts, and arrange matters so that when it ends people will be able to regain their self-respect and to look each other in the eye."

She hardly allowed him to finish. "Henry said something else. He said he thought he knew who you really were. I think that's why he died. Not for the gold, though you took it since it was there, but because of what he knew."

He made no answer, though, under the brim of his hat, his eyes narrowed to slits. In the taut quiet, the sound of a limb falling from high up in the treetops and thudding to the ground was like a blow. The wind was rising, growing cooler. Overhead the clouds thickened, becoming darker.

At last Ransom spoke, the words a soft rasp of sound. "And you, Miss Mason? Do you think you know? Did your brother reveal to you just who he thought I might be?"

"Do you really think that you would be free at this moment if he had?"

Lettie held the hard gaze directed to her with a great effort, held it partly from pride, partly from the knowledge that to avoid it would be to court disbelief and therefore death. There was nothing to indicate that he would let her go even if he accepted what she said; still, there was always a chance.

Oh, if she only had a pistol! Henry had shown her how to shoot years ago. A heavy army-issue Colt would give her the advantage, would allow her to take the Thorn back to Natchitoches and turn him over to the authorities. He would not expect her to be a threat; that was something he reserved for himself.

It did not do to think of such things. Instead, she concentrated on the man's appearance, trying to impress it on her memory. It was difficult to do at the distance he had maintained between them. His eyes were indistinct under the shadow of his hat brim, but it appeared they might be that indeterminate color known as hazel, something that might explain the different eye colors attributed to him. His hair, where it could be seen, was a dull dark brown, and his skin was rather swarthy. His features were obscured by the mustache, which extended in a drooping curve onto his angular cheeks, though they appeared regular enough, with a hard, cynical cast. He might have been an attractive man once, in a raffish fashion, before he had been marked by the life he had chosen.

Alerted by the searching intensity of her gaze, Ransom took a step backward, at the same time making a swift gesture of dismissal. "I advise you to go home while you still can. Not just back to where you are staying, but home to the North, where you know what you are doing and can meddle in local affairs in safety."

A sharp retort rose in her mind, but she suppressed it. Her voice soft and yet dry, she said, "Your concern is overwhelming. I take it that you are releasing me?"

"I never held you," he answered with equal softness. "If I had, you would have known it when I let you go."

Lettie stared at him as her heart began to jar in her chest and a curious languor crept along her veins. She could feel the heat of a flush spreading upward until it reached her hairline. Fear and revulsion swept over her in waves, but beneath it was something that she recognized only vaguely and yet which left her aghast. It was a definite response in the innermost reaches of her being to the leashed strength and the sheer male force she recognized in the man before her. It was a betrayal, one for which she despised herself, though she could not deny it.

Wrenching her gaze from his by will alone, she swung around in a swirl of tan skirts and plunged away from him.

The climb back up the slope to where she had left the buggy was the longest one Lettie had ever made. She could feel the Thorn's gaze upon her, was aware of his satisfaction with the way the exchange between them had gone. She half expected him to come after her, to lay hands upon her, to say he had changed his mind and she could not go. There had been the timbre of a threat in his last words that made it seem entirely possible.

Once in the buggy, she sat with her hands clenched in her lap while long tremors shook her from her head to the tips of her high-button shoes. She could not understand what had just happened to her, could not believe that she had spoken as she had to her brother's killer. The things she had said came back to ring in her ears, and she was amazed that she still lived. Not that she would take any of it back. The pleasure of telling the Thorn to his face exactly what she thought of him would have been worth the cost, was worth even the self-knowledge she had gained.

She had left the tablecloth that had contained her lunch beside the spring as well as her hat. It didn't matter; she wasn't going back. Gathering the reins, slapping them against the haunches of the mare, she turned the buggy and sent it wheeling in the direction of Natchitoches.

The wind fluttered the hood of the buggy and whipped the sand raised by the horse's hooves, whirling it up into Lettie's face. The sky grew darker. Now and then there came the distant rumble of thunder, but the rain held off.

The road wound endlessly. It had not seemed so far coming as it did now on the return journey. She felt driven, as if the furies were on her trail, and once she thought she heard an echo of horse's hooves as if she was being followed. Imagination, she told herself, or else an echo sent back by the woods; why would the Thorn want to follow her? Still, she sent the horse along at a brisk pace and cast as many anxious looks behind her as she did at the dark clouds gathering in the sky.

It was odd how alike the rutted roads looked traveling in this direction. The impression of a main military high-way was much less. Lettie paused several times as the road forked, uncertain of which branch or turning to take. She always chose what she perceived to be the most well-trav-eled road, but as time passed, as nothing she saw looked familiar and the landmarks she expected to see failed to appear, the fear that she had made a mistake grew. She searched her map, but without the sun as a guide or some hint of where she was, it was useless. She fully intended to ask the first person she saw to direct her, but there had been no houses, no settlements, no other travelers for miles.

Her arms and shoulders ached from the unaccustomed

strain of driving. She found that she was clenching her teeth and forced herself to relax. Ahead of her was a ford for some creek that should not have been on the road she was traveling. With a frown between her eyes and her mouth set in a straight line, she guided the horse down the incline that led to the creek and under the huge cypress trees draped with moss that stood with their roots in it.

Two men, with long, rough hair under shapeless hats and faded ill-kempt clothes, astride wild, stunted-looking horses closed in on Lettie from either side. So overwrought was she that she did not stop to question their purpose but snatched up the buggy whip. As they came alongside the buggy, reaching for the reins, she struck them with all her strength.

They howled and fell back. She lashed the chestnut mare onward, forcing her into the water with its muddy, wheel-hugging bottom and up the bank on the other side. Lettie could hear their yells and curses and the splashing of their mounts as the men spurred them after her.

Then came the crash of a shot, a keening sound, and a hole was ripped in the glazed leather of the cover above her head. Her face set in a grim mask, she laid the whip on the mare again.

Then from farther behind her came the thudding sound of a horse ridden fast. More shots exploded, one of them ricocheting through the treetops. One of her attackers yelled, bawling out an oath. The two men spurred hard, leaning low over their mounts' necks as they passed the buggy in a clatter of hooves and through fountains of water. They surged up the slope of the creekbank and galloped away down the road.

Lettie called to the mare, pulling her in, gentling the blowing horse to a stop. The mare needed to rest and so did she. It would also be polite to thank whoever had frightened away the two men. He was crossing the ford behind her, drawing even with the buggy.

The Thorn tipped his hat but barely pulled in his mount. The words clipped, he said, "Are you all right?"

Disbelief and the remnants of fright she had had no time to acknowledge until now compressed Lettie's voice. "Yes, certainly."

"You made a wrong turn. Bear right at the next crossroad and that will take you to a ferry that crosses the river. You'll be below Natchitoches, not at Grand Ecore. Take the next right turn on the other side to go back to town."

Before Lettie could open her mouth to speak, he kicked his horse into movement and rode away. She stared after him, her chest tight.

Never, never in her life had she been so mortified or so enraged. There was not another human being who had the power to so overset her emotions as this man had. It was incomprehensible. She was usually quite calm and rational, even staid, in her actions. The fault was the Thorn's, because of the things he did and said, his total lack of ordinary regard for people's feelings.

But what did she expect? He was not an ordinary man. He was a rider of the night, a thief and a murderer. For her to be upset was not unnatural, though she must control it. She would do just that. She would drive herself back to Splendora, very carefully, and if there was any kind of benign providence, the next time she saw the Thorn it would be in a courtroom where he was being tried for murder.

Lettie set the horse in motion once more and refused to look up as thunder growled in a dull bass overhead.

By the time she reached the river, the sky was so dark that it might have been nearing evening. The constant grumble of thunder was like far-off cannon fire, and light-

ning made white flares overhead. Rain was beginning to
fall, dimpling the water. The far bank was almost lost in
a gray, obscuring curtain. The rope cable used to pull the
railed wooden platform of the ferry back and forth stretched
across to the other side, but the ferry itself was a dim shape
of railings and uprights against the far shore. Beside the
muddy trough that served as a landing, a man draped in
an oilskin poncho sat his horse. Lettie knew who it was
even before she pulled to a halt beside him.

Neither spoke for a long moment. The rushing sound
of the river and the spattering of the rain filled the stillness,
growing slowly louder.

The rain began to drip from the brim of the Thorn's
hat. His shoulders moved in a gesture that might have
indicated resignation. He turned from the river to meet
her searching gaze.

"There is a small problem. The men who shot at you
crossed here ahead of us. By the time I reached the riverbank, they were three-quarters of the way over. They
are holding the ferry."

"Holding the ferry? What do you mean?"

"I mean, they are preventing the ferryman from bringing
it back here."

"Why would they do that? Did they think you were after
them?" Her voice was sharp, but she did not care.

"They knew it."

A gust of wind whipped rain in under the top of the
buggy. Lettie gasped at the cold wetness, wiping her face
with her hand. She looked around for shelter. There was
a large oak with spreading branches down a muddy lane
to the right. Beyond it was what appeared to be a lighted
window in a low shape like a small house. She lifted the
reins.

Lightning lighted the sky, giving a blue cast to the features of the Thorn. He leaned in the saddle and reached

out a hand to catch her reins. "Not that way. Trees, and whatever may be under them, make fine targets for lightning."

"The cabin then—"

"It belongs to the man who works the ferry, but I don't think his wife will appreciate company or that you want to stay there. Three of their five children are down with scarlet fever, and both grandmothers are on hand to help."

Eight people in the one-room cabin and scarlet fever. Was he telling the truth? There was no reason she could see for him to lie. The buggy rocked in the wind. There was a curtain that could be pulled to keep out some of the rain, but it was so fragile with age and disuse that as Lettie tried to unfasten the thing with one hand, it tore into dusty strips. A tree branch with fluttering green leaves went whirling across the road, followed by stinging bits of bark. The mare reared and whinnied. The Thorn wheeled to go to the mare's head before she could bolt.

Lettie dropped the broken curtain so that she could use both hands to hold the reins. She looked again at the tree and the low shape of the cabin. Above the wind she shouted, "Maybe they have a barn!"

"Just a shed!" came his answer. He watched her for a moment. With a soft imprecation, he turned away, then swung back again. His face was grim as he called, "Come on, I can show you a place."

She was a fool to take him at his word, a fool to follow him, but she seemed to have little choice; neither she nor the horse could stay out in this storm. It might be wiser to take her chances with a bolt of lightning, but she had the distinct feeling that it would be dangerous to let the Thorn know she thought so. At any rate, it was too late for objections. He was leading the mare in a turn so that they were headed back the way they had come.

The promised shelter sat at the end of the track some

yards off the main road. Built of logs, perhaps half as wide as it was long, it was quite small, little more than a hut. To one side was a lean-to sagging with the weight of a Virginia creeper vine. Off to the right was a large spot of blackened ground and timbers that looked as if it was from a burned building.

The Thorn stopped beside the buggy as Lettie pulled up. He reached for the reins. "You get inside. I'll see to your horse."

Lettie was only too glad to comply. The skirt of her carriage dress was soaked to the knees with rain, and her bodice was so damp and clammy that every gust of wind seemed to penetrate to the bone. That she could be so cold now when she had been so insufferably hot earlier was unbelievable.

Her hands were shaking as she climbed down and hurried to pull open the door of the hut. The wind snatched the flimsy panel of split logs from her hand and sent it smashing against the wall. She grabbed for it, then fought it shut as she whipped herself inside, closing out the sweeping sheets of wind-blown rain. There was no inside latch, but the tight fit at one corner where the door sagged kept it in place.

Lettie stood in near darkness. There were no windows in this small building, no other entrance or exit except the one through which she had come. Faint glints of grayness shone through the unchinked logs, but that was the only light.

As her eyes began to adjust, she could see the pale shape of her own hand, but little more. To make matters worse, the dense gloom seemed to be alive with small rustling noises. They were caused, she thought, by the wind through the cracks shifting and stirring what appeared to be a pile of cornhusks against the back wall. She could not be sure that was all, however. The place smelled of dried corn and mildew and mice.

She stood still, listening. Above the storm, she thought she heard the Thorn speaking to the mare in the lean-to and the animal's snuffling response. Was that a scrabbling noise of tiny, clawed feet? She couldn't tell. She was not afraid of mice, had never been one to scream and climb on chairs when they appeared, but neither did she like the thought of one running under her skirts and climbing among her petticoats. Either they had to go or she would.

Taking a deep breath, she slowly bent and caught her soggy skirts in both hands, lifting them above her knees. With a quick running step, she dashed among the corn-husks, kicking the pile so that they flew up around her, scattering across the rough, warped floorboards. A mouse squeaked and ran, vanishing down a knothole. Another scuttled toward the corner. Lettie went after it. It leaped up and slipped away through the opening between two logs just as the door flew open.

"What's going on in here?" the Thorn demanded.

The wind behind him flapped his oilskin and sent the cornhusks whirling. A blowing mist of rain spattered across the floor, wetting half the hut. The open door let in the gray-purple light.

"Getting rid of the rats," Lettie snapped. "What does it look like? Would you close the door!"

Ransom choked on a laugh that he turned at once into a cough. He had expected to find her subdued and fearful, even backed in a corner. He should have known better. Just as he should have known she would have slender and altogether delectable legs. He moved to comply with her request. There was rich amusement in his voice that he did not trouble to hide as he said, "Need any help?"

Was he daring to laugh at her? Belatedly, she remembered to let go of her skirts. They dragged at her waist with their heavy wetness. "Thank you, no. What is this place?"

"A corncrib. Have you never seen one before?"

"Not," she said with glacial politeness, "to my knowledge."

"It's used to store the corn crop until it can be shucked and the kernels removed from the cobs for feed or else taken to the gristmill. The people who lived here were burned out, not by the Yankees but by a fireplace fire that spread to the barn. This is all that's left."

There was a slithering, sliding sound as he finished speaking. He appeared to be removing his oilskin, taking off his hat, and slinging water from its brim. Her voice sharp, she said, "What are you doing?"

He paused. "Making myself comfortable."

"But I thought—that is to say, you aren't staying?"

"Now why would you think that?"

"You have foul-weather gear, and there must be other things you have to do, other places you must go to."

"Not," he said, mimicking her earlier chilly accents to perfection, "to my knowledge."

What he was doing was dangerous and Ransom had the liveliest awareness of that fact. He preferred to think of it as something preordained, even though he knew better. He should leave her in this shelter, mean as it was, and ride on; he might have done just that had he not felt to blame for her being there.

He had followed her earlier because they had both been going the same way, back to Natchitoches, but he had deliberately allowed her to take the wrong turn when he could have stopped her. He had wanted to know if her deviation from the correct route was accidental or if there was some reason for it; he had been curious about what she would do when she discovered her error, if it was one.

And it had seemed best that she not know he was behind her. The less anyone knew of his movements the better, of course, but he also didn't want her to feel that he was menacing her.

But because he had kept quiet, she had been attacked at the ford by those two pieces of scum. Instead of being at Splendora where it was safe, she was here, and so was he. She should not be left alone, not simply because it was rough country but because the two on the other side of the river might come back. He was responsible. He would stay, her self-appointed guardian. Whether she wanted one or not.

Lettie made her decision before he finished speaking. If he was staying, she certainly wasn't. She moved toward the door with swift, determined steps.

He dropped his hat and oilskin to one side and stepped in front of her. "Going somewhere?"

"Yes." She tried to move around him.

He blocked her way. "I can't allow it."

"You can't stop me." She sidestepped.

"I think I can."

He put out his hand, catching at her arm. She jerked away.

He closed in upon her, his movements swift and silent and forceful. She only had time to throw up her hands, then she was pressed against the wall with his hard fingers imprisoning her wrists on either side of her face.

She kicked out and felt the hard toe of her high-button shoe slam into his shin. He exclaimed under his breath but only turned slightly, leaning closer. His hard thigh and calf came up against her legs, holding her immobile.

"Correct me if I'm wrong," he said in rasping annoyance, "but it seems we have been in this position, or something very like it, before."

"Let me go." She could feel the butt of his holstered

revolver against her abdomen. It was a frightening reminder.

"With pleasure, if you will sit down and be still. You
have no need to be afraid of me."

"How can I be sure?"

It was a moment before he answered, and then the words
were taut and evenly spaced. "You have my word."

"That isn't much of an assurance, particularly from my
point of view at this moment." She swallowed hard. There
was such implacable strength in his hold and something
more that she had felt once before, something she did not
care to name. The effort to keep her anger and will high
was so great that a shudder ran through her, followed by
another and another.

Abruptly he released her, pushing away and stepping
back until his shoulders were against the opposite wall.
"Go on then, if you think your chances are better with the
two men out there."

"They—they are on the other side of the river." The
catch in her voice was caused by her trembling, nothing
more.

"Are they?" His laugh was low and hollow. "You only
have my word for that."

It was true. She lowered her hands, clasping them together as she tried to think. "I s-suppose it was a l-lie about
the ferry and the scarlet fever?"

"Was it? Now I wonder what my reason can have been?
Do you think I lust after your beautiful body?" The gibe
was at himself as much as at her. He did want her. That
was the reason he had taken his hands off her as quickly
as possible, the reason for the distance between them at
this moment.

She drew in her breath with a gasp. "How dare you say
such a thing."

"Why should I not say it when you think it?"

"I think n-nothing of the kind!"

"Oh, you acquit me of the desire to ravish you? Now, let me see. I could have killed you long since if that had been my fancy. What then can I want, except . . . shelter?"

"How very affecting, to be s-sure," she returned with scathing sarcasm, "the m-misunderstood man with every hand turned against him."

"You have no idea. It seems I offend everyone and please none."

"Perhaps it's your m-manners!"

"A wicked thrust. Permit me to mend them by offering you a blanket. I fear you have become a little . . . chilled." He bent over the small heap that was his oilskin and brought a rolled blanket from under it. Straightening, he tossed it to her.

So dim had it grown in the corncrib that Lettie did not see the blanket coming toward her in time to catch it. It struck her a soft blow in the chest, then, as she fumbled for it, fell to the floor. She knelt swiftly to pick it up. There was a strong smell of horse about it, but it was dry, protected as it had been by the wide skirt of the Thorn's poncho. It was also warm to the touch.

She should refuse it. She knew that much, but the faint hint of warmth was so enticing that it was impossible to do so. With trembling fingers, she shook out the folds and swung the blanket around her, pulling it close about her shoulders. In a tone that had an ungracious ring even to her own ears, she said, "T-thank you."

"Delighted to be of service. Shall we sit down, or would that be too compromising?"

Lightning crackled so brightly outside that it lit up the corncrib with its glowing silver fire. In that instant of luminescence, Lettie could see the ironic twist of the man's lips. "You're enjoying this!"

"Am I? Now why should that be?"

"Because you think I'm trapped here with you, and you know I would rather be anywhere else, anywhere at all."

"You think I wouldn't?"

Something in his voice puzzled Lettie. She was silent as she considered it. He waited for a moment, as if for her answer, then when she made none, turned from her and picked up the oilskin poncho. He shook the water from it, and though it was difficult to tell what he was doing in the dimness, she thought he turned it inside out and bent to spread it over the cornhusks.

"Madame," he intoned with a movement that might have been a gesture of presentation, "your couch."

The storm showed no sign of abating. Rain pounded on the roof and poured off it in splattering streams. It lashed against the walls, blowing into the crib, seeping in wet tracks over the logs. Thunder made a rolling roar. A chill draft blew across the floor, swirling grit and bits of trash into the air and stealing under Lettie's wet skirt hem to increase the gooseflesh that pebbled her skin.

It seemed foolish to continue standing, yet imprudent to sit. But was it, in truth, any more imprudent than remaining under the same roof as the Thorn? She could not think of how she had come to this or what it meant. All she knew was that she was miserably wet and cold and that if she remained standing she was very likely to shake so uncontrollably that she would fall down.

Moving with the stiffness of reluctance, she stepped to the poncho-covered heap of husks and knelt upon it, then sank down to sit with her back against the log wall. She flinched a little as the Thorn moved toward her, then lowered himself onto the poncho beside her. She clutched the blanket around her, her every muscle stiff with resistance, though it seemed a waste of effort to protest. He made no move toward her, however.

After a time, she cleared her throat. Above the sound of the rain, she said, "What will happen if the ferryman isn't allowed to come back in the morning?"

"There are other roads, other ferries. I'll direct you."

"My landlady is going to be worried. She may send out a search party."

"Is the warning for my benefit or for yours?" His voice was hard, though it still had that husky edge that was peculiarly his own.

"Certainly not for yours!"

For his benefit! Did he actually think she meant to warn him that there were men coming who might take an interest in his presence? She would enjoy seeing him captured, taken away in chains. Or would she? Angel and devil, Henry had called him. He had killed her brother, but had saved her from death or some even more unthinkable fate. He had treated her with shocking familiarity, but had also been considerate. His nearness frightened her, but at the same time it made her aware, to her guilty shame, that she was a woman and he was a man.

"I've told you, you have no need of protection."

She did not answer. He was dangerous. She must not forget it.

Beside her, he shifted, drawing up one knee and resting his hand upon it. Lettie turned her head sharply toward him. The faint light gleamed for an instant on the leather of the revolver holster at his waist. She drew a deep and silent breath, her eyes narrowing before she turned her gaze away.

What if she captured him herself, forced him to ride with her to Natchitoches, then turned him over to Colonel Ward? Her quest could be ended here and now. Her brother's letters would be enough to allow the authorities to hold him until his guilt, or the innocence he claimed, could be proven. All she had to do was move a little closer to him and snatch the revolver that was so close at hand. It would be, in many ways, a vindication.

A shiver of apprehension ran through her, and she huddled into the blanket. The Thorn turned his head to peer at her. His voice was carefully neutral as he spoke.

"You would be more comfortable if you got out of your damp clothes."

Lettie opened her mouth for an acid retort, then closed it again. An awkward movement or two would not seem strange while she was in the act of undressing. Not that she meant to remove more than her bodice and skirt under any circumstances! But there could be little harm in that much; the dark gray dimness would prevent him from seeing her plainly, and in any case she could use the blanket as a shield.

She moistened her lips. "You—you could be right."

Ransom's brows drew together in a frown. Her agreement was the last thing he had expected. The strain in her voice was also puzzling. Then, as he saw her bend her head and begin to fumble with the buttons of her bodice, a tight feeling grew in his chest, cutting off his air, threatening to choke him. The desire that stirred in his loins was so strong that he pressed his back against the wall and clenched his fists, afraid that he would betray himself.

The blanket slipped from Lettie's shoulder, but she let it go for the moment. How very wanton she felt, preparing to remove her clothing in front of a man, regardless of the reason. She was aghast at her own temerity but no less determined because of it.

As the last button slipped free of its hole, she spread the edges of her bodice and shrugged it off her shoulders, leaning first toward the Thorn and then away from him as she freed her arms from the sleeves. Drawing off the garment and folding it in half, she laid it to one side, then reached behind her back to unfasten her skirt placket. She got to her knees when it was done, lifting the skirt and shifting to free the hem that was caught under her before drawing it off over her head. The last was accomplished with more of a flourish than was necessary. The skirt cascaded down to land with a portion of its fullness across the Thorn's lap. She murmured a word of apology and reached to gather it up. Through the damp material, her fingers brushed his thigh, the holster. She began to pull the skirt toward her, slipping her hand under it.

In that moment, she lunged for the revolver. Her fingers closed over it. She flung herself back, sliding, pushing away.

Ranson felt the revolver leave the holster, but so intent had he been on the pale satin gleam of Lettie's skin, the molded shape of her camisole and corset cover in the gloom, and also on her exploring touch, that it was an instant before he could make himself believe what she had done. He wrenched himself upward with a gathering of powerful muscles, preparing to launch himself after her.

"Stop!" she cried. "I'll shoot!"

He tensed into rocklike stillness, an oath rising to his lips. The epithets continued in fluent self-scorn. Hearing them, Lettie felt the rise of triumph, and a soft laugh escaped her.

"Yankee witch," he said, the word both a salute and a curse. "I won't forget this."

"I hope not. Throw me the blanket."

He was immobile for long seconds, then slowly he moved to obey.

"Carefully," she warned.

The blanket sailed toward her, thrown hard, but this time she was ready. She caught it with one hand, shook it out, then draped it around her, all without removing her gaze from the shadowy figure of the man on the corn-husks. Inching back against the wall, she lowered herself to the floor and leaned back.

He snorted, a sound of derision. "Now what?"

"Now," she said sweetly, "we wait until morning."

5

*T*ime dragged. The storm slackened and started to move off to the northeast, but the rain continued. The floorboards on which Lettie sat grew hard. Her eyes burned from staring into the dimness, watching for any hint of movement from her prisoner. The question began to haunt her: What was she going to do when darkness fell completely and she could no longer see or when she began to grow sleepy? If she had a rope, she could tie the Thorn up. It was possible, of course, that he had some of the same thin grass rope on him he had used to restrain her at Splendora, but to find it she would have to search him, and that was too risky by far. All she could do was guard him.

The Thorn did not help matters. He settled into the pile of cornhusks, sliding down until he was using the lowest log of the wall behind him for a neck rest. Now and then he stretched as he relaxed or smothered a yawn, for all the world like a man readying himself for the night. She did not expect him to be petrified with terror, but his lack of concern, once past the first surprise, was annoying. It was also suspicious. For that reason, she watched him with extra care, her grip on the revolver so tight her fingers ached.

All she saw was a faint blur of movement. Something struck the floor in the corner to the Thorn's left and rolled. So tightly strung were Lettie's nerves that she swung the revolver and pulled the trigger. The gun roared, spitting flame and smoke. The rolling thing burst into fragments with one piece skittering into the corner and spinning to a stop. Immediately she swung back to cover the Thorn.

He had not moved. He was staring at her. With amazement in his voice, he said, "You can shoot."

"What was that you threw?" Hard on her words, she realized that the object, light and cylindrical, had to have been a corncob.

"I didn't throw anything. Must have been a rat."

The mock innocence of his words was too much, on top of his elaborate surprise at her skill. She pointed her weapon in the vicinity of his foot. "Oh, yes, I see! There's another one!"

It would have been all right if he had not moved. She meant only to give him a start by shooting into the floor beyond his boot in retaliation for the way he had made her heart leap. Instead, he heaved himself away from her, rolling. The bullet struck his foot. He let out his breath in a grunt of pain.

The explosion of the shot died away. Gunsmoke, blue and acrid, swirled in the dimness. Lettie shook off her blanket, lowering the revolver as she leaned toward him. "Are you hurt?"

He pushed himself to a sitting position and crouched over his foot. There was a wet red gleam across the instep. Lettie strained to see, rising to her knees and inching forward.

He sprang with the swift and effortless uncoiling of the muscles of a hunting cat. She saw him coming. She tried to bring up the gun, but it was too late. He crashed into her, driving her back. She struck the floor with a jarring thud. He landed on top of her, his weight driving the air from her lungs in an anguished burst. He reached for the revolver. In desperation, she threw it from her. It clattered on the boards, bouncing, sliding to the far wall. As he whipped his head up to follow its flight, she shoved him with both hands. He rocked backward and she twisted, kicking at him, scrambling, clawing the floor as she dragged herself from under him, trying to reach the weapon.

He caught her waist in a grip like an iron barrel hoop, clamping her to him. She was lifted, then turned in a dizzying swing as he rolled with her and thrust her upon her back among the cornhusks. Blinded by a red haze of shock and distress, gasping for breath against the tight clasp of her corset and his hold, Lettie lay rigid.

The anger that had driven Ransom—anger for her attempt to injure him, for the trick she had played and for his own gullibility in being fooled by it—seeped away. In its place welled white-hot desire. The blood sang in his head, and the feel of her warm curves under him was an enticement impossible to resist. He craved the taste of her mouth the way a drunkard craved drink. It was madness, and yet the wild and wet night was closing in, its darkness forcing on them an intimacy that would never come again.

Lettie sensed the swing of his mood. Her eyes widened as she stared up at his broad form looming over her. She wanted to cry out, to protest, but could not make a sound. Her heart thudded in her chest and her breathing deepened, becoming quieter. She felt strangely bereft of will, paralyzed by an intimation of danger, by ancient curiosity, and by something more that had to do with the nerve-straining closeness of the man who held her. She was quiescent; her hands, which were trapped between them, rested on the hardness of his chest under his coat. She was acutely aware of the dry rustling of the husks under them, the drum and splash of the rain, and the clean, starched smell of his clothing combined with the male scent of his body. Aware, too, of his sudden indrawn breath, as of some decision made, and the slow, almost hesitant descent of his shadowed face toward her before his mouth touched hers.

He was a murderer, but his kiss was warm and sure, beguiling in its sweetness, tantalizing with the faint irritation of his mustache. He was a killer, but his arms were cradling, firm yet gentle. He was an outlaw and a rebel, but there was something inside him that some part of her recognized and rose to meet.

Nothing had prepared her for this betrayal of her own senses, her own bodily responses. It was beyond belief. She despised this man, wanted to see him hanged. She knew she should strike out at him, should struggle to be free. That she could not confused and shamed her. Until she grasped at an idea with relief, the idea that her very stillness might become a weapon. Her fiancé had been quite distracted while kissing her. Perhaps this man might be the same. A moment of inattention, and she could break free and reach the revolver. All it would take was a moment.

His lips upon hers were gently caressing as he brushed their smooth surface, tasting the moist line where they met and probing their vulnerable corners. The sensation was exquisite. It awakened such tingling and heated sensitivity that Lettie's lips parted in surprise. Ransom took instant advantage of that inadvertent invitation, deepening his exploration. The velvet roughness of his tongue touched hers, twining, abrading, enticing in amorous play.

He spread his hand at her waist, smoothing the heavy satin and steel ribs of her corset that covered that trim indentation, sliding lower to her hip, drawing her closer against him so that she was molded to his long length. She felt the rigid heat of him, sensed in some recess of her brain the intensity of his need and the firmness of his control of it. A tremor ran through her at the liberties he was taking, and involuntarily she pressed closer. Her arms and legs felt leaden, while in the lower part of her body grew a burning ache that seemed to fuel the delicious torpor that gripped her. At any moment she could and would break free of it to find the gun. Soon. When the time was right.

He blazed a trail of molten kisses along the curve of her cheek to the turn of her jaw, pausing at the delicate hollow under her ear, inhaling the fresh fragrance of her skin at the base of her neck. His warm breath wafted over the gentle curves of her breasts, which were pushed up by her corset, before he pressed his lips to the valley between them. He brought his hand up to cup one mound that was covered by her lawn camisole, shifting his attention to it, moistening the fine material with his tongue as he teased the nipple underneath to hardness.

Feeling her breasts tightened with unacceptable desire, Lettie acknowledged a flutter of panic. This was too new, too far beyond her experience to be treated so lightly. She must stop it, but how was it to be done without incensing him to the point of forced assault? Before she could find the means, she felt his hands at her waist once more, felt the quick compression of her ribs and then the release of her corset hooks. The small cry of protest she made was lost in the gasp of relief forced from her as her lungs filled with air. An instant later, he took her lips once more, his hands gently, confidently marauding.

She would hold him from her until she could form the words that would protect her. She shifted her hands, spreading her fingers as she increased their pressure against him. The movement brushed open his coat. She felt the taut bands of muscle that wrapped his chest under her fingertips and palms. The discovery was engrossing. Without conscious thought, she allowed her touch to linger, exploring the hard contours and planes, the tight, flat coins of his paps. The linen of his shirt was a barrier. The sudden need to have it removed, to feel his skin against hers was so strong, so startling that her hands clenched upon the material in a wracking spasm, and she felt the rise of such heat that her body seemed to glow with it.

In unerring answer to that convulsive movement, Ransom wrenched open the buttons of his shirt and stripped it off with his coat. It was only when he drew her against him that Lettie realized the buttons that fastened her camisole had been slipped from their holes and that she was naked to the waist. Her breasts, exquisitely sensitive, brushed the soft matting of hair on his chest. She caught her breath with the pleasure of it, a pleasure that mounted to her head, destroying thought.

Lost, she was lost in the incredible sweetness of his mouth, the fascination of the sensations he aroused, and the wild and voluptuous urgency of the race of the blood in her veins. She had never felt like this, never dreamed it was possible. It was frightening, yet irresistible magic.

He loosened her petticoats. Rustling softly with starch, they were drawn from her to be cast aside. Her pantalettes followed, as did his trousers and underclothing. The touch of his hands and mouth was constant, pervasive, invasive. It glorified her, incited her to imitation. Never, never had she been so close to another human being. Never had she been left so little privacy, so little modesty, or needed either less. Never had she been handled with such assurance or with so much abiding care.

She was a virgin, and if he had not known, he soon discovered it and eased the way for her with infinite art and patience, providing bliss as an antidote to pain. As a cure, it was peerless.

Hot and strong and vital, he pressed into her. Now above her, now drawing her upon him, they strove among the cornhusks. Joined together, male and female, they moved in passionate wonder to the ageless and wild rhythm. It tensed their muscles and heated their bodies, beat in their blood and echoed in their hearts. It transformed them for a single bright and blinding moment, fusing their spirits for that brief time, giving them ineffable grandeur. But it could not make them one.

It was some time later when Ransom stirred. Raising himself to one knee, he raked together the husks that formed their bed and spread a petticoat over them. He found and straightened the blanket, then lay down and reached for Lettie. His voice carefully neutral, he said, "Come, you'll be more comfortable."

"I'm comfortable here." That she was lying naked on the floor made no difference. She pulled her shoulder from his grasp, moving away a few inches.

His chest rose and fell in a silent sigh. "Do you expect an apology? You won't get it."

It was an unreasonable attitude, and he knew it. He was sorry, more sorry than he could say. He had wanted to think her deliberate removal of her outer clothing a provocation, had managed to let his fury at being duped and shot by her convince him that it was so, at least for a short time. Deep down, he had known better. It had been no more than an excuse to do something he had wanted to do since he had first held her at Splendora. The proper thing, the only honorable thing now was for him to offer her the protection of his name. And that was impossible. What else was there, then, except to play the complete scoundrel?

"All I want," she said, the words muffled as if she was hiding her face in the curve of her arms as she lay on her stomach, "is to be left alone."

It was odd how much that simple declaration hurt. He set his mouth in a grim line as he reached for her once more. "Too bad."

Lettie heard the derision in his tone and also a note of the same assurance that had so easily led her astray. She jerked away, surging to her hands and knees and scrambling from him. She struck something cold and metallic. The revolver. It skidded a few inches and she pounced on it. As she brought it up, she used both thumbs to cock the hammer.

The metallic double click was loud in the darkness of the corncrib. Overhead, the rain whispered down, quiet now but relentless. Lettie's breathing sounded loud in her ears, and she controlled it with an effort.

"Now what?" the Thorn said.

Lettie gave a short laugh as the answer came to her. "Now you leave."

"What?"

"Get your clothes and get out."

There was a certain humor in the situation. Ransom's mouth quirked before he spoke. "You would send an injured man out in the rain?"

"I somehow doubt you are hurt enough to matter."

"You're a hard woman, Letitia Mason."

"Not hard enough, or you would be dead."

It could not be denied. "Are you hard enough to shoot a man at all?"

"Try me and see," she returned in cold tones.

The temptation to do just that was almost overpowering. She had been tried enough for one day, however. The best amends he could make at this moment might well be to leave her this small victory. His voice tinged with admiration, he said softly, "Another time."

She didn't trust him, not even when she heard him move to gather his clothes. It had been too easy. She had expected, had been afraid, that he would force her to pull the trigger. Once she would have said that she could do it without remorse. That was before she had drawn blood, his blood. The thought of injuring him further made her feel ill, though he seemed in no way incapacitated by his nicked foot. She was taking no chances, however. Holding the gun level on the moving shadow of his form, she backed to the side wall of the crib and eased along it as far away from him as possible.

She heard the slither and slide as he got into his trousers and shirt, the stamp as he pulled on his boots and settled his feet into them. He bent once more, perhaps to find his coat and oilskin poncho, then came the sound of his footsteps moving toward the door. He paused.

"Would you send me out among enemies without the protection of a weapon?"

There was something in his tone that disturbed her. She shut it out. "What would you have me do? Give up my only defense?"

"You need none from me, this I swear. And while I am with you, you need no other protection."

"If what just took place is an example of your protection—"

"I did not say that I would not hold you . . . or taste your sweet lips . . . or touch the perfect twin hills of your—"

"Get out!"

His chuckle had a ragged sound. The door opened and then closed. He was gone.

Lettie let out her breath, her shoulders sagging in relief as she lowered the gun. She closed her eyes and leaned her head back against the wall. Tears gathered, burning as they pressed for release. She swallowed hard, reaching up to wipe the overflow with the heel of her hand.

Dear God, but she had been a fool. She was well served

for blithely driving out into the wilderness alone. She could not think of why she had done it, except that she had not quite believed in the danger. There were few places in the East where a woman alone was not safe. The only salve she could find for her pride was that no one need know. Even if she had the right to claim assault, she had no intention of making her humiliation public.

She was not sure what had happened to her. She felt as if she had dishonored her brother's memory, her family, and, most of all, herself. Such a thing must never happen again. She would see to it that it did not, but, more than that, she would see that the only other witness to the whole degrading incident, beginning at the spring and ending here in the corncrib, did not live to tell of it. The Thorn was not only a murderer; he was a sneaking despoiler of women. He must not be allowed to get away with his crimes.

Cool, wet air drifted around her bare flanks and she shivered violently. Stumbling a little, she moved to the pile of cornhusks and dropped down on her knees, groping for her clothes. She put them on with shaking fingers, buttoning the last button to the throat. The blanket had been left behind, and she wrapped it tightly around her as she sat bolt-upright against the log wall. Her eyes burned as she stared into the darkness, waiting for daylight.

Lettie must have slept, though it seemed she only closed her eyes for an instant. A noise jerked her into alertness so suddenly that every nerve leaped and jangled. She grasped the revolver and struggled out of the blanket. Pushing to her feet, she moved with stiff steps to the door. The rain had stopped during the night. The gray light of dawn was filtering through the cracks in the log walls and between the loose planks of the door. She leaned to peer through a crack.

In the direct line of her vision, standing in front of the

corncrib, was the buggy. The noise she had heard was the rattle of it being brought out of the shed. On the weed-grown track beyond it was a flicker of movement. It was the form of a man on horseback riding away in the early-morning mist.

The Thorn had not gone far when he left her, or so it appeared. He must have spent the remainder of the night in the shed with the horses. He had hitched the buggy and led it out for her before taking his leave. How very chivalrous of him, she thought with acid irony. It was a pity he had not shown more of such an instinct earlier.

It was when she mounted the buggy that she found the locust. Dry, prickly, and pale tan, thrust through with a vicious black thorn, it lay on the leather seat. She stared at it with all the horrified revulsion she might have felt for a snake curled to strike. Her first impulse was to crush it or to cast it from her at the very least. She reached out to pick it up gingerly.

It was feather-light and delicate, and it clung to her fingers with its tiny claws, every one intact, as if it would never let go. The thorn that pierced it was polished to gleaming perfection, hard and black and without blemish. The two specimens were each perfect in their way; they were also perfect reminders of the folly of which she was capable and of its consequences. She would do well to remember. Taking her handkerchief from her pocket, she wrapped the symbol of the man called the Thorn in it and placed it carefully on the seat beside her.

When Lettie reached the river, the ferryman came from his house with his coffee cup in one hand and a biscuit in the other. He was tall and rawboned, his features obscured behind a straggling mustache and beard that grew nearly to his eyes. He kept up a string of questions and commentary as he pulled the ferry across the river.

He hated like Hades that he hadn't been able to take

her across the evening before, especially with it setting in to rain and all, but there hadn't been a consarned thing he could do; there had been a time when he had been mighty fearful that he'd be lucky if he ever crossed again himself. He would have invited her to have a bite of breakfast, but the thing was, there was sickness in the house and he didn't think he'd better. Anyway, he was glad she had found a dry place to spend the night. No, he hadn't seen anything of the man who had been chasing the pair that had held him up. Must have gone back t'other way. He sure hoped the scare she'd had didn't put her off this part of the country. They needed schoolteachers.

As loquacious as the man was, his attitude was comforting. It seemed that there was nothing particularly unusual in being stranded for the night, that she was more to be pitied than censured because of it. It was good to realize that everyone would not instantly place the worst construction on her escapade, even if it was deserved.

Regardless, it was a relief when Natchitoches was behind her and she finally reached Splendora.

Aunt Em scolded and exclaimed, but after a long look at Lettie's pale face, sent her to her room with promises of a breakfast tray and a bath and with orders not to emerge until she was rested. It was Mama Tass who toiled up the steps from the outdoor kitchen with the breakfast tray, and Lionel who manhandled the long zinc bathtub of the type known as a julep tub—a bath thought to be efficacious for the relief of a julep-induced hangover—into the room. The boy also brought the cans of hot water to fill the tub. He had no other duties at the moment, he said. Mast' Ranny was still asleep. He had been taken by one of his headaches right after she had left the day before and was shut up in his room.

Lettie did not expect to sleep, not in the middle of the morning with the sun shining outside. Not when she was a fallen woman, sore in body and conscience. But the bed was soft, the sheets smooth, and the breeze drifting through the open window, gently billowing the muslin curtains, was fresh and scented with magnolia. The strain and guilt of the night seemed far away. She stretched, feeling her lips curve into a smile for no reason as she stared up at the tester above her. She closed her eyes.

It was late afternoon when she awoke. The room was quiet and still and overly warm. Outside her windows, the sun was casting sharp and slanting shadows across the veranda floor. A murmur of voices came to her. Through the gauze weave of the curtains, she could see the shape of a man standing at the veranda railing. For an instant, her heart jarred against her ribs, then she recognized Ranny's quiet, almost diffident voice and the higher tones of Lionel in answer.

How very lazy she felt. There was no exuse for such self-indulgence; she did not know why she had succumbed to it so easily. She was no highly bred Southern belle prone to giving way to the least weakness. In truth, beyond a bit of soreness, she felt little different, scarcely changed at all by the ordeal of the night. Hiding herself away, licking her wounds, and feeling sorry for herself was not going to mend matters. She must take hold of herself and get on with what she had come here to accomplish.

She knew it was not possible to see into the bedchamber from the outside through the muslin curtains; still, she dressed herself in a corner well out of the line of vision of anyone on the veranda. She brushed her hair and twisted it into a thick coil on top of her head for coolness, then, because she was already warm, bathed her face and hands in the basin on the washstand. As she patted her face dry, she looked in the mirror. How very flushed and overheated she looked, and how stifled. She put down the linen towel and, on impulse, unfastened the cuffs of her sleeves, rolling them to the elbow. Then she released the two top buttons of her high collar. That was better, but she really must buy at least one or two dresses more suited to the climate.

Ranny turned as Lettie emerged on the veranda. A slow smile lighted his face, kindling the soft blue of his eyes. His gaze rested for an instant on the white hollow of her throat that was exposed by her open collar, and a corner of his mouth quivered before he ducked his head. "Afternoon, Miss Lettie."

Lettie divided a smile between the man and his companion. "Good evening, Ranny. Lionel told me you had not been well. I hope your headache is better?"

"Much better. And . . . you?"

The question was abrupt, as if he was embarrassed to ask or else cared strongly about the answer, which was, of course, unlikely. She smiled with an assumption of ease. "If you mean have I recovered from my outing, yes, indeed."

"You should have let me go with you."

The warmth in her face faded like the sun going behind a cloud. "Yes, perhaps I should."

It had been wrong of him to remind her, Ransom thought. He was going to have to remember that her smiles were for Ranny, for the child-man she thought he was and not for the one he was in truth.

To distract her, he said, "I've been thinking about what you said."

"About what?"

"About teaching me. Do you still want to?"

"Certainly. I would enjoy it very much, if you care to learn."

"If you will teach Lionel, too."

Lionel, who had been following their conversation with some interest, opened his eyes wide. "Aw, Mast' Ranny!"

Ranny grinned at him. "I'm not doing it by myself."

"It's not fair!"

"Your daddy will like it."

The boy hung his head. "He don't care."

"Yes, he does," Ranny said quietly. "He does."

Lettie thought she understood them, though she could not be sure. Lionel's father, Ranny's manservant before the war, had apparently deserted the boy, leaving him in the care of his mother, Mama Tass, while he went off to enjoy his freedom. It spoke well for Ranny that he was trying to give his young friend a good opinion of his father, deserved or not.

"I will be glad to teach Lionel," Lettie said. "It will be good to have company for the drive to the school every morning, not to mention two friendly faces in my class."

Ranny sent her a brief glance from under his lashes, then shook his head. "No."

"But I thought you said—"

"I would rather learn here."

Oh, but you wouldn't be the only adult," she said earnestly. "There will be quite a few others, men and women who have been slaves all their lives or who have lived so far back in the wilderness that they never learned to read."

"Here," he repeated. "With Lionel. And the others."

"The others?" she questioned, at a loss.

"From the quarters. My people."

He meant the people of Splendora who still lived in the quarters behind the house. "They could come to the school."

"But they won't. They have to work so they can eat. And some will be too afraid."

She lifted a brow. He had a point, one that she would like to take up with the officials at the Freedmen's Bureau. "I understand. I'm sure I could teach you in the evening."

"We could start now, the three of us. Here?"

His smile was so guileless, so expectant, that she hadn't the heart to refuse him. In any case, it would take her mind off things she would just as soon not dwell upon.

Lettie had brought with her a few primers and readers since she had been advised that such things were in short supply. She also had a small slate and a box of chalk. She brought these things out and spread them on a table on the veranda. She and Ranny and Lionel spent a hilarious half hour with their heads together, drawing letters. Lionel apparently had had some instruction, for he could not only write the letters of the alphabet but could form simple words. Ranny tried diligently, sticking the tip of his tongue out of the corner of his mouth in his concentration, but his letters had a tendency to stagger over the slate in such a comical fashion that Lionel smothered giggles behind his hand. The harder Ranny tried, the worse it became until the reeling letters began to look downright tipsy.

Lettie, frowning, gave a slight shake of her head at the young boy for his lack of compassion. She put her hand over Ranny's strong, brown fist to guide him. He allowed her to move his hand without hindrance while he turned his head to look at her. So near was he that only inches separated their faces. She was snared by the steady light in his eyes, alerted by the glint of humor she saw in their depths.

She caught her breath, then gave his hand a push that made the chalk squeak on the slate. "You're doing it on purpose!"

Lionel burst out laughing and fell from his rocking chair to the floor, where he rolled back and forth. Ranny grinned and gave a sheepish nod.

"Why?"

"You wanted to teach me."

"You might have told me I was wasting my time!"

"There could have been something I didn't remember. Besides . . ."

"Besides what?" she asked with deep suspicion as he paused.

"You're pretty when you are being so—so . . ."

It was Lionel who supplied the words, "So stiff and mean like a schoolteacher!"

"How else should I be?" she said with a frown, not quite sure whether she was offended or not.

Ranny tipped his head to one side as he surveyed her without answering. "*Very* pretty."

She gave him her most severe look, though she could not prevent the faint twitch of a smile at the corner of her mouth. "I can see that I'm going to have to prepare a test for both of you to see how much you already know."

"Tomorrow," Ranny said with finality. "Can you read to us now?"

"Read to you?"

Lionel sat up and clasped his arms around his knees. "Sometimes Miss Em reads us stories all about knights and soldiers, like *Ivanhoe*."

"Does she?" Lettie considered the idea. Anything that encouraged either of them to read must be good, she supposed, and for the moment she did not feel up to the mental task of constructing a test. "I suppose I could do the same if I had a book."

"I'll get one!" Lionel yelled. He leaped to his feet and raced into the house. He was back in an instant with a leather-bound volume in his hands, a tale by Dickens. He handed it to Lettie, then settled at her feet. Ranny leaned back in his chair, stretching his long legs out before him. Lettie set the slate and chalk aside, then opened the book and began to read aloud.

She held the book in her lap, turning the pages with one hand while the other rested on the arm of her chair. She had read only a few paragraphs when Ranny reached to touch the back of her fingers with one hand. He smoothed the fine skin at the bend of her knuckles, then traced the almond shape of her nails. He turned her hand palm-up, following the lines that crossed it with one finger before branching off to investigate the blue veins that pulsed in her wrist. At last he curled his fingers around hers, clasping them in a firm but light hold.

She raised her head to look at him, an inquiry in her brown eyes. He met her gaze, his own clear. The veranda was shaded, but the afternoon sun seemed to cast the reflection of its bright golden glow over him, giving him a burnished look. So perfectly regular were his features, so crisp and vital his hair, and so bronze his skin that he did not look quite human. The jagged scar, cruelly outlined by the harsh light, increased the impression. There was something disturbing about him, a sense of great promise lost or, perhaps, of a masterwork wantonly damaged, forever marred. She felt it inside like an ache.

"Do you want me to let go?" he asked.

"No, I don't suppose."

He gave her a slow smile that seemed to make the light in his eyes burn like a steady flame. "Good. It makes me feel . . . better."

Her mouth curved in answer for an instant before she returned her gaze to the book. However, as she found her place once more and began to read with slow emphasis, it was as if she could feel the warm strength of his grasp seeping into her, supporting her.

It was the effect of simple human contact, of course, but curiously enough it made her feel better, too.

*T*he next two days at Splendora were uneventful. Lettie, with little to do and an ingrained dislike of being idle, offered her services to Aunt Em. In company with the older woman and Sally Anne, Aunt Em's niece who was still visiting, she helped about the house: polishing furniture, plying a needle through torn linens, pulling weeds from the front flower beds, preparing the endless array of vegetables that was put on the table.

She learned to hoe in the garden and to identify the young growth of such exotic crops as okra, squash, sweet potatoes, the love apples more correctly known as tomatoes, and also the collard greens and cow peas that had once been raised for the slaves but were now considered acceptable for everyone. She was also taught to distinguish the young plants of marigolds and zinnias, or old maids as Aunt Em called them, common flowers that would brighten the vegetable garden in midsummer and provide bouquets for the house.

Among the outbuildings on the place was a cabin containing a spinning wheel and a loom. In it, Aunt Em carded wool and cotton and spun it into thread, then colored the yarn using homemade dyes, such as brown from the hulls of black walnuts and blue from indigo she had grown herself. She then wove her own material for coverlets and curtains. She had made many a shirt and pair of trousers for the Confederate soldiers, she said, every fiber and stitch a product of Splendora. Watching the older woman at the loom was absorbing, and Lettie was even allowed to weave a few inches of cloth, though Sally Anne warned her with a smile not to make it perfect or she might find herself with shuttle in hand every day.

The poultry yard was another interest of Aunt Em's. There she raised everything from bantam chickens, with the appearance of animated hat decorations and the disposition of scrappy streetfighters, to great, gawky, and superior-acting turkeys that were so delicate of constitution that they had to be petted and protected every minute of their lives; from commonplace Leghorn chickens to French geese and rare Chinese ducks. The older woman also kept a pair of peacocks that screamed at each other constantly like an irate husband and wife to the point where Aunt Em swore she was strongly tempted to find out what the Persians had found to their taste in peacock meat.

In theory, the poultry stayed in their yard fenced in by tall, half-rotted, and rather drunken-looking palings. Actually, they were out of it more often than in. They roosted at night in the fig and peach trees behind the kichen building and made their nests in the brier thickets that had grown up around the slave cabins. One wise old hen, more enterprising than most, had found a cabin with an open door and made her nest in the blackened and empty fireplace.

It was necessary to make a circuit of the various nesting places every day to gather the eggs, otherwise the hens would lay a clutch of a dozen or so, then stop laying and sit on them to hatch them. As long as the nests were never full, the hens continued producing eggs for most of the year, eggs that, when sold in town, gave Aunt Em her pin money. Evidence that the hens, as well as the ducks and geese and turkeys, were better at hiding their eggs than the humans were at finding them was plain in the numerous small groups of young chicks and ducklings and goslings that fluttered here and there, scratching among the flowers and tempting the barn cats as well as the owls, hawks, and foxes that crept out of the surrounding woods at night.

Another use for the poultry was to supply feathers for pillows and mattresses. On the third morning after Lettie's visit to the spring, she and Aunt Em and Sally Anne were reworking pillows on the veranda. They were sewing fresh cases out of striped ticking, fluffing the old feathers and adding handfuls of new down, then stuffing the cases and sewing up the ends.

It was pleasant on the veranda with the fresh morning breeze wandering along its length, now and then wafting the scent of flowers to them. Lettie had never felt that she was the sort of woman who had a need for constant companionship; still, it was also enjoyable getting to know the other two women.

Lettie, rubbing her nose, which itched from the flying bits of feathers in the air, while also trying to stitch up the end of the plump pillow she held under her arm without squeezing out its stuffing, sent the older woman a quizzical glance. "What a busy person you are, Aunt Em, always at some task. I can almost regret having anything to do with taking your slaves from you."

"Whatever are you saying, child? I do less now than I ever did before the war."

Before the war. It was a phrase heard again and again. Though in the past few decades there had been the Seminole Indian War, the War for Texas Independence, and the Mexican War, there was never any question of which war was meant. Lettie ceased sewing, saying with interest, "Surely not?"

"Oh, but it's the truth. There were always forty or fifty

people to be looked after, to be kept fed and with clothes on their backs, not to mention seeing to it that they were healthy."

"But there were servants to do the work!"

"While I sat in the shade sipping lemonade and fanning myself? Tell me, dear, does your mother have hired help in the house in Boston?"

"Why, yes, a cook and a maid, and sometimes an extra woman during the spring cleaning."

"And do they do their jobs without somebody right behind them to see that they are done properly?"

Sally Anne looked up from where she was loosening a knot of feathers. "Or without being shown how to do them time and again?"

"I see what you mean," Lettie said with a wry smile.

"In a city like New Orleans, it may have been a little easier," Aunt Em said with a judicious twist of her lips. "A lot of what we made from scratch at Splendora could be had out of the store there, and was fairly cheap since it didn't have to be shipped upriver. But here in the country it was different."

"Nicer," Sally Anne said.

"Quieter, less sickness, less gossiping and carrying on," Aunt Em amplified, then gave a short laugh. "It was downright boring at times, but we could always get up a dance or a quilting bee or a fish fry on the creekbank. Kinfolk came and stayed on for days, sometimes weeks, and there were always weddings and birthings. No, I wouldn't have changed with those city ladies for the world. I liked planting and watching my chickens and seeing the seasons come and go before the war, and I like it now."

"You make it sound almost—not primitive, but rather like the days of the early settlers."

"And why not? When I came here thirty-five years ago as a girl, that's the way it was; this was the frontier. We came by ship to New Orleans from Georgia and then up the river by steamboat. From there we put everything we owned in wagons pulled by oxen, including my mama's big armoire and tester bed that her grandmother had given her, and hauled it into the depths of the wilderness. My father had bought a place north of here, good, black bottomland, but he cleared it himself and built a house of logs with the trees—though later he built a big house with lumber. There were bears and wolves and panthers then, and the nearest doctor was thirty miles away. When I married James Tyler and we moved to Grand Ecore, I thought I had come to the city. But it really wasn't that different."

Aunt Em's husband had been killed trying to swim his horse across the Red River during a flood; Lettie had learned that much already. Ranny's mother had died of consumption when he was small. Instead of going back to her family at her husband's death, Aunt Em had moved in to take care of young Ranny, allowing her husband's holdings to revert to the two brothers who were left. Then Ransom's father had been felled by a stroke during a heated argument over secession the year the war began. With Ranny in the army and later incapacitated, the responsibility for the running of Splendora had fallen on Aunt Em.

"I think it's wonderful the way you have held this place together, making it produce a living," Lettie said.

"Don't let Ranny hear you say that, please. He helps all he can, but he feels terrible that he can't do more. He worries about the way I should be living, the way the house looks and the fences and the fields. I see him looking at it all sometimes, as if he is remembering, and it just breaks my heart."

"He does a great deal. Yesterday I saw him plowing with a mule in one of the back fields."

Sally Anne carefully removed a feather that was stuck

to her lip before entering the conversation. "Yes, and last night he had another one of his headaches."

"You can't tell him anything," Aunt Em said with a sigh. "He just won't listen." She turned to Lettie. "He pays attention to you during the lessons. I've been meaning to tell you how grateful I am to you for taking the time with him, and with Lionel."

"And Peter," Sally Anne added. Her son had joined the lessons when he discovered they were taking place.

"It's been fun, really, though I don't know how much any of them is learning. They are such cutups."

"It's been good for Ranny, I can tell. Not just the learning, but having you speak so naturally to him. A lot of people don't know how to act with him, especially young women."

"They are either tongue-tied," Sally Anne said, "or else they chatter as if their salvation depended on it. And that's only if they can't find an excuse to stay away from him."

The older woman shook her head. "It wasn't always like that."

"Heavens, no!" Sally Anne grinned, though there was a faraway look in her eyes. "Half the belles in the parish were wild about Ranny before the war. And you should have seen the way they flocked around when Bradley first brought him back, when he was unconscious. His bed was piled three-feet deep in fancy embroidered and crocheted pillows. Lionel and Peter made themselves sick on the cookies and candy that he was in no shape to eat. Someone had to dust the house every day because of the carriages coming and going on the drive, with girls begging for just a glimpse of him. But all that ended the minute they learned he wasn't quite right."

"I wish you wouldn't put it that way, Sally Anne." Aunt Em's tone was fretful. "He's just a little slow."

"I know, I know, and I'm sorry, but he might as well be a complete imbecile the way he's treated."

"He's far from that." Lettie placed another stitch in her pillow before sending a quick glance to Ranny's cousin. The flush of anger across Sally Anne's cheekbones gave a nice color to her face. She was very attractive and still less than thirty. It was odd that she had not remarried. Or perhaps it wasn't. So many of the men her age had not come back from the war. Moreover, there was a tendency in the South, or so Lettie had heard, to view widows as having buried their hearts in the grave, a tendency that must be doubly hard to overcome when the dead husband was a war hero who had sacrificed his life for the Lost Cause. It was also possible, however, that Sally Anne's affections were given to the cousin that she defended so warmly.

Aunt Em's hands were still as she looked out over the veranda railing. "It hurts me when I think of Ranny never marrying, never having children. He used to be so good with babies, not at all afraid to hold them like some men. And there's Splendora. What will happen to it, and to him, when I'm gone?"

There was, of course, no answer to be made to such a question. Sally Anne said, "He's still good with children, like Peter."

Quiet fell as they returned to their sewing. Lettie thought of Ranny and Peter, and also of Lionel, as the three of them had set off down the drive earlier. They had carried their fishing poles and a jar of earthworms that they had dug up behind the kitchen for bait. They were going to try their luck at Dink's Pond, and possibly along the river. The two boys had skipped along to keep up with Ranny's long strides, chattering to him as if he was their age, which in a way he was. There was indeed something affecting in the thought that he would never enjoy the rights and pleasures of normal manhood.

Pity did not seem proper, however. There was about him, in all situations, an innate dignity that forbade it.

"Someone's coming," Sally Anne said.

The young woman's voice sounded flat, stifled. Lettie was not surprised to see a blue uniform when she looked up, though it was a little unusual that the man wearing it was driving a smart black buggy with yellow wheels and silver fittings. It was Colonel Ward who got down in front of the gate and, removing his campaign hat, came up the walk.

His greeting was easy and natural. Aunt Em, as if to make up for Sally Anne's silence, was most affable, offering coffee or tea and cake.

"Thank you, ma'am, it's kind of you, but not just now. I had a few free hours and I thought to look in on Miss Mason, maybe see if she might like to go for a drive."

He was speaking to Aunt Em, but the words, and his smile, were for Lettie. She returned it. "How thoughtful of you, but, as you can see, we are in the middle of a . . . ticklish job."

"Which makes no difference whatever!" Aunt Em declared. "Go along with you now. Sally Anne and I can finish here. You'll be wanting to see a little more of the countryside and there won't be many chances once you start teaching."

"No, really. I hate to leave a job half done."

"Nonsense. Go on with you."

"Well, if you're sure, then."

Lettie would have protested further, but it seemed that Sally Anne might be more comfortable if the colonel's presence was removed. Setting her pillow aside, Lettie rose and stepped into her bedchamber to fetch her hat and gloves and also to smooth her hair and brush away any clinging bits of down. A few minutes later, she and the officer in blue were bowling away down the drive.

"This is very nice of you," Lettie said.

"It's my pleasure. Besides, we Yankees have to stick together in enemy territory."

She sent him a quick upward glance. "Do you really still think of it like that?"

"Sometimes, such as just now with the young widow. The women are the worst. Southern men may forgive and forget; Southern women, never. Though if Congress doesn't end this mess soon, we'll never overcome the bitterness. But that isn't what I intended to talk to you about when I asked you to come with me. I wanted to be sure you are being well treated and that you are satisfied with your lodgings."

"Yes, on both counts," she answered, following his lead, and then went on to talk of other things.

He asked if she had gone, as planned, to the spring. She told him she had, but gave him to understand that nothing had come of it. She had told no one anything different since her return, had not even mentioned the pair who had attacked her. To do so would mean explaining how she had escaped them, and as she did not want to cast herself in the role of a heroine and had no intention of bringing up the name of the Thorn as her savior or in any other capacity, it seemed best to remain silent. That did not prevent her from asking her escort if anything had been heard of the man during the past few days.

The colonel's face took on a grim cast. "You might say so. Last night he stopped a detachment of my men who were escorting a prisoner into town. The prisoner was old man Jim Hathnell, a cantankerous old goat who the day before had fired a double-barreled shotgun at the troopers who came to serve him with his eviction notice for non-payment of taxes. The Thorn claimed the old man was near blind with cataracts, couldn't tell the difference between troopers and jayhawkers. He even dared to ask what had become of a man's right to defend his home! And he was also kind enough to advise us not to waste our time looking for our prisoner because the old man would be on his way to Texas to stay with his granddaughter."

"Was it true about the man being blind?"

"I don't know. Probably."

"And you're sure it was the Thorn?"

"He left his calling card, though the troopers swear he was seven feet tall, as round-bellied as an ox, and spoke with a German accent. Of course they may have been trying to account for the fact that one man was able to hold up the six of them and not only take their prisoner but leave them bootless and on foot thirteen miles out of Natchitoches."

"It seems incredible."

"It's damned—downright annoying! I can't understand what he thinks he's doing. The things he has pulled are so different it makes no sense. It's almost as if he's doing his best to confuse us, or else he's touched in the head. I swear you'd think he was running a one-man campaign to right the wrongs of the world."

"Angel and devil," Lettie murmured.

"Exactly."

She stared ahead of her for a long moment, snared in memories of a dark corncrib and the terrible magic there could be in a caress. She closed her eyes to banish the images, saying abruptly, "I suppose you sent men out on all the roads to Texas?"

He gave a short nod. "Not that I expect them to bring back the Thorn or even old man Hathnell. Even if it wasn't a ruse to make us chase off in the wrong direction, there was nearly enough time before my men walked back into town for anybody to reach the Texas border. It's not more than forty or fifty miles any way you go."

Since she was interested, the colonel pointed out the roads that led south and west to Texas as they passed through town. The two of them drove southeast along the river, passing through cotton fields that marched in green rows to the horizon and past shanties where Negro children played or big old houses that were falling into ruin, seeing only now and then a well-kept dwelling that looked as if it might house prosperous owners. Where the road began to leave the river, they took a narrow track that wound back to the water. At the end of it, they pulled up to rest the horses on a bank overlooking the channel.

"I wish there was more time," Thomas Ward said. "There are a lot of places I'd like to show you. Just a few miles below here is the community of Isle Brevelle, the home of several families, most related, of what are known here in the state as *gens de couleur libre*, free people of color. They are fascinating people of mixed French and African blood who count among their ancestors one of the earliest merchant-soldiers to settle at Natchitoches during the French regime, a Monsieur Metoyer."

"Yes, Henry wrote me about them."

"They consider themselves to be a third caste, nonwhite but definitely not Negro. They were once wealthy, owners of hundreds of slaves, and highly educated—many of them were sent to Paris for continental polish. Now their way of life is gone."

"I believe the funeral earlier in the week was for one of them?"

"Right. He was a man who had lost everything he valued, the only way of life he could bear to live."

The fortunes built by these free people of color had been tied to the slave economy and so had been forfeited. The freeing of the Negroes had also tended to lower the social barrier between the free people of color and the former slaves so that they were gradually losing the special status they had once held.

"It's terrible, really. You have to pity them."

The colonel nodded. "They have become very clannish, avoiding strangers who don't understand who and what they are. It's hardest on the younger ones, those old enough to marry. I understand it was once the practice to supply large dowries for the daughters in order to find Caucasian husbands for them. The money for that is gone and they hold themselves above the freedmen with pure African bloodlines. Now they marry only among themselves."

"How complicated everything is," Lettie said, her tone baffled, "not at all as I expected."

"I know what you mean. Did Henry tell you about the McAlpin plantation?"

"I don't think he did."

"It's supposed to be the setting for Mrs. Stowe's *Uncle Tom's Cabin*. Robert McAlpin was a bachelor from New England; some say he was a family friend of the Stowes'. At any rate, he had the reputation locally of being a cruel master to his slaves and apparently he's the model for the villainous Simon Legree."

"I've never read the book." It was, she felt, a damning admission.

"I tried once, but it was heavy going. From what I remember of it, I can't think that Mrs. Stowe was ever in Louisiana or at least in this part of the state. It's funny when you think of the influence the book had."

"You know, Colonel," Lettie said with some asperity, "you are beginning to sound more Southern than the Southerners."

His laugh rang out loud, the skin around his green eyes crinkling and his mustache rising at the corners. "It happens to us bluebellies sometimes, it really does. But if you are going to take me to task, Miss Mason, you really ought to call me Thomas."

"I'll do that, if you will call me Lettie."

Theirs was a short acquaintance for such informality, but the circumstances were unusual and there seemed to be no harm in it. The colonel was an attractive man and good company. Lettie liked him, not only because the two of them were, in a manner of speaking, compatriots, but because he was plain-spoken and without pretension. It made her feel much better knowing that he was in command at Natchitoches, even if he didn't approve of what she was trying to do.

In a strictly superficial way, he reminded her of the Thorn. It was the mustache, no doubt, and his height. Hirsute males seemed to be everywhere she looked these days. Facial hair was the fashion. Though beards were not in favor, the mustache was a masculine glory, from the thinnest pencil-line on the upper lip to the full, flowing masterpiece that merged with muttonchop whiskers in front of the ears. This prevalence did not help her to determine what the Thorn looked like. She had only seen him in either shadow or darkness. He had appeared nondescript, really; tall, but no more so than many of the men she had met lately, such as the colonel and Martin Eden, who had been introduced to her at Aunt Em's, or even Ranny for that matter. It was possible, of course, that the image she had of him had been carefully contrived; he was apparently very good at disguises.

It was time for the colonel and herself to return to Splendora. Her escort turned the buggy and they started back the way they had come. Lettie sat in silence for long moments. Finally she spoke.

"There's something that bothers me about Henry and the payroll. My brother was a cautious man, and he suspected that the Thorn had some kind of inside knowledge about the movements of the gold. It seems unlike him to set out alone with the shipment in his saddlebags. I can't believe he wouldn't have waited for an escort."

Thomas Ward's green eyes were dark as he turned toward her. "What are you getting at?"

"Why did he do it? Was he perhaps under orders?"

"To my knowledge, Henry acted on his own initiative."

The man most likely to have ordered her brother to take the risk was sitting beside her. There was no reason he should deny having given the order, however. Or was there? Colonel Ward was also one of the few people who would know the exact movements of the payroll: when it reached Natchitoches, where it would be stored, when and how and by whom it would be transported to Monroe.

She was being foolish. Thomas Ward was an officer of rank in the United States Army. He would not stoop to such treachery.

And yet it might well be hard for him to watch other men making themselves rich on the spoils of the defeated South. He had hinted before that he felt he was being used by such scavengers. In addition, it was obvious that he lacked the patriotic zeal for the Northern stand on Reconstruction that might have been expected from a man in a Union uniform. He would not be the first to have divided loyalties stemming from the recent conflict.

"I still don't understand it," she said, keeping her voice even and free of accusation with an effort. "Were there many people who knew when the payroll would be going out?"

"Three or four, not that it means anything. If a man was watching, the heavy saddlebags used for the trip would have been enough to arouse suspicion."

"All the more reason to wait for an armed escort."

"So it would seem. I don't know if there is any satisfactory explanation. It was just one of those things that happen. It's hard to guard against them when there are men like the Thorn and his ilk who are willing to take any risk to get what they want."

Lettie pursued the matter no further, but directed the conversation toward the more mundane subject of books, leading from there into her bout of reading with Ranny and the two boys and then quite naturally to her teaching experiences. Their conversation was easy, lightened by laughter and mutual understanding. In many ways, due perhaps to the colonel's uniform and military way of looking at things, it was not unlike talking to Henry. By the time they reached Splendora again, her doubts about him seemed so heinous that she was tempted to apologize. She did not, but when he asked her if he might call on her again, her reply was a shade warmer than it might have been otherwise.

They were standing at the gate where he had walked with her after helping her down from the buggy. There was no one on the veranda, and the aromas wafting from the direction of the outdoor kitchen suggested that the others might be making ready for the noon meal. The colonel took her hand and rubbed his thumb across the fine skin of its back.

"You're an unusual young woman, Miss Lettie, to travel so far alone and to lend your time and skills to try to help out here in the South."

She shook her head with a smile. "My family thinks I'm headstrong, not to say as stubborn as a Missouri mule."

"I think you're a marvel, though I'd like to be able to protect you from the trips like the one you made to the spring. I'd like to protect you from the competition I'm going to have, too. The men have found out that there's a girl in the vicinity who not only talks like they do but is considerably more than attractive. Pretty soon Aunt Em is going to have to take a stick and knock the men in blue off her veranda like chickens off a roost."

"She should be very good at that."

"You think I'm joking, don't you?"

"Well, exaggerating just a little."

"Wait and see. And you had better brush up on that phrase your mother taught you that goes "But this is so sudden!"

"So long," she said, her eyes sparkling, "as I don't need it just now."

"I'm making no promises." He pressed her hand and released it, but then reached to place one finger under her chin. "Hold still a minute, will you? There's something I've been wanting to do for the last hour."

"What?" She drew back, suddenly wary.

His voice rich with laughter, he said, "Not what you think, though I'm more than willing. You have a feather caught in your eyelashes."

"A what!"

"Well, a piece of down. Hold still."

A moment later, she felt a touch at her closed eyelids. When she opened her eyes, he carefully showed her the small piece of white fluff. "There. Proof." He blew the piece of feather away, then took the hat he held under his arm and settled it on his head. "I'll call again soon."

"Do that, and bring your friends," she called after him as he turned and walked away.

"An unkind cut," he said over his shoulder, but when he stepped into his buggy and gathered up his reins, he was smiling.

Lettie waved, then turned and went to the house.

Under the magnolia tree at the side of the house, Ransom

straightened from where he leaned against the trunk in the deep shade. He stared after the buggy, his eyes crystalline with self-knowledge, though there was resignation in the hard set of his mouth. He had no right to feel jealous, none at all.

*F*resh eggs, warm from the nest, for breakfast, that was
the lure. The hens began cackling out their pride in their
laying endeavors by a good sunrise. Lettie, awakening early,
set out in the dew to find them. When her apron, which
she had taken to donning for the random jobs she did
around the place, was full of eggs, she turned toward the
kitchen.

The sound of raised voices stopped her in the middle of
the path. She recognized the irate tones of Mama Tass
mingling with the deeper ones of a man of her own race.
The last thing Lettie wanted to do was become involved
in a private quarrel; still, she could not stand there with
her fragile burden for long.

Aunt Em, with her no-nonsense manner, would doubtless know how to settle the altercation, but though Lettie
looked hopefully toward the house, there was no sign of
the older woman. Even Ranny's appearance would be welcome since Mama Tass had a noticeable tendency to give
him her undivided attention when he was on hand. He
was awake, for she had heard movement in his room as
she left the house earlier, but he was nowhere around
now. The only living thing in sight was the calico cat that
came stepping down the walk toward her to wind about
her ankles and a half-dozen chickens scratching with extreme industry around the nearby herb bed.

The voices ceased. When they did not begin again after
a few seconds, Lettie breathed a sigh of relief. She started

forward, only to be stopped short once more as Mama Tass spoke again, her voice throbbing with despair.

"You gonna get yourself killed, that's what's gonna happen."

"I have to help my people."

"By lettin' these carpetbaggers use you?"

"If they're using me, I'm also using them. Our reasons are different, but we want the same thing, a voice for the freedmen."

"You can't say much if you're dead! If you want to help somebody, help your boy Lionel, help me, help the folks here at Splendora. We all need you, and this is where you ought to be!"

"I don't owe Splendora a thing!"

" 'Course you don't!" Mama Tass said with heavy irony. "Just your life that Mr. Ranny saved for you time and again, just the learning that makes you think you can be a senator—"

"Representative."

"Don't correct me, boy! And don't forget the clothes on your back was bought by Miss Em. Not to mention every bite of food that goes into your son's mouth and mine."

"How can I forget, when you won't let me?"

"I won't let you because I know a thing or two about being grateful, because taking care of ourselves is what being free's all about. And I know a thing or two about the white folks, and they've about had a bellyfull of being told what to do by Yankees and trashy black folks. You don't need to run with that crowd. You do, and one night the men in white sheets will hang you from a tree limb."

"I'm not afraid of them."

"That's just fine, but it won't keep your neck from stretching, and I didn't raise you to hang!"

It was her son Bradley, Ranny's former manservant, whom Mama Tass was addressing. He was apparently paying an early-morning visit, since he lived in town, or perhaps he had spent the night with his mother and son as he sometimes did. To be caught listening would be a terrible embarrassment. Lettie looked around her. She could not pass the kitchen without being seen from the open door, but she could circle it to the rear and perhaps unload her apronful of eggs in the dining room.

She stepped back and trod on the calico cat. The cat howled and clawed at her ankle, then fled, hissing. Three chickens, scratching and pecking with a wary eye on the cat, flew up squawking. Lettie, off balance, stumbled backward away from the flapping wings and sat down abruptly on the ground. There was an ominous cracking noise.

From the upper veranda of the big house came a peal of high boyish laughter. Lettie looked up to see Lionel leaning over the railing and pointing, while Ranny, trying to hide a grin, emerged from the house, running down the steps.

The heat of a flush rose to Lettie's hairline, one not at all cooled by the seep of wet stickiness she could feel through the front of her skirts. Never, but never, in her life had she encountered such a series of indignities as had plagued her since she had arrived in Louisiana. She was at a loss to understand it. Her life heretofore had been sedate and proper. It may have been a little dull, but it had also been decorous and reassuringly safe. She felt as if she had forfeited that safety along with her self-respect. How it could have happened, she was not sure. One thing seemed to have led to another. She had made mistakes and paid for them. Their price, she discovered as she sat there on the ground struggling with a strong desire to burst into tears, was higher than she had thought.

Ranny stopped in front of her and went down on one knee. He reached to take the gathered corners of her apron in one hand while with the other he grasped the upper portion near the waistband.

"Untie your apron strings," he said.

She did as he said, releasing the apron to him. He took the fullness of it all into his left hand, forming a sack, then extended his right to her as he rose. She put her fingers in his, looking up at him with a smile that was a little tremulous before allowing him to draw her to her feet. His strength was unexpected. She came up against him before she could stop herself, resting there for an instant before she stepped back.

Ransom stood holding her hand; feeling the imprint of her firm breasts where they had pressed against his arm; staring at the soft pink tint of her cheeks, at the moisture that made her eyes liquid and hugely bright, at her lips so softly parted. A wave of desire swept through him with such force that he felt as mindless and immature as he could hope to appear.

"Mast' Ranny? What's going on? You two come in here so's I can cook your breakfast and get it out of the way."

Bless Mama Tass, Ransom thought. She was an old tartar but a wise woman. He let go of Lettie and stepped back, allowing her to pass in front of him before he followed her toward the kitchen.

Mama Tass's son Bradley, who had given himself the last name of Lincoln, was of medium height, stocky, and well-formed. His resemblance to his mother was marked, his skin a rich brown, his features clean-cut, and his eyes sharp with intelligence. He greeted Ranny with easy affection, though he seemed wary of Lettie, treating her to his best English and rather forced interest.

"So you're the new teacher? How have you found the South so far?"

"It's difficult to say," she answered, disconcerted by the directness of his words.

"Not exactly the way you thought it would be?"

"Not precisely, no."

"No turreted castles, no gilded carriages, no groveling former slaves singing praise at being released from their chains? It's a little late for all of that. What's left is ruins and hard work, the aristocracy of the hoe—unless you want to count the Knights with white sheets in place of armor?"

"Bradley?" Mama Tass gave a shake of her head as she looked at her son.

"I'm here to work," Lettie said, the words carrying quiet dignity.

"I thought you were here about your brother, with teaching as an afterthought?"

"Bradley!"

This time the warning in Mama Tass's voice was stronger. She stood at the foot of the table where the rest of them had taken seats. In front of her were two bowls, one holding the cracked eggs still encased in the apron that was draped over the sides, the other ready to receive the ones that were uncracked as Mama Tass inspected them.

Annoyance raced along Lettie's vein, a reaction partly due to the man's manner and partly because what he was saying was the truth. She arched a brow. "Are you suggesting you don't need help, Mr. Lincoln?"

"I'm saying I'm tired of people coming down here who claim to want to help us but are really after their own advantage."

"Hush up, Bradley!" Mama Tass said, but it was Ranny, rather than her son, who turned his attention to her.

Lettie ignored the byplay. "I assure you, I have nothing to gain! But as long as you receive the help you need, do the reasons it's given really matter?"

"They matter because of a few facts that you and your kind never quite understand, Miss Mason. We may be former slaves, but we have our pride. But most of all, we are Southerners, too."

Lettie stared at him for an instant, then a smile crept

into her eyes, warming them. "Yes, I think I see. Tell me, when you were with Ranny in the war, did you ever fire at the enemy?"

"I wasn't supposed to, but when you're standing in the midst of an army with a musket in your hands that you've been reloading and two thousand men in blue coming pouring over a hill doing their level best to kill you, you don't think about why they're coming. You don't think about much at all except staying alive."

Ranny, at the end of the table nearest Mama Tass, reached over and took an egg from the bowl closest to him, turning it in his hand.

Lettie went on. "You saved the life of your master when he was injured, I think, and spent time with him in a Union prison camp?"

"If you're trying to say that I'm different, you're wrong. There were thousands like me. If I saved Ransom, he did the same for me a dozen times over. What was I supposed to do when he was hurt? Desert him? I was his body servant from the day he was weaned. We grew up together. We were Don Quixote and Sanchez, always off on some crazy quest, the more desperate the better."

"Oh, Bradley," Ranny said, his voice soft and sad as he tossed the egg in his hand, catching it with delicate precision, "you talk too much."

It seemed almost a threat. Lettie could not tell whether Bradley perceived it that way or not.

The black man looked at Ranny and at the egg, and his dark brown eyes filled with an appreciative yet somber light. "My regret is that circumstances have removed the need for my services, and so I am forced into becoming the manservant of the radical Republicans."

Ranny placed the egg back in the bowl. He met the eyes of the man across the table. "I'm still your friend."

"Yes. Still."

Bradley Lincoln reached out his hand. Ranny clasped it. Mama Tass, with a small sniffing sound, picked up the egg bowls and turned toward the stove. Lettie watched the look that passed between the two men and felt a knot form in her own throat.

At the same time, she had the disturbing feeling that there was something she had missed. It was not the first time she had noticed it. There were crosscurrents in the relationships of these people that they seemed to understand by some instinct she did not possess. It made her feel like an outsider. She was one, of course, and yet it was irksome to be constantly reminded of it. They did not mean to do it; she absolved them of that charge. It was simply a fact she could not overlook. She wondered if it was possible for someone like her ever to belong. It did not seem likely.

The dance that was held on the veranda of Splendora that evening stemmed solely from a saddlebag full of lemons. It was Colonel Thomas Ward who brought them, fresh off a boat from New Orleans. He came after supper, also bringing three of his fellow officers.

"It's an invasion," Sally Anne said under her breath as they cantered up the drive, and, in truth, it seemed to be one before it was done.

Of the three additional soldiers, one was from New York, one from Maine, and one from Tennessee. They came up the steps, their faces wary but hopeful, their hats under their arms, their hair carefully combed. "Why, they're just boys," Aunt Em said, and struggled up out of her rocking chair to go and greet them.

What she had said was true and yet untrue. They were not that old in years, but they were seasoned veterans. They talked softly and grinned often as they began to relax;

still, there was resolution and assurance behind their quiet manners.

Lettie had been afraid they would be snubbed, perhaps repulsed. She should have known better, she realized on second thought. Hospitality and innate courtesy would require a polite reception, if not a warm one. The men had their entrée through Colonel Ward; it would be up to them to ensure their welcome in the future.

They attempted to do that in part with small gifts, beginning with the lemons. They were brought forth, fat, yellow globes juggled with no small difficulty from the saddlebags to the veranda. Another man produced a cone of sugar wrapped in brown paper, and yet another a tin box of marzipan, while the third brought out a fiddle in a leather case. The lemons and sugar were exclaimed over with suitable fervor and expressions of gratitude, then dispatched to the kitchen by Lionel and Peter with instructions for lemonade. Soon they were all sipping the tart beverage, talking wistfully of slivers of ice with which to chill it, as in times past, and listening as the sound of the fiddle, sweet and rather doleful, drifted over the veranda and out into the gathering twilight.

The welcome of the next man to ride up to the gate was never in question. Johnny Reeden swung down from his mount, digging a harmonica from his coat pocket as he came up the walk. Ranny, seeing the instrument, gave a theatrical groan that was echoed by Lionel beside him.

Johnny beamed with malicious pleasure. "I knew you would be overjoyed. There I was, feeling melancholy, and I said to myself, Now which of my friends should I choose to share my sorrows? I was riding in this direction when I heard the fiddle music and knew immediately that I had my answer! Some things are directed by a higher power."

"Not many," Ranny said.

"You," Johnny told him, "are a pessimist." In a pretense at huffiness, he sat down on the steps, turned his back, and raised the harmonica to his mouth.

Lettie expected to have her ears assaulted. Instead, the music of the simple mouth organ rose clear and true, blending in perfect harmony with the fiddle, adding richness. There was heart-catching emotion in the flowing sound and a degree of pathos that was unexpected from the laughing, red-haired young man.

Johnny and the man in blue from Tennessee gave them "Lorena," "Rock of Ages," "Old Folks at Home," and "Rocked in the Cradle of the Deep." Just when everyone was nearly in tears from such lugubrious selections, they swung into "Oh! Susannah" in such lively fashion that Aunt Em began to tap her foot, and the moths clustering around the pair of oil lamps that had been brought out of the house seemed to flutter back and forth in time to the music.

In the midst of the gaiety, Martin Eden drove up in a surrey. He had with him a vivacious young girl, Marie Voisin, the daughter of a near neighbor, the girl's mother, Madame Voisin, as chaperone, and a friend, Angelique La Cour. They had been taking the evening air when they saw the lights and heard the music. Curiosity compelled them to discover the cause.

Introductions were made. More glasses were brought out and lemonade poured. The marzipan was passed around. The music resumed and the tempo of the evening picked up perceptively.

Marie Voisin, dark and vivacious, flirted as naturally as she breathed. She was interested in everyone and everything; her questions flew thick and fast, and her liquid brown eyes sparkled with zest. Madame Voisin, comfortably ensconced beside Aunt Em and nibbling on marzipan, was indulgent. The friend Angelique was less animated but spoke easily enough when Marie turned to include her in the conversation.

Who began the dancing was difficult to say. One moment everyone was sitting, talking, swinging their feet, and slapping at the occasional mosquito; the next they were up and pushing the chairs and lamp tables back against the wall. No one seemed to think it was unusual. It was treated rather as a natural opportunity, one that must be seized.

Lettie whirled around the floor with Thomas Ward, then went from one to the other of the men in blue in such quick succession that she was soon breathless and feeling the pull of a stitch in her side. Marie and her friend Angelique were just as much in demand and just as obliging. Even Aunt Em sashayed about to the rhythm of a reel, holding up her skirts and tossing her head. Sally Anne, on the other hand, pleaded fatigue and, though she was pleasant enough about it, refused to take the floor. Nothing, seemingly, could change the young widow's mind until Ranny pushed away from the wall where he stood and moved to bow in front of her.

The music was slow, a waltz tempo. The pair revolved down the long veranda, their movements gliding, perfectly matched, infinitely graceful. Ranny bent his blond head toward Sally Anne, and she looked up at him with a smile that had the look of wistful enjoyment. They seemed to inhabit a world of their own, one removed from the noise and laughter around them, one softer, more gentle and delicately colored than that where ordinary mortals were forced to abide. Lettie, also circling in the arms of the colonel, watched them and gave a small unconscious shake of her head.

"What is it?" Thomas Ward asked. "Surprised?"

She gave him a brief smile. "Yes, a little, to be honest. I rather expected him to be clumsy on the floor."

"I suppose there are some things you don't forget unless, of course, the bodily responses are damaged."

"Yes," she said in agreement. "I was thinking, too, that they are both casualties of the war, in their way."

"Are they? Tyler may be, but if the lovely widow is a casualty, it's by choice."

"Because she refuses to dance with the Union army?" Lettie lifted a brow, her smile quizzical.

"Because she's hiding behind those widow's weeds she always wears."

"Maybe she can't afford anything else."

"Maybe she feels safe."

"Who's to say she doesn't deserve any safety she can find?"

"Such as marrying Tyler and playing mother to him as well as to her son. It would be a terrible waste."

Lettie said no more, but her gaze on Ranny and the woman in black was wide and speculative.

Their numbers increased. Mr. Daniel O'Connor, the tax collector, arrived in search of Colonel Ward. He had been told, the Irish carpetbagger said, that the Union commander was visiting the Tyler house. He hoped he didn't intrude? 'Twas the last thing he wanted to do.

The man was invited to join them, if with little enthusiasm, and offered refreshment. He accepted, grimaced at the taste of the tart lemonade when he had apparently expected something stronger, them moved aside with the colonel for a few minutes.

Their business transacted, the two men looked toward where Lettie stood against the railing, fanning her flushed face. The colonel started toward her and the carpetbagger trailed along at his heels. As they neared, Lettie heard O'Connor, a short, plump man whose clothes were too brightly colored and of too tight a fit, speak to Thomas

Ward in what he undoubtedly thought was an undertone. "By the way, what's the high yellow girl doing here?"

"What do you mean?" the officer said, pausing to look down at the other man.

"Over there. The quadroon from down Isle Brevelle way."

He was indicating Angelique, who was dancing at that moment in the arms of Martin Eden. Lettie stared at the girl. Could it be true? Her skin was the color of overrich cream and her hair jet-black and thickly curling. Her appearance was a bit exotic, but Lettie had thought that perhaps she had a strain of Spanish or Mexican blood, an inheritance from the Spanish post that had shared the Texas-Louisiana frontier with Natchitoches for decades during the French and Spanish regimes. Angelique was well known by the Tylers, apparently, and accepted as being some distant family connection of their Voisin neighbors.

"Are you sure?" The colonel's voice was blank.

"Sure as shootin'. Saw her at her old man's place not a week back. A choice piece, one I wouldn't mind looking after for a few weeks." He nudged the man beside him in the ribs.

Thomas returned no answer. The two men moved on to stop before Lettie, and the tax collector was presented to her. Before there was time for more than a brief greeting, a blue-coated officer approached and swept Lettie away. She was not sorry. O'Connor was of a type she could not stomach, crude and grasping, pretentious and porcine. It was he whom the Thorn had recently left tied to a lamppost with a sign around his neck. It was possible that in this case the Thorn had reason for what he had done.

Claiming exhaustion after an hour, Johnny Reeden put down his harmonica and staggered toward the lemonade pitcher. The dancers collapsed in the chairs along the walls or hung over the railings in search of a cooling breeze. Sally Anne, who was nearest to the lemonade, poured Johnny a glass of it and put it in his elaborately trembling hand. He reeled away, making it as far as the chair that sat between the rocker Lettie had claimed and the straight chair on which Ranny reclined with his long legs thrust out before him.

"For a man sunk in melancholy," Lettie said to Johnny, "you make lovely music."

"A woman of rare discernment." He toasted her with lemonade. "But you can't see the black pain in my heart."

"Of course I can. It's caused, I suspect, by boot black."

"You think I'm shamming? I'm cut to the quick!"

"Oh? Then we should soon see the truth of it."

"Heartless." He swung around to Ranny on his other side. "I appeal to you, my friend: Did you ever see a more heartless female?"

Ranny held up his hand as if warding off a blow. "Don't ask me, Johnny."

"Coward! Great oaf of a coward, deserting your friends at the first hint of trouble."

"Who, me?" Ranny was the picture of innocence.

"Certainly you, you dumb Adonis. What a fine thing it is when a man can't even insult a friend and have him know it."

"You want to insult me? I'm insulted, then."

Johnny gave a moan and dropped his rust-colored head in his hands. "You aren't."

"Yes, I am."

"Aren't."

"Am."

"Aren't."

"I am."

"You are, and I'm an addlepated idiot."

O'Connor, still at the railing beside the colonel, gave a snort. "That makes two."

There was a hush. The exchange between Johnny and Ransom Tyler had been the merest banter, good-natured and easy, between friends of long-standing. It had been an expression of closeness rather than an insult.

That Ransom Tyler's circumstances were known to all those present was plain, for though he was officially their host, few other than his immediate family spoke to him directly. Whether from embarrassment or indifference, they had tended to ignore him or else to patronize him. The gratuitous disparagement spoken by O'Connor seemed to Lettie one of the most ill-bred and stupidly vicious remarks she had ever heard. That Ranny understood could not have been clearer, though his face as he looked at the tax collector was closed-in, without expression, and he moved not a muscle. Anger boiled up inside her.

"Two of what, Mr. O'Connor?" She raised her voice, its pitch clear and slicing and as cold as her smile as she asked the question.

"Why, two—that is . . ." The man blustered to a stop, his face reddening as he looked around him for support. "I don't rightly know what you mean."

"Indeed? I thought it was you who meant something."

"No, ma'am, nothing at all. I've clean forgot what I was saying."

The look the short, fat man gave her was livid. Lettie returned it with a chill smile, then deliberately turned her gaze away. There was a concerted rush of talk as, by instinct, the others tried to cover the moment of awkwardness. She let it wash over her while she sat back in the rocking chair. She was astonished at herself. She could not think what had possessed her to defend the owner of Splendora. She hardly knew herself at all these days.

"Bravo, Miss Lettie, ma'am," Johnny Reeden said in quiet tones, "here's my hand."

She gave him hers because it would be impolite to refuse. In some confusion, she said, "Such atrocious manners. I couldn't let him get away with it."

"No, I understand. It was for Ranny."

"Not really—you mustn't think it was anything personal. I was just annoyed."

"The best kind of champion, an angry one."

"I can't explain it—"

"No need. You did it, and that's enough. Principles are lovely things."

He smiled, a movement of his lips that did not quite reach his eyes. Lettie met his gaze and suddenly it occurred to her that his melancholia was real and blighting. There was no reason for it that she could see, and yet it was there. It was disturbing, both its presence inside the laughing young man and her own sensitivity to it.

The soldier with the fiddle picked it up and began to scrape out another tune. Ranny reached out to pluck Johnny's harmonica from his friend's pocket and put it to his lips. He played very well, though with less verve than Johnny had displayed, and he had to fend his friend off with his elbow as Johnny kept trying to regain his property.

It was a relief to Lettie to be asked to dance by Martin Eden. She was able to leave her uncomfortable introspection behind while she parried his compliments, which became more outrageous the less she responded. Martin was gallant and handsome, a man of dark and smiling charm; it was perverse of her to remain unimpressed. But though she enjoyed his company, after a few moments her attention began to wander.

The hour was growing late. Lionel and Peter, after ripping up and down the outside stairs, trying to walk the veranda railing like a tightrope, and sneaking two pieces of marzipan for every one they were given, had finally settled down against the wall. The younger boy was nearly comatose, staring glassy-eyed at the company. As Lettie watched, Ranny handed the harmonica back to Johnny and moved toward Peter. He reached down and pulled the boy to his feet, then herded him into the house, presumably to the trundle that was stored under his mother's bed in the chamber they occupied next to Lettie's. After a few moments, Ranny returned and went to sit against the wall beside Lionel, talking quietly to the boy.

Ranny's relationship with Lionel and Peter was interesting. Sometimes he allowed them to lead him around by the hand, as docile and uncomplaining as some big friendly dog. Other times, he seemed to lead them, using persuasion and cajolery and, when that failed, a little bullying rather like a slightly older brother. To Lettie's knowledge, they never offered any real resistance to his suggestions; still, she was forced to wonder what he would do if they did. There was strength in that magnificent body—she had seen it once or twice—but was there any force of will? It mattered very little, of course, but she wished she knew.

"How does he do it?"

Lettie dragged her attention back to her partner. "I beg your pardon?"

"Our Ransom doesn't do a thing, never did, but the ladies can't keep their eyes off him. Even now you can see them watching him."

"Envious, Mr. Eden?"

He gave her a confiding smile and shook his head with a motion that made the dark curl that fell onto his forehead dip lower. "Hardly. But it's one of those phenomenons like a full moon or a shooting star; people just stop to look, particularly women."

"You've known him a long time?"

"We were all boys together, Ransom, Johnny, and I; we

did our fishing together, our courting, and our fighting. I'd say I know him about as well as anybody, better than most."

"You don't call him Ranny like the others."

"That's a nickname of recent years, one I don't particularly like. He was always Ransom before he came back from the war and I see no reason to change just because he's not quite the same."

"Is he . . . very different?"

He shrugged, a wry smile tugging his mustache up at one corner. "Yes and no. I find myself watching him at times like everybody else, trying to decide. I think what I miss most is his sharp wit—there was a time when he could nail you to the wall with a word—that, and the fun. Lord, but we used to laugh. He could do some of the wildest things, say some of the most hilarious things, and never crack a smile. I do miss him."

"I believe he's recovered many of his faculties compared to what he was like when he first regained consciousness here at Splendora. I don't suppose there's any chance that he could—"

"After all these years? Not likely. But if you see any sign of it, let me know. I owed him twenty dollars—in gold, not Confederate script—when that shell exploded!"

Lettie smiled at his sally. They whirled past where Ranny sat. Lettie's skirts brushed his boots on the somewhat narrow dance floor. The blond man drew them back, as if afraid they would soil her gown, but did not look up.

Lettie, turning her attention back to her partner, gave the handsome Southerner a speculative look. Another tall, mustachioed man. A small frisson of anxiety moved through her and then was gone. Surely if she had been intimate with him, if he was the Thorn, she would know? Surely there would be something in his manner to give him away, some suggestion of familiarity, of triumph? She had to think so, or else the strain of being in the company of men, of wondering if each one she met was the man who had made love to her in the darkness, would become intolerable.

It may have been the irritation of her nerves brought on by her thoughts that made her wish, abruptly, to get beneath the smooth and urbane manner of the man who held her.

"You fought for the South, Mr. Eden, but now you cooperate with those in power. Tell me, are you a Union sympathizer or just an opportunist?"

He stiffened, missing a step as temper flashed in his brown eyes. He recovered quickly and murmured an apology, his expression wry. "You're very straightforward, aren't you?"

"Does the term opportunist bother you?"

"Of course it does!"

"I seem to remember that you don't like scalawag, either."

"No, but I prefer it to being called a Union sympathizer. That, at least, I'm not."

"But you cooperate, anyway."

"We lost the war. It was a hard and dirty and glorious fight, but we lost and we have to live with that fact. It seems to me that we can stand on our pride and be ground into the dust or we can cooperate and slowly rebuild our fortunes and our future. I say I'm a reasonable man; others say I'm a scalawag and refuse to shake my hand. So be it."

If his tone was defensive, it was not surprising. His stand seemed most realistic to Lettie, however. She told him so and was just a little ashamed of the impulse that had made her bait him when she saw the relief in his face.

The party began to fade away. Daniel O'Connor, after a dance with Angelique, took his leave. If he said anything improper to the girl, she gave no sign of it, though afterward she went and sat beside Madame Voisin for some time, watching the others, particularly Martin Eden, though he paid her scant attention. Madame Voisin herself, a short while later, began to smother yawns and called to her daughter to hurry and finish enjoying herself. Johnny and the soldier from Tennessee, bowing to the inevitable, announced the last waltz.

Lettie was standing beside Sally Anne, talking with the young widow and Martin while Ranny lounged nearby listening, when she saw Colonel Ward coming toward her. She had already turned, ready to give him a smile and her hand for this final dance, when the military commander bowed before the other woman.

"May I?" he asked, his expression grave and his stance rigid as he held out his arm in invitation.

Sally Anne's face turned pale, but she spoke without hesitation. "It's very kind of you, but I'm rather tired. Excuse me this time, if you please."

"There may never be another."

"I'm sorry, but I can't."

Thomas Ward stood his ground. "Is it the uniform, the accent, or is it me?"

Martin, frowning, took a step toward the colonel. "You heard what the lady said."

"Please, Martin," Sally Anne said softly, putting her hand on the Southerner's arm.

"Unfortunately," Thomas said, "I didn't hear the answer to my last question. I must ask you to allow the lady to speak for herself."

"This is a private home and you are a guest. You can't force yourself upon a woman, regardless of your military jurisdiction." Martin's hands were clenched into fists.

Thomas ignored the remark. "Mrs. Winston, all I ask—"

"Did you hear me?" Martin demanded, reaching out and pushing Thomas's shoulder.

"Too well," the colonel snapped, squaring back up to him.

"Then back off!"

"The hell I will!"

Martin Eden pushed Thomas again. The man in blue gave with the shove but, in a quick, hard movement, dragged Martin toward him, pitched him over his hip, and slung him to the floor.

The veranda shook with the thudding fall. Sally Anne screamed and covered her face with her hands. Lettie stepped back in sudden apprehension, catching the arm of the other woman to draw her with her. Martin shoved himself to his elbow. He fumbled inside his coat and a derringer, small and deadly and silvery in the lamplight, appeared in his hand.

The colonel stopped still where he was bent over the crouched form of the other man. The other men in uniform, already moving toward the altercation, halted, freezing in place. Aunt Em and the rest of the women turned with their mouths tight and their eyes wide. Lionel, standing with his back to the wall, looked ready to bolt. The music twanged to a stop. Tension stretched as tightly as the bow in the fiddler's hand.

Then, like an eagle striking, Ransom moved. His hard, booted foot caught Martin's wrist. The derringer flew up, discharging in an exploding roar into the ceiling before clattering to the floor. Martin cursed and grabbed his hand. The colonel let out the air in his lungs with an audible sound. Sally Anne cried out, then flung herself on Lettie and began to sob. Ransom bent to pick up the small gun, then stood holding it as if not sure what to do with it.

"Good gracious," Aunt Em cried. "Ranny, put that thing down and help Martin up. Colonel Ward, I'll thank you to give him a hand. And you, Martin, remember who you are and where you are. Hush that noise, Sally Anne, and let this be a lesson to you. And the rest of you had better volunteer to fix my ceiling or I'll have the stripes from your sleeves so fast it'll make your heads spin!"

It was precisely what the moment needed, the voice of authority, the hint of humor. Martin, on his feet, rubbed his elbow, gave a dazed shake of his head, then thrust out his hand to the colonel. "I don't know what came over me, sir. My most sincere apologies."

"I may have been out of line," Thomas Ward said readily enough as the men shook hands. He looked at Sally Anne. "I meant no harm, however."

Tragedy had been averted by swift action, common sense, and manners. Lettie recognized that fact easily enough, but what she could not quite comprehend was the speed, indicative of lightning-quick thought, with which Ranny had moved. Instinct again? The remnants of his old military training and experience? Whatever the cause, for an instant, the way he had struck out at Martin had reminded her of the Thorn. The force she had wondered about earlier had certainly been there in that brief space of time. She found, quite illogically, that she did not like it.

It was not to be expected that the visitors would tarry under such uncomfortable circumstances. They departed with many farewells and expressions of pleasure and much pretense that everything was as it should be. Still, within a very short while, they were gone and the dust was settling on the drive.

Lettie and Aunt Em gathered up the sticky glasses and stacked them on a tray while Ranny and Lionel returned the chairs and tables to their proper places. Mama Tass, who had no doubt been watching from some vantage point, came bustling out to wipe the tabletops with a wet cloth and to take the tray of glasses away to the kitchen.

Aunt Em started toward the open doors that led into the

great central hall. Lettie had begun to move after her when the older woman turned back, looking to where Ranny stood leaning with one shoulder against a column and his hands in his pockets.

"Coming, Ranny?"

He turned from his absorbed contemplation of the night to look at his aunt, then glanced down as Lionel came and put a small brown hand on his arm. Only then did he turn his gaze to Lettie. It came to him with unexpected strength that there were times when he despised the role he had given himself. If he was not locked into his pose of a bumbling idiot, he could have made his bow before Lettie this evening and swept her into a dance; could have held her in his arms, breathed the scent of her, made her laugh in that quick, surprised way that she had, perhaps even persuaded her to walk with him out under the magnolias.

But he had done none of those things. He had, instead, watched her dance and smile with other men and pretended not to care while he felt as if he was exploding silently inside. The result was that he had done a stupid thing. He had attacked Martin when he drew his gun, rather than simply stepping between his friend and Colonel Ward as he should have done. How much of that had been due to the danger of the moment and how much due to a need to display his heroics in front of this woman was a question he did not care to examine. Nor would he.

"Coming," he answered his aunt in his softest voice, and gave his hand to Lionel.

*T*he moonlight was disturbing. Lettie lay for some time watching it stream through the muslin curtains, turning them to panels of silver-gold gauze. The air in the room was close and overwarm, almost too thick to breathe. She was tired, but sleep seemed far away. She felt peculiar, edgy, though she refused to consider why or to think of anything else beyond that simple fact.

The door of her room stood open to encourage the free passage of air through the house. It served also to conduct sounds. She could hear the steady ticking of the clock in the parlor, Aunt Em's soft and even snoring, and the occasional snap and creak of boards and beams in the attic. To these noises was added the scratchy chorus of night insects, creating a quiet cacophony that wore on her nerves until she began to feel that she must sit straight up in bed and start to scream.

It was intolerable.

Lettie sat up and groped over the foot of the bed for her dressing gown. Pushing aside the mosquito netting that hung from the tester, she slid out of the high bed, thrusting her arms into the sleeves of her dressing gown at the same time. Barefooted, she padded to the window, opened the jib doors, and stepped out onto the veranda. She paused, a faint tremor moving through her as she recalled the last time she had ventured out like this; then, with a quick toss of her head, she moved to the railing. That incident with the Thorn had been the purest mischance, an accident, as had been her meeting with him at the spring. It could not happen again.

She stared out into the warm, scented night, leaning forward with her hands on the railing and her elbows stiff, locked. The darkness seemed alive. It had a presence of its own that invited, almost coaxed, her to come out into its softly moving shadows. The moon was waxing, nearly three-quarters full in the black, silk-lined arch of the sky. Its serene face was a beacon, one that held a benign promise.

Lettie pushed away from the railing, then swung her back to it. She closed her eyes and shook back her hair as she breathed deep. Fanciful. She was full of fancies these days. The air was fresh out here, and she liked being free of the confinement of her room. That was all. The night was simply a time without sunlight; there was nothing special about it.

The double entrance doors leading into the house stood open to catch and circulate the stray breezes. Lettie, staring at them, thought she would never become used to that habit, though she could readily see that tightly closed windows and doors would be stifling in this climate. Still, it indicated a level of trust that seemed foolhardy under the present unsettled circumstances. She could not decide if that trust was due to the Southerner's belief in his fellow man or merely to his dependence on his ability to protect himself. Either way, it bothered her.

On several occasions she had awakened toward the middle of the night when it became cooler and got up to close her own door. She had noticed that Ranny's door was often closed then also. It was possible he felt the need of that protective gesture just as she did.

The wide hallway was like a dark tunnel through the house. The open doorway at the far end was a dimly lighted rectangle giving on to the rear veranda. The open space did seem to be creating a draft; the edges of a crocheted lace cloth hanging over the sides of a small table were moving gently, ghostlike, in the dimness.

The need to feel that coolness, momentary as it might be, was strong. Lettie moved toward the doorway, reentering the house. Her footsteps soundless on the wood floor, she eased past the parlor on the left and her own bedchamber door opposite, past the dining room in the middle of the house and the bedchamber occupied by Sally Anne and Peter, and on toward the last bedchambers at the back of the house, those opening onto the rear veranda. From the one on the right, that of Aunt Em, still issued the rhythmic noises of deep sleep. The faint sheen of light on the mahogany panel on the left showed that Ranny's door was closed.

Abruptly, Lettie came to a halt. There was a strange bundle lying on the floor outside the door of the bedchamber belonging to the owner of the house. She took a step nearer. The bundle stirred, gave a sigh.

Lettie gasped on a soft laugh. It was Lionel, sound asleep on a rug. How very medieval.

She could not think, however, that the boy was there at Ranny's orders. Ranny had gone to bed soon after the evening party had broken up. Perhaps he had had another of his headaches after the excitement and Lionel was staying close in case he was called in the night. He was a most loyal companion with a true affection for his large charge.

Stepping lightly so as not to awaken the boy, Lettie moved on. Emerging on the back veranda, she angled across its width to the right end where a bright wedge of moonlight lay. She stopped at the side railing and leaned her shoulder against the corner post. To her left lay the kitchen with its slate roof shining dully and beyond it the row of cabins at the edge of the field. To the side, behind the kitchen, was the overgrown orchard, while closer at hand so that it almost merged with it was an alley of crepe myrtles interplanted with a dense tangle of rambling roses.

Something moved among the crepe myrtles. Lettie, catching the flicker from the corner of her eye, stiffened. A moment later a bird flew up with a sleepy squawk and the calico kitchen cat stalked out of the undergrowth, twitching its tail at the loss of its sport and midnight meal.

Lettie castigated herself for her jumpiness as she relaxed again. She lifted her gaze to stare at the moon. She could feel its light on her face like a touch. It gave her a deep sense of pleasure, one she surrendered to for a brief moment.

The radiance poured over her, giving her skin the soft luster of pearls and settling in the waves of her hair like pale fire. It edged her dressing gown in silver gilt, forming a glowing nimbus around her body that made her look ethereal, not quite real.

Ransom, where he had stepped back in haste into the dark shade of a spreading pecan tree, stood transfixed. His chest swelled, and he pressed his hand against the trunk of the tree beside him until the faint ridges of the bark pressed into his palm. He did not move for a long moment, then slowly the tension seeped away. The temptation to approach Lettie once more in his present guise had been nearly irresistible, but it was not an indulgence he could afford.

This Yankee schoolteacher was more than a minor impediment to him; she was fast becoming a major threat. This was the second time she had stood between him and his refuge. It was unintentional, of that he was almost certain; still, Aunt Em's decision to take in a boarder had complicated his activities beyond measure. More than that, her presence did strange things to his power of reason. She was dangerous. It was possible that something would have to be done about her.

He could not think what it might be. He had expected her to flee from Louisiana in horror and disgust after the incident at the corncrib. That she had not done so left him with mixed feelings of puzzlement, distraction, and an odd, debilitating tenderness, feelings compounded by the sure knowledge that he had a problem.

Aunt Em herself, bless her, never gave him cause for worry. Though she was apt to say that she hardly closed her eyes at night, she always sank immediately into the deep sleep enjoyed only by those with kind hearts and clear consciences. With a little help from Lionel and Mama Tass, he had been able to come and go at will.

The decision to keep his aunt in ignorance was something that often troubled him, but it could not be helped. She was a dear but completely incapable of dissembling for long. She was sure to become flustered if questioned, or else forget and give him a sound scolding instead of treating him with the patience and compassion due to one with his supposed affliction. No, the way he was handling his aunt was for the best. That the same could not be said about Letitia Mason, was, he knew well, his own fault.

His face bleak, Ransom retreated a step, then another. Swinging around, he circled with stealth toward the kitchen.

There came to Lettie the faint sound of water splashing. She straightened, trying to locate it, and finally turned in the direction of the kitchen building. Alarm raced with the blood in her veins, then was slowly replaced by curiosity. There was nothing furtive, nothing secretive about the noise she was hearing.

A man stepped from the kitchen door out onto the walk. Lettie made a swift movement toward the hall of the house, then stopped short. How foolish of her. It was only Ranny.

He came toward her along the walk with free and easy grace, his movements unhurried. He wore only a pair of trousers and had a towel slung around his neck. His hair glistened wetly and he ran his fingers through it, raking it back in a quick gesture that sprayed water droplets like silver rain into the air. Water beaded on his bare torso, glittering upon the golden furring of hair on his chest. As he approached the house, he was humming quietly to himself.

Lettie walked to the head of the flight of steps. Her voice soft but carrying, she said, "What are you doing up?"

He stopped just below her and looked upward, his song dying away. A smile spread over his face. "Miss Lettie."

"I asked you a question," she reminded him. It was not really suspicion that prompted her but rather a niggling feeling that it was not normal for him to be out at night.

He laughed up at her. "Swimming."

"Alone?"

"It was hot. Lionel was asleep." There was a trickle of water running down his chest, a trickle still dark with brown dye. He wiped it hastily.

"Do you do it often?"

"No. Only sometimes."

"In the river?"

Ransom calculated swiftly. Not the river, for Aunt Em would be upset if she heard of this supposed midnight swim and thought he was fighting the river currents. There was only one place left. "Dink's Pond."

"And no one minds?"

"I don't tell them. You won't tell, will you?"

Instead of answering, Lettie sighed. "I wish I could have gone with you."

The suggestion was so unexpected that it took Ransom's breath. He had a flashing vision of what it would be like: the two of them disporting themselves, naked in the murky waters of the pond, their wet flesh shining in the moonlight, gliding together. Lettie didn't know what she was saying, of course. Or perhaps she did, only it was Ranny she was saying it to, someone she considered safe, someone less than a man. Annoyance as unreasonable as it was real moved over him.

"Come now," he suggested, his voice soft. "I'll go again."

Why she had mentioned such a thing, Lettie could not have said. The thought of acting on it was alluring and yet frightening. She stared down at Ranny. The moonlight gilded the planes of his face and chest, highlighting the superb musculature of his body while leaving his eyes in shadow. It turned the tousled wetness of his hair to shining gilt and gave the drops of water on his skin the sparkle of diamonds. A peculiar sensation invaded the center of her being. Unconsciously, she raised her hand to her throat, gathering the edges of the opening of her dressing gown together.

It was embarrassing that she should feel this awareness of Ranny as a man. It was doubtful that he saw her as anything more than a chance companion, like Lionel. She had no desire for it to be otherwise, and yet she felt his ability to look at her without awareness very like an insult to her femininity. It was ridiculous, but she had a strong desire to test whether he would respond to a warm smile in the same way that other men did. The impulse within herself was horrifying, so much so that she backed away from him.

"Don't go." Ransom was contrite the moment he saw the change in her face. He put his foot on the bottom step and began to mount upward.

"It—it's late."

"Yes. Stay. Talk to me."

"I can't."

He stopped. His voice grave, he said, "Are you afraid?"

She was, afraid of herself, of the new and sensual part of her nature that had been revealed to her.

Before she could speak, there was a shuffling step in the hall behind her. Lionel, his voice thick with sleep and yet shaded with concern, cried, "Mast' Ranny, you all right?"

"I'll talk to you in the morning," Lettie said hurriedly to the man on the steps. Turning, she fled into the house.

In her room once more, Lettie shut the door behind her, slipped from her dressing gown, and climbed into bed. She lay down flat on her back with her hands at her sides and her eyes so tightly closed that her lashes felt meshed together.

It didn't help. The images she had been keeping at bay for three days flooded in upon her. The Thorn. The rain. The corncrib. Her incredible lack of self-control.

What had come over her that she could permit a vile murderer like the Thorn to take liberties that she had refused to Charles, the man who had loved and wanted to marry her? It was true that the Thorn had been in a fair way of taking those liberties whether she permitted them or not, but she could not think, looking back, that he would have forced himself on her if she had struggled. What was so reprehensible in her mind was that she had not fought him, had not made the least protest.

Physical passion, it was said, was an overwhelming force. She had never believed it. She had thought instead that it must be no more than an impulse that was controllable by the intellect. Never had she suspected that she was capable of being affected by it. She had felt, with good reason, that her nature was moderate, even a little cool. She could not understand what had happened to her, could not accept that she had been so wrong about herself.

Was it possible that the difference was in the man who had held her? Such a thing made no sense. She despised the man who styled himself the Thorn, hated him and everything he did. She fully intended to see that he was brought to justice. If the opportunity came, she would destroy him as she might the mosquito that whined outside her netting.

Or would she? She could have shot him dead, but she had not.

The truth was, there was something inside her that responded to the touch of the Thorn as it did to no other man. That it was against her will, against her principles made no difference. It could not be denied. The question was whether that weakness was an indication of other wanton tendencies within her, such as her desire to have Ranny recognize that she was a woman. She prayed that it was not, or that if it were, she could continue to suppress it so that she need not admit it.

The morning brought the news that the Widow Clements, whose house and lands were to be sold at auction that afternoon, had awakened the night before to a strange noise and found a bag of gold on the table beside her bed. The bag was tied up with a piece of yellow ribbon to which was attached a locust and a thorn.

The tale was a three-day wonder, one much discussed on Splendora's veranda by the visitors who came and went. O'Connor, the tax collector, had stamped up and down and made a great many threats, predicting that the twenty-five hundred dollars he had added to the five thousand already on the Thorn's head would see the man caught and hanged.

The widow kept her property. There was nothing to prove that the money she had used to buy it back in at the sale had any connection with the sum that had been taken from O'Connor. Widow Clements, with great presence of mind, had destroyed the symbols left for her, though she had spoken of them in the greatest secrecy, of course, to her friends.

Colonel Ward took a philosophical view of the event. So

long as a man wanted to risk his life for such a quixotic cause, there was little he and his men could do to stop him. It would be as well, however, if the Thorn did not try to rob the tax collector again. O'Connor had requested and received permission to keep a squad of soldiers with orders to shoot to kill with him while traveling about his business in the countryside. The army had no choice but to comply.

Thomas's lack of heat was perhaps characteristic, but it may also have been occasioned by the fact that his views were expressed to Sally Anne during an afternoon drive. After succeeding in his campaign to achieve her company, he was hardly likely to offend her by appearing too anxious to capture one who was becoming a hero to her country-men.

The commander had arrived with a box of chocolates and a small bottle of attar of roses for Aunt Em's widowed niece. He had begged Sally Anne's pardon once more for his conduct the evening before and followed it by a plea that she come out with him for a drive to show that she had no ill feelings. Sally Anne, it was plain, had no idea where to look, much less what to say, particularly since Peter was staring at the chocolates, a rare treat, with avid longing in his big blue eyes.

Inspired, the colonel, included the boy in the outing. Peter insisted that Lionel should go also. Sally Anne, a gleam of amusement in her eyes at the thought of two wriggling, chocolate-smeared boys between her and the Yankee colonel on the buggy seat, had assented with the proviso that the chocolates must go as well.

"Dear me," Aunt Em said as the quartet drove away. "I hope Sally Anne minds her manners."

"Are you afraid Thomas will use his position to retaliate if she insults him?" Lettie asked. "If so, I think you mis-judge him."

"Heavens, no, but Sally Anne, for all that she's such a quiet little thing, is capable of making the drive most uncomfortable for him."

"He'll recover."

"It was nice of him to wish to make amends, but really I think he should have taken you with them instead of Peter."

Lettie could not prevent a chuckle. "As a chaperone? I think the two Sally Anne has with her will be more than adequate."

"No doubt," Aunt Em agreed, smiling in her turn, "but the colonel first came to see you."

"I like him well enough, but I have no claim on him!"

"You need not take me up so quickly, Lettie. It's a pity, though. The colonel is such a nice man."

Ranny, sitting on the steps breaking a stick into little pieces and throwing them in the yard, looked up at them. "A pity," he repeated, his tone guileless.

Lettie sent him a quick glance, but it was impossible to tell whether he mocked her or his aunt or, indeed, anyone at all.

As the summer advanced and the warm days lengthened, more travelers passed through the Natchitoches area. They could be seen in town buying supplies, asking for information about the roads ahead, consulting the doctor, attending church services on Sunday. Lettie, shopping in town with Aunt Em, saw them on the streets, dispirited men and women with children either subdued from weariness or else wild with the escape from the constant plodding along the road. They aroused Aunt Em's ready sympathy so that she often struck up a conversation, learning where they had come from and why, and sometimes inviting them home to dinner.

Some of them had sold up homes in Arkansas and Tennessee, Mississippi and Alabama and Georgia; many had simply left them behind with a sign tacked on the door reading G.T.T., Gone to Texas. For some, the land had been played out, depleted of its nutrients by years of planting without adding anything back to the soil so that the yields were scanty and the price a man could get for it just wasn't enough to live on. For others, the tax collector, whose bite had become bigger every year since the war, had finally swallowed the whole thing. For many more, the move was brought on by fear of the increasing violence in the night as groups of men fought back against the government that had been foisted upon them. And then there were those who had decided, finally, that they could not abide with honor where they were and so were heading to Mexico and Central America to join friends and families who had already emigrated.

Most carried everything they owned in the world in a single covered wagon pulled by mules or oxen, with chickens in crates slung underneath and a cow and a dog tied to the back. They were a fair indication of the kind of small farmers—men who had owned four or five slaves at the most—who had been and still were the major landholders of the states south of the Mason-Dixon line. Some families, however, required a train of wagons to transport their goods and furnishings. Through the ends of the canvas covers could be glimpsed the sheen of gold-leaf mirrors and polished rosewood, and when the wheels fell into potholes, the jangle of piano wires or the tinkle of crystal could be heard.

The latter type of traveler most often had guards, hardeyed men who carried rifles across their saddle horns. The single wagons were not so well protected. Now and then a man rode into town looking for word of a family who could be traced as far as the Red River but who then seemed to have disappeared.

The jayhawkers were suspected, though nothing could be proven. Wagons could easily be burned or driven across the state line into Texas and sold. There was a ready market for horses, oxen, and other livestock in Arkansas as well as in Texas. Valuables could be disposed of to unscrupulous storekeepers. Bodies could be buried anywhere in the deep woods or thrown down the nearest well if that was more convenient. The backwoods families, clannish and self-sufficient in their isolation, did not encourage anyone to ask questions, and prying around their barns and outbuildings could be downright dangerous.

They were not all so unsociable, however. It seemed that Aunt Em was related on her mother's side of the family to many of the people who lived along the creeks and bayous and swamps in the deep woods. A cousin who lived some eight or nine miles from Grand Ecore on the opposite side of the Red River was marrying off his daughter, the last of five, and was throwing a party to celebrate. Aunt Em was obliged to go, even if she had not wanted to, which she certainly did. Friends and relatives would be coming from miles around; news and gossip would flow along with the homemade blackberry and 'possum grape wine and the corn whiskey. It would be a good time to catch up on what was happening with everyone. Sally Anne and young Peter would go, and of course everyone wanted to see Ranny. Lettie must come along, too—it would be a good opportunity for her to meet people, become acquainted.

Ranny did not go after all. During the morning, he had developed a headache so severe that it blurred his vision. Lettie had made a trip into town for Aunt Em to replenish his supply of laudanum and had met Johnny Reeden. Being at loose ends, Ranny's friend had returned with her to Splendora for lunch. When he heard of the wedding, he had offered his services as escort at once. It was just the kind of frolic he enjoyed, he had said, and he had been wondering what he was going to do with himself for the evening.

The home where the wedding was to be held was a dogtrot house built of weathered cypress. It had a single large room on either side of the open central hall, a sleeping loft, and a porch at the front and back. There was no formal parlor since the beds the large family ordinarily slept in crowded both of the main rooms, leaving only an area around the fireplace where guests were invited to sit. One room had been completely cleared for the wedding ceremony and the dancing and feasting afterward, however, and spare chairs were lined up and down the dogtrot and against the wall of the porches to allow for the overflow.

The ceremony, a Protestant one, was simple. The bride wore a gown of blue lawn and carried a bouquet of white and red roses in a silver foil holder. The groom had on his best suit with a white satin waistcoat and a white satin bow pinned to his lapel. The preacher, a circuit rider in a black tailcoat and dusty boots, pronounced the words over them. There were a few tears, a great many hugs and kisses, and then a rush toward the refreshment table.

In deference to the preacher and many of the women who practiced temperance, there was no liquor in the fruit punch. It was available instead in the kitchen or out in the front yard where the men and boys were gathered around the buggies and wagons. There was also fried chicken, chicken and dumplings and chicken dressing, ham, corn fritters, fried apple pies, coconut pies, lemon pies, egg custards, hot rolls, and, of course, the wedding cake, a confection made with a frosting of coconut and many egg whites.

The food was served on plates that were taken away to be eaten wherever there was a place to sit, from the table in the outdoor kitchen to the front steps. There was a short period when few sounds were heard other than the clattering of knives and forks on plates. When the men were through eating, they put down their dishes where they finished with them. A squad of older women and young girls went around gathering them up and bearing them away to the kitchen to be washed. Then the men and a few older women cut off chews of tobacco or dipped snuff from bottles with a twig, while the unattached boys and girls and young married couples began to call for the fiddlers, harmonica players, and banjo pickers.

After the first waltz by the bride and groom, the music was lively and fast, being mainly reels and square dances, with now and then a polka or schottische. The dresses of the women were of calico and gingham, with here and there one of silk or satin, though most were homemade. The fragrances they wore were of roses and lilacs and apple blossoms, fresh and wholesome. The men smelled of bay rum and corn whiskey and the camphor that had kept the moths from their suits. The odors mingled in the warm night with the lingering aromas of the food. Faces were flushed and voices full of lilt and gaiety. Feet shuffled and stamped in the inevitable grit on the floor. The floorboards sprang up and down and the walls seemed to shake as the lines of dancers in the reels went down the dogtrot.

The children who had been brought were put down on pallets in the loft to sleep with a few older women to see that they didn't fall down the stairs. The older men, the bearded patriarchs escaping from the noise, gathered on the back porch to spit their tobacco juice into the yard and to talk of crops and horses and politics and, in lowered voices, the night riders.

Lettie, strolling out for a breath of air, overheard a few words, enough to identify the subject if not the substance of what was being said. The moment she was seen, however, the men fell silent. She was not surprised; still, it was frustrating.

Finally the bride and groom left the party, driving away in a buggy with white ribbons tied to the struts and a collection of old shoes dragging behind. There was some talk of a charivari, a serenade with bells, banging pots, and other noisemakers, since it was well known that the couple was going no farther for the night than the house of the bride's older sister. The mother of the bride squelched the idea with great firmness, however, and the fiddlers struck up another reel instead.

Aunt Em danced with the father of the bride while Lettie whirled with Johnny Reeden, but they did not linger long afterward. Ranny's headaches were much too frequent these days; Aunt Em was worried about him and wanted to get back. They were among the first to leave, and the chorus of good-byes and urgings to hurry back was loud, following them for some distance down the drive.

Since the buggy was not big enough to hold all of them, they had fitted a wagon with rocking chairs for the excursion. They had a lantern with them to light the way, but the moon was so bright that it was not needed. The sand of the wheel tracks in the road gleamed as white as the satin bridal ribbons they had seen so much of that evening. Johnny, in the driver's seat, sent the wagon along at a steady pace that fanned their faces with the breeze of their passage. Relaxed, full of good food, pleasantly tired, they were quiet as they rolled along.

Aunt Em, something of a matchmaker as Lettie was beginning to discover, had insisted that Lettie ride beside Johnny while she and Sally Anne sat in the back with Peter on a pallet between them in the wagon bed. Johnny's attention, however, was on his driving. Lettie allowed her mind to wander, thinking of the friendliness and good nature of the people she had met that evening, of the hard life they were living and yet their obvious enjoyment of it.

It did not, apparently, take a great deal to be happy. Why, then, could she not reach that state?

Still, everything was not as it seemed, she thought, remembering the fragment of talk she had overheard. Some of the men at the wedding were among those who donned sheets and rode about the countryside terrifying the freedmen and carpetbag officials.

"Tell me something," she said to the man beside her after a time. "Is there really all that much secrecy about the night riders, or do men shut up like clams about them when I appear because I'm a woman?"

Johnny swung his head around sharply. He stared at her for a long moment before he grunted. "Depends on which night riders you mean."

"What?"

"Some call the Knights of the White Camellia night riders, some give that name to the jayhawkers."

"I suppose I meant the Knights, the ones in white sheets."

"The jayhawkers wear sheets, too, when it suits them."

"That must be rather confusing."

"It's intended to be."

"Yes, I see," Lettie said slowly.

"As to why they don't talk in front of you, being a woman is reason enough, but it's also because you're a stranger."

"And a Yankee?"

"That, too, though the other things strike a man first."

"Thank you," she said, her tone dry in response to the humor in his voice. "It's easy to see what the jayhawkers are after, but don't the Knights realize that the kind of violence they employ won't work?"

"What else do you suggest?"

"The political system, of course."

"They can only vote if they dishonor themselves, and even if they do that, the ballot box is controlled by the radical Republicans, who are backed by the military. Moreover, Congress, which is to say the rest of the United States, has refused to recognize the Democratic representatives elected before the Reconstruction laws went into effect, and there's less hope to think they would recognize them now. What else is there?"

"Meetings, petitions?"

"Meetings are forbidden, petitions ignored, those, anyway, that ever make it to Washington."

"But how is the whipping and hanging of Negroes going to help?"

Johnny shook his head. "They are caught in the middle, poor devils. The radical Republicans are using them; the Knights see it as necessary to show them the consequences of allowing themselves to be used. The Negroes have also, let it be admitted, become the scapegoats for the frustration and blood lust of a few who spent five years killing men and now can't accept the fact that the war is over and they were beaten."

"It's horrible."

"Agreed. It's also human."

"I shudder to think so."

"Human beings are capable of great good but also of great evil."

"Whatever they do, the choice is theirs," Lettie said firmly.

"Is it? Sometimes I wonder."

There seemed to be no answer to that. Lettie let it go as she mulled over what he had said. The way he explained it, the motives of the Knights were a little more understandable, but she felt instinctively that they could not be right.

From behind her came a gentle snore. Turning, Lettie saw that Aunt Em had nodded off to sleep, but Sally Anne was still awake, staring out into the stretch of woods through which they were passing. Lettie, exchanging a smile with the other woman, faced forward again.

There was a strong smell of smoke in the air, but there were no houses near to account for it. Then, as they topped a small rise, the orange glow of what appeared to be a campfire could be seen around the next curve. It was hidden from sight for a moment as they rounded the bend, coming closer. The road straightened. Abruptly, they were upon it.

Lettie had a confused impression of an unhitched wagon with the canvas cover ripped open; of a man huddled next to a woman with a child in her arms beside it; of two men in sheets, their hoods thrown back to expose their faces; and of a clumsy, overweight priest on a donkey so swaybacked that the priest's feet nearly touched the ground. The priest held a revolver in his hand.

"What the hell!" Johnny said under his breath, and began to saw on the reins, pulling the wagon up.

Their appearance around the curve seemed to galvanize the scene they had come across, for in that moment one of the men in sheets turned, springing for his horse, while the other swooped toward his gun, which lay on the ground.

"Halt!" the priest shouted. The report of his gun rang out, once, twice.

The man reaching for his gun pitched forward and lay still. The other screamed and cursed as he lurched against his saddle, but his foot was in the stirrup and his horse reared and plunged around, covering him from fire, before bolting into the night with the man clinging to the horn. The woman screamed and moaned, cradling her crying baby between her husband and herself while he enclosed them in his arms, screening them with his body. The donkey brayed and kicked. The priest threw one long leg up and over the animal's head, kicked free of his stirrups, and sprang to the ground, landing with amazing lightness for one of his bulk.

Johnny had brought the wagon to a stop. He handed the reins to Lettie and jumped down, but stood where he was with one hand on the wagon seat. In the back, Aunt Em was awake and grasping the arms of her rocker with white-knuckled hands, while Sally Anne knelt in the wagon bed hugging Peter who, frightened at the noise, had begun to cry.

Quiet descended, broken only by the sobbing of the child and the retreating hoofbeats of the escaping man. The priest moved ponderously to where the fallen man lay. He turned him over, raised an eyelid, then made the pious sign of the cross and bowed his head for a brief prayer. Rising to his feet, he walked to the couple beside the wagon. He reached out to the child, a small girl with curling blond hair, speaking softly, huskily as he took her tiny hand in his. The little girl ceased crying except for a small sob or two as she stared at him in wonder.

Lettie felt a pain like a sudden blow in her chest. She couldn't breathe, couldn't speak, though she stared so hard at the priest that her eyes burned. It couldn't be. Not with that big belly, that round face. But the voice, the voice.

The priest inclined his head in parting, moved to the horse of the fallen man, and stepped into the saddle. "Forgive my haste," he said to the company at large, "but I have urgent business elsewhere. I will report this sorry business to the authorities, never fear. Bless you, my children. Remember: *Bona mors est homini, vitae qui exstinguit mala.*"

He swung the horse around.

"Stop him!" Lettie said. She looked at Johnny, but he was staring at the priest, his face white, and his hands on the wagon seat were shaking with the uncontrolled tremors of palsy.

The priest saluted her, smiled, and rode away. No one moved until he was out of sight.

"Goodness, sugar, what's that you've got, some nasty bug?"

The woman's voice was high and scolding with the passing of her fright as she pried the object from her child's hand. The locust shell fell to the ground and rolled lightly in a stray puff of wind. There was no thorn.

Aunt Em made a choked sound. The man beside the wagon touched the insect shell with the toe of his boot. "A strange kind of priest," he said, "but God knows where we'd be now if he hadn't happened along."

"We'd be dead, that's where!" his wife said.

Sally Anne, stirring, asked, "What was it he said in Latin?"

"Good is a man's death that destroys the evils of life."

It was Lettie who answered her, the words forced from her. She had never seen a man die before. Never.

The sound of her voice seemed to release Johnny. He laughed, a strained, hollow sound, as he stepped forward, moving toward the man and his wife as if to offer his services.

"That's what the good father said, isn't it? Bless us, but that's exactly what the man said."

*R*anny came ambling out of the house carrying a lamp to light their way as they straggled up the steps of Splendora. Aunt Em had brought him a piece of wedding cake wrapped in a napkin. When they were settled in the chairs of the sitting area in the hall, he sat munching on it, sharing a bite or two with Peter, who leaned against his knee, while he listened to the story of the shooting. His interest was not overpowering, or perhaps it was only that the effects of the laudanum he had taken earlier were just beginning to wear off, for he yawned through the confused tale as Sally Anne, Johnny, and Lettie added bits to what Aunt Em was saying. His attention was given mostly to Peter, who was still white and subdued and had a tendency to cling to his big playmate.

Aunt Em blessed herself a half-dozen times as she described in detail the palpitations of her heart during the brief incident. She was sure that the disguised priest had been about to truss up the two would-be robbers and leave them for the authorities when their wagon had appeared around the curve, but she could not suppress a shudder and a fear that he might just as easily have robbed the travelers himself or shot both of the men he had caught in the act in summary justice. Her faith in the goodness of the Thorn, after seeing the swiftness with which he had moved to kill, seemed shaken. She wondered aloud who he might be, putting forth the names of various men. There was a great deal of discussion about the size and experience and skill with weapons of the different men, but no conclusions were reached. There were just too many who were of the right height and build, and practically any man in the area had, from long years of hunting, considerable prowess with guns and knowledge of the country.

The time spent exclaiming and considering and describing their horror and disbelief during the incident served to calm them all. Aunt Em, after saying for the third or fourth time that she did wish she could have persuaded the travelers to come back with them to Splendora for the night, finally fell silent. Almost immediately, however, she remembered her duties as a hostess and suggested making coffee while wishing for something stronger.

"Not for me," Johnny said, getting up from his chair, "I'd better be getting down the road."

"You don't want to drive all that way this late," the older woman said in shocked tones. "Why not just stay with us? The trundle in Ranny's room is all made up, just like always."

"Mama will wonder where I am."

"She won't mind this once."

"You don't know Mama."

"At least have some coffee, so you don't fall asleep on the way."

"I don't believe I'd care for it, though I won't say no to a glass of water."

"Why didn't you say so before!"

"Don't get up," Johnny said quickly, waving her back down in her chair. "I'll step out to kitchen."

Lettie rose from where she was sitting. "I'll get it; I wouldn't mind some myself."

"I'll just come with you," Johnny said at once.

Lettie, who was beginning to gain some insight into the

character of these people, did not argue. Johnny's offer, she realized, was as much because the way to the outdoor kitchen was dark at this time of night and she was a woman presumed to be in need of protection, as to save her the trouble of waiting on him, though the last was an added aspect. The courtesy was innate, based not simply on good manners, which could be taught, but on concern for other people, which was learned only by constant example. It was a phenomenon she had met with often since she had been at Splendora, not something reserved to Johnny. It made her feel warm inside every time she came across it. She was going to miss it when the time came to leave.

"I don't suppose," Johnny said, looking around hopefully when he had set the lamp he carried on the kitchen table, "that there's any bicarbonate of soda?"

"I'm sure there must be."

They found it on one of the open shelves on one wall. Johnny mixed a spoonful of it in a small amount of water and drank it down, then stood pressing his abdomen while he waited for the sovereign remedy for a troubled stomach to work. Lettie dipped a glass of water for herself from the bucket that sat on the workbench, then got another glass for Johnny and handed it to him. The black smoke and fumes coming from the lamp they had brought with them were bothersome in the heavy air, and she stepped away from them to the open door. She leaned on the frame, breathing deeply of the soft night air and sipping her water as she looked out into the darkness. After a moment, she turned back to Johnny.

"You know who the Thorn is, don't you?"

Water from the glass he was lifting to his mouth slopped over the rim and down onto the front of his shirt and waistcoat. "Good Lord, lady, just look what you made me do!"

"Don't you?"

Brushing at the water on his clothing in comical dismay, he did not look at her. "What makes you think so?"

"You stared at him this evening as if you had seen a ghost."

"Well, what am I supposed to do, ignore it when a man is killed in front of me?"

"Oh, come, you faced men on the battlefield and probably killed your share. There could have been nothing unusual in that. It was the man behind the priest's disguise that startled you."

"You're wrong."

"Am I? You know, it stands to reason that the Thorn is an ex-Confederate soldier. A man with his strength and stamina and peculiar abilities must have been in the middle of the fight. It stands to reason, then, that he should be near the same age as you and Ranny and Martin Eden. If he has made such a stir now, he must have been well known to the community before the war. How could you not know him?"

"Easily. He could be anybody from anywhere; some stranger passing through on his way to Texas, a Northerner with Southern sympathies, a straggler from the Union army, a conscript-dodging jayhawker, anybody."

"If that was the case, you wouldn't have recognized him and you wouldn't have been so disturbed."

"You don't understand."

"Don't I?"

Johnny stared at her, then drank down his water and set the glass aside. "It wasn't the Thorn, it was the little girl. I keep thinking about her. She was so small and sweet, the same age as my little sister who died a few years back, before the war. If the priest—the Thorn—whoever he may be—hadn't come along just then, what would have happened to her? Her parents would have been killed. Those two pieces of scum would have taken her and— I can't bear to think about it, but I can't stop."

There was a raw sound in his voice and horror in his eyes. Lettie could not doubt he spoke the truth, but was it the full explanation for what she had seen? She could not tell, nor could she continue to question him in the face of his distress. Concern for others was not restricted to the South.

The reason behind Lettie's need to know the identity of the Thorn remained the same, but added to it was one more thing. She required some means to connect in her own mind the man who had killed her brother with cold calculation and had made love to her in a darkened corncrib with the man who had saved her from the jayhawkers and had appeared as the avenging priest and prevented the death of the travelers. How could a man be a murderer and thief and the champion of justice and defender of those in danger at the same time? It made no sense. And yet she could not think that the evidence collected so carefully by her brother was wrong. It almost seemed that there were two men riding in the night.

Angel and devil.

That explanation was too simple, however. There must be another one. Perhaps the Thorn meant to confuse the issue with his good deeds. Perhaps there was in him a streak of knight-errantry or, like Johnny, he had a fondness for small girls as well as large ones like herself. Or possibly he resented the encroachment of the jayhawkers upon his territory and sought to dissuade or destroy them. Whatever the reason, she would find it. She must. To discover the identity of the Thorn was, she had decided after long hours of cogent thought, the best way to find and stop the man himself. And the best way also to regain her self-possession.

. . .

The summer advanced, though the heat-drugged days seemed to slow to a crawl. The colonel and his men were frequent visitors. They sat on the veranda fanning themselves with their campaign hats and laying wagers among themselves as to who was quick enough to catch two of the flies that buzzed around before a count of twenty. Aunt Em held court, her scepter a fly swatter with a four-foot-long handle with which she whacked the pesky creatures and anyone else who became too brash. The flies were inescapable, attracted by the lemonade. Bringing the ingredients for the refreshment had quickly become a tradition with the Union soldiers.

Sally Anne lingered at Splendora. She tried several times to return to her father's house, but there was such a chorus of protests that she always abandoned the move. Her son's voice was among the loudest; Peter was enjoying his lessons with Lionel and Ranny. Aunt Em forbade her niece to go on the grounds that if she did her old aunt would be danced off her feet during the impromptu cotillions. Lettie begged her to stay so that she would not have to take all the soprano parts during their singing sessions alone or entertain all the lovesick swains who would be left behind. Thomas Ward declared that he would be lost without her smile, and his men swore, with varying degrees of fervor and on various objects from the stars to tombstones, that they would die of heatstroke if she took her cool blond loveliness away. Ranny gave no reasons. He simply said, "Don't go," and Sally Anne stayed.

Whether from the warm weather, the lightness of her spirits due to the pleasant company, or some other cause, Sally Anne began to soften the severity of her mourning. First a few silk flowers appeared under the brim of her dark straw bonnet. The ornament made of her husband's hair in the shape of a heart was replaced by a gold locket, which hung from a blue silk ribbon. A shirtwaist of white linen given to her by Aunt Em was paired with one of her black skirts, and color was added at the waist by a belt of blue silk faille. Finally a day came when the young woman asked Aunt Em to ride into town with her to select a length of material for a summer gown.

Aunt Em insisted that Lettie go with them. Between the two of them, they persuaded Sally Anne to take not only a piece of lavender lawn, suitable for half-mourning, but also another of white shadow-striped dimity embroidered with small bouquets of violets. The last was a gift from Aunt Em or, as she put it, from her chickens who provided the egg money.

Handling the light, airy fabrics, Lettie became aware as never before of the heaviness of her own clothing. In a burst of enthusiasm, she bought herself a length of the dimity, though one embroidered with roses; a piece of voile in a color called French vanilla that was edged with broderie Anglaise scallops, plus the white taffeta to go under it; and also a piece of calico in a delightful coral and aqua stripe.

It was an odd thing, but the new finery, when made up, caused Lettie to feel not only cooler but lighter of spirit, more carefree. It was apparent that Sally Anne's had much the same effect on her, for her smiles came more frequently and her light laugh could be heard often on the warm air. There was little danger Lettie would forget that the many compliments that came her way when she wore her new garments were caused as much by loneliness and propinquity as by the way she looked in them; still, there could be no doubt that the effort she and Sally Anne had made was appreciated.

Colonel Ward, in particular, applauded the change in the young widow. He presented her with flowers and equally florid compliments, with books and bonbons and even a few verses in his own hand until the poor woman stammered and blushed rosy red. She finally used up a not inconsiderable store of excuses for not driving out once more with him in the evening so that she was forced to go if merely to stop him from asking. After a time, it was the excuses that stopped.

The lessons Peter so enjoyed absorbed Lettie also. They had been moved from the veranda to one of the slave cabins behind the house. The cabin, shaded on one side by the spreading umbrella of a chinaberry tree and on the other by the gnarled limbs of an ancient live oak, was small but serviceable, and perhaps one of the coolest places on the plantation.

Lettie, with the help of Mama Tass and Ranny, had swept the accumulated debris from it and scrubbed it with lye soap and carbolic in steaming hot water. Aided by one of the men on the place and hindered as much as helped by Peter and Lionel, Ranny had cut back the encroaching blackberry vines, shrubby growth of French mulberries, and sweet gum saplings. Then they had whitewashed the cabin inside and out. Four crude benches had been made by placing boards across upturned kegs. Slates and chalk had been brought from town. Then the instruction had begun.

Each morning Lettie spent two hours with Ranny and the boys, and in the evening she devoted two more hours to any of the former slaves of Splendora who wanted to learn to read and write and do sums. It was engrossing, fascinating, if sometimes frustrating work. It was also rewarding.

By degrees, her evening class grew larger, drawing not only from Splendora and the people there, most of whom were Mama Tass's brothers and sisters, nephews and nieces, but also from the neighboring houses. More benches were constructed, more slates bought, and still there were times when not all of the people wanting to learn—old women with their gray heads tied up in kerchiefs; young ones large with child and with other children dragging at their skirts; half-defiant, half-grown boys and older men straight from the plow with bent backs, swollen knuckles, and dirt under their fingernails—could find places.

Each and every one of them had a terrible yearning to better themselves and to relieve the burden of their ignorance. And yet many of them had never been exposed to the printed word, to the plethora of ideas and images contained within the covers of a book. They had never tried to form a letter, never tried to draw or to write with a stick in the dirt. They did not lack understanding or ability so much as the very concept of either. A few were quick to grasp at knowledge; some gained it slowly but steadily; while for others there seemed to be a great barrier against it inside of them, as if it were so totally beyond their experience that they were separated from it by an unbridgeable chasm. The first group gave her fine visions of herself as some mythical goddess spreading enlightenment, while the last made her feel stupid and without talent as a teacher, as if it were in some way her fault that she could not transfer the skills she held to them.

There were just as many highs and lows in teaching Ranny and the two boys. The hours spent with them contained quiet satisfaction and a great deal of merriment, but also some of the same pressures. Peter's level of intelligence was perfectly normal for his age, while Lionel and Ranny were so nearly equal according to her tests that she usually constructed a single lesson for them. She had attempted once or twice to persuade them to join the class in the evening, but every time they seemed near to agreeing, Ranny was stricken by another of his headaches. Since he seemed consistently free of them in the morning, she finally ceased to mention the change.

It was Ranny who caused the problems. His progress

was erratic. He seemed to advance and retreat according to his mood, state of health, the weather, and even whether Lettie was holding his hand or not. It sometimes seemed that the harder she tried to force the pace, the slower he became. There were occasions when he stared at her with an expression of such vacuity that she was exasperated to the point of screaming, even ready to think he did it on purpose to annoy her. And then there were the times when he displayed such flashes of stabbing intelligence that she was pierced to the heart by the realization of what he had lost.

One such incident took place not in the schoolroom but in Aunt Em's front-yard garden at sunset. Lettie had been clipping a few blooms to put in the lovely Old Paris vase that sat on the table beside her bed. Attracted by the mind-swimming fragrance of a bed of flowering tobacco in full bloom, she moved toward it. Her approach startled a cloud of butterflies into flight. They fluttered around her, their wings making a soft and delicate clattering. Their coloring was a velvety brown-black with the edges of their wings braided with gold and speckled with a line of blue. One settled for an instant on the curve of her breast and another on her skirts. She stood still, holding her breath in enchantment.

She had not known Ranny was there until he stepped out from behind her. He eased around her until they were facing each other; then, his face absorbed, he reached out his hand toward the butterfly on her bodice. There was neither threat nor apprehension in his movements. He touched her breast with his forefinger, gently nudging the butterfly, and the beautiful insect climbed confidently on it.

"*Nymphalis antiopa,*" he said softly on a note of satisfied wonder, "the mourning cloak."

Just as quietly, Lettie said, "You collect butterflies?"

He shook his head. "I could never stick a pin in them."

"The name you gave it was Latin, you know, and quite correct."

He looked up, his gaze clear and plainly startled, and then it became slowly opaque, like the drawing of a curtain. "Was it?"

"Do you know the names of any others?" There was an urgency in her voice as she asked it.

But the moment was gone. "No," he answered.

Later, in the night, Lettie began to think. Butterflies and locusts. Latin names and Latin quotes. And on the night when they had seen the Thorn disguised as a priest, Ranny had been at Splendora guarded by Lionel, felled by one of his headaches. Or had he?

She was being ridiculous. Surely the man who sat across from her at the supper table, meekly accepted her strictures on the sloppiness of his lessons, fed the chickens in the backyard—sometimes scooping up a strayed and peeping chick and carrying it around in his shirt to save it from the cat until it could be restored to its mother—could not be the same man who had shot down a murderous jay-hawker, stolen the prisoner of a squad of soldiers and set them afoot without their boots, and made a laughingstock of the tax collector O'Connor? Surely golden-haired, smooth-shaven Ranny could not be the ruthless mustachioed giant who had taken her upon the cornhusks? Surely she would know it if it were so, surely she would sense it?

And yet he was a strange man, was Ranny. And because he was tall and broad and strong, because of what he had once been, glimpses of which she had seen herself and had heard about from others, she must eliminate him before she could go on to consider who else might fit the part.

The headaches would be her excuse. After the days and weeks she had been at Splendora and the time she had spent teaching Ranny, it could not be thought surprising if she showed concern for him. In all truth, she *was* troubled by the frequency of the recurring pain in his head. Such pain was not normal, despite his injury. It was possible that it was a symptom of something gone wrong, some pressure against his brain caused by fluid or possibly a splinter of bone from his skull that should have been removed. Someone should encourage him to see a doctor. But it seemed that because the problem had gone on for so long without worsening, everyone just accepted it.

There was, she suspected, little money for journeying from one doctor to another in search of a cure, but that was no reason to ignore the situation. Means could be found if it was necessary. Injuries to the brain were not something that could be taken lightly. They could cause paralysis, madness, even death. How terrible it would be if any of those things befell beautiful, gentle Ranny. It did not bear thinking of.

What was required for this test of him was simply another night when he retired early after asking for his laudanum. Lettie had not long to wait. At the dinner table on that particular night, Ranny was silent, only answering the questions put to him in monosyllables and often resting his head on his hand. He did not mention his pain, he never did. His eyes simply took on a glassy sheen and, a short time later, he murmured his excuses and left them.

There had been no company that evening. The three ladies and Peter moved from the dining room to the sitting room in the hall. Aunt Em took out a sheet to mend, Sally Anne picked up her embroidery frame, and Peter sprawled on the floor playing with a top and a piece of string. Lettie settled into a corner of the settee to read a few more pages in a volume of Thackeray that she had found in a book cabinet.

The minutes ticked past, punctuated by the chime on the quarter and half hours of the clock in the parlor. Layers of smoke from the lamp chimney hung in the still air. From outside came the constant whirring of crickets and peeper frogs. The calico cat stalked through the open back doors, rubbed around Aunt Em's ankles until she nudged it away, batted Peter's top here and there, then leaped up to curl itself in Sally Anne's lap.

Lettie looked up, yawned, read another page, then yawned again. Aunt Em gave a tremendous yawn in imitation, then laughed with a shake of her head. Lettie smiled in return, but a few minutes later, she yawned again. She put her book aside and said her good-nights.

As she had expected, Aunt Em was not long in following her example. Sally Anne, with an ingrained habit of accommodation, sought her bed at the same time. There was the sound of movement and faint voices from the next room as Peter was put to bed in the trundle. At last everything was still.

It seemed safe enough to suppose that if Ranny was the Thorn, he could not be in the habit of leaving the house until well after everyone else was in bed. It was difficult to wait longer; still, Lettie held her impatience in check until Aunt Em's soft snores had been drifting through the house for nearly an hour.

When she left her room, however, she made no special effort at stealth and carried a bed candle. Hers was not, on the surface, a clandestine errand; it would be foolish to go about it on tiptoe. On the other hand, she did not wish to awaken the whole house, so neither did she announce her purpose with any unnecessary noise. Her footsteps did not even disturb Lionel on his rug outside Ranny's door. She had to reach over him in order to knock.

He came awake then. Seeing her looming above him, he gave a choked gasp, then scrambled to his feet. "Miss Lettie, ma'am, what you doing? You not going to wake Mast' Ranny?"

She summoned a smile. "I just wanted to check on him."

"But he's sleeping!"

"I won't wake him, then."

"You can't go in there!" Lionel's eyes were dark and shining with alarm, though he kept his voice low. "You a lady and Mast' Ranny is a gentleman. It ain't right."

"I only want to help."

"Mast' Ranny be mad if I let you in."

Lettie was sorry to upset the boy, but it could not be helped. She did not wait for an answer but put her hand on the doorknob, gave it a twist, and pushed the door into the bedchamber. Lionel put out his hand, as if to catch her skirts, but snatched it back without touching her.

Her candle made no more than a small pool of golden light in the large room. It moved with her as she neared the bed, turning the curtains that swayed at the windows to wavering columns of pale yellow and making the high bed with its mosquito netting look like a draped catafalque. The top sheet was turned back and rumpled. There was no one under it.

Lettie walked to stand at the foot of the bed, then skirted the end, sliding her left hand along the sheets until she stood beside the pillows.

She had not wanted to be right. She had not thought she could be. For a single aching moment, she was sorry that she had made the discovery, even wished that there was some way she could undo it. To think that Ranny, with his quiet sensitivity and puckish humor, was a fake pained her more than she could have imagined. The knowledge was like a poison; she felt stunned, numb, and nerveless. She stood, breathing deeply, slowly, trying to control the press of burning tears behind her eyes.

A voice, deep and quiet, and infinitely soothing, sounded from the window behind her. "Did you want something, Miss Lettie?"

She swung around in a swirl of skirts, her heart lurching and her eyes widening in disbelief. "Ranny! Where did you come from? I thought—"

"I couldn't sleep. I stepped outside."

Her heartbeat was declining, though her knees were still weak with the relief. She felt a strong inclination to laugh out loud. Instead, she pressed her hands together in front of her and took a deep breath. Almost as an afterthought she noticed that he seemed to be wearing only his trousers, as if he slept without a nightshirt and had donned the minimum needed for decency before going outside. She looked away in confusion. Color rose to her cheekbones as she searched for something, anything, to say.

"You couldn't sleep? But you took laudanum."

"It doesn't always work. Not anymore. Not for me."

The laudanum from the opium poppies lost its power if used over a long time unless the dose was increased. Even then there were limits to the amount that could be taken. Apparently Ranny had reached it, not surprising considering how long he had needed it.

"I'm sorry," she said, and meant it. "I . . . only came to see if there was anything I could do."

If Ransom had not heard her voice as she spoke to Lionel when he was halfway down the steps, he would be long gone by now. She was going to drive him madder than she thought he was already. He was becoming quite adept at flinging his clothes off and on for her, though it might have been more useful, more likely to curtail her inconvenient concern, if he had appeared stark naked. But since he had been forced to return, he might as well receive some benefit from it.

He looked at Lionel, who hovered, grimacing his regret and blamelessness, in the doorway. "It's all right," he said. "Go back to sleep." When the boy had backed out and closed the door, he turned once more to Lettie. His smile coaxing, he said, "Talk to me. That will help."

It was most unconventional, being alone at this hour in a man's bedchamber. But surely there could be little harm in it.

"I can talk for a few minutes," she agreed with caution, "but could I get you something first, perhaps a glass of water?"

"No, thank you."

"It . . . might be better—cooler—if we went out on the veranda."

It might, indeed, be better. Ransom stepped back and held the curtain aside. As she came nearer, passing through the window opening, he took the candle she held from her hand and blew it out.

Lettie stopped. "Why did you do that?"

"Draws mosquitoes. The light."

"Oh, yes, I suppose so." He had reached to set the candle holder on a table and was holding back the curtain. She moved on ahead of him, groping a little in the darkness until her eyes became accustomed to it.

There was a bank of clouds hiding the moon and a sultry feel to the air. It was possible it would rain by morning. It was not much in the way of conversation; still, in order to restore some sense of normalcy, she said as much.

"It's possible," he agreed, his tone grave.

She grasped at the next thought to rise to her mind. "Do you think it would help if I massaged your temples and the back of your neck? I do that for my mother sometimes when her head pains her."

"If you like." She could do anything she wished if it involved touching him, he thought with certain self-knowledge.

"If you will sit down then, I'll try."

"While you stand? No. You take the chair."

"But I can't reach—"

"You can like this," he interrupted her as he took her arm and pressed her into the chair. When she was settled, he lowered himself to the floor to sit at her feet. He turned his back to her, clasped his arms around his knees, and waited.

Even in the dimness she could see that his back was broad and ridged with the shadowed outlines of muscles. She could feel the heat of his body and smell the faint male muskiness of him. She put out her hand involuntarily, then drew it back. She felt a little dizzy, the result of the shock she had had, no doubt. How very strange.

His head. He was in pain. That was her purpose here on the veranda and she must remember it. Lifting her hands, she called upon her strength of will and reached out to touch him.

His hair was silky and thick under her fingers, his skull well-formed, symmetrical. The scar at his temple was a series of ridges around a jagged depression, though the bone under it seemed solid, intact.

She focused on where she thought his pain must be centered, imagining it in her own brain, trying to think what movement might soothe it. She massaged his temples in slow, firm circles, letting her fingers glide over his hair and stroke back above his ears.

He gave a soft sigh. She redoubled her efforts, transferring her attention to the back of his neck. She kneaded the taut muscles and tendons there. His skin was warm and supple under her hands. Her palms, flat against him as she followed the line of his neck with her thumbs, tingled with an odd vibrant life.

Ranny leaned into her movements, absorbing them. To the comments she thought to make, he gave answers that grew briefer as the minutes passed. He leaned his head back, rolling it on his neck, as she returned her attention to his temples once more. Just as she thought he was near somnolence, he sighed and reached up to catch her hand. He turned it to place a kiss in the palm.

"Miracle fingers. It's better, much better."

Lettie's shoulders ached from her sustained movements and the awkward position she had held as she leaned forward to reach him. She did not regard it as long as it had been useful. "I'm glad."

Ransom was not nearly as torpid as he pretended to be. It simply seemed best that she cease her ministrations before he could become addicted to them. He had been enjoying her touch far too much. It gave rise to all sorts of impulses, most of which would shock and enrage her if she ever learned of them. There was one, however, that seemed innocent enough to receive at least a hearing. And it might also serve to give her thoughts a new direction, to put to rout her obvious suspicions.

"Miss Lettie?"

"Yes, Ranny?"

The calf of her leg was pressed against his side. Lettie could feel the rise and fall of his breathing and the firm contours of the muscles that covered his ribs. She should move away, but for the moment she could not bring herself to make the effort.

"Do you like me?"

"What a question! Of course I do."

"Sally Anne likes the colonel."

"I suppose she may."

There was something in his voice that made her wary, though she could not put a name to it. She wished that she could see his face, could look for the sparkle of humor that she had come to recognize as preceding one of his practical jokes. He still sat with his back to her as he stared out through the veranda railing.

"I saw her kiss him."

"Did you now?" she said with some severity. "You shouldn't spy on them."

"I didn't. I just saw them under the magnolia tree."

"Anyway, it's none of your business."

"No. But Aunt Em says it's bad to drink from the same glass as other people. Kissing looks worse."

Lettie's voice quivered with amusement. "I daresay it may look that way."

"Have you ever done it?"

"Really, I don't think—"

"Did you?"

"I may have, once or twice."

"Did you like it?"

It was a moment before she answered, and then her tone was flat, compressed. "It was . . . bearable."

He winced in the darkness but refused to abandon the line he had taken. "Would I like it?"

"Ranny! I have no idea."

"Would you kiss me? To see?"

The request was so humble, if also a bit pressing, that she could not be insulted. His interest, she thought, was more academic than salacious. She had brought the situation, one in which he could put such a question to her, on her own self. There was no one else to blame.

She asked, "Are you sure you want to do that?"

"I'm sure," he said, turning to face her and rising to one knee. "Don't you want to?"

His voice held a timbre that was unconsciously seductive. She felt a frisson move along her nerves, coming to rest with a flutter in her throat. What could it hurt, after all? "I don't suppose I mind."

A small surge of pure triumph brought Ransom to his feet. He made no sudden move, however, but reached to take her hand and draw her up to stand in front of him. He did not release her, only lifted her hand instead to place

it on his shoulder while he circled her waist with his arm.
He felt no resistance, no fear or strain. He could have
groaned when he thought of the difference between this
time and that in the corncrib. It could not be erased, but
it might be mended at least in part. But even if it was not,
it was good to know that he had not completely destroyed
her trust, good also to know that poor Ranny held no terror,
no disgust, for her.

He was so near. His hold was light, yet commanding.
The strength of the shoulder under her hand seemed to
promise difficulty in evading what was to come should she
change her mind. She had no wish to do that. There was
inside her an unexpected stir of anticipation. Her heart
began to race and she stared up at him, her eyes shadowed
in the darkness and her lips parted.

He bent his head. His mouth touched hers, gently molding to its smooth contours. It was heated, beguiling in its
sweetness. He moved his lips infinitesimally upon hers, as
if in wonder at their soft yet resilient fragility. The touch
was tentative, without force, yet firm.

Lettie swayed closer, wanting, expecting him to deepen
the kiss. He remained passive yet kept the contact, as
though entranced by the sensation. It came to her that he
did not know what to do. She lifted her hand to the back
of his head, threading her fingers through the thick waves.
Greatly daring, she brushed his mouth with hers, then
allowed the tip of her tongue to flit over the warm surfaces
of his lips. He seemed to stiffen with surprise before, as
if obeying some natural impulse, he followed her lead,
meeting her tongue with his own, advancing, retreating,
inviting her direction.

The sense of being in control, of being the instigator,
was heady, enthralling. It made her feel both gratified and
delightfully wicked. Swift and turbulent desire raced along
her veins, invading her mind, her senses, and destroying

thought. With a soft murmur in her throat, she pressed against him. Her breasts brushed his chest, the nipples hardening, as she invaded his mouth and encouraged him to do the same in return.

His arms closed around her. He tangled his fingers in the soft knot of hair at her nape, then swept his hand down her back, past the narrow turn of her waist to clutch the curve of her hip and to hold her against the lower part of his body. Through the layers of her skirts she felt the firm rigidity of him.

Lettie was recalled to herself with wrenching abruptness. This was Ranny. She gave a low cry as she dragged her mouth from his. Pushing away from him, she stood, aghast, clasping her arms across her chest. Her lips throbbed, and in her brain burned a single refrain. How could she? How could she?

"Miss Lettie?" His whisper was agonized.

"Please—please don't worry," she said, gaining some control of her shaking voice on the second try. "It's all right, really. I think I had better go in now."

"Must you?"

"It would be best."

Best for him, necessary for her. She swung away from him. She had only gone a few steps when he called after her.

"Miss Lettie?"

She paused without turning her head. "Yes?"

"I could drink from your glass."

The trace of insouciance in his voice was welcome. He had not been hurt. She gave a small choke of laughter that had the sound of incipient tears. "Thank you, Ranny."

"No, Miss Lettie," he answered. "Thank you."

10

The hall was a thousand miles long. By the time Lettie reached her bedchamber and stepped inside, she was gasping on a sob. She ran to her bed, went up the bed steps, and flung herself on the mattress to bury her head in her arms. Hot tears squeezed from between her lashes and dropped with small plopping sounds on the coverlet as shame for what she had just done washed over her.

To make love to a man like Ranny was the same as seducing a young boy. To take advantage of him, to rouse the base male desires inside him that he could not be expected to understand or control fully was the act of a conscienceless wanton. That he had begun it was no excuse. The responsibility for the way it had ended was hers.

Wanton. Harlot. Jezebel.

She deserved all those names and more. She wished she could turn back the clock, could have this past hour to live over again. She would not betray herself in such a way if given a half a chance.

But perhaps it was better to know what she was really like. She could be on her guard against it.

It was so much worse than she could ever have imagined. She had thought she was depraved for being able to feel vivid carnal pleasure in the arms of a thief and murderer like the Thorn. That she had come near to the same emotions in that brief kiss exchanged with Ranny marked her as beyond redemption.

To think that if she had never left Boston she might

never have suspected it. She must guard her secret well. No one must know how easily she could be led astray, God help her.

There was one who knew, however, one from whom she could not hide her nature. That one was the Thorn.

The Thorn, a man of disguises, a man who might be walking among them all every day. A man who might have looked at her a hundred times and smiled, thinking of how she had responded to him, knowing what she was like. She writhed in misery at the very idea.

She must take care. No one must have the opportunity to point a finger at her. She would be as modest and circumspect as she had been taught to be. And never must she be alone with a man. Not even one like Ranny. Especially Ranny.

It was not, as it happened, an easy vow to keep. Splendora, it seemed, was always full of men. Like an invasionary force, they progressed from the veranda to the hall sitting room and parlor, and on into the dining room where Mama Tass fed them with fried chicken and beaten biscuits, baked ham and cow peas and her special lemon pie. Their numbers increased like the hordes of Tartary, but there were always the regulars, Johnny Reeden and Martin Eden and, of course, Thomas Ward. Men could not be avoided, and in any case, as Lettie discovered, trying only drew attention to her. All that was left was to be pleasant but remote, to set herself at a distance by her coolness.

There came a Sunday when the only guests, other than Sally Anne and Peter who could not be counted in that category, were the regulars plus O'Connor, who had arrived late. The afternoon was hot and airless. It had not rained in nearly three weeks, not since the deluge when Lettie had visited her brother's grave. The burning sun had siphoned away the moisture, usually so abundant, until the leaves on the trees hung limply, the flowers in Aunt

Em's garden drooped, and the grass and weeds had begun
to take on a parched appearance. The last of the magnolia
blossoms had turned copper-brown, and the petals on the
roses on the arbor over the gate had shattered, littering
the ground underneath like pale pink snow. The illusion
should have been cooling but only seemed to make the heat
worse.

They sat on the veranda hoping, for the most part in
vain, for a breath of air. The ladies plied their fans and
encouraged the gentlemen not only to remove their coats
and cravats but also to open the necks of their shirts and
roll up their sleeves. Even so, they wiped perspiration from
their brows and waved whatever they could find, from
handkerchiefs to hats to sheets of newspaper, before their
faces.

"Is it this hot very often?" Colonel Ward asked with a
sigh.

Johnny snorted. "You think this is hot, just wait until
summer's really here."

"It gets worse?"

"I should say. Why, compared to August, this is a cool
spell."

Martin sent Johnny a look of weary disgust. "It's hotter
than hell's hinges, as my old granddad used to say. Don't
let him fool you."

It was, indeed, a scorching day. The floor of the veranda,
even with its canvas cover, was so hot where the sun struck
it on one end that it was impossible to stand on it with
bare feet. They all knew this for a fact because Lionel and
Peter had tried, hopping and yelping, until told to desist.
They had wanted to see if it was really possible to fry an
egg there, after Johnny had been unwise enough to utter
the old saw, but Sally Anne had vetoed that suggestion
with such heat-induced annoyance that the two boys had
retreated to the dense shade under the magnolia where

they showed every sign of preparing to take a nap. Lettie wished that she could join them since it appeared cooler there. Like Thomas, she felt the heat more than those who had been bred to it.

Thomas wiped a bead of sweat trickling down his nose. "How do you all stand this for three months?"

Aunt Em looked at him with sympathy in her faded blue eyes despite the mockery of her lifted brows. "You all?"

He grinned at her, unrepentant. "Isn't that correct usage?"

"No, indeed. If you're going to try to talk like a Southerner, at least say 'y'all.'"

"Yes, ma'am. How do y'all stand it?"

"What? Oh, the weather. Well, tell me this, how do y'all stand snow and ice for three or four months of the year?"

"We're used to it."

"There you are, then." She gave a decided nod. "You'll get used to the heat, too, in a few years."

"Years?" There was mock despair in the word.

"When you blood thins down so it runs faster."

From far away came a mutter of thunder. Conversation, such as it was, came to a halt as they stopped to listen. The distant sound had come once or twice before. This time it seemed louder, as if it might be moving nearer.

O'Connor finally broke the silence. "What with the weather, I reckon they'll be burying the travelers this afternoon."

"What travelers is that?" Aunt Em asked, her voice sharp.

"You haven't heard? There was an old man and woman found late yesterday afternoon by a couple of boys looking for blackberries. They had been robbed and killed and dragged into the woods a short piece. There was sign of a struggle in the road and a set of buggy tracks leading away. It appears they weren't moving to Texas but were just passing through, maybe on the way to visit relatives in Natchitoches."

Sally Anne shuddered. "How awful."

"That it is. Whoever did it was a fiend. He cut the woman's throat, but he stood on the man's back and twisted his head to break his neck."

"Mr. O'Connor, please!" Aunt Em exclaimed.

At the same time, Martin said with distaste, "Not in front of the ladies, sir, if you don't mind."

Johnny made a sound of distress, his face under his fair skin turning pale and then fiery red. Ranny, the mild interest he had shown in the story fading from his features, put out his hand and clasped his friend's arm.

It was Sally Anne who filled the awkward pause that followed. "Whoever is doing these terrible things is getting bolder, or so it seems."

"Or more careless," Thomas said. "Men who get away with their crimes a few times finally come to think they can get away with anything."

"Monsters" was Aunt Em's pronouncement. "Isn't there something that can be done about it?"

"The situation is a bit murky," the colonel said, wiping his brow once more. "My job here is to prevent political disturbance, not to interfere in local affairs. My intelligence officer has done a certain amount of investigation of the activities of a criminal nature, especially as they touch the military, but I've had no mandate from my superiors to search out and destroy whoever is behind them. The sheriff here, on the other hand, seems to think that it's a military problem, part and parcel of this business of the Knights of the White Camellia—or perhaps I should say that's his fear."

"Do you think so?" Lettie asked.

"It may be, then again it may not. But the result is that

while we wait to see who has authority, these attacks continue."

"Dear me," Aunt Em said, her tone pensive. "What's going to come of it?"

Thunder made a distant hollow bumping. A puff of air stirred the leaves of the trees to a dry rattle and brushed along the veranda. The katydids, making a constant buzzing chorus among the trees, sang louder. They were silent for a few seconds, then began again. A tree frog croaked in raucous counterpoint. A pair of doves in the fields behind the house called, a mournful, hopeless sound. The rumbling came once more.

Conversation lagged, becoming no more than a low and desultory series of remarks. Ranny left his seat and stretched full length on the floor between Lettie's chair and that of his aunt. Within seconds, it seemed, his face was composed and peaceful with sleep.

Lettie watched him with concern as well as with a nebulous, only half-admitted sense of pleasure. He was wearing another of his faded blue chambray shirts, one of what seemed to be an endless supply. Its softness seemed to emphasize the bronze of his skin and the rugged strength of his body, but also to deepen the shadows under his eyes. He often dropped off like this in the middle of the day, seemingly able to snatch a few winks almost anywhere. What troubled her was that it did not seem quite normal considering the early hour he usually went to bed. She was afraid his abnormal need for rest came from the same source as his headaches.

The summer storm advanced, rising up in slow majesty out of the southwest. The dark blue-black clouds loomed higher and higher. The sun dimmed and was lost to view. Out at the fence, O'Connor's buggy horse shook his stubble-trimmed mane now and then, sensing the weather change. Aunt Em suggested that he be taken to the stable with the other mounts, but the tax collector waved away the offer as too much trouble.

The wind rose, and they lifted heated faces to it. It sent dust devils spinning along the drive and rocked the branches of the trees back and forth. The first scattered raindrops began to fall, making wet splatters in the dusty dirt between the flower beds. The smell of it, musty but refreshing, rose around them.

Lightning flashed and crackled. Peter and Lionel, disturbed from their nap, had ventured from under the magnolia to caper about in the warm drops. Now they gave a leap and a yelp and scampered for the veranda. Ranny woke and, smothering a yawn, sat up and clasped his arms around his knees.

They saw the main body of the rain coming, a solid, marching gray curtain dragging over the treetops. It reached them in a whispering rush. The drops fell in fat warm blobs, steadily increasing in number. They rattled down in earnest, becoming a drumming roar. Harder and harder they fell, pounding on the roof, spilling, spouting from the eaves.

Lettie was fascinated by the storm, by its sheer elemental power and the unbelievable torrents of water. The crashing thunder and brilliant, stabbing lightning were more violent than any she had ever seen before. She could not bear to leave it and go inside. The others also lingered on the open veranda.

Then came a slashing flare of lightning that seemed to rend the heavens like a fiery sword, followed immediately by an enormous, explosive roar of thunder. Sally Anne gave a small cry and covered her ears with her hand. Aunt Em jumped up.

"That's it! I'm going in! The rest of you can stay out here and be burned to a cinder if you want."

There was a rush for the door. Laughing, wiping blown rain from their arms and faces, they trooped into the house.

The strong draft created by the hallway channeled the wind through the old building so that already the heat that had hung in the rooms was gone. Aunt Em, alerted by curtains billowing and flapping in every bedchamber, sent out squads to put down the windows. They did not close off the hall, however. The wind swirled through it, setting the lusters on the lamps to tinkling and slapping the overhanging edges of the crocheted cloths on the tables.

It was a nice place to be, there in the long hall. As the rain showed no sign of slackening, a pair of lamps were lighted against the storm's gray dimness and everyone settled down on the chairs and settee near the front doors to enjoy the unexpected coolness.

The afternoon stretched long before them. A checkerboard, cards, and dominoes were brought out and they set about amusing themselves with varying degrees of anticipation and reluctance. When the games palled, Sally Anne suggested charades, and that held them for perhaps an hour until the titles and clues became so silly that even Peter rolled on the floor in disgust with his fingers over his eyes and his thumbs in his ears.

"I know," Lettie said, "we could get up a play. Didn't you tell me, Aunt Em, that there are trunks of costumes in the attic? And I saw a book of plays just last week in the cabinet."

"A grand idea," Johnny said. "I bet that's the same book we used to use."

"Yes, indeed," Aunt Em agreed. "Ranny, Johnny, why don't you go up and—"

"No," Ranny said, without looking up from the game of checkers he was playing with Lionel.

"Whatever do you mean?"

"The costumes are gone. You gave them to Mama Tass."

"Why, I never—at least I don't think I did."

"Told her to make quilts."

"Did I? How vexing, but I suppose they were needed at the time."

Costumes and disguises. Lettie looked at Ranny for a long, considering moment. No. He had passed his test, and his indifference to the subject as he concentrated on his game was complete. She glanced at Colonel Ward, who was also watching the master of Splendora. It was a pity she could not tell him that his suspicions were unfounded, but she supposed that he would learn.

Another game of dominoes began, pitting Aunt Em and Sally Anne against Thomas and O'Connor. Martin Eden stood behind Sally Anne's chair, directing her play and leaning over her shoulder often to point out unnoticed points, much to the annoyance of the colonel. Johnny, rubbing a hand over his carrot curls, wandered in the direction of the back doors. He stood leaning against the frame, staring out at the falling rain. Lettie watched the game for a few minutes, but then, when Ranny's friend did not rejoin the group, got up and moved down the hall to join him.

Johnny turned his head to give her a troubled smile but did not speak. His face appeared drawn, as if he had aged ten years in the past hour. She could not say that she knew him well, and yet she had seen so much of him in the past weeks that she felt that way. In any case, there were some people you simply liked on sight, people you could feel closer to in a moment than you could others in years. Johnny was one of them.

"Is something wrong?" she asked quietly.

He seemed to collect himself with an effort. "Wrong? Where did you get that idea?"

"I just thought you were upset. I still think so."

He stared at her for a moment, then looked away. "I've never been good at hiding things."

"Is there anything I can do to help?"

"I appreciate the offer, but there's nothing anyone can do. Don't worry about it. I got myself into this mess and I can get myself out."

The look in his eyes did not go with the nonchalance of his words. "This mess, would it have anything to do with the deaths of that man and his wife they found?"

The blood drained from his face, leaving it waxen. "God. Ranny said you were smart."

Lettie refused to be diverted. "You knew them."

He squared his shoulders. "Please let it go. It . . . isn't something I can talk about."

"In that case," she said, her eyes darkening with slow comprehension, "you must have some idea who did it."

He took a long step away from her, out onto the veranda, beyond sight of the others. She hesitated, then moved after him and caught his arm. He jerked it from her grasp, then shuddered with a strangling sound in his throat. "I didn't know. I swear I didn't know."

Lettie looked over her shoulder, then drew him farther away from the doorway where the sound of the falling rain would cover their voices. "What is it? Are you mixed up with the Thorn?"

"The Thorn? God, no! If it were just him."

"Then who?"

For a taut instant she thought he was not going to answer, then it came pouring out of him, the words stuttering, tumbling over themselves.

"It's the jayhawkers, only that's a nice name for common, murdering outlaws. I used to know some of them, used to hunt with them before the war. I rode with them one night for a lark, just to take some horses into Arkansas to be sold. Turned out the horses were stolen. They divided the money with me. I took it because I needed it—my mother's heart—but never mind that. Then I was in and I couldn't get out. They threatened to tell Mama. It would kill her, I know it would. I took messages about the movement of money and people, but I thought the jayhawkers were just thieves. I didn't know they were torturing, killing."

His voice fell away to a whisper leaden with grief and guilt. Lettie thought rapidly, but there seemed to be only one answer. "You should go to the sheriff or to the colonel."

"I'd be arrested, the story would have to be told. They might even hang me as an accomplice. Mama would be so ashamed. And even if I didn't hang, the outlaws would kill me."

"You can't go on as you are."

"I have to."

"Maybe—maybe you could go away for a time, maybe to Texas like so many others."

"The outlaws would catch me before I got to the state line. They're everywhere, always watching."

"But surely there's something that can be done."

"Nothing. I've thought until my brain feels on fire, but there's not a thing that can be done."

"I won't believe there isn't something."

He moved his shoulders as if they held a great weight. "I could always shoot myself and get it over with."

"Don't talk like that," Lettie said sharply, disturbed by the acceptance in his stark words. "We'll put both our brains together."

But the words were mere bravado. No answer came. She thought back over what he had said, weighing every word.

Abruptly, she said, "Messages from whom?"

He gave a raw laugh. "You don't want to know."

"Why not?"

"To say would sign my death warrant sure enough, and maybe yours as well."

She stared at him. Finally she said, "Whoever he is, he sounds ruthless."

"It's as good a word as any. He likes his position and won't let anything jeopardize it. He used to take the messages himself but quit when it looked as if he would be found out."

"The information in these messages, how does he come by it?"

"Gathers it here and there. It isn't hard. Only I never knew what he was doing with it. I never knew what a fiend he could be—I still can't quite believe it. It just doesn't seem possible. I feel so stupid that I didn't—"

Johnny broke off at the flicker of movement in the hall doorway. Sally Anne appeared in the opening.

"Whatever are you two up to with your heads together out here?" she called.

"Just watching the rain."

It was Lettie who answered, her tone consciously light as the woman tripped out to join them, with Martin and Thomas sauntering close behind her. The others followed, straggling out one by one to stand leaning on the railing, breathing the rain-washed air.

The storm had rumbled away. The rain was tapering off and a watery sun was peeping through. In a few minutes the rain stopped altogether. In the east a fragment of rainbow appeared. The afternoon had advanced toward evening, and the light had a greenish pink cast caused by the sunset. The call of a mockingbird perched on the kitchen chimney had a clear, melancholy sound.

With the way to the kitchen clear once more, coffee was made and passed around with pound cake, and glasses of spirits, good whiskey brought by O'Connor, were given to those who wanted them. It was, in a sense, a stirrup cup, for the party began to break up afterward and Lionel was dispatched to the stables to bring the horses around to the front.

O'Connor said his rather brusque good-byes and marched to the gate ahead of the others, who were making more lengthy adieus. The tax collector had his hand on the latch when he turned back.

"Oh, by the way, Mrs. Tyler. You're related to Samuel Tyler down the road at Elm Grove, I think?"

"Yes?" There was tension in Aunt Em's voice. The tax collector, given his access to records as well as his frequent visits, had to know the exact family connection and that of Sally Anne also.

"His house is going up for sheriff's sale. Nonpayment of taxes."

"I never!" Aunt Em gasped. Sally Anne put her hands to her mouth, though she made no sound.

O'Connor gave the younger woman a glance, though if he felt the slightest sympathy there was no sign of it on his face. With a sharp nod that could, if they pleased, be taken for a farewell, he settled his hat on his head and pushed the gate open, letting it thud shut behind him on its weighted chain. Climbing into his buggy, he drove away at a smart trot.

Sally Anne turned to the older woman. There was quiet dignity in her tone as she spoke. "It's been a lovely visit, Aunt Em, but I believe it's time I went home." She glanced at the others. "If you will all excuse me, I will go and pack."

She turned and went into the house. Thomas Ward took a quick step after her. "Sally Anne?"

The blond woman did not look back, nor did she say good-bye.

. . .

Lettie tapped on Aunt Em's bedchamber door. She could not think what the ethics might be concerning what she was about to do. She knew very well that Johnny had thought she would respect his confidence, but she had not promised secrecy.

She had also wrestled with her conscience over Johnny's confession. His actions had led to the deaths of innocent people, and they had certainly been made with the knowledge that he was dealing with outlaws. But he had been forced into the role he had played against his will. So far as she could see, he was guilty of stupidity for getting mixed up with such evil men, but little more.

Ranny's friend needed help. She herself could not think where to turn to gain it for him. Aunt Em, with her calm manner and stout good sense, in spite of her habit of exclaiming, was one of the few people Lettie thought might give advice without either condemning Johnny or flying into a panic. That the older woman might feel he would be best served by calling in the sheriff was a chance that must be taken. It was not possible to sit back and do nothing, allowing him to continue on his present course. If he were not caught with some message and hanged for his involvement with the outlaws, he would inevitably be drawn deeper into their crimes. No, she must act.

The older woman was dressed for bed. She invited Lettie in with the utmost cordiality, then shut the door and returned to her seat before her dressing table. Busily braiding the gray strands that hung over her shoulder, she nodded at a slipper chair. "Sit down, child, and tell me what I can do for you."

Lettie did not hesitate but told her the details of Johnny's dealings with the outlaws just as he had given them to her, as well as the suggestions the two of them had considered and discarded between them as a solution. "The thing is," she said when she had finished, "I can't think of anything else that might help."

"Goodness me," Aunt Em said in pain and dismay. "To think of this going on right under my nose. Poor Johnny."

"Do you think he's right about his mother? That seeing him in jail could kill her?"

"I suppose it's possible. She's always been sickly."

"Then what can we do?"

The other woman pursed her lips. "There is one last possibility that comes to mind."

"And that is?" Lettie urged.

"You won't like it."

"How can I not if it might work?"

When Aunt Em only watched her with a shrewd, considering look in her eyes, a virulent doubt struck Lettie. She could not mean—no, it couldn't be.

"The Thorn." Aunt Em raised a hand and went on before Lettie could open her mouth. "Now listen before you start. I know you think he's Satan himself, but he has helped people. He did take old man Hathnell from the soldiers and get him across the line into Texas. What he did for him, he can do for Johnny. It's not so far away that Johnny couldn't send for his mother after everything dies down. The Thorn not only knows the back trails and hidden ways to cross the line, he might be able to give Johnny a disguise that would make it easier."

"He also might cut his throat if he's the leader of these outlaws!"

"Pshaw!" Aunt Em said with vigor. "They sound to me like a bunch of lawless men taking advantage of a lawless situation. There's not a single story told of the Thorn that connects him with other men. He always plays a lone hand."

"That's all very fine, but even if it would work, how is the Thorn supposed to know that Johnny needs help?"

"I was talking to Widow Clements in town the other day, the woman, you remember, who got the money for her taxes from him. She told me a tale, just a whisper, mind, because we live near to Dink's Pond. Seems that there's a hollow tree where people can leave messages. I don't know how she knew of it, unless the Thorn told her he could be reached that way in case of need. But it's supposed to work."

"You are suggesting we just . . . write him a note telling him Johnny needs him, and that will be sufficient?"

"I don't think it would be a good idea to mention Johnny. The note could be found by someone else, you know. We could just say that we would meet him at an appointed place and time."

"Meet him!"

"How else are we to explain?"

"Perhaps you can do it, then."

"I don't think that would work. It will have to be at night, and my vision isn't too good after dark. Besides, the meeting place will have to be some distance away, somewhere safe for him."

"For him! What about us?"

"I know it could be a bit dangerous. That's what I'm saying, that it will be better if there are two of us."

"Or three. Or four. Or a maybe hundred?"

"We would have Johnny with us on the way there. On the way back, I just don't know."

"Johnny could go alone."

"So he could, but would he? I have a feeling that he might get to thinking about his mother and turn around and forget the whole thing. That wouldn't help matters."

"No," Lettie said with a defeated sigh. She would not

think of what she would say when she was face-to-face with the Thorn again. Perhaps she need say nothing. Maybe she could stay in the wagon and let Aunt Em talk. "Very well. What are we going to put in this note?"

By the time the thing was written, the oil in Aunt Em's lamp had burned low and the wick was sputtering. The wording was simple, giving a time and place for the meeting and communicating the fact that the matter was urgent. It was agreed after some discussion that in order to prevent interference from anyone who might read the note by accident, the place of the meeting must be indicated in a way that only the Thorn would understand. There were a number of places Aunt Em knew of which had a connection with his past exploits, but the trouble was that other people also knew of them. Lettie ventured to suggest the spring as a site, but that was too distant as well as too difficult to hint at without giving it away.

When Aunt Em suggested the corncrib where the house had burned near the ferry below Natchitoches, the same one she had spent the night in, Lettie knew a moment of panic. How could the older woman know the Thorn was aware of it since she had told no one of her adventure there with him? It seemed, however, that this was one of the places where it was rumored that he sometimes stabled a spare horse. Aunt Em thought it the very spot and suggested with some relish that they designate it for their purposes as the "place of the corn." There was a terrible inevitability about it. Feeling as if caught in the coils of some monster of her own making, Lettie could only agree.

It was the following afternoon, during the heat of the day when it was least likely that anyone would be stirring about, that Lettie set out for Dink's Pond with the message in her apron pocket. It was not to be supposed that the Thorn would check the hollow tree before nightfall, if at all. The less time the note stayed in its hiding place, the better.

Lettie had covered perhaps half the distance to the pond. With every stride, she grew more heated and less certain of what she was doing. The impulse to turn back was strong. It was only the thought of Johnny and the look in his eyes that drove her on. Learning people's secrets meant assuming obligations, making one a hostage to compassion.

So intent was she on the problem that she heard nothing until a soft footfall came behind her. She swallowed a cry and whirled.

It was Ranny. "Don't do that!" she snapped, made more incensed by his instant and gratified grin.

"Where are you going?"

"For a walk."

"Can I come?"

"I don't think so."

"Why not?"

The question was completely logical; still, it was annoying how quickly he could get to the point with his few words. "I would rather be alone."

"Are you meeting someone?"

"No!"

"Are you afraid of me?"

"Of course not. Why should you think such a thing?"

"You don't talk to me anymore. You get up and go away."

Lettie had not expected him to notice her attempts at withdrawal. That he had gave her a pang. She wondered if it was meant to, then dismissed the idea as unworthy. "I'm sorry."

Ransom gazed down at her, studying her face. She was too pale, and the spinsterish tightness of her features, nearly banished during the past weeks, had returned since that night on the veranda when Ranny had kissed her. He had sought to give her thoughts a new direction. It seemed he might have succeeded too well. He hovered now between an impulse to provoke her into a show of spirit and the need to discover why she was walking so purposefully toward Dink's Pond with a square of paper very like a note showing through the fabric of her apron pocket. Curiosity won.

"We can talk and walk now," he suggested.

She laughed at his single-mindedness. She could always send him on some errand while she found the hollow tree and completed what she had come to do.

As it happened, it was Ranny who found it.

Lettie, uncertain precisely what she was looking for, wandered in circles, peering here and there. She had, somehow, envisioned a dead trunk without leaves, some huge old sentinel impossible to miss. There was nothing in the area, nothing anywhere around the pond, that looked in the least like that.

She glanced at Ranny, wondering if he knew of the proper tree, debating the wisdom of questioning him about it. A flash of inspiration came as a rabbit hopped out of the woods on the opposite side of the pond.

"Where do rabbits stay in the winter? Do they hibernate this far south?"

"Hibernate?"

"Sleep for the winter."

"Oh. Don't you know?"

There was a faint tremor of humor in his tone, but she assumed it was amusement for her city ignorance. "I asked, didn't I?"

"They sleep some, come out on sunny days. They use brier thickets, piles of brush, things like that."

Exasperation touched her. She controlled it. "Hollow logs?"

"Sometimes."

"Are there any around here?"

"One," he answered promptly. "It's over there. I used to hide things in it."

She looked at him sharply. "Things?"

"Fish flies. A chew of tobacco one time. I got sick. So did Martin and Johnny."

He led her toward a tree that looked perfectly sound, with a full canopy of leaves. At its base, however, was a cavity that looked as if it could easily be the den of some small animal, and a few feet above the ground was a narrow slot just big enough to admit a man's hand. Lettie put her own hand into her apron pocket, fingering the note.

"Do you suppose there's a snake in there?" As he shook his head, she went on. "It looks like a good place for one to me."

"No. See?" He put his hand into the slit and pulled it out again.

"Is it deep?"

"You can see."

Carefully palming the note, she put her hand into the hole and drew it out again, empty. "You're right. Thank you for showing it to me."

"My pleasure." His voice was soft, the look in his eyes unaccountably warm.

Lettie gave him a smile that barely curved the corners of her mouth. "Shall we go back to Splendora now?"

*L*ettie had a feeling about the appointment with the Thorn, and it was not a good one. A dozen times she decided she would not go, and just as often, as she thought of the relief and hope that had appeared on Johnny's face when she and Aunt Em had told him what they had done, she changed her mind again. It was extraordinary to her how much confidence both Johnny and Aunt Em could place in the Thorn, given the stories circulating about him. It was almost as if they were willfully ignoring his more discreditable exploits. She could not forget them, any more than she could forget the night in the corncrib. That she was returning there of her own will was beyond belief. She could not feel that any good would come of it. Ill-conceived, ill-fated, how could the entire project be anything but a disaster?

She was not surprised when things began to go wrong during the morning of the day before the one that was set for the meeting.

Aunt Em, going into the poultry yard to feed her flock, spotted a fat hen that looked perfect for a pot of chicken and dumplings for dinner. She gave chase in her most stealthy and experienced fashion. Just as she bent over to snatch the hen's legs from under her, a pugnacious rooster came fluttering up in defense and spurred Aunt Em in the arm.

The wound bled profusely but was not deep. On the older woman's instructions, Lettie washed it with soap and water and tied it up with a bandage. Aunt Em went about her work. The hen was caught and put into the pot. By late evening, however, the older woman's arm had swelled and was extremely tender. Aunt Em rested it upon the table and enjoyed her meal of dumplings.

With the morning, Lettie's landlady was listless, and she turned white around the mouth at the sight of food. She was feverish, and there were angry red streaks running up her arm. The doctor was sent for and, when he came, recommended soaking the arm in hot water to which a carbolic solution had been added. Aunt Em obeyed the instructions, also soaking it in hot salt water. The redness and swelling began to subside, but the fever and infection had made the older woman, as she herself put it, as weak as dishwater. She was obviously in no condition to go rambling over the countryside at night.

So Johnny and Lettie set out alone. The two of them elected to ride instead of driving the buggy. It would not only be quieter and faster, but it would give them more freedom of movement should the need arise. The sidesaddle found for Lettie was an old one with most of the padding gone from the seat and knee rest, a lack she was going to feel come morning, but its benefits outweighed that drawback.

The riding habit she had brought South with her was of wool crepe and much too heavy. She had pulled from the armoire instead a plain poplin skirt with a black band at the waist that she donned with a simple tucked lawn shirtwaist. If the fluttering of her skirt now and then showed the hem of her petticoat and the leather of her riding boot to the knee, it hardly mattered. The whole point of this evening's excursion was that they be seen by as few people as possible.

Accordingly, they crossed the river at Grand Ecore, avoiding the more direct and shorter route that led through

Natchitoches. Once on the other side, Johnny took the lead, guiding them along the back roads. Lettie tried to watch the different turns he took and the branching cross-trails through the deep woods, but was soon hopelessly confused in the gathering darkness. Her only recourse on the return journey would be to go back by way of the ferry below Natchitoches, the one she had taken last time. That would also be the safest way for her, no doubt, once she was alone.

They held their pace to a steady lope, one that ate up the miles but did not strain the horses or call too much attention to their passage. Lettie's thoughts did not keep to such an even pace. She alternated between what she was going to say to the Thorn to persuade him to help Johnny and wondering if he would come; between what the man would think when he saw her and regret that she had not informed Thomas Ward of the meeting.

It puzzled her that, since the means of contacting the Thorn was known, someone had not informed on him to the military before so that a trap could be set. Of course, it stood to reason that a man of his experience would be extremely wary of that possibility. He would be unlikely to approach any meeting without careful reconnoitering. Whatever else he might be, she did not make the mistake of thinking him a fool.

The corncrib was just as she remembered it, squat and dark and nearly overgrown with briers, sumac saplings, and sedge grass. They pushed their way through to the lean-to and tied up the horses in its concealing shelter. They did not go inside but stayed instead with the animals, partly to keep them quiet and partly because Lettie preferred it.

She and Johnny spoke now and then, though more for the sake of the sound of a human voice than because they had anything to say. Lettie was, for the most part, with-drawn, brooding. She refused to allow her mind to drift to what had happened to her inside the building behind them. There was no point in raking over the coals; she had burned herself enough at that task. She could not excuse her conduct, but neither did she see any benefit in exploring it yet again. Johnny was also morose, with a tendency to jump at every noise from the thud of a falling limb to the hoot of an owl. Long periods fell when they were silent, each wrapped in his own problems. At the same time they kept a sharp vigil.

After an eternity, there came the distant sound of a wagon. It drew closer, rattling and squeaking and bumping as if it might fall apart before it could round the bend and come into sight. Above its noise came the cheerful quaver of an old woman singing a hymn at the top of her lungs.

The wagon appeared around the curve. A lantern hang-ing on a hook on the wagon bed lighted its way, casting jiggling, bouncing shadows over the trees and revealing as ramshackle a rig as ever rolled down a road. The boards of the wagon bed jostled, the wheels wobbled on their axles, and the mule between the shafts was flop-eared, sway-backed, and appeared to be plodding along with his eyes closed. Between the woman, the equipage, and the steed, it was a sight to behold.

The wagon came even with the track to the corncrib. Suddenly it swerved down the side trail. It was pulled to a halt with such wrenching ineptness that the mule nearly sat back on its shaky haunches. The old woman, still hum-ming, climbed down and traipsed with high-stepping strides through the briers.

"Yoo hoo! Oh, yoo hoo! Are you there?"

"My God," Johnny said under his voice.

"Yes, we're here," Lettie called out in low, tight tones

to stop the yodeling. Motioning to Johnny to stay back, she moved out of the lean-to and into the shifting light of the lantern. "Who are you?"

"I've been sent to take you to the man you want to see, dearie. Come along and get in the wagon."

"How do we know this isn't a trick?"

"You don't, but if you can think of another way to find out beside coming with me, dearie, you're welcome to try."

"Please don't call me dearie."

The woman gave a cackle of mirth. "As you like, sweetheart. Are you coming? You and the gentleman you've got hid back in there?"

Johnny stepped forward. He gave the old woman a hard look, then moved past her and climbed into the wagon. Lettie followed with stiff reluctance. Only the Thorn could have sent this foolish and noisy old woman. Using her as a courier was either a stroke of genius or the act of an idiot. The only way they could discover which was to take their lives into their hands and go with her.

"There's a quilt back there in the wagon bed, one I stitched myself. I'd be obliged if you would both lie down and cover up with it."

They complied. What else was there to do? Lettie expected the quilt to be musty and smelly. Instead it was fresh and clean, with the fragrance of herbs clinging to it. She settled herself as best as she could on the hard boards, lying shoulder to shoulder with Johnny. The wagon was backed, then jerked forward into a steady, bone-jolting pace. The old woman lifted her voice again in screeching assault upon a hymn. Lettie, trying to ignore the singing, lifted a corner of the quilt, keeping watch out the back of the wagon over the way they were going. It might be good information to have.

In due course, they came to a log cabin set well back from the road under a pair of spreading pin oaks and with a single lamp burning in the window. A pair of yellow curs ran out, barking, as they drew up. They quieted at a single command from the old woman, as if recognizing the voice of their mistress. The woman reached into the wagon bed and threw back the quilt.

"Come on into the house, now. Step quick, that's a good boy and girl!"

A moment later, they were inside with the door closed behind them. The elderly woman shuffled to the lamp and moved it from the window to the eating table in the center of the room. The room was small. Fitted out with a fireplace, a pair of rocking chairs, a dresser for dishes, and the table, it served as sitting room, kitchen, and dining room. Through a door was another room, little more than a shed, that might have been for sleeping. The interior of the cabin was spartan but scrubbed to astringent cleanliness.

In the lamplight, the old woman's face was round and cut by deep lines. Her bulbous nose supported a pair of gold-rimmed spectacles and the brows above them were thick and gray. On her chin was a large black mole. Her gray hair was tucked under the faded gray sunbonnet she still wore. She was rather tall despite her bent back, but her body was round and shapeless in the faded gray dress with its sagging hem.

She gave them a hearty smile as they stood regarding her. "I have some coffee made. You'll be wanting a cup to help you stay awake tonight."

The coffee was hot and strong and black. The old woman served it to them in enameled tin cups at the rough, hand-built table, then sat down herself.

As Lettie sipped the brew, she considered their position. The cabin was not more than four or five miles from the corncrib, with only a single turn to reach it. She thought she would have no difficulty in returning to the horses, or in finding the cabin again, for that matter, if it were necessary. She pondered the Thorn's connection with the elderly woman. It might be that he used her house as a way station, a convenient hiding place, or somewhere to change into his many disguises. She sent the woman a glance. Their hostess stared back, her eyes unblinking.

"What is your name, if I may ask?" Lettie said.

"You can call me Granny. I don't think we need more than that."

"You live alone?"

A chuckle greeted the question. "In a manner of speaking."

"Are you related to . . . the man we seek?"

"You're just full of questions, aren't you, sweetheart?"

There was harsh amusement in the old woman's voice. It raised an echo in Lettie's mind. A shiver ran along her nerves. In the act of lifting her coffee cup to her lips for a final swallow, she sat staring at the creature across from her.

Johnny set down his cup. "Let's stop fencing. When is the Thorn coming?"

It was Lettie who answered, her words measured. "I don't believe that he will."

"What do you mean?" Johnny demanded.

"I think he's here already."

The woman smiled and then crooned in a voice that became more husky and masculine with every word, "Oh, clever, sweetheart, very clever."

Johnny uttered an oath, his eyes widening with shock. He swallowed. "I should have known."

"I would have been devastated if you had. Tell me, Miss Mason, what was it that gave me away."

"I'm not sure," Lettie said, her brown-eyed gaze still on the face of the Thorn made up like a hag. When dressed as a priest, his nose had been narrow and thin. Its broadness now was probably due to gum rubber and who knew what trickery, all as false as his sagging bosom. "Something in your voice, perhaps. Or maybe it was the way you looked at me."

"Next time I'll have to be more careful."

"I trust there won't be a next time. I am here only because of Johnny."

The Thorn barely glanced at him. "Your interest being strictly humanitarian?"

"My interest being none of your business," she said without expression. "I'm told you can help him, if you will go to the trouble. I take leave to doubt it, but you may prove me wrong."

"Lettie!" Johnny protested, his gaze anxious and still a little confused as he looked from her to the Thorn in his ludicrous disguise.

"Your confidence puts me on my mettle," the Thorn drawled. "By all means, let's hear how I may be of service and the reasons why I should exert myself."

Lettie set her coffee cup aside, her lashes shielding her gaze. It had been a mistake to permit her animosity to goad her into plain speaking. It would not help Johnny to antagonize this man. She gathered her thoughts as she took a deep, calming breath. When she began to speak, telling Johnny's story once more, her tone was more conciliatory.

Johnny allowed Lettie to explain as she would, interrupting only once or twice with a few words of clarification. He sat with his gaze on his enameled cup as he played with it, only glancing up now and then at the Thorn with uneasiness in his eyes.

When Lettie had finished, the Thorn turned to Johnny. "It's your decision to go to Texas?"

"Not exactly. There's my mother to think of, but I don't know what else to do."

"You let her know you were going?"

Johnny gave a slow shake of his head. "She was bound to ask questions if I did, and I couldn't bring myself to tell her the truth."

"I'm inclined to agree that Texas is best. You can write your mother a note and I'll see that she gets it."

"That's decent of you."

The Thorn pushed at the spectacles sliding down his nose as if it, or something, annoyed him. "You can't leave without telling her some tale. Not only would it upset her more than is apparently good for her, but she would most likely call out the sheriff. The result of that, I have every reason to think, would be that I would be blamed for your disappearance."

A sheepish look mingled with concern moved over Johnny's face. "I wasn't thinking."

"There's pen and paper in the next room, also another dress and bonnet. I suggest you make use of them."

Johnny shoved back his chair and got to this feet, then, as the implication of what had been said reached him, he stopped. "Hey, wait a minute. Dress up like a woman? Me?"

"Only for an hour or two tonight, until I can get you to a better hiding place while arrangements are made."

"I thought we would ride hard and fast for the line."

The Thorn gave him a level look. "That's the best way I can think of to attract attention, if that's what you want."

"No. No, I'm sure you know best." Johnny moved toward the rough door that led into the next room. He was almost to it when he stopped and turned back. There was a thoughtful frown between his eyes. "You know, the way you look as an old woman reminds me—"

"Most old women look about the same," the Thorn said easily.

"No, but that costume, that nose—"

"You can tell me about it later."

"I could swear—"

"Later."

There was a note of command in the single word that Johnny obeyed instinctively, though he shot a final glance at the other man before he stepped into the other room. The Thorn waited until the door had shut behind Johnny before turning to Lettie.

"Now," he said, his tone not a whit softer, "tell me what reward I can expect for being so obliging."

"Reward?" Lettie repeated the word as if she had never heard it before.

"What did you expect? That I would do it out of charity or for the sake of your smile—which I have yet to see, by the way."

"I should have known better than to expect anything other than the most callous conduct from you."

There was such contempt in her face that Ransom felt an intense need to see what it would take to displace it. "So you should."

"I have no money with me. However, if you will name your price—"

"In gold? How mercenary you are, a typical Yankee shop-keeper's daughter. I had in mind a finer and sweeter coin."

She stared at him until her eyes began to blur, until fear and the hysterical desire to laugh at the farcical nature of the suggestion that hung in the air between them threatened to choke her. That it had been put forward by a man who appeared uncannily like an old woman only added to the bizarre unreality.

She cleared her throat, speaking with an effort. "Such as?"

"Oh, Miss Mason," he said, his tone mocking, "you are a sad flirt."

"And you are a cruel tease," she cried, rising to her feet and leaning over the table. "You don't really mean to barter a man's life against—against—"

"Your charms? But of course I do."

"It's barbaric! And insulting."

"Insulting? It seems to me to be placing a rather high value on them."

"You can hardly expect me to agree!" She swung away from him, folding her arms across her chest and clasping them tight.

"I don't think you are the kind of woman who would consider the few minutes of her time I ask for to be more treasured than a human life."

Ransom sought not just to substitute fear for the contempt in which she held him, but for something to use as a distraction once more. He and Martin and Johnny had once done a skit as the three witches from *Macbeth*. Something about his hag's costume must have reminded Johnny of it. It was important that Lettie not be allowed to dwell on the little his friend had been permitted to say.

More important to him, however, was his need to know how she would answer his outrageous proposition, to gain some idea of how she felt, to learn if the moments they had shared in a corncrib haunted her as they did him. He needed to know if, given excuse enough, she would come to him again, despite the conventions that forbade it, despite her fears, despite the wild tales that turned him into a bloodthirsty beast. He wanted, in short, to know if she desired him as he did her.

In the jangling silence that held them, an idea occurred to Lettie. She considered it, rejected it, then came back to circle it cautiously in her mind. "You—you weren't joking, weren't just . . . trying to annoy me?"

He looked at the taut set of her shoulders, heard the appeal in her voice, and he almost agreed. But there was something tentative about her words that made his pulse leap, overriding his better instincts.

"You don't really think that."

She drew a deep breath. "Then what can I say? As you pointed out, it would be too callous of me to refuse."

It was an agreement made under duress, one she had no intention of keeping. He would not find her an easy conquest, not a second time. She could be wrong, but she did not think he would take her in front of Johnny. He had said that he would transfer Johnny to another place of hiding. That would give her some time to escape.

She should have known he would exact a price for his help. If the truth were faced, she had expected something of the kind. Certainly she had known there would be trouble. Given the character of this man, how could it be otherwise?

"Lettie—"

"Miss Mason to you."

The correction sounded overly prim to her own ears, but she could not bear to hear her name on his lips. She was not surprised that he knew it; he seemed to know everything. She turned to give him a defiant stare, then quickly lifted one hand to her mouth to hide a flash of humor. The suppressed desire in his eyes did not sit well with his disguise.

He glanced down at himself, then chuckled in his turn. "It is ludicrous, isn't it. I'll have to change before I return."

"And this change, will it be with or without the mustache?"

His eyes, she saw in the lamplight, were hazel, that color that is a mixture of all others, though for the moment they appeared more gray, reflecting the gray clothing he wore.

"Which would you prefer?"

She lifted one shoulder. "It matters not at all."

"Perhaps I'll surprise you, then."

"Or you may be surprised," she said with her most dulcet smile.

He lifted a brow, but before he could speak, the door to the other room opened and Johnny emerged. Qne look at him in his woman's costume was enough to show how gifted an actor the Thorn was. Where Johnny strode with flapping skirts, the other man had walked with the rolling and rather halting gait of an old woman with overstretched pelvic bones from childbearing, unevenly distributed adipose, and tender joints. His hunched shoulders and bowed back had, until he discarded the pose, seemed natural. It was uncanny, almost frightening, as Lettie thought of it. It meant that he could be anyone, that he could be watching her, laughing at her at any time, while she never knew. It was not a new thought or a pleasant one, and yet she could not get it out of her mind.

Johnny came to Lettie and took her hand. His face was earnest and his voice gruff as he spoke. "I hate good-byes, but I don't guess I'll be seeing you again. I'll never forget you, though, or what you and Aunt Em have done for me."

"Oh, please. Anyone would have done the same."

"Nobody did," he said simply, "except you."

"I—I hope you'll forget all of this, and that you will be happy."

He smiled, though there was pain in his eyes. "I'll try. I sure will try." He lifted her hand, pressed it to his lips, then replaced it at her side. He turned away.

The Thorn moved to the door and held it open. Johnny stepped toward him.

Johnny, with his red hair and stocky build, was nothing like Henry, and yet for some reason he reminded Lettie of her brother. There was a hard knot in her throat as she called, "Take care."

He glanced back, smiling. "That I will."

The door closed behind him and the Thorn. Moving to the window, Lettie watched as the wagon pulled out of the yard, the two figures huddled on the seat with their bonnets pulled around their faces like old women. In a few short minutes, the rattling of harness, squeaking of wheels, and plodding hoofbeats receded. Finally it died away altogether.

Lettie eased the door open a crack, drew it wider, just wide enough for her to pass through. She closed it carefully behind her. Her footsteps light, her movements agile, she moved down the steps and across the yard to the narrow road. Then she picked up her skirts and began to run.

She ran until she had a stitch in her side. She walked until it eased, then ran again. Her hair, loosened from its knot at the nape of her neck, spilled over her shoulder and left a trail of pins behind her. Her boots were heavy, not made for such effort; they soon rubbed a blister on her heel. She stopped and pulled them off, walking in her stockinged feet as she carried the boots under her arm. The dust sifted through the cotton stockings, collecting in a fine grit between her toes. She ignored it.

She could not ignore the sounds that pursued her, the calls of night creatures, the scuffling noises in last year's dead leaves beneath the undergrowth. A dozen times her heart jarred against her ribs in apprehension as she thought she heard hoofbeats behind her, but it was only the echoes of her own footfalls.

When the real hoofbeats sounded, she disregarded them for long seconds. She was almost to the turning for the road that the corncrib was on and knew she could not be far from it. There was a stretch of thick woods here that seemed to hold sound so that she could hear the whisper of the sand under her feet as it shifted. Then she realized that the hoofbeats were coming faster than she could possibly travel.

She plunged off the road into a sumac thicket and knelt among the saplings, peering through the leaves. A body of horsemen, five in number, clattered past. She caught a flash of white. White sheets. She and Johnny and the Thorn were not the only ones abroad in the night. She crouched lower, shivering. They did not check but rode on out of sight.

It was some time before Lettie could move. She was holding on to a sumac sapling, ready to drag herself upward, when she heard another horseman approaching. She went still, her teeth clenched against the pull of a cramp in her right leg. The man passed by at an easy lope. His hat was pulled low and his head tilted, as if he were listening. It was almost, she thought, as if he were keeping a safe distance between himself and the men ahead of him.

The man vanished into the darkness. Quiet returned. The dust settled. Lettie stepped back into the roadway. She began to run again, though she looked often over her shoulder.

Her chest was heaving and the hair around her face was damp with perspiration when she reached the corncrib. She stood with her back against one of the lean-to posts for long moments, gasping, trying to catch her breath.

At last, her chest still heaving a little, she leaned over and tried to draw on her boots. Her feet were swollen and sore, and entirely too filthy. There was a piece of tattered rope hanging on a nail on the wall, and she looped the boots together and threw them across the pommel of her saddle.

Time was passing. She checked her cinch, pulling it tighter, and spoke quietly to her horse as it sidestepped in the darkness. When the animal was calm, she pulled herself into the saddle. She sat for a moment wondering what to do about Johnny's horse there in the lean-to with her own. The Thorn knew where it was, she decided after a moment. Let him worry about it. Perhaps he would take it to Johnny's mother with the note Johnny had written her. Bending low to avoid the lean-to roof, she rode out into the night.

She saw no one on the road to the ferry as she retraced the route she had taken from the corncrib once before. It was with intense relief that she saw the gleam of the water, the low road leading to the ford, the ferryman's cabin set back among the trees. Dogs ran out barking as she came near. A man appeared around the house carrying a lantern in his hand. He stopped, then, as he saw her, started toward her with a lanky, weak-kneed stride.

"I hope I didn't wake you," she called as he came nearer. "It's important I cross tonight."

"No, ma'am. Had a sick horse in the barn."

His voice was so drawling and thickened that she suspected he had been drinking while attending his animal. It didn't matter so long as he was sober enough to get her across the river.

She dismounted and led her horse toward the ferry. The man followed along behind her. He held his lantern low to show her where to walk, but it gave off only a feeble light, being an ancient affair of pierced tin.

The ferry, like a barge with rails, rocked as she stepped aboard. She urged her mount toward the end and tied the reins to the railing, then moved back toward the front on the opposite side to even the weight. The ferryman set the lantern down on the bank, released the rope that held the ferry, shoved off, then jumped on board.

Lettie glanced at the man as the boat dipped to his weight. He wasn't as thin as he had appeared, or perhaps as she had remembered, though his beard was just as thick and scraggly. She wondered if he had left the lantern behind on purpose or if he had forgotten it. He paid it no attention, certainly, but put his hands on the ropes that controlled the ferry and began to pull hand over hand, like drawing water from a well.

The ferry glided into motion, drawing away from the bank. The lantern light diminished, the rays falling away until only a glowing yellow spot was left. Darkness closed in around them. The sound of the river, gurgling, rushing around the boat, grew louder. The water swept away on either side, catching and refracting the faint gleam of starlight so that it appeared gray beneath the black press of the night. As they neared midstream, there was a sense of isolation, as if for the brief moment that they floated there between the two banks they were utterly alone, stranded together in the swift flow of time and the river.

The ferry stopped.

Lettie turned her head to look at the ferryman. He straightened away from his rope, then moved toward her. He came to a halt not two feet away and spoke in that husky voice that alone of every sound she had ever heard could send chills of degrading excitement along her spine.

"Surprise."

There was no reward for virtue, none for trying to do what was right; she had known that for years. Regardless, it did not seem fair that she should strive so hard to escape what this man wanted of her, only to run full-tilt and barefoot into his trap.

"No," she whispered.

"I have your word."

"Why? Why are you doing this?"

"Because I must."

It was true. He had known she would be gone when he returned to the cabin, and he had just as surely known where he would find her. He could no more prevent himself from riding ahead to intercept her than he could have stopped breathing. It was a weakness, and he knew it. Still, his memories of the night they had shared fired his blood, while her unattainable beauty haunted his dreams. He admired her intelligence and her courage. He would like to gain her respect, her liking, but since that was impossible, he wanted to taste her mouth and to hear the blood sing in his ears. The risk was great, but he accepted it because the reward promised to be greater.

His words sent a painful fluttering along Lettie's nerves. There was in them a note of finality that told her more certainly than her own senses how complete the trap was. She could expect no help from the ferryman, who must have been bribed to remain in his bed. The late hour made it unlikely that anyone would come to demand the ferry. The river was wide and deep with treacherous currents, and in any case she could not swim.

There were those who would say that she should plunge into the water before accepting certain dishonor, but she could not think they had ever been in her position. In any case, she suspected the Thorn would only dive in after her.

Her hesitation had nothing to do with the man himself. Of course it did not. The weakness in her limbs and the drumming of her heart were caused by her exertions and her very natural fear. She was aware of his size and strength as he stood so close to her, and of something remorseless and daring in his manner that stirred sensations she would rather forget.

With loathing in her voice that was not entirely directed at him, she said, "You really are a fiend."

"Do I frighten you, Lettie? That was not my intention."

"What was it, then? To simply appear and have me run straight into your arms?"

"That would have been nice, but no, I fully expected to be forced to come and get you."

There was a smile in his voice that she could not see for the darkness and the damnable false beard that obscured his features. "Oh, it's all very amusing for you, isn't it? You'll forgive me if I fail to see the humor!"

"Lettie . . ."

He lifted a hand as if he would touch her. She backed away, searching her mind for something more to say to distract him, moistening her lips with her tongue. "Johnny—is he safe? Well hidden?"

"Oh, yes," he agreed easily as he moved close once more, "I keep my bargains."

"Are you saying I don't? It was no bargain, it was blackmail!"

"Only an exchange of favors."

"If it's so small a thing, why go to so much trouble? Why not just let me go?"

"Because you agreed," he said, then went on, his voice dropping to a husky sound. "And because the thought of you, the feel of your softness in my arms, the taste I had of your sweetness, is driving me mad. Because I want you as I've never wanted anything in my life, and there is no other way I can have you."

He had not meant to say such things any more than he had intended to barter Johnny's life for her surrender when he had set out that evening to keep the appointment. It had happened, one thing leading to another until it came to this, the two of them facing each other on a ferry dipping with the wash of the river. He should stop, here, now, and take her back to Splendora. Every instinct of chivalry pounded into him from childhood demanded it. But there were other instincts more insistent. She had made a promise. He had heard it spoken, seen it in her eyes. He would not allow her to disavow it. He could not.

He reached for her, his hands closing warm and strong around her upper arms, drawing her to him. Lettie, caught off guard by his unexpected declaration and the despair that edged his words, was nearly too late as she brought her hands up to brace them against his chest.

"No!"

"For Johnny's safety, Lettie, and my sanity?"

The plea was whispered. He bent his head, his lips hovering above hers, their touch feather-light, tingling.

"No."

Her voice sank to a trace of sound. There was no strength in her arms. Her will fought that weakness. And lost.

His mouth descended upon her lips, his beard tickling and yet caressing the sensitive corners. Somewhere deep inside she felt a strange, shifting sensation. Desire, like the slow seep of an opiate, suffused her. For a moment longer fear and pride and conscience warred inside her, along with sharp concern for what this man was going to think of her; then, with a soft sound of distress, she let them go, swaying, molding herself against him.

Ransom's chest swelled, his grasp tightened with fierce, protective joy as he accepted that surrender. Slowly, carefully, he set himself to reward it.

What was it about this man that sapped her initiative and fired her senses? Lettie could not tell. She only knew that his lips burned and enticed and fueled her desperate pleasure, that she had no will, no strength. Shivering, with eyes tightly closed, she felt the sear of his lips upon her eyelids, her cheekbones, the curve of her jaw, and the tender turn of her neck. She smoothed her hands over his back, over the corded tendons and muscles, and knew that, deny it though she would and despite her unfeigned rage and attempts to escape, she had wanted this, had been waiting for it. God forgive her.

The waiting was no more. He eased back a step and took her hand, turning with her toward the rail. He lowered himself to the wooden deck with his back against an upright, drawing her down to lie half across his lap, cradled against his drawn-up knee. He removed his hat and laid it aside. There was calm deliberation in his movements, as if he would be neither stopped nor hurried but meant to take what joy there was to be had in the moment.

Lettie could feel the strong beat of his heart against her, could sense the probing of his gaze, though it was doubtful that he could see any more of her than she could of him. It was better that way, infinitely better. As he tilted her chin with his strong fingers, she lifted her mouth to his without restraint. Once more his beard tickled. Half enchanted, half repulsed, she knew better than to ask him to remove it. Firmly attached with what must be spirit gum, the disguise was better in place, for her sake as well as his. She was not sure she wanted, at this moment, to know who or what he was.

He spread her loosened hair over his arm, smoothing its silken strands. With consummate care, he opened her shirtwaist and drew back the edges, at the same time sliding the straps of her camisole from her shoulders. He cupped a breast in his hand, gently circling it, touching the alabaster skin as if its texture and firmness gave him pleasure. He brushed the nipple with his thumb, bringing forth exquisite sensations that caused it to contract into the shape of a berry that he took into his mouth.

"Delicious," he whispered, "delicious."

Casually, as if the movement was accidental, she touched her fingers to the strong column of his neck and trailed them down to the open collar of his shirt. She dipped into the hollow at the base of his throat, counting the steady beat of the pulse that throbbed there. By degrees, she eased lower to the buttons of his shirt, loosening them slowly, unobtrusively, one by one. He permitted the familiarity in a show of elaborate unconcern as he found the secret of the catch at the band of her skirt and freed it to push the heavy material and the petticoat underneath down around her hips.

Absorbed, each pretending not to notice what the other was doing, they undressed one another. She plowed the hair on his chest into furrows with the tips of her fingers and followed the descending triangle to the hard, flat expanse of his belly. He kissed the hollow between her breasts and set them tingling with sweeps of his beard before diving to plunge his tongue into her navel. She pressed her palm to his lean, hard-muscled flank, slowly grasping. He flicked his tongue along the sensitive skin on the insides of her knees, one after the other, and would not let her close them. With the tip of one finger, she traced, marveling, the faint ridge along the underside of the silken length of his swordlike member. He scoured a hot wet path to the apex of her thighs and, ignoring her gasping protest, tasted the honeyed essence of her, probing, until she lay in silent, trembling wonder.

It was at first a shared jest, that half-playful wooing. Time was elastic, a thing that seemed to stretch endlessly. The pleasure of it held them in a powerful bond, heated and liquid and without limit. But by degrees it lost its humor, becoming a thing of taut muscles and stretched nerves, of heated bodies, of pounding hearts and harsh, straited breathing.

Holding Lettie close, Ransom spread her skirts and placed her on her back upon them. She gripped his arms for an instant, as if in panic, though it might have been in a paroxysm of suppressed desire. Either way, there was a remedy. He caught her to him and rolled so that he was upon his back and she lay on his hard length.

"My treat," he said, and moved slightly, nudging her softness, to make his point.

Exhilaration for her freedom and a curious kind of passionate gratitude seized Lettie, blending with the vibrant, aching pressure of desire. Holding her breath, she eased back upon him, giving a small cry as the entry was made, then taking him deep and deeper still until he filled her, was a part of her, seemingly inseparable. She moved upon him then, grasping his muscled shoulders, her hair swinging around them like a golden-brown flail. He aided her, finding her rhythm, holding it in endless strength. The pleasure escalated, burgeoning upward from their joined bodies, bursting in her brain. Lettie was molten inside, her body incandescent, transformed.

It burst over her, the healing eruption of liquid fire. She gave a gasping moan and went still. In that instant he heaved himself up and over, plunging into her so that the receding waves of her turbulent joy took with them the last vestige of her tension, and she sobbed in an aching, infinite relief so unexpected that tears rose in her eyes and trailed in hot tracks into her hair.

Ransom held her, rocking her gently with the declining movements of the old ferry, staring with hot eyes into the darkness.

The jest, it seemed, was on them. It was rich but rather cruel, and not unexpected.

The breeze drifting over the water dried the film of perspiration that covered them, cooling their heated bodies. A mosquito whined around their heads. Ransom stirred, reaching for the white blur of Lettie's petticoat to draw it over her.

It was caught. As he tugged at it, he found that she was holding it in her fist. She swallowed, a difficult sound thick with tears, and wiped her face with a furtive movement. Ransom eased from her to rest on one elbow. She turned on her side with her back to him. Tightness invaded his chest. He touched her shoulder, then took his hand away again. He opened his mouth to speak, and in his distress, he could not think of how he was supposed to sound. Alarm touched him. It cleared his brain as it had always done.

He said quietly, "I'm sorry."

Her throat closed at the harsh sound of pain in his voice. She could only shake her head.

"It won't happen again, you have my word. Please—"

She took a deep breath, choking a little. When she spoke, the words were nearly unintelligible. "It isn't you."

"Not . . . ? What is it, then? Are you hurt?"

"No. It's . . . me."

"I don't know what you mean. Tell me." He caught her shoulder and rolled her toward him, his voice urgent.

"I feel—I feel like such a harlot." It was not as hard to say as she had thought it would be. This man did not pretend to be upstanding and God-fearing; he would not judge her.

His body stiffened as he lay against her. The soft sound he made was not unlike that caused by a hard blow to the heart.

"I'm not blaming you," she said hastily, scrubbing her face with her petticoat, trying to control herself enough to make sense. "It's just that I—that I should fight you and I don't, and I should hate you and I can't, and I shouldn't—shouldn't—"

"You should never, never enjoy physical love because good women don't."

"Yes," she said, and blotted fresh tears with something like desperation.

He ground out an epithet that made her stop and stare at him there in the darkness before he asked, "Who told you that?"

"Everyone says—"

"They're wrong! The fact that you feel pleasure when I touch you means nothing except that it's the way the female body is made, or the male for that matter. It's the brightest gift one human being can give another, our sole reward for being born. There would be something wrong with you if you were incapable of feeling it."

"Then why—"

"Why do they say it? Ignorance and stupidity. Or maybe it's just a convenience to fearful fathers and selfish husbands, who, you will note, make no bones about their own pleasures."

"Oh, but—"

"You are as the good God made you. Can it be wrong?"

It did not seem so when he spoke with such firm conviction. She was growing calm enough to feel a little resentment at being set so firmly among the ignorant, however, even if he had not meant it that way. With some asperity, she asked, "How do you know so much about it?"

"There was a buxom widow during the war. I was on reconnaissance when the battle lines shifted and I was caught in enemy territory. The lady hid me in her barn for three weeks. I was as green as a watermelon in May when I went in, but considerably riper when I came out."

"Three weeks?"

"Well, I had a trifling injury in the leg. She said it needed exercising. Come to think of it, she may have been right."

There was entirely too much levity in his voice. "Your legs and feet seem prone to injury—and to giving you excuses for lovemaking. How is your gunshot wound?"

"What?"

"Your foot, where I shot you."

"That's long healed," he said, then added hastily, "though a little stiff at times, such as now."

"I don't believe a word of it." She gave him a look of dark suspicion.

"What, no offer of exercise?" He reached to take the petticoat from her grasp, then brushed the palm of his hand over the globe of her breast, molding it gently to fit his hand. He moved closer, pressing against her thigh.

Her eyes widened as she felt the turgid length of him once more. "Not again!"

"I assure you, it's possible."

"It can't be necessary!" There was less force in her voice than she had intended as the effects of his ministrations spread through her. She wanted to be miserable and guilty, but somehow the need for it was gone.

"That is a matter of opinion."

"Your foot—"

"—is fine, but there is another part of me that isn't. Don't you feel the least little need of . . . ripening?"

She bit her bottom lip to keep it from curving at his

wheedling tone. He leaned to brush her lips with his, flicking his tongue along the line of her teeth set in the soft skin. She released her breath in a sigh. She whispered, "Maybe . . . just a . . . little."

There was a mount waiting for the Thorn on the opposite side of the river. Lettie did not ask where it had come from, and he did not explain. She preferred not to think that he had planned the way the evening would end from the very beginning, but the only other explanation was that he had reached the ferry far enough ahead of her to give him time to transport his mount across the river.

There was little doubt in her mind that he was the man who had passed her while she crouched on the trail, the man behind the night riders. Still, the only way he could have been prepared for her at the ferry was for him to have known exactly what she meant to do and how he would counter it. It was uncomfortable to think that she was so transparent or he so calculating. The proper description might be determined rather than calculating, determined to collect what was owed him. She did not care for that view of him, either.

Riding along beside him in the night, Lettie began to think it was possible that Aunt Em could be right about the Thorn. Nothing that she had seen of this man, nothing she had received at his hands, gave her reason to believe that he was a killer.

Henry must have been wrong, misled by circumstantial evidence. The culprit he had sought, the murderer loose in the countryside, must be one or more of the outlaws Johnny had spoken of, a man who masqueraded in a sheet like the Knights of the White Camellia at times but who could also strike down a victim in broad daylight if the reward, such as an army payroll, seemed worth the risk. It made sense.

It made sense because she wanted it to make sense, because if the Thorn were innocent of spilling her brother's blood that would make what she had just done all right. That was all.

She glanced at the tall shape of him beside her. If she really thought her brother was wrong, she would ask this man to remove his disguise. She could not do it. Whether the cause was something in the Thorn or some failing in herself, she did not know, but it was an impossibility. Curiosity burned inside her, and yet . . . and yet . . . To know could mean terrible embarrassment. It might also mean that her conscience would require her to inform the authorities. Or if she did not, she would feel responsible, would be responsible, for everything laid at his door from this moment. It was true, of course, that her failure to ask made it so in any case.

They came at last to Dink's Pond. He reined in and she stopped beside him.

"So silent," he said, his voice low. "More guilt?"

It was startling, this ability of his to understand her when he hardly knew her. "It's the way I'm made; I can't help it."

"There's no need to take pride in it."

"Pride!"

"Accepting the blame for what other people do is as much a form of arrogance as claiming the credit."

"We have a responsibility toward other human beings."

"Let me speak plainly, love. You are not responsible for anything I have done or may do in the future."

"But . . . if I could stop you?"

"Try, by all means."

"Now who's being arrogant!"

He reached across the space between them to catch her hand. "Oh, I am. Will it serve?"

Her annoyance faded, though she could be no less than honest as she answered, "I'm not sure."

He heard the pain in her voice and wished with sudden savagery that he had the right to banish it. Or had at least exercised sufficient self-control not to put it there in the first place. His best instincts seemed to vanish when he was with her. Knowing the cause didn't help. Or give him confidence. There was only one thing to be done, now.

"I'll say good-bye here. If I don't see you again—"

The stifled sound that Lettie made was so soft that she did not think he could have heard it, and yet he paused for so long that she flushed, afraid he was trying to think of some way to take his leave without hurting her. Keeping her voice even with an effort, she said, "Yes, if?"

"Forget," he said, his voice harsh. "Forget what happened between us. Never bring it to mind. Let it be as if it never took place."

"And is that what you will do?"

His grip on her hand tightened for an instant, then he raised it to his lips and pressed a kiss into her palm. Carefully, he placed it on her knee. When he answered, there was a trace of dry humor once more under the steel of his words. "No," he said, "but then I have no conscience."

It was a lie; she knew it as she watched him ride away. She was less certain by the time she reached the stables at Splendora, and not sure at all when she was safe at last in her own bedchamber. She had thought he was worried about her, but his greatest concern might have been for himself. Forget, he had said, but was it because it was better for her that way or because she would have less to remember to tell the authorities?

He was safe, if he only knew it. She could think of no way to approach Colonel Ward, or the sheriff for that matter, without telling him of how she had come by her information, how it was that she could describe the Thorn, if not accurately, at least more closely as to height and body build than most. That was something she had no wish, could not bear, in fact, to disclose to a living soul.

The auctioning off of the Tyler place, Sally Anne's home, was held on a bright and hot morning near the end of June. The proceedings were to begin at ten. The crowd began to gather at sunup. By the time Aunt Em, Lettie, and Ranny with Lionel arrived at nine, there was no place before the house, on the drive, or along the edges of the road for a half mile in either direction to leave a wagon. It was just as well that they had walked.

They joined the family—Samuel Tyler and his wife, Sally Anne and Peter, Sally Anne's sister and brother-in-law and their two small children—on the veranda. The women all wore black. Sally Anne's father, a man with a shock of white hair and thick gray brows who might have been leonine in appearance if he had not been so thin, sat staring into space and gripping the arms of his chair. He shook off his lethargy enough to rise to his feet when the ladies appeared and to shake hands with Ranny, gripping his shoulder. Mrs. Tyler, short and plump and with traces of blond still in her gray hair, gave Aunt Em a tight hug and, smiling gallantly through rising tears, thanked her for coming. Their voices were soft and subdued. Most of the women held handkerchiefs. Their visit had every appearance of a condolence call and served much the same purpose, that of support for the grief-stricken.

A bottle of sherry was produced. "Damned locusts won't get this," Mr. Tyler said as he poured it out and passed it around. They sat sipping the mellow golden wine and talking of the weather, pretending not to hear the people tramping through the house behind them or to see those that straggled up the drive.

They had descended like the locusts they were called,

the carpetbaggers. They were the ones with the money these days. They swarmed in and out with their women, most of whom were of less than sterling virtue, on their arms. They turned up their noses at the horses as less than purebred stock, sneered at the carriages with their split-leather seats and glazed paint, and joked about the various uses that could be found for several hundred field hoes. They sat in the Sheraton chairs one after the other, looked at the bottoms of vases for markings, and flicked the crystal with their fingernails to make it ring. They wondered how in the world the high-ceilinged rooms were kept warm in the winter, while conceding that they were more comfortable than expected in the present warm spell, and disagreed about what it would cost to hire enough Negro maids to keep the place decently dusted. They made disparaging comments about the furnishings: on the state of the silk hangings, "Threadbare, positively rotten, and so faded you wouldn't think they had any color to begin with!"; the Queen Anne table and chairs, "Ugly bowlegged things, aren't they?"; and the coin silver tea service, "Hardly a scroll on it, too plain to be worth much." With notebooks in hand and pencils in their fists, busily figuring, they trailed out again to the front steps where the proceedings would be held.

Lettie, hearing the broad and rather hard accents of the Northeast, was ashamed, not just of the ignorance displayed but of the lack of consideration. Anyone who came up the drive must know that the family was still in residence. The only conclusion to be drawn was that they knew and didn't care. To them anyone so poor, or with so little sharpness that they had lost their fortune down to the roof over their heads, could not matter.

"Now you aren't to worry about a thing," Aunt Em was saying to her sister-in-law, Sally Anne's mother. "Everything is ready at Splendora. You and Samuel can have the middle bedroom, Sally Anne and Peter can move in with me, and the others can have the sleeping loft to themselves. We'll make out fine, and just think what fun we'll have, all being together?"

"You are a dear, Em. It's terrible that we have to put you to so much trouble."

"Nonsense! No trouble at all."

It was a familiar exchange, one that had been repeated at least a dozen times in the past few days. Lettie paid little attention to it and so had time to notice Sally Anne's abrupt stillness as she sat staring down the drive. Turning her head swiftly in that direction, Lettie saw a man, wearing a blue uniform, on horseback. It was Thomas Ward.

Lettie looked back at Sally Anne. The woman gave her a tired smile. "I never expected it of him. I suppose I should have, but I didn't."

The colonel, as he neared the house, looked up. He removed his hat, tipping it as he leaned in a half bow from the saddle. Sally Anne looked away as if he was not there. Thomas's face tightened. Lettie deliberately lifted a hand to wave. She understood how Sally Anne must feel, but that did not keep her from wanting to shake the other woman. If Thomas Ward was there, it was not to take advantage of the Tylers' misfortune.

Or was it?

The auctioneer, banging his gavel and raising his voice in a self-satisfied shout, began the business of the day exactly on time. Lot after lot of items came under his hammer, starting with barrels of ropes and tools from the outbuildings, carrying on with the farm animals and furniture, and ending with barrels of china and books from the house. Every lot, every item, was bought by Colonel Thomas Ward. He was not troubled by the angry looks and snide remarks from the bidders around him. He did not look at Sally Anne or her family. He paid no attention, or so it seemed, to what he was buying or how much it cost.

But he would not be outbid. Some tried it, only to go down in defeat. As the others saw what was happening, they began to drift away. By noon, the drive and the front yard had been cleared of carriages, wagons, and horses, and the lawn was empty. The auctioneer, taking his helpers and the colonel's hefty bank draft with him, had gone away. Thomas Ward was left in possession.

He mounted the steps to the veranda where the family still sat. He removed his hat and gave a curt bow, then put the black felt headpiece under one arm and clasped his wrist with his other hand. He glanced at Lettie and seemed to take courage from the fact that she at least acknowledged his presence by looking at him.

"I apologize," he said, "for that vulgar display. I didn't know how else to go about it."

Sally Anne's father got to his feet at last, holding himself stiff and straight. "You were quite within your rights, sir. I congratulate you on an excellent purchase, and I assure you that we will be out of the house by nightfall."

"Not on my account, I beg you. It's my hope that you will remain, all of you, as my guests."

He had their attention now.

"I beg your pardon?" Samuel Tyler threw his head back and looked down his nose with a fierce frown.

"I have no intention of putting you out of your home. I only ask that you permit me to call now and then—on your daughter."

Sally Anne came to her feet with her blue eyes, usually so serene, glittering with rage. "Colonel Ward, I take leave to inform you that though you have bought our home, you have not bought me!"

Thomas looked at her with confusion and the dawning of anger in his eyes. "I never thought it."

"No? It seems odd to me that this is the first time I have heard of your great desire to call, the first I've seen of you in weeks!"

"There were arrangements to make for funds and I didn't want to intrude or have it look as if I were assessing the property."

"If by that you mean me—"

"I didn't say that!"

"Are you positive you don't want to dispense with the formalities and just move in? Why pretend, since you have made so sure of me?"

"I'm not—"

Sally Anne would not let him finish, though for those who could hear it there was pain threading her angry tirade. "Why go to the trouble of paying court when money will do? Why not just hand me a roll of bills and lead me to my bedroom? That's the way men like you usually get what they want, isn't it?"

"What I would like to do," the colonel began, putting his hands on his hips, "is lead you out to the woodshed—"

"Stop!"

It was Ranny who spoke, coming to his feet with a smooth surge on that single word. His voice was not loud, but there was something in it that cut through the building quarrel like a keen sword. He looked from Thomas to Sally Anne and back again. His tone flat, he said, "This is silly." Then, without a backward glance, he walked away along the veranda and down the steps.

There was absolute silence for the space of ten seconds when he had gone. The colonel raked his hand through his hair and clasped the back of his neck. He sent a quick glance at Sally Anne, then looked at the floor. "I'm sorry if I offended in any way. I only meant to help."

Sally Anne said nothing. Lettie, watching the movement

of the woman's slender throat and the shimmer in her eyes, thought it was because she could not. Mr. Tyler gave a heavy sigh.

"I am sure, Colonel Ward," the older man said, "that my daughter regrets anything she may have said that was unseemly. Regardless, you must see that what you propose is impossible. We cannot accept your charity."

A stubborn look came over Thomas's face. He straightened his shoulders. "It isn't charity."

"Whatever the term you choose, it would not be proper for us to live here under the circumstances you have described. It is a question of something that has caused a great deal of hardship in this part of the world, and probably will cause more, but something to which we cling now as never before. That thing, sir, is pride."

There was an implication—unintentional, Lettie was sure, but there all the same—that pride was something with which the colonel must be unfamiliar. Thomas Ward did not take offense. He stared at Sally Anne's father for a long moment, and when he spoke, his voice was tentative.

"As you wish, sir. But there is an alternative. Could you, perhaps, square it with your principles to accept me as the holder of your mortgage?"

"With the same provision as before?"

Thomas did not so much as glance at Sally Anne. "By no means."

"I see." There was a flicker of regret in the older man's face before he pursed his lips in thought.

"However," Thomas said, "I have formed a deep attachment to this area and would like, someday, to live here and own land. I know next to nothing about the farming methods that work best, a problem I would like to remedy. It would be a great service to me, sir, if you would permit me to visit from time to time and go over the fields with you."

The men regarded each other intently for long moments. At last a smile began to lift the lines on Samuel Tyler's face. He gave a snort of wry laughter and rose from his chair to step toward the colonel, clapping him on the shoulder. "I think I can put my hand on a bottle of bourbon, if my wife doesn't have it packed in the bottom of her trunk. Come on inside and let's talk about this over a drink."

It was a male conspiracy. Lettie, looking from the two men to Sally Anne's suspicious frown, fought to keep the smile of appreciation from her lips. Whether it would work or not was impossible to know, but at least now there was a chance. Ranny, with his simple and decisive intervention, had given it to them.

He had one to offer Lettie also.

Lettie, Ranny, and Lionel were in the schoolroom as usual the following morning. Peter was absent, though the problem was a cut foot, according to the note that had been sent, rather than anything to do with the events of the previous day. The morning was unsettled, with high moving clouds coming and going across the sun. Because of the fluctuating light, Lettie had moved her chair closer to the window in order to see her book better as she read from *Great Expectations*. Ranny sat at her feet with one shoulder braced against the chair leg as he held her hand, playing with her fingers as usual. Lionel lay on the floor nearby in his favorite position, staring at the ceiling with his hands clasped behind his head.

Lettie came to the end of the chapter and closed the book. She looked at her lapel watch. "Nearly noon. That's it for today."

Lionel turned his head. "Just one more chapter? Please?"

"If you haven't had your fill of school, there are those sums—"

"I think I hear Mama Tass calling me to dinner!" he

exclaimed in sudden energy, and, jumping up, made a dash for the door.

Lettie let him go. She could not blame the boy for not wanting to work. It was a lazy day. She leaned her head against the back of her chair and looked down at Ranny.

He was watching her. He had always done that, but lately there was something unnerving in the concentration he bent on her. For an instant, she was caught in the deep and unwavering blue of his gaze. The clear light falling from the window beside her fell fully upon his face, gilding his skin, striking into his eyes.

Lettie realized suddenly, as she looked closer at him in that lambent glow, that the color she thought she saw in the irises of his eyes was false. It was actually a mixture of blue and green and brown enclosed in a gray outer ring. His eyes only appeared blue as a reflection of the chambray shirt he wore, one of the many that made up his wardrobe. How odd that she had never noticed it before. She supposed that she had received an impression at their first meeting, one there had been no reason to doubt.

Hazel. Hazel eyes. It was not an uncommon color. Not at all.

"Miss Lettie, will you marry me?"

Her thoughts scattered. "What did you say?"

"I said—"

"Forgive me, Ranny. That's all right, I know what you said. It just . . . took me by surprise. What I would really like to know is why you said it." She felt as if she were prattling nonsense, but she needed time to think, time to discover if this was another of his jokes.

"I would like to be married to you."

"Now why? Is it maybe because of the colonel wanting to marry Sally Anne?"

"No."

The word was hard. He looked down, shielding his eyes

with his gold-tipped lashes as if he was either hurt or offended. Her voice soft, she asked, "Why, then?"

He looked up again to meet her gaze, his own open, totally vulnerable, though a pulse throbbed beside the scar on his temple. "Because I want to take care of you. Because I want you to live with me. Because I want to be with you my whole life long."

Tightness invaded Lettie's throat. For a long, breathless moment, she knew an insane impulse to agree. He was so very dear, so touchingly handsome in his incapacity. There was such goodness in him and an odd kind of strength that went beyond the physical power of his body. It would be so easy to take him, to care for him, to teach him the pleasures of love she had been shown, to allow him to love her. Their children would be beautiful.

Dear God, what was she thinking!

Ransom watched her face, the moist softness in her eyes and tremulous curves of her mouth, with his heart suspended in his chest. He saw the faint flush that seeped into her skin and felt a stirring of hope for the gamble he had made, one crafted with care over these many endless days since he had held her on the ferry. Then came the shock, driving the color from her features and turning her eyes black. His grasp on her hand tightened.

"Don't look like that," he said, his voice rough.

She gasped and summoned a shaky smile. "Oh, Ranny."

He had to help her. "You don't have to. It's all right."

"I wish—I really wish I could." She reached out to touch his hair, running her fingers through the soft, blond strands. "You should have been married long ago, when everyone else was doing it at the start of the war, when all the girls were chasing you."

He sat very still under her hand. It had been a long time since she had touched him, a very long time. "I didn't want them."

"You don't want me, either. It wouldn't be right."

"Why?"

"I'm not good enough for you," she said, her voice low and etched with acid self-knowledge.

He saw what he had done to her, saw and felt it cutting into him, deep and deeper still. He wanted to explain, to remove her pain, to take the blame upon himself where it belonged and make it right. His mind was blank except for one thing.

"I love you."

The tears rose in her eyes, clinging to her lashes. "Oh, Ranny. It's a strange thing, but I think that in a way I love you, too."

"Then take my name."

His name, a man's most valuable possession. She might have succumbed to the promise the day before, when she had been afraid for nearly a week that she might be carrying the Thorn's child. Today that possibility no longer existed. If she was dispirited and too inclined to tears, doubtless the cause could be laid to the time of the month. But that had nothing to do with Ranny. She summoned a smile.

"I can't do that, you know. Your aunt wouldn't like it. People might even say I did it for Splendora."

"You can have Splendora."

He was so stubborn but full of his own guile. Lettie tried a different tack, allowing her voice to rise with annoyance. "You think I would marry you for money, any more than Sally Anne would take the colonel?"

"I don't care why."

"I can't do it."

"You love me a little. You could love me more."

To say the words gave him such ease that it hardly mattered how she answered. He had accepted the fact that she was not going to say what he wanted to hear. There had been a chance, a very slight chance, that she might, though the dark shadows under her eyes this morning had made him fear that her need was past, even if his was not. Now all he wanted was to see what she would say to his ingenuous pleas, to watch her face and judge what she really was like, how she really felt. And not to betray himself by suddenly snatching her out of her chair and into his arms on the floor, if it took every ounce of his willpower. There was a fragment of a poem running through his mind, from where he did not know.

> *O Western wind, when will thou blow,*
> *That the small rain down can rain?*

"I might, but it wouldn't matter."
"It would to me."

> *Christ, that my love were in my arms*
> *And I in my bed again!*

But, of course, she had never truly been in his bed. Would she ever be?

"Please," she implored him. "Don't say any more."

He stared at her for a long, considering moment. What was a pleasure for him was torment for her. He should have recognized it before. He gave an abrupt nod. "I won't, then, for now."

His understanding was so unexpected that gratitude welled up inside her. On impulse, she leaned over and brushed his forehead with her lips. The curve of her breast pressed for an instant upon his shoulder and her knee touched his chest. That contact, brief as it was, sent a wave of desire flooding in upon her. She drew back as if from a hot stove.

She met his gaze, her own despairing, and saw that his eyes were pools of stillness, guarded, protective.

There was the scrape of a footstep at the door. "Well, well, teacher," Martin Eden drawled in lazy humor, "if this is the way you conduct class, when do I start lessons?"

Guard yourself from the heat, my dear, not only for the sake of your health but because warm climates are known to weaken moral fiber.

Lettie dropped her mother's letter on the table and propped her elbow beside it, rubbing her forehead with her fingertips. Lately, some of the comments in her family's letters struck her as being not only uninformed but ridiculous. They seemed to think the entire state of Louisiana was a disease-ridden marsh peopled by cruel, hot-tempered men who deserved to be ground under the heel as punishment for their crimes against humanity. The thought of Ranny, Samuel Tyler, or any of the men she passed in the street in Natchitoches in that guise was ludicrous. They were simply men who had used a feudal system sanctioned for hundreds of years to build a way of life. It was not their fault that industrial societies, such as England and New England, that no longer had anything to gain from such a system had decreed, suddenly, that it was base exploitation and must be ended. No reasonable man could deny the truth of that statement; likewise, no reasonable man could, or should, have expected people with millions invested in slavery to end the practice overnight. The war had been a tragedy, but what was happening now was an outrage. She saw that so clearly that she could not think why it had ever seemed otherwise. It was a measure, she supposed, of how much she had changed.

That she had changed greatly, she knew well. The idea her mother had expressed concerning the climate was one she herself had accepted once. Not anymore. She had seen no moral laxity during her stay. The warm weather might encourage more interaction among people and allow them to venture farther from restraining supervision, but whatever happened came from the people themselves, not the heat. She should know.

She ought to leave, nonetheless, to go back to Boston where she belonged. She wasn't doing any good, wasn't making any progress in finding Henry's killer. All the things that she had thought she would do—and that her sister and her brother-in-law continually harped upon—such as hounding the sheriff and exhorting him to greater efforts, she now saw as useless. What should be done instead, she could not tell. She had made no efforts for some time, not since the night on the ferry. Her only usefulness was in teaching, and she often wondered if there were others who could do it better, with more patience and concentration than she could summon lately.

Lettie pushed the letter to one side and leaned back in her chair. She had heard from her mother, her sister, one or two cousins, and her best friend in the past two weeks, but the letter that Johnny had promised had not arrived. Aunt Em said not to worry, that he was getting settled, finding something to do with himself, making ready to send for his mother. He would write when he had his affairs in order. Still, it was troubling. She kept thinking of how quickly the Thorn had returned from hiding him, how quickly he had stripped off his disguise as an old woman. Nor could she forget the dangers that Johnny would have had to run to reach the state line. It wasn't that she actively doubted the Thorn. She was just uneasy and would be until she received word that Johnny was all right. She thought that Aunt Em, for all her confident air, was the same.

The older woman had weathered the blood poisoning from the rooster's spur in fine form. The wound on her arm was still purplish, but it had healed nicely. She was back at her regular tasks, as well as being involved in putting up jars of the blackberries and plums that the children from the quarters picked and brought by the bucketful, or else making jelly and jam and cordial from the juice. She churned butter from the milk of a cow that had "freshened," or calved, and sold it to the townspeople who drove out for it, as well as for the buttermilk that was left from the process and the fresh eggs for which Aunt Em was famous. Her profit, she declared, was being eaten away by Ranny and Lionel, who insisted on a huge breakfast of biscuits and butter, eggs and ham, milk and fresh jam every morning. There was no heat in her complaints, however; she always beamed as she watched them eat.

Food, cooking, planning what to eat, and eating it was so much a part of Aunt Em's daily routine that it wasn't surprising when she declared that the Fourth of July would be celebrated with a "fish fry." What was surprising to Lettie was that there would be a holiday declared at all. That was until Aunt Em pointed out with some tartness that many an ancestor of the people of the lower states had fought for their freedom from the British, too. Northerners, she said, had no monopoly on Independence Day.

They converged on the riverbank early while the dawn coolness still lingered and the sun was just lifting a brow above the horizon. The early start was a bit perplexing until it dawned on Lettie that they were all expected to catch their own fish for the feast.

Other than the Splendora household, which included Mama Tass and Lionel, there were the rest of the Tylers from Elm Grove, plus Martin Eden, who appeared to be squiring Sally Anne for the day; a full contingent of the military, with the colonel prominent among them; and even the tax collector, O'Connor.

Lettie felt a bit sorry for the Irishman. No one seemed to have invited him or to have a liking for his company; he had just appeared as they were setting out. A more sensitive man would have stayed away, but it seemed that Splendora was one of the few places where the man was tolerated, and so he pushed in regardless.

He was rather pathetic as he stood around the edges of first one group and then another, making a comment now and then but never really being drawn into the different conversations. He was pointedly snubbed by Samuel Tyler, who walked away whenever he approached, and once Sally Anne drew her skirts back as if he might contaminate them as he walked by. The soldiers exchanged quips with him, however, and Ranny smiled at him and offered him a fully rigged fishing pole. He took the pole with transparent gratitude though he only grunted his thanks.

Red River was named for its rusty color, which came from the soil, washed from the surrounding fields and the iron ore hills farther north, that muddied it during the winter and spring runoffs. There was always a faint reddish tint to it, though it was less obvious in summer.

Fishing the Red wasn't easy. They had moved upriver, away from Grand Ecore and the high bluffs nearby, bluffs from which a lovelorn Indian maiden was supposed to have leaped to her death. It was not the supposedly haunted location that caused them to seek other ground, however, but the problem in getting down to the water. The level of the river was fairly low in the section finally chosen, leaving here and there a shelving sandy bank to stand on. The edging of willow and sweet gum and dogwood trees mingled with hardwoods, all hung with gray rags of Spanish moss, gave some shade, but also made it difficult to move up and down and presented a hazard to getting a hook in and out of the water.

The only person who elected not to wet a hook was Sally Anne's mother. The older woman spread a quilt for the youngest members of the party, Sally Anne's sister's two children, who were little more than crawling babies, and sat beside them flapping at gnats and mosquitoes with a leafy switch. The rest spread out along the water's edge, most of them wandering up and down surveying the possibilities of floating logs, crooks, bends, and stumps as "fishy" looking places, likely hiding places for fish. It seemed the best-looking ones were always the most inaccessible, either choked with trees or fronted by steep, muddy banks.

Peter and Lionel, their faces narrow-eyed with concentration, settled down with a can of worms and a forked branch broken from a handy tree to receive their catch between them. They scowled and made hushing noises at everybody who came by in their anxiety that the scaled monster they sought would be scared away.

Aunt Em and Mama Tass, veterans of bank fishing, had brought wooden buckets to sit on. They turned them bottom-up and sat down on them with businesslike determination. Samuel Tyler wandered away downriver, squinting from the sun to the tree shadows cast on the water and muttering to himself.

The men in blue, or rather in pieces of their blue uniforms combined with whatever civilian clothes they happened to have, had hauled a wooden boat with a square prow and stern to the river. Three or four of them piled into it and poled up and down, tangling their lines, hooking each other's hats, and generally having a fine time.

Lettie, with Ranny just along the bank below her and Martin, O'Connor, and Sally Anne above, settled down near where an uprooted tree trailed its still-green branches in the water. Ranny had shown her how to bait her hook, sliding a wiggling worm on the evil-looking barb without a trace of compunction. Her line was of black silk and the pole of bamboo cane cut from a veritable cane forest in back of the old blacksmith shop at Splendora. Some four feet or so from her hook, fastened to her line, was a piece of bobbing cork carved more or less in a sphere. It had been provided by Colonel Ward, another of the army's contributions to the outing, in addition to the boat, the usual lemons, and a pair of rubber ground cloths that would later become their tables when it was time to eat. Lettie, unsure of what to do with her fishing gear, watched as Ranny gave his hook and line a careless flip out into the water. She tried her best to do likewise.

The sun crept higher in the sky. The day grew hotter. Flies buzzed around them. The whine of mosquitoes was an irritant, but it was even more nerve-wracking when they were silent since it meant the vicious little insects had found likely spots to sample their victims' blood.

Now and then came a yell as someone's cork went under or they pulled in a gleaming sun perch or big blue gill. Sally Anne caught a grindle two feet long and several pounds in weight. It was fun to pull in, she said, but it wasn't worth the worm, being a trash fish full of tiny bones embedded in meat like cotton. Martin and Colonel Ward nearly came to blows over who was going to take it off her hook. Martin won the honor, though it was possible that the colonel, looking at the fish that resembled some prehistoric creature with teeth like a crosscut saw clamped around Sally Anne's line as it made grunting, grating noises, may have given in gracefully. By the time Martin had removed the hook and line, he was hot, flustered, and swearing. He threw the grindle, by that time thoroughly dead, into the bushes.

A short time later, there came a loud grunting and squealing from the direction in which the fish had been thrown.

Lettie swung around to look at Ranny, her eyes wide. "What's that?"

"Not the grindle." He didn't look up from his cork.

"What, then?"

"Hogs."

"Hogs?"

"They clean up the mess. They like fish. Or anything else."

"Ugh."

He shrugged, giving her a smile. "Better than letting it lie there and smell."

He had a point. Any fish not kept at least half-alive in water would soon spoil in the heat.

The hogs trotted off. Quiet returned. Ranny caught a fish that glittered red and blue and gray. Lettie pulled up her line and looked at her worm. It was still there. Ranny caught another sun perch.

Lettie sent him a frown. "Why are you catching fish and I'm not?"

"You drowned your worm."

It sounded like a terrible thing to have done, but it hardly seemed to matter since the poor thing was going to be eaten by a fish.

"So?"

"So put on another one."

"This one still looks all right to me."

"You," he said solemnly, "are not a fish. He needs it to be wiggling."

She made a face. "It sounds like torture."

"That's the way things are. Haven't you ever been fishing before?"

"No," she said, her voice defensive.

He gave her a slow grin. "Why didn't you say so? Put on a new worm."

Lettie, her lips curled in disgust, stripped off the dead bait and carefully threaded a new, desperately wriggling specimen on her hook. Holding it in her fingers, she sent her teacher a pained look. "Now what?"

"Put it in the water."

"Right." She plopped the line and hook into the river.

"Give him a little air now and then. Move your hook around."

She obeyed his instructions and also the others he gave her at intervals, but it didn't help. After a time, she moved farther along the bank, closer to Martin. O'Connor seemed to be having about the same luck she was, for he shifted also, throwing his hook back in the water between Martin and Lettie.

At a shout of triumph from Aunt Em, Lettie craned her neck in that direction. The older woman was pulling in a huge, slick, silvery gray fish that appeared to have whiskers.

"Channel cat," the older woman called in answer to a faint question from somewhere beyond her. Aunt Em's skirt was nearly to her knees as she perched on her up-turned bucket. Under it, she had on what looked to be a pair of men's trousers. Her head was covered by a battered old man's hat to keep off the sun. The outfit was immensely practical and looked just as comfortable.

Lettie had worn her oldest skirt and shirtwaist and shabbiest shoes, but she still felt overdressed compared to the others. Even Sally Anne had on a faded and patched gown that fell short of her ankles.

With a glance around to be sure no one was watching, Lettie rolled her sleeves up past her elbows and opened her collar wider for coolness. She unbuttoned the few buttons on her low shoes and kicked them off long enough to remove her stockings and put them in a rolled ball in her pocket. Then she put her shoes on again.

The river flowed past with the sun glittering on its surface like billions of tiny flashing mirrors. It swirled sometimes into patterns, making little gurgling sounds, carrying bits of bark and leaves and spent tree blooms. A dragonfly, a beautiful insect of iridescent blue-green with black gossamer wings, landed on the end of Lettie's pole. A great white crane flapped by overhead with slow, majestic beats of its wings. Birds called back and forth in the trees around them. It was so calm and lovely, so peaceful there with nothing to do but watch a bit of floating cork.

Her cork! It was gone. She snatched at her pole, jerking it straight up. The line stretched taut for an instant, then, as the fish got off the hook, it snapped out of the water, flying up, reaching high, higher. The end of the black line struck a tree limb high above her to her left with the hook whirling. It caught. It hung.

Getting a hook hung was nothing unusual from what Lettie could tell, but she had yet to see anyone, even young Peter, hang theirs in a treetop. Pink with annoyance and chagrin, Lettie yanked on her pole. Nothing happened. She thrashed it back and forth. The line whipped and vibrated and the tree limb shook up and down as if in a gale, but her hook did not come loose. Bits of green leaves and bark showered down on O'Connor, who looked up at her line caught on the tree limb above him. He had the effrontery to laugh.

"It's blue gills we're fishing for, Miss Mason, not blue birds," he said.

Lettie looked over her shoulder at Ranny, farther along the bank now and absorbed in removing another fish, this time a blue gill, from his hook. There was no help there at the moment. Turning back, she took her pole in both hands and gave it a tremendous pull toward her.

The tree limb bent double. With a loud and sudden crack, the hook popped free. The limb flew up and the small tree thrashed. Something long and thick and writhing fell from a higher tree branch. It struck O'Connor on the shoulder, tumbled down his shirt front, then hit the ground with a heavy, slapping thud. The tax collector gave a hoarse yell.

"Snake!"

O'Connor jumped back, stumbling, cursing, dropping his pole. The snake righted itself and slid with a soft rustling into the water. O'Connor rounded on Lettie.

The danger was over, though there had been a moment when Lettie had been ready to break and run. As she saw the tax collector's livid face and thought of his undignified scramble away from the snake and the snake's huffy departure from the place of its disturbed rest, she gave a choked laugh and clapped a hand over her mouth.

O'Connor's pasty-white face turned red with rage. He stalked toward her. "What in the name of bloody hell do you think you're doing?"

"I'm sorry! I didn't know it was there." Lettie was genuinely contrite.

"That was a cottonmouth moccasin; I've seen 'em before. I could have died if it'd bit me!"

O'Connor was upon her. His eyes glittered, and there were great beads of sweat on his upper lip. He reached and caught her upper arm, and she could feel the tremors of shock still rippling through him.

Abruptly, Ranny was beside her. He clamped hard fingers on O'Connor's wrist, wrenched the man's hand from Lettie's arm, and flung it back at him.

Martin also came striding up, a frown on his handsome

face. "Dammit, O'Connor, it was an accident. What are you so fired up about?"

O'Connor looked at them. He muttered, "I can't stand snakes."

"Neither can I, if it comes to that." Martin's tone was hard in its significance.

"Are you insinuating—"

"I'm stating a fact, no more than that." Despite his words, Martin's eyes narrowed as he spoke, as if he would not back down from the challenge if the tax collector meant to make one.

"Please, I am sorry," Lettie said in an effort to smooth over the situation that had boiled up so suddenly.

O'Connor shifted his gaze away from Martin and back to Lettie. "It's my belief Miss Mason has a liking for such low company. I hear she was seen one night not so long ago with a man who looked mighty like the description of our noble Robin Hood, the Thorn."

Lettie gasped. She sensed the stiff attention of the other two men as they stared at the tax collector.

"Who says such a thing?" Martin demanded.

"I'm not saying, but it would be interesting if there was any truth in it."

Martin gave Lettie a swift glance before turning back to her accuser. "My God, man, the Thorn killed her brother. If I hear any more such slander, somebody's going to be sorry."

"Are you threatening me?"

"Are you the one who's supposed to have seen her?"

"Of course not!" The reply was short, flustered.

"Then you have nothing to worry about. I think, however, that it might be better if you forgot about fishing for today. Your company can no longer be pleasing to Miss Mason."

The dismissal was more than a little high-handed.

O'Connor's face tightened. "I've lost my taste for both, anyway."

Ranny made a soft sound, moving forward. O'Connor stepped back hastily as he saw the expression on his face, then retreated another step. He looked at the three of them and his thick lips took on an ugly twist. "I won't forget this."

Martin curled his hands into fists as he drawled, "I trust not."

It was the last word. O'Connor only glared and turned away, trudging where he had left his buggy. The three of them watched him go. When he was out of sight among the trees, Lettie turned to Martin.

Before she could speak, he said, "I apologize for my language in front of a lady just now."

"I didn't regard it, I assure you. Thank you for coming to my defense."

"My pleasure, but Ranny was there before me."

"Yes," Lettie agreed, smiling, and swung around to speak to Ranny. But he had turned his back and was already walking away, returning to his fishing.

The incident caused scarcely a ripple. No one seemed to have noticed much beyond O'Connor's departure. There was a yelled inquiry or two, but Martin smoothed it over by simply calling back that the tax collector had gotten too hot and decided to call it quits. There was no grief over the news.   .

Lettie's hook had straightened from its bout with the tree limb and she had lost her worm. She eyed the hook with some doubt, wiped it on her skirt, then, copying a move she had seen Aunt Em make, put it between her teeth and gingerly bit down on it. It served nicely. The hook looked like a hook once more. She baited it again and slung it back out into the water.

Her pretense of competence at the art of fishing did not

serve to distract her from the problem that faced her. She had been seen with the Thorn. True, there was some uncertainty about it, but the fact remained. Her name was being bandied about among the men in town. She had been foolish to think that she could ride through Natchitoches, no matter how late, and be safe from prying eyes. She had tried to dissuade the Thorn from accompanying her, but he had been concerned for her safety. It would have been funny if it had not been so disturbing.

She had been right earlier, she should go home.

She was jerked from her reverie by the sight of her cork going under the water once more. She let the fish take it for a second or two. It was heading for a log. If it swam under it, she might never pull it in. Lettie sidestepped and gave a strong yank on her line. Her foot came down on a dead limb. She knew what it was, and yet the thought of the snake had not been far from her mind since it went into the water near her feet. She shifted too quickly just as the fish tugged. Suddenly there was nothing under her but the muddy, sloping bank. She slipped, threw up her hands, and slid with a stifled cry into the river.

The water was no higher than her knees here near the bank. She floundered for an instant with arms outstretched, but her feet were too deep in the soft mud of the river bottom for her to fall. With a soft oath, she began to turn back toward the bank, lifting a foot from the squishy, sucking ooze and swinging around in her heavy skirt that was wet to her thighs. Her shoe came off. Balancing precariously, she felt for it.

"Need some help?"

It was Ranny at his most laconic, his tone resigned. He was kneeling on the bank with one hand held out to her and the other holding on to a tree trunk.

"I will never," she announced in doleful tones, "be a fisherman."

"Fisherwoman."

"Whichever."

She reached out for his hand, but he withdrew it abruptly to point. "You're losing your pole."

The fish was still on the line and was towing her floating pole out toward the middle of the river. She plunged after it, splashing waist high. She grabbed the end of it and towed it toward her. Lifting the pole, she shouted as she saw the huge red sun perch flapping and dangling on her hook. She swung the fish toward her, grasping the line just above it. Twisting around, she laughed up at Ranny. "Look! I caught one."

She was breathless and flushed, she had muddy water on her face, and her hair was coming down from its pins, hanging in tendrils, but she was warm and happy and beautiful, and there was not a trace of tightness in her smile. Ransom felt his heart constrict, felt the cutting blade buried inside him slice deeper. He had been so jealous of the few words of appreciation she had given Martin a few minutes before that he had wanted to throw him in the river. Now it was all he could do not to pull Lettie out and make love to her there in the mud. He was losing control, had had very little, in fact, since he had met her. He was going to have to do something, but what it could be he had no idea.

"Yes, you caught one," he said, his voice carefully neutral. And felt like crying as he watched the joy fade from her face.

They cleaned the fish they had caught and cooked them there beside the river. Mama Tass had built a fire and let the wood burn down to a bed of coals. A great iron pot with a bail was hung from a support over the heat and was filled with lard that was soon so hot it rolled as if it were boiling.

The first food to be fried was the "hush puppies," spoonfuls of uncooked cornbread into which had been stirred chopped onions and hot peppers and even a little fresh corn from the garden. They puffed up crisp and golden-brown on the outside and moist and spicy on the inside. Next the fish were dredged in salted cornmeal and plunged a few at a time into the hot fat. Last of all to be cooked were the potatoes. Sliced into rounds like cookies, they quickly became tender and golden.

It was while the potatoes were cooking that the Voisin family—mother, father, daughter Marie, and her friend Angelique La Cour—drove up. In addition to a croquet set to aid their welcome, they had with them two watermelons the size of beer kegs and with rinds so dark green they were almost black. Nothing was needed, however; company was always greeted with pleasure, and there was never a shortage of something to eat. The newcomers were made much over, and the watermelons were put into a water-filled tub and set in the edge of the river to cool.

Finally, everything was ready. The rubber ground cloths were spread in the shade of a grove of oak and ash trees. The food, piled on huge platters, was placed on the cloths along with a supply of tin plates, forks, and a pile of old napkins. Quilts were spread about the edges to deter the ants and to make for comfortable seating. Peter and Lionel were put in charge of handing out the lemonade as Lettie and Sally Anne poured it. Aunt Em's cucumber pickles and bottled tomato relish were passed around along with sliced onion.

The smell of the woodsmoke and the delicious aromas rising from the black pot, plus the exercise of the morning, had made everyone ravenous. They all helped themselves from what was there and then, balancing their plates on their laps, fell to eating. They largely discarded their forks as they picked the fish apart to look for bones and held the hush puppies to bite into them. Frequent recourse was made to the napkins to wipe greasy fingers and mouths, but no one complained. Instead, praise poured in upon Mama Tass, particularly from the Union soldiers who declared with extravagance that they hadn't known such good food existed.

Finally the last hush puppy was eaten and the last potato snatched from the platter. There was an offer of muffins for dessert, but few were accepted. It was agreed by voice vote that they tarry to visit for an hour or two or three before cutting the watermelons. There was no hurry. It was a long time until dark.

The dirty dishes were given a scrubbing with sand and rinsed in the river, then wrapped in the rubber cloths and bundled away into the wagons to discourage the gathering flies. The older women rambled away along a wagon track to "walk off their meal," taking the two younger children with them. Sally Anne and her sister, with Marie Voisin and Angelique, the colonel and Martin and a lieutenant from Maine, cleared most of the leaves and trash from a clearing and set up the croquet set. The rest of the men and boys lay back on the quilts, moaning about how much they had eaten, until here and there they began to snore.

It really was difficult to keep awake after the big meal on such a warm day. It was pleasant in the shade with a faint breeze rustling in the leaves overhead and the sun making a scattered pattern of moving light over the quilts and the faces of those lying on them. Lettie sat on a corner of a quilt with her back to the trunk of a big ash. Through half-closed eyes she watched the others, too content and somnolent to move to a more comfortable position.

Ranny lay not far away. He was flat on his back with his hands behind his head. Just beyond him were Peter and Lionel, both in the same position. A smile twitched Lettie's lips as she noticed the boys' mimicry.

Her gaze went back to Ranny. Was he asleep? It was impossible to tell. His chest moved with a regular rhythm and his eyelids were still, but sometimes when he lay like that on the veranda he would suddenly open his eyes and smile at her, as if he could feel when he was being watched. His headaches had not been so frequent lately, so perhaps he was sleeping better.

There was a spot of muted sunlight the size of her hand across the lower part of his face. It made the bronze of his skin look translucent, and in it she could see the faint stubble of his closely shaven jaw. It was darker than his hair, almost brown. It was odd how men's mustaches and beards were often a different color from their hair, sometimes a different color from each other.

Her mind was drawn inexorably to that night on the ferry and the false beard the Thorn had worn. She could not think of why she had not snatched it off, had not been able to understand it in the many days since. The excuses she had given herself had no weight. The truth was, no matter how she might try to hide it, that she was a coward. She was, in some deep recess of her being, afraid to know who he might be, afraid of what the knowledge might mean to her.

Mustaches. That was what she had been thinking about.

Most of the men spread out before her had them, and most of them were brown. Martin Eden's had a trace of red in it. Why had she not noticed that before?

Of course, in his guise as the old lady the Thorn had not worn a beard, nor had he as the priest. He might have had time to grow one since, though it would have been obvious in its stages of regeneration. Perhaps he was even now wearing a false mustache while he waited for his real one to reach full luxuriance? Or possibly he never had a real one in order to give himself more diversity? She should probably have been looking for a man who was smooth-shaven all this time or else one with a false mustache.

She was so sleepy that she wasn't making sense. Surely a false mustache would be too dangerous, too obviously fake in the light of day? Or was that what everyone would think? So the Thorn would then do the opposite? He was bold and clever and daring. He might.

Dear heaven, but he was bold.

No. She would not think of that. She would not.

She was no longer sleepy.

Lettie got to her feet as quietly as possible and moved away from the quilts. The sparkle of the river attracted her and she walked toward it with her head bent, her hands clasped behind her back, and her steps swinging as she kicked at her skirts. They had dried quickly in the heat, but now had a wrinkled stiffness about her ankles so that they felt almost as if they had been starched. Looking up as she neared the water, she caught sight of the soldiers' boat, which was beached on a section of sandy bank shelving off into the water. She changed direction to move toward it.

The boat, built of nearly indestructible cypress wood, was heavy and unwieldly out of the water, though easy enough to handle when afloat. Its pole lay in the bottom along with a short-handled paddle. Lettie did not trust the currents of the river's channel with only herself to guide the thing, however, so made no move to get into it. She only put her foot with its mud-caked shoe on the low gunwale and set the boat rocking.

"Climb in," Martin Eden said behind her. "I'll be your boatman."

She turned to smile at him. "Would you?"

He gave her a small bow. "It would be my privilege."

The consummate Southern gentleman, always ready to be of service. She was charmed, as she was supposed to be. The gallantry and the coquettish response was, she had discovered, almost like a game, a kind of half-humorous ritual between a man and a woman. The more appreciative a lady was, the more gallant the gentleman became, but the sparkle in their eyes as they moved through the ancient game was, she also realized, only partly for the parody.

She stepped into the boat and moved to seat herself on the crosspiece in the prow. Martin shoved off and, as the craft glided into the water, leaped aboard.

The rocking of the boat was an inescapable reminder of another craft, another time on the river, another man. Or was it the same one? Martin did not seem to notice the sudden tautness of her face and body, but gave her a wide smile as he took up the paddle and began to pull upstream against the current.

"You're different from when you first came here, you know."

"Am I?" She forced herself to relax, though she leaned to trail her fingers in the water as an excuse not to look at him.

"Not nearly as distant or as proper."

"Dear me," she said, her tone mocking, "is that good?"

"There, you see what I mean? Not so long ago you would have pokered up and said something freezing like 'Indeed.' "

"I expect you're right, and I probably should now."

"No, no, it's too dampening. A man must have encouragement."

"Must he? Now why?"

The sun was hot on the water and so glaring she could hardly see. She was sunburned already, she was afraid, and tomorrow there would be a harvest of freckles across the bridge of her nose. She didn't really care, but sunstroke she could do without. The top of her head was blistering to the touch as she reached up to lay her hand on it.

Abandoning flirtation, Martin said, "You should have brought a hat or a parasol."

"Now you tell me."

"There's a bit of shade under that tree down there. We'll make for it."

It was a tree whose roots had been loosened so that it leaned out over the water. Martin dug in his paddle, and they were soon gliding into the dark patch. Lettie, a laugh in her voice, said, "Watch out for snakes."

"And spiders," Martin agreed, and used his paddle to brace the boat against the overhanging tree trunk, slowing and finally halting their progress. The boat thumped against the tree roots as it rocked in the current.

The sun was still hot, the water still blindingly bright, but at least the top of her head did not feel as if it might catch fire at any moment. Lettie also had had time to collect herself.

"I suppose you know," she said, "that you have left the field with Sally Anne to the colonel."

"Ward overplayed his hand at the auction. He should have known better."

"So you aren't worried? But he seems intent on making a recovery."

"He's welcome to try."

"Would you mind?"

But he was giving nothing away. "It would be most indiscreet of me to say in my present company. A gentleman doesn't talk about one lady to another."

"Who told you that, your mother?"

"A lady friend," he admitted with a wry laugh that tilted his mustache upward at the ends.

"And, anyway, you have known Sally Anne all your life and I'm a virtual stranger. I am properly chastened."

"I somehow doubt it," he said. "There are depths to you

I never expected. Tell me about this midnight ride with the Thorn."

"There's nothing to tell," she protested. "It's all a silly mistake."

"Is it? Then why are you blushing?"

It was not hard to summon indignation. "I didn't care for Mr. O'Connor's insinuations. And it's extremely hot!"

"You forget that I also saw you kissing Ranny. I don't remember, somehow, my teacher ever kissing me even when I was a boy. And Ranny is not, despite circumstances, a boy."

"It . . . was just an impulse. He can be very sweet."

"So can I," he said, "with the proper, or improper, encouragement."

He put down his paddle and eased off the seat, moving toward her, going down on one knee in the middle of the boat. He took her hand and pulled, drawing her toward him. The boat, released from its temporary mooring, began to drift downstream again.

She could have resisted, could have said something brittle and amusing or else something cold that would have stopped him. Her gaze, however, was on the glint of brown in his dark mustache. Closer she came to him, closer. There was satisfaction in his eyes, eyes that were brown, not hazel.

The mustache was real, each individual wiry hair growing from the skin. It was carefully waxed and combed and slightly curled at the corners. His lips below it were firm, ready. They touched hers.

She set her hands on his chest and gave him a hard push. He overbalanced, teetered, then went over the side with a splash that sent cascades of water in every direction and set the boat to bobbing. He went under, then surfaced thrashing and spluttering as he tread water.

"What did you do that for?" he yelled after her as the current carried her away.

"Ask your lady friend!"

"I doubt she could tell me about you!"

The implication was obvious. "Yes, and you're not much of a gentleman, either!"

He was swimming with easy strokes now. Let him swim, then; she would be damned before she would make any attempt to pick him up in the boat. She would get herself back to the bank without his help. She reached for the paddle and, regaining her seat, dug it into the water. Bending into it, using the strength of her anger, she sent the boat heading for the tree line. As she looked at it, however, she saw that they had drifted nearly back to where they had started. Ranny was there on the bank. Waiting.

When she was a few feet from the sandy shelf on which he stood, Lettie gave a last, hard pull with the paddle. The front end grounded on the sand. Ranny reached and dragged the heavy craft higher, beaching it. Without a word, he steadied it while she stood up, then put his hands on her waist and lifted her out.

Her voice was curiously subdued when she finally spoke. "Thank you."

He looked down at her, a hard light in his eyes and his hands on his hips. "Tell me something," he said. "Do you kiss all the men?"

She felt as if he had slapped her. "Good gracious, no," she cried, borrowing one of Aunt Em's exclamations though she gave it a scathing ring, "only the handsome ones!"

She gathered up her skirts and stamped away with her head high. Ransom, staring after her, knew with rueful certainty that he deserved just what he had got. It had been too tempting to use the license allowed to Ranny to say precisely what he thought. He would not do it again.

Swinging away, he shoved the boat off and leaped into it, pulling toward where Martin was splashing and cursing in the river channel.

14

The rooster was young and proud and somewhat confused. He began crowing at a little after ten o'clock in the evening and did not stop for four hours, until he was so hoarse he sounded like a creaking gate. Then he began again at five in the morning. It would not have been so bad except that he had chosen the magnolia tree not far from Lettie's bedroom window for his combination roost and perch. She endured the crowing the first night and the second. On the third night she lay listening and wincing and wondering how Aunt Em could sleep through such a racket. After two hours, Lettie could stand it no longer.

She got out of bed and put on her dressing gown, impatiently dragging the long braid of her hair from inside the collar and throwing it back over her shoulder before jerking the belt into a slip knot at the waist. She pushed her feet into her slippers and strode from the room with very little attempt to be quiet. If everyone in the house wasn't still awake, the little noise she made wasn't going to rouse them.

Halfway down the hall, her conscience pricked her and she began to tiptoe. There was no sign of Lionel outside of Ranny's door. That did not mean that Ranny was free of his headache tonight and was resting without laudanum, but rather that Lionel's father, Bradley, had been due for supper with Mama Tass. There had been some mention of him staying the night, as he had done several times in the past few weeks when he visited his mother and his son.

She eased out of the house and down the back steps. She thought longingly of a good supply of bricks to throw at the rooster, but such a thing was not to be had. There was, however, a bucket of cucumbers sitting at the door of the kitchen. These were so big and shaded with yellow that just that afternoon Mama Tass had culled them before slicing the rest for pickles. Lionel had been told to take them to the hog pen, but he had been distracted from the task by Peter, who had been dropped off to play while Sally Anne and Colonel Ward went for a drive in the cool of the evening.

It was a night of bright moonlight. Lettie could see perfectly well as she carried the bucket of cucumbers around the end of the house and let herself in at the side gate of the picket fence encircling the front yard, heading toward the magnolia tree. The rooster stopped crowing and began to cluck with a slightly worried sound as he saw her coming. Lettie set the bucket down and chose a cucumber. It was darker under the dense shade of the thick-leaved magnolia. Locating the rooster by the sound he was making, she shied the cucumber in his direction.

The missile sailed through the branches with a mighty clattering before falling with a thud to the ground. The rooster squawked and shifted his position but would not be dislodged. Lettie picked up another cucumber. The rooster had fallen absolutely silent. She thought she saw his shape against the moonlight sifting through the leaves. She drew her arm back to throw.

Something in the quietness of the rooster and of the night, or perhaps it was the faint sound of hoofbeats carried on the still night air, arrested her movements. Still holding the cucumber, she turned toward the road before the house.

She saw the light, like a red eye, of the torch first. It

came nearer, burning brighter as the sullen throb of hoof-beats became a muffled thunder. The moonlight poured down relentlessly, gleaming on the white sheets that lifted and flapped in the wind of the passage of the night riders, the Knights of the White Camellia. It caught the hoods with the holes cut for eyes, giving them the sepulchral look of apparitions from hell. That the effect was deliberate did not make it less terrifying.

Where were they going? What was their purpose?

The answer was not long in coming. The riders turned in at the drive of Splendora. They slowed to a trot as they came toward the house, swinging into single file as they passed the front gate. The torch sent showers of sparks floating back over their heads. It illuminated the band, so they could be counted off one by one to the number five. The costumed men did not stop but continued on along the track that passed around the house and led toward the old slave quarters.

Lettie watched them disappear from sight, then dropped the cucumber she held and picked up her skirts. Breathless with fear and an odd possessive anger that these men should dare to trespass on Splendora, she ran toward the corner of the house, whirled through the gate, and sped past the kitchen building along the path that also led toward the quarters.

She could see the torchlight ahead of her, floating, dancing in the air as it was carried. It was a beacon. Tripping over tufts of grass, blundering into spiderwebs wet with dew, she followed it.

It stopped in front of the cabin that belonged to Mama Tass. There came a harsh call.

"Bradley Lincoln! Come out of there!"

The men sat fanned out in front of the house with a view of the side windows. Lettie, half hidden behind a fig tree, saw a shadow at one window that she thought was

Lionel. She did not wait for more, but turned and ran back toward the main house.

She plunged along the path, heedless in the darkness, trying to be quiet, holding her skirts well above her knees with one hand while the other was clenched into a fist. Her one thought was of Aunt Em and her brisk common sense. The older woman would know what to do, would know how to stop what Lettie feared was about to happen. She could reason with the men, use her authority and the weight of her years to force them to leave the property.

A faint shadow moved at the side of the kitchen. Lettie's heart leaped with a sickening jolt. She crashed into a solid, iron-hard surface. Bonds, strong and unbreakable, closed around her. A hand clamped across her mouth. She was assailed by familiar and terrible sensations, a sense of recognition. Then a voice whispered in her ear.

"Be still. It's only me."

Ranny.

A violent shudder rippled through her. She was quiescent. She nodded. Slowly, carefully, the hand was removed. Ranny's arms loosened. He stepped back.

Lettie felt suddenly chilled, confused, as if a protective shield had been removed. She gave herself another small shake and wrapped her arms around her chest. She swallowed. Her voice so low it barely stirred the air, she said, "It's Bradley. The Knights are after him."

"I know."

"We have to get Aunt Em."

"No. You go into the house."

"What? No! We have to do something."

"I'll do it."

"You can't!"

"Don't be silly. I can." He shifted, and the moonlight caught blue gleams from the double barrels of the shotgun he held in his hand.

"You'll get hurt."

"I won't. Go into the house."

"I can't let you go alone. I'll come with you."

There was never, Ransom thought with bitter admiration, a more meddlesome, exasperating female. It was dangerous for her to see him take action as Ranny, but it was equally dangerous for him to use the strength and force of will that it would take to put her in the house where he longed for her to be. There was also scant time for persuasion, even if he could arrange reasons for it in Ranny's simple speech. Never before had his role been such a handicap.

"All right," he said without expression. "Come on, then."

Lettie longed to be able to rouse Aunt Em. She would know how to deal with Ranny as well as the situation. Or would she? She might also be flustered and distraught. In any case, there was no time. If she left Ranny and went back to the house, he would run into danger before she could return with his aunt.

What was he going to do? The question beat in Lettie's brain, turning her mouth dry and her limbs stiff as she followed him. She could not remember when she had been so apprehensive or felt so helpless. Not even when she had faced the Thorn for the first time had she been so afraid. There had been only herself at risk then. This was different.

Ranny's movements were sure and quiet and amazingly swift. He had the advantage of knowing every inch of the way, and he had as good as told her he knew what to do. Still, she had not expected such decisiveness. It was difficult to keep up with him as he circled the quarters, coming up on the back side of the delapidated cabin across the dirt lane from that of Mama Tass. It almost seemed as if he wanted to leave her behind.

They stopped in the deep shadow of a tangle of Virginia creeper and honeysuckle that had grown up into a huge old cape jasmine shrub. The jasmine was in bloom, the flowers carrying a scent so heavy that combined with the honeysuckle it was nearly overwhelming. Aunt Em would not allow the plant near the house because its scent reminded her of funerals. It surrounded them, heavy, stirring, with an undertone of death in the scent of the decaying yellow blooms still clinging among the dark green leaves.

Lettie pulled aside a dangling length of vine and looked across the way. At first she saw only moving forms and the flare of the torchlight, and, incongruously, the white gleams of the moonflower vine at the end of Mama Tass's porch. Then, as her eyes adjusted, the breath stopped in her throat. She felt Ranny grow rigid beside her.

Bradley had been dragged from the cabin and was stripped to the waist. There was a red sheen of wetness on his cheek. Mama Tass, in a long white nightgown, was kneeling in the doorway, pleading over and over with agony in her voice. Lionel hovered behind her, his eyes wide with terror but his hands knotted into fists at his sides.

The Negro man was hustled down the steps and shoved against the porch near one of the posts that supported the roof. He was pushed against the post and his hands were fastened together at the wrists. The men who had tied him stepped back. The leader of the night riders got down from the saddle with slow deliberation. He took a bullwhip, long and black and lashed at the end, from his saddle horn and began to flip it out so that it uncoiled on the ground.

The man behind the mask lifted his voice. It was neither rough nor harsh, but sounded instead cultured, tight with distaste, resigned. Vaguely familiar.

"This is in the way of a warning. It's nothing personal,

understand; we just can't have you setting yourself up as a mouthpiece of the damned carpetbaggers. You don't want to be any representative. Believe me, you don't."

The men in sheets moved back. Their leader swung the whip behind him with his hand low so that the snaking length stretched out straight along the ground. He took a deep breath, moved his shoulders to loosen his coat, and began to bring his arm up and forward in a great swing.

"That's enough."

Ranny moved out into the open, stepping into the road. He held the shotgun cradled under his arm, but his finger was on the first of the two triggers and his other hand rested under the double barrel ready to bring it up.

The leader slewed around. His voice was querulous but hard when he spoke. "Stay out of this, son."

"This man is my friend. This is my land. Get away from my friend. Get off my land."

There was a moment of utter quiet. Lettie's burning gaze clung to Ranny. The wavering glow of the torch turned his hair to red-gold silk and glazed his skin to a bronze sheen. The moonlight added a trace of silver gilding and threw his shadow like an enormous black genie before him. For an instant it was as if he were not quite of this puny world, but was rather like some ancient god of war, magnificent and terrible in his simple wrath. There could be little doubt that he would pull the trigger of the weapon in his arms. Moreover, there was a sense that he would do so without compunction, without the least regard for the consequences. It was unnerving. Horrifying.

And yet he was so vulnerable there with his damaged faculties, one against many. His understanding was such a fragile thing that he might be tricked, overpowered, beaten senseless, if not worse. The thought of it made Lettie feel sick. The pounding of her heart was so hard and suffocating that she felt as if she swayed with it where she stood. Never in her life had she been so frightened for another person. Never. Not even for Henry.

If Ranny should be struck on the site of his old injury, he might die. To think of him, with his sweet nature and gentle teasing laughter, dying on a night of such moonlit splendor was more than she could bear. To see him killed while she stood by would maim her in some way that she did not quite understand.

Lionel had gone to kneel beside his father, fumbling with his bonds while keeping one wary eye on the men who now stood with their backs to him. Mama Tass was crying, a soft wailing that had the sound of ageless anguish.

The leader took a step toward Ranny with his whip trailing in the dust at his back. "This has nothing to do with you, son. You're interfering in something you don't understand. Go on back to bed and let us deal with it. That's the best way."

"I understand. Get off my land."

"This is our lives, our families, our homes, our land we're dealing with here. Everything we ever dreamed of and worked for is being taken from us. Friend or enemy, black or white, doesn't matter. We have to take a stand."

The leader twitched the whip a little behind him, straightening it. He meant to use it, to stun Ranny or, perhaps, if he was good enough with it, to snatch the shotgun from his hands. Could Ranny see it? Did he realize?

"It matters to me," Ranny said, his gaze square on the eye slits in the sheet covering of the leader.

The man stepped forward again. He held out his free hand. "You don't want to hold a shotgun on your friends and neighbors. Give me that thing."

The other men were easing apart, getting ready to rush

Ranny when the moment came. At any moment, as soon as the leader was close enough, the lash would whip back and forward.

Lettie stepped from her hiding place. She moved out into the golden wash of moonlight, out into the road. Her head high and her arms swinging, she walked to Ranny's side. Her voice rang out, clear and carrying.

"I would take care if I were you. He is single-minded when he decides what he wants to do and very, very fast."

The leader glanced at Lettie, then looked back at Ranny. His manner was more angry, less coaxing. "Hand me that shotgun!"

Ranny lifted the weapon, centered the black holes of the gun barrels on the man's chest. There came a hair-raising double click as he pulled the hammers back. His eyes were bright in the flickering torchlight with what might have been laughter, rage, or a touch of madness as he said, "Which end?"

Not a sheeted figure stirred. Somewhere a whippoorwill called, and the ignorant rooster in the magnolia crowed as if in answer. A breath of air lifted the sheets and sent the smoke of the torch flying in a long, gray plume. The night was abruptly hot, stifling.

"I think," Lettie said, "that it might be best if you did as he told you. Carefully."

The leader made a brief gesture with his head. The others began to back away, their eyes on the gun Ranny held. They took the reins of their mounts from the man who held them as well as the torch and swung into their saddles. The leader coiled his whip with slow care, a gesture of his defeat and of his refusal to preside over a complete rout. Slipping it over his arm, he climbed onto his horse, then sat looking down.

"We won't forget this."

Ranny answered before Lettie could speak. "Don't."

They rode away. The red eye of the torch grew smaller and finally disappeared along the road. Bradley, free of his bonds, stepped toward Ranny. His face was gray under the brown of his skin and yet it was transfigured by the dawning warmth of his smile. "I won't forget it, either."

Ranny held out his hand and they hugged each other in the sudden joy of relief. Ranny gave a soft laugh. "We saved our hides again."

"One more time," Bradley agreed, "especially mine."

Ranny sent Lettie a quick look. "Miss Lettie helped."

"So she did," Bradley agreed, turning to her. "I'm grateful, believe me."

"You're welcome." If her tone was ungracious, she could not help it. She could not forget the danger this man had brought down on them all. "Why do you think they waited until you came here?"

"It's quieter, more isolated, and, so they thought, less likely to be interrupted than in town."

"You take it easily."

The black man shook his head. "It wasn't unexpected."

"Then why aren't you armed?"

His mother came bustling up, her fear turned to anger. "Because he's stupid, that's why; stupid to get mixed up in this mess, stupid to come here, stupid to let them take him out without a fight."

Bradley shook his head. "If I let them teach me their lesson, they let me go. If I kill or even injure one of them, I'm a dead man. Dead men don't become representatives."

"Representative for who, son? Them carpetbaggers? They're the enemy. Don't you see that? They don't care about you; they don't know you and don't want to know you. They just want to use you, and then they'll throw you away like a rag too used up to wash."

"I still have to try. I can't not try."

It was the same quarrel and the same haunting fears.

No one seemed to notice or care that Ranny had been drawn into it, that he had made enemies who could destroy him, enemies who could come again at any time, appearing out of the night. Lettie thought of that moment when she had been afraid he would be tricked, defeated, and an icy chill moved over her. She could not bear to stand there a moment longer being polite and calm. She had to get away.

"Excuse me," she said. "I'll see you in the morning."

Only Lionel murmured an answer as he clung to Bradley's coat and also to Ranny's hand, which he had taken as he moved to stand beside him. Lettie walked away, keeping her back stiff and straight. When she could no longer hear their voices, she increased her pace, taking long, quick strides. Faster and faster she went until she put her head down and began to run.

What she was running from, she did not know, unless it was from Ranny. Or herself. There was something wrong, terribly wrong inside her. She wanted to weep and could not, wanted to cry out with the pain of it and would not. All the old wives' tales about southern climes might be true after all, for there was something in her heart and mind that made her feel what she ought not feel, think what she should not think, want what she must not want. She thought she had conquered it, but she was wrong. It was even stronger now, possibly stronger than she was.

She had almost reached the bottom of the back steps when she heard the quick, soft footfalls. In a frenzy, she snatched up her skirts and began to leap up the wide treads. She reached the top and fled across the veranda.

She was caught just inside the dark hall. Ranny grasped her arm and whirled her around. She staggered, tripped, fell against him as her long braid whipped around to lash across his bare shoulders. His arms closed around her. She stood in the circle of his arms, her chest heaving and her breath coming in ragged gasps. She was aware with every ending of her nerves of her nakedness under her nightgown and dressing gown, of her soft curves just brushing the hard angles and planes of his body.

"What is it, Miss Lettie?"

It was the soft concern that broke her control. With a sound of anguish in her chest, she flung herself against him, going on tiptoe to clasp her arms around his neck and to press her forehead into the hollow of his collarbone. The sense of comfort and safety she felt was false, but for the moment it was enough.

Ransom held her close and felt the trembling, like the vibrating of a taut violin string, that shook her and the desperate tightness of her grasp upon him. He stroked her braided hair and murmured quietly he knew not what and cursed himself and wars and politicians. He was close, so close, to picking her up, taking her into his bed, which was so near, and letting her guess as he made love to her just who and what he was. His courage failed him, not because he feared what she would do, but because he could not stand to see her hate him.

And yet, she was a sensitive woman, his passionate prude, and he was beginning to think that her hate would be easier to bear than this tortured affection—he would not call it love—she had conceived for Ranny. He almost wished she would guess. There had been a time when he thought she had, but he had been too panicked by the idea to do anything other than to cover his tracks and bluff his way through. It had been too soon. Now, if she asked him, if she wanted to test him, he might find the strength to allow it and to give her whatever else she might possibly want of him.

He bent his head, brushing her forehead with his lips, pressing light kisses along her temple, her cheek. She lifted her chin to give him her lips, her fervor a delight and a promise that made his arms tighten involuntarily. The kiss deepened, a meshing of tongues in clash and play, a torment to strained senses, and a delight. He followed her lead, pressing as she retreated, tracing the edges of her teeth with his tongue. Entranced by her sweetness and the ravishing tenderness of her surrender, he lost touch with who he was and of his purpose. Until he tasted the salty wetness of her tears.

Gently, lingeringly, he ended the kiss, flicking the corners of her mouth, slanting a last, moist brush across the sensitive indentation of their perfect, generous bow. He sought Ranny's soft, lilting tones. Found them.

"Is there more you can teach me?"

She didn't laugh. She stared up at him, dazed, hardly aware of what he said or the hot tracks of wetness on her face. What occupied her senses, her mind, was the warm and firm pulsing of him against her in arousal. She had done this to him, had made him long for something more that he could not have. She had introduced him to the torture of desire, something not easily controlled, as she had learned to her cost. It could be she had infected him with her own malady of immoral longing, had given him something that would make it impossible for him to go on as he was, innocent, joyously childlike in his man's body. It was thoughtless and cruel of her, and quite possibly a greater threat to him than any gathering of night riders.

She must do what she could to mend matters. Her voice husky, almost breaking with the ache of tears, she said, "No. No, Ranny, there is nothing else."

"Are you mad at me?"

"How—how could I be? And are you annoyed with me anymore, as you were at the fish fry?"

"Not so long as you kiss me, too."

"I was wrong to do that. I shouldn't do it again."

"If it was wrong, nothing is right."

Sometimes he made such sense, even if what he said

was quite unanswerable. She could not think, could not reason with him now. Perhaps another time, when she was calm and had thought in advance of what must be said.

"Let me go, please. It's right that I leave you here and go to my room."

"Why did you run away?"

"I was overwrought."

"What does over—"

"Afraid. It means afraid. I didn't know how much until it was over."

"Afraid for me?"

Sometimes he was too acute. She lowered her gaze and placed her hands on his chest, pressing until he let her go. She stepped back, breathing easier. "For all of us."

"Bradley and Lionel and Mama Tass—"

"And me."

"You don't ever have to be afraid with me."

There was something in his voice that brought the return of tears, so nearly conquered, to her voice. "I know," she whispered. "I know. It would be best if you were afraid with me."

With a strangled good night, she left him. He was still standing there, a dark form against the wide moonlit square of the open doorway, when she stepped into her bedchamber and closed the door panel behind her.

15

"*I* still can't believe it! Where in the world was the Thorn when we needed him? He would have sent those Knights in their silly white sheets about their business in short order!"

Aunt Em bent to give a hard yank to a handful of pea pods in her annoyance, stripping them from the waist-high vines and casting them into the pan she carried on her broad hip. Lettie, picking peas in the next row over in the vegetable garden, was not sure what to say to mollify the older woman. Some comment appeared to be required of her, however.

"Ranny handled it well enough without him."

"Bless his heart, he did, didn't he? I'm so proud of him. I just wish he had peppered a few backsides with his shotgun. To think of those high-and-mighty Knights actually daring to ride onto our land and tamper with our people. It makes me so mad I could jump up and down and scream."

Our people. It was a term often applied to the former slaves. It had a possessive ring, and at the same time there was something protective, almost familial about it. Lettie had come to see that the slave and master relationship was more complicated than she had ever dreamed. Nor had it been dissolved, not completely, by war and freedom. For good or ill, the majority of Negro men and women of the South were still dependent for the necessities of life on their former masters. Until they could provide for themselves, they would never be really free. For the time being, they were a burden that had to be carried without hope of return. And when it was lifted, if it was ever lifted, both races might well have lost as much as they had gained.

"At least Mama Tass's son was unharmed."

Lettie shifted the pan on her hip and bent to snatch a drooping stalk of peas in the hull. It was nearly too hot to breathe. The glare of the sun was blinding and the heat reflecting up from the sandy ground caused a trickle of stinging perspiration between her breasts and along her shoulder blades. Bees hummed and wasps danced over the new blooms on the pea vines. Now and then lizards, green chameleons and also gray-blotched ones with blue throats, darted here and there. The cloth sunbonnet on her head made her feel hotter, but it at least kept the top of her head and her nose from burning.

"Yes," Aunt Em agreed, her tone grim. "I don't know where it will all end, I really don't. I don't want the Knights coming after Bradley, but on the other hand, Bradley has no business getting mixed up with the Republicans. He'll wind up getting himself killed for nothing and leave Mama Tass and Lionel grieving. He thinks the riffraff at the state capital is going to give his people what they want, when he ought to know it's something that will take time and work. The Knights think they can scare people like him when they ought to know it will just make them more set on getting their way. The Republicans think they can keep us down now that they have their heel on our necks, when they should realize that it will cause our men to rise up in righteous wrath, even if it's in secret. It's enough to make a body wonder if men ever think what they're about."

"I expect that if everyone worried too much about other people and what they need and want, nothing much would get done."

"You're probably right." Aunt Em sighed, then repeated

for the fourth time that morning, "But what I really can't understand is how I came to sleep through the excitement. I'm not that heavy a sleeper, not really."

Lettie, her voice soothing, said, "There wasn't that much noise."

"I didn't even hear the rooster that woke you up. We'll have to catch him and clip his wings. There's no other way he'll change his roost; that's the way they are, creatures of habit, like the rest of us. But," she went on in a sudden reversion to the previous topic, "you and Ranny could have waked me!"

The reasons why they had not done so were many, and Lettie had no wish to talk about them. She merely signified her agreement while keeping her head bent so that her sunbonnet hid her face as she continued to pick peas.

The colonel found them in the garden. They raised their bent backs and shielded their eyes with a hand against the sun as he rode around the end of the house and cantered down the track toward them. They were so nearly at the end of their rows that they were able to grab the last few peas and go to meet him.

"It's too hot for this kind of labor," he greeted them. "Two such lovely ladies should be lying in the shade with a book in one hand and a fan in the other."

"While the peas dry on the vine? A scandalous waste! But what brings you out in such weather?"

"If we can all go and sit on the veranda where it's cooler, I'll tell you about it."

"Just where we were heading," Aunt Em said, but though her tone was jovial, even welcoming, the look in her eyes was wary. Lettie was also less than easy. The colonel's words were pleasant enough, but his manner was more than a shade formal.

Ranny and Lionel, cutting palings at the edge of the woods to be used to repair the chicken yard, the better to pen the roosters and chickens, joined them on the veranda. Nothing was said, but it was apparent that they had seen the arrival of Thomas Ward and had come to see what was happening.

When they had all had a glass or two of cool fresh-drawn water from the well to allay the effects of the heat, they sat enjoying the vagrant breezes that crossed the veranda and talking of this and that. After a time, Aunt Em, growing impatient, brought the conversation to a head.

"I suppose you have heard about our excitement last night?"

The colonel lifted a brow in inquiry. "Can't say that I have. What took place?"

He was told in detail, with many exclamations and applications to Lettie and Ranny for corroboration. The officer was silent for long moments when Aunt Em was done, his green gaze considering. Finally he said, "I know the experience was upsetting, but it's getting to be a common occurrence. Unless you can supply the identities of the men under the sheets, I'm afraid there isn't a great deal the army can do."

"I wish I did know who they were! I'd go straight to them and give them a piece of my mind, that's what I'd do. The very idea!"

Thomas turned to Lettie. "You said they spoke of themselves as neighbors. Did you recognize any of their voices?"

She had thought that something in the voice of the leader reminded her of Samuel Tyler. It seemed so unlikely, however, that she could not say it. To bring the military down on Ranny's uncle for so small a cause would be unforgivable. "No, I'm afraid not. The sound was muffled by the sheets, you understand, and of course they didn't say a great deal."

"I suppose they didn't."

Lettie, glancing at Ranny in the chair beside her, found

him looking at her. It happened so often she was not surprised. She smiled a little, but his gaze remained closed, without expression, as if his thoughts were elsewhere. It was disconcerting.

It was also reassuring since it seemed that she and the emotions she had aroused had not taken over his attention to the exclusion of all else. He leaned back in his chair, relaxed and yet alert, with his water glass resting on his knee. His shirt clung to his broad shoulders and his hair was damp around his hairline from the perspiration of his labors. The scar at his temple seemed darker and more noticeable this morning, perhaps because the blood was nearer to the surface from the heat and his exertions.

The colonel was speaking. "Of course, if Bradley wants to file a complaint and can give us something to go on, we will be glad to look into the incident. Is he here now?"

"He left for town early, just after breakfast." Aunt Em set aside her water glass and reached to pick up the enamelware pan of peas at her side. Settling the pan in her lap, she selected a pod and began to shell it in a motion so practiced it did not distract her from what she was saying. "I somehow doubt that he will be able to tell you any more than Lettie and Ranny, or that he would if he could. What he's doing is unhealthy enough as it is, but it would be even more dangerous for him to make a complaint."

"Yes, we've run into that before."

"It's a sad situation, but there it is."

There was a brief pause. Thomas left his chair and went to lean with his shoulder against one of the square columns and his hand resting on the railing behind him. It was a position that put his back to the bright light beyond the line of the roof while they all faced it. His face was grim as he looked at them in turn, and there was about him a sudden air of authority.

"The incident last night is not why I'm here, nor is this, unfortunately, a social call."

Aunt Em's hands stilled. Ranny turned to look at the colonel with a frown between his eyes. Lettie, for no reason that she could think of, felt a sudden dread, a need to prevent the man in blue from going on even as she waited for him to do so.

"I have to tell you that yesterday evening at dusk the body of a man was found in an abandoned well some miles from here. The body was identified this morning as that of Johnny Reeden."

The handful of pea hulls that Aunt Em held, about to drop them in a bucket placed for them, fell to the floor with a soft clattering. "Oh, dearest God, no!"

"He had been dead some time," Thomas went on, "as much as two weeks, possibly more, but identification was established by his clothing and the papers found on him." He took an envelope from his pocket and opened it to remove a small object, then held it out to them. "This was discovered inside his shirt."

The thing he held in his fingers was a crushed locust shell pierced by a needle-sharp thorn. It was stained a rusty red with what could only be dried blood. Johnny's blood.

Lettie felt sick, physically ill, with the images Thomas had conjured up, with the grief and rage rising white-hot and deadly inside her. Nothing, nothing she had ever endured in her life had prepared her for the rending horror of the knowledge of how she had been used and betrayed— and of why it mattered so terribly. She could not move, could not speak or breathe for it.

"Don't," Ranny said, the word compressed as he reached out to close his hand around her fingers where she gripped the chair arm. "Don't look like that."

There was a white line around his mouth, and stark grief and pain shimmered in his eyes along with an element of confusion over his friend's death. His concern was for her, however. His clasp was firm, offering support, comfort, if she would accept them. Lettie felt a small giving sensation inside her, felt a measure of her distress recede. She turned her hand palm-upward, taking Ranny's, returning the pressure and the comfort with gratitude.

Aunt Em closed her eyes. With one hand at her throat, she said in ragged tones, "Please, Thomas, put that thing away."

The colonel returned the locust shell to its envelope without looking at them. "Forgive me if I've upset you. For the sake of past friendship, I wish that things could be different, but I have to inform you that this is an official inquiry."

"Official," Aunt Em echoed.

"There are questions concerning the object I just showed you and Johnny's death that require answers."

"I see." The older woman's face was abruptly haggard, years older. "Very well, ask what you must."

Colonel Ward gave a nod and then straightened to his full height, his bearing more military. When he spoke, his voice was neutral, without a trace of its customary warmth.

"We have, of course, talked to the victim's mother, Mrs. Reeden. According to her statement, her last communication with her son was a letter received just under three weeks ago. In this letter, now in our possession, Johnny Reeden said that he was in trouble and had been persuaded that the best thing for him to do was to go to Texas. He said that you, Mrs. Tyler, and also Miss Mason were going to help him, that you knew someone who would see that he got across the state line safely. He told his mother not to worry, that he would send for her when he was settled." Thomas Ward turned to Lettie. "The letter was dated the same day that you, Miss Mason, are said to have been seen with the Thorn."

The connection between the three of them, Johnny, the Thorn, and herself, was made with such suddenness that Lettie was caught unprepared. The formal use of her surname while it was made was doubly disturbing. What was she to say? How was she to answer without exposing the whole sordid episode? It was not only herself who would be implicated in Johnny's death. There was also Aunt Em.

She lifted her chin, her eyes dark but steady. "Are you accusing me of something, Colonel?"

Aunt Em broke in before he could reply. "I don't believe it! I don't care what you say or how you twist things around, I won't believe that the Thorn killed Johnny. There was no reason for it, not for him."

"The fact remains that he did."

"Fact? You call it a fact because of a locust? Anybody could have put that thing on Johnny when he was dead."

"Anybody?"

"Anybody who wanted to make it look as if the Thorn was guilty."

"Don't you think that's a little unreasonable?"

"Not at all. You don't know—"

It was the opening the colonel had been waiting for. "No, but I'm trying to find out."

Aunt Em licked her lips, her faded blue eyes haunted. She sent a quick look to Lettie, then her shoulders sagged. "Well, I don't suppose it matters now if it's told. It can't . . . hurt Johnny any longer."

There was complete quiet as Aunt Em, faltering now and then, told of how Johnny had confessed to getting involved with the outlaw clan, of how he had been blackmailed into carrying messages, and of how devastated he had been to discover that he had been a party to murder.

"Lettie discovered the mess he was in. He told her, too,

that the only solution to it that he knew of, was to put an end to his life. How could we not help him?"

"I don't suppose," the colonel said with irony, "that it occurred to you to send him to the sheriff or to me?"

"Certainly it did, but the same thing that caused him to become a messenger for the outlaws in the first place made that impossible. He couldn't bear for his mother to know what he had done or to have her face the public disgrace."

Lettie spoke up. "He was also positive that if he went to the authorities, the outlaws, or their contact in town, would kill him."

"He didn't mention names?"

Lettie gave a slight shake of her head. "He said it would be too dangerous for me to know."

"So you arranged with the Thorn to give Johnny safe passage to Texas. Did you never think that might be like turning him over to the hangman?"

"That's a terrible thing to say!" Aunt Em protested in indignation.

"A terrible crime has been committed."

"The Thorn didn't do it. If he said he would see him across the line into Texas, he saw him across the line. All I can suppose is that Johnny turned back for some reason and that he met some of the outlaws or even this man from town, who had figured out what he meant to do and decided to kill him for it."

"And he just happened to have a locust with a thorn handy?"

"Maybe the Thorn gave it to Johnny earlier as—as some sort of keepsake! I don't know! I only know that the Thorn couldn't have done this. It doesn't make sense."

"Unless he is either the leader of the outlaws or their contact? Or unless Reeden stumbled on to his real identity during the ride?"

"I don't believe it," Aunt Em repeated, folding her arms and rocking back in her chair.

Lettie hardly heard the older woman's stubborn answer. In her mind was the scene that night in the cabin. Johnny in his old woman's clothing, the Thorn in his. What was it Johnny had said? *"You know, the way you look as an old woman reminds me—"* He had not been allowed to finish the sentence. Had his memory been jostled by a resemblance, by some past incident that had given him an inkling of who the Thorn might be? It was possible. It was only too possible.

The colonel's voice, low and biting, broke in upon her thoughts. "You seem determined to champion the man, Mrs. Tyler. Could it be you know him personally?"

"I wish I did."

"Is that your only answer?"

Ranny had been following the interrogation with frowning concentration. Now he spoke. "Colonel, I will tell you as I told the men in sheets. This is my house. That is my Aunt Em."

Colonel Ward turned his head to stare at him, then gave a brief nod before swinging back to the older woman. "I'm sorry if I offended. I will endeavor to cut this short. It's fairly obvious, Mrs. Tyler, that if you don't know the Thorn, you at least know how to contact him. Tell me, how is it done?"

It was a question that had been inevitable from the beginning, from the moment the Thorn's name had been linked with Johnny and the two of them. There seemed to Lettie no way that the truth could be avoided, no way Aunt Em could keep from explaining about the message in the hollow tree and thereby betraying the Thorn into the hands of the Union army. But did it matter? Was there really any reason, now, to shield him?

Aunt Em had regained her self-possession and her wits

during the course of the argument, however. Now she looked squarely at the colonel and told a lie that would have her on her knees before nightfall. "It was a chance opportunity, almost an accident, one of those things that seem meant at the time. Who's to say it wasn't?"

"Meaning?"

"The ways of the Lord are mysterious."

"You know very well what I am asking," the colonel said, his face flushed. "If you think you are aiding in some heroic cause by protecting this man, you are making a serious mistake. For every good deed he has done, there has been an evil one that wipes it out, and then some."

"It was the purest coincidence, I tell you. Wasn't it, Lettie?"

It was an appeal she could not refuse. Lettie could not brand Aunt Em a liar at this moment, even if she regretted it later.

"So it was. I happened upon him coming from Dink's Pond one evening. I heard no dogs, but I suppose he was being careful to confuse his trail. I believe it was you, Colonel, who told me he used it now and again for that purpose?"

"A second chance meeting?"

For a moment she thought the colonel might know more than he was saying, then she remembered. The visit to her bedchamber on the night of her arrival. "Strange, isn't it?"

Her flat, unemotional tone seemed to disconcert him for a moment. Only for a moment. "I thought you were convinced the man killed your brother? What changed your mind?"

What, indeed? She wished she knew. "I was persuaded otherwise for a short time. I see now it was, as you said, a serious mistake."

Lettie was trembling. Ransom could feel it in her tight grip upon his hand. He was afraid for her, afraid as he had never been in his life. It was peculiar to be forced to sit and listen with scant intervention while his fate was decided, but he could summon little interest. His concern was for Johnny's death, Johnny whom he had sent, laughing, on his way across the state line, and for the woman at his side. Lettie's restraint disturbed him as much as it surprised him. He had sat waiting for her bitter denunciation of the Thorn, for her to give her fullest cooperation to the Union commander by exposing the location of the message tree. That she had done neither affected him with an odd jubilant disquiet. He would give all he owned, all he was or ever hoped to be, to know what she was thinking, what she felt, what her trembling meant.

Weak. She had been morally, mentally, physically weak. She had permitted liberties, had given herself, to a murderer. She could not blame the climate, the circumstances, or even the Thorn. There was no one to blame except herself. She was debased beyond saving, a pitiful creature enslaved to a sensual nature.

Oh, but how was it possible that the man who had held her, had joined with her in such rapture, could be a cold-hearted killer? It could not be.

He had come to her with blood on his hands. What an exciting chase it must have been for him, to run her down on the ferry and take her in payment for saving Johnny, knowing all the while that it was Johnny's life that was forfeit. Her murderous lover.

Still, he had been so tender, so exquisitely gentle in his strength, so loving.

Tender and cruel. Gentle and savage. Good and evil.

There had to be some explanation. Perhaps there were two of them? Two night riders claiming to be the Thorn?

She was looking for excuses for the sake of her conscience. There were no excuses, just as there was only one Thorn.

Aunt Em was so sure he was innocent.

She was a wonderful woman, but deluded. As deluded as Lettie herself had been to believe in a chivalric righter of wrongs. That was only in legends, lovely old tales of knights and honor and great deeds carried out against impossible odds. If such things had ever taken place, they did so no longer. Men only acted when they were forced to do so to save themselves, or when there was something they hoped to gain, such as a woman's favors.

"All I've done, all I'm trying to do, is to see that as few people as possible are hurt—"

Words. Empty words.

Ranny was pressing her hand, a warning to recall her attention. Aunt Em was standing. The colonel, it seemed, was preparing to go, for he had his hat in his hand. Lettie, summoning at least the appearance of composure, allowed Ranny to pull her to her feet. With his hand under her elbow, she moved to the top of the steps as the Union commander trod down them.

He turned at the bottom. "Oh, yes. There is one other thing. The funeral will be this afternoon; where and when I don't know, but I expect the notices will be up in an hour or so, if they aren't already. I'm sure you will all want to attend."

The funeral notices were tacked on posts and on trees here and there in Natchitoches and for some distance out of town on either side. The black-bordered placards, printed with the proper sentiment under a design of a weeping willow and lettered by hand with the time and place, were already curling in the heat when the party from Splendora drove past them later in the day. The service for Johnny would be held at a small church in the country south of town.

Aunt Em had taken food to Mrs. Reeden's house as was the custom, driving there with it the instant it was prepared, well before the noon meal. She had returned a short time later. Her face was pale and her eyes were red from weeping. Johnny's mother was prostrate, she said, and seeing no one.

The church of white clapboard sat beside a winding, back-country road. Its narrow width and steep roof gave it the same look as a thousand such churches from New Hampshire to Texas, though the shingles were of cypress that could only have come from the swamps of Louisiana. The congregation was Methodist, the preacher a tall, lanky man with arms too long for his sleeves and a prominent Adam's apple. He made one of a quartet of men who sang a Wesley hymn, then moved to stand in the simple pulpit looking down on the flower-covered wooden coffin before him.

The congregation fanned themselves, enduring, since they could not change it, the heat caused by the hot day and the press of bodies in the small church. The air was thick with the smell of overwarm humanity, good clothes brought out of the back of armoires, hymn books, and varnished walls—all of it overpowered by the heavy, cloying scents of the wilting cape jasmine and honeysuckle that had been massed around the coffin to overcome the faint but unmistakable odor of death.

The preacher, mopping his face with his handkerchief, which he sometimes held to his nose, did not give a long eulogy. He finished his remarks, gulped for air, then motioned the pallbearers forward. They carried the coffin on their shoulders out the front doors and into the churchyard.

A grave had been dug beside a row of graves that was each marked with a rust-colored iron rock tombstone. They set the coffin down beside it.

Johnny's mother, moaning, barely able to walk so she had to be supported on both sides, followed the coffin to the graveside with other relatives. A chair was brought for her and she collapsed into it. The people gathered around, shuffling their feet, clearing their throats. Here and there a woman sniffed and held her head up to keep from crying. Beside Lettie, Aunt Em was blotting unembarrassed tears. Not far away stood Martin Eden, with his hat under his arm and his gaze straight ahead. Beyond him, on the edge of the crowd, was Colonel Ward, with Sally Anne and her family nearby.

The pallbearers stepped back from their task and stood shoulder to shoulder, their heads bent under the blistering sun, their hands clasped behind their backs. The preacher stooped and replaced flowers that had fallen off the coffin as it was set down. Then he took his Bible from under his arms and began to read.

" 'To every thing there is a season, and a time to every purpose under the heaven. . . .' "

Lettie allowed her gaze and her mind to wander. Scattered here and there in the graveyard were other graves marked with iron rock, some even piled with it. There were many, however, of engraved marble. In the corner was one grave with a tall monument that was covered by a small wooden structure and surrounded by an iron fence, like a dwelling for the dead. Cedars were planted here and there, along with cape jasmines and roses and evergreen periwinkle. Most of the graves were scraped clean of grass, but a few were overgrown. On nearly all of them was a vase of some kind—some expensive, some cheap—filled with the stems of dead and blackened flowers.

Her attention was drawn back to the grave. Ranny was

one of the pallbearers. He stood staring at the ground, the sun striking golden gleams in his hair, his face flushed with what might be heat from his black suit and his exertion, but was more likely emotion. Johnny had been his friend, perhaps his only real friend.

The preacher concluded his reading, said an amen that was echoed with deep voices among those standing around the grave, then closed his Bible. He moved toward the bereaved mother, bending to console her. The brief, simple ceremony was over.

Almost. Ranny took a harmonica from his pocket. Looking neither to the right nor left, asking no one's permission, and needing none, he cupped it in his hands and lifted it to his lips. He took a deep breath, let it out, took another. He began to play.

The pure, mournful sound rose, each note carefully, perfectly drawn, floating gently on the warm air. The clear, sweet melody spoke of friendship and laughter and camaraderie, of battles and long marches and lonely campgrounds. It spoke of Johnny, with his red hair and freckles and love of life, his wide grin and quick, barbless wit, his tact and ready understanding. Wordless, unspeakably poignant, it was a tribute, a requiem, and a cry of grief.

Listening, Lettie thought of Johnny with trouble on his face, trouble that had turned to relief and to trust. They had failed him, she and Aunt Em. She had led him to his death, given him over to his killer. She had been one of the last people to see him alive. He had said to her, "I don't guess I'll be seeing you again." And he hadn't.

The last clear notes of the harmonica died away. Johnny's mother was sobbing. The other women wiped their eyes. Men blew their noses and looked around to see if anyone had noticed. One or two went up to Ranny and shook his hand. The rest began to move away slowly, pausing in groups of three or four to talk in subdued voices.

Mrs. Reeden was surrounded and taken to where a buggy sat at the nearest edge of the graveyard. Aunt Em went to speak to Sally Anne and her family, and they began to move back toward the church and their own buggy that waited beyond.

Lettie stood still, her gaze on the coffin heaped with flowers. Johnny was dead, and she had helped to kill him. And if that was not enough, she was protecting the man who had murdered him by her silence. She could make excuses, could say she was doing it for Aunt Em, but the truth could not be denied. The same weakness of the spirit and the flesh that had allowed her to give herself to the Thorn was preventing her from turning him over to the justice he deserved.

She was depraved. She had known that as she watched Ranny and heard him play for his friend. He was so simple and good. What she was doing to him was wrong, so wrong. It would be better for everyone if she went away.

She would go back to Boston where she knew what was expected of her, what was permitted and what would be scorned. She would go now, while it was still possible that she might regain a sense of who and what she was and what she must do with the rest of her blighted life. But first there was something she must do if she was ever going to be able to regain her self-respect, something she should have done weeks before when it would have served a worthwhile purpose, that of saving a life.

To her shame, she did not want to do it, even now. To her shame. The tears welling in her eyes threaded through her lashes and tracked slowly down her face.

A resolve, once taken, should be carried through as soon as possible. So Lettie had been taught, and so she did. When she and the others returned to Splendora, she went to her room, took off her hat and gloves and put them away, then sat down at the table where she wrote her letters. She drew paper toward her, unstoppered the ink, dipped her pen, and began at once to write.

The pen nib made a scratching sound that was loud in the quiet of her room. The smell of the ink was bracing. She did not pause to think; what was the need? She had composed what she must say on the drive back from the funeral, in the long twilight hours on the veranda, during the empty hours of the night, over and over again, waking and sleeping, for weeks.

The sense of finally doing something that was right sustained her until the last line was written and she had signed her name. A teardrop—where had it come from?—dropped on the page. She reached quickly for the blotter and held it on the drop until it was absorbed. The word where it had fallen was blurred. Let it go; she could not bear to write it out again.

She folded the paper with care and set it aside. Taking another sheet and positioning it in front of her, she dipped her pen again. She sat with the nib poised and ready. No words came. She put her pen down and put the paper away. It would be just as well if she delivered this message in person. She would do it in the morning, early.

The sun had gone down and shadows were gathering in the room. It was the blue hour of dusk when the summer heat began to loosen its iron grip. Through her open windows she could hear the murmur of voices from the veranda where Ranny and Aunt Em were sitting to catch the stir of the evening breeze. Somewhere in the fields behind the house a pair of doves were calling. The sound was plaintive, nearly despairing.

Lettie picked up the folded letter. She pushed back her chair and moved toward the door. She passed the dressing table and for a moment her reflection slid across the mirror above it. She paused, startled. Pale and composed and tight-lipped, her hair drawn back and severe, her mirrored image might have been that of her own grandmother, as in her picture that hung in the stairwell of the house in Boston. Swinging away, Lettie went quickly out of the room.

The smell of chicken roasting with garlic and onions and other herbs hung in the backyard near the kitchen. Mama Tass could be heard rattling silver and shaking pots on the stove. It would not be long before dinner was announced. She would have to hurry.

The sky in the west was shaded with lavender and gold. The colors had dyed the glassy surface of Dink's Pond. The water, smelling faintly of fish and decaying vegetation, appeared placid. It was deceiving. Insects skated across it or hovered, nervously dancing, above it. There was a plopping sound and a small wave now and then as a feeding fish broke the surface. A slight roiling at the edge was the activity of young frogs and fingerlings. The arrow shape in the water was the track of a snake. The upright form in the shadows was a blue heron standing motionless on one leg, waiting for its supper.

Wherever there was life, death waited. It could not be avoided. But no man had the right to beckon it forward for another. No man.

There was the hollow tree. Lettie put the letter inside it and withdrew her hand.

Pain assailed her, settling in her chest. The Thorn would come and stand here where she stood now. He would put his hand inside and take her letter, touching the paper she had held. He would read it, and perhaps he would smile.

She put her hand out to the tree for support, leaning her forehead against the living wood. She had known it would be hard, but not this hard.

Betrayal.

He had betrayed her. He had taken her body and her

spirit and changed them in some strange manner so that she hardly knew herself. He had awakened those primitive responses that lie dormant inside most civilized human beings. Helped by this damp and warm land where life was so abundant, helped even by Ranny, he had turned her into the kind of harlot who could love a murderer.

Love.

It did not seem possible. She hardly knew him. He came and went in a hundred disguises, a hundred moods, none of them ever quite the same. But he had touched her and held her and kept her from the storm, and there was in the taste and feel and sight of him something that her mind and body craved, something beyond desire, something that had no other word to encompass its meaning except love.

If she did not love him, why did his betrayal cause such anguish? Why did she feel as if in betraying him she was destroying herself?

She could not stand there forever. It was growing dark and she would be missed. She preferred that Aunt Em and Ranny not know what she had done, not while they could stop it. They would have to know when it was over, of course; there was no help for it. They would think that she had betrayed them, too. She was sorry about that, desperately sorry.

It could not be helped. The decision, the only one possible, was made. Now all she had to do was live with it. If she could.

She straightened, turned. Picking up her skirts, she walked back toward Splendora.

Ransom stepped out of the willows on the far side of the pond. He stood staring after Lettie with narrowed eyes and his hands resting on his hips. When she was out of sight, he began to make his way toward the hollow tree.

16

One twilight was very like another. The sun went down, the light faded, night came. It had been happening for thousands of years and would happen for thousands more. The only difference in this one from all those these many weeks past, or indeed from the evening before when Lettie had left her note in the tree, was that there was a wind blowing from the southwest. Hot, dry, and fitful, it rustled the leaves on the trees until they clashed like small paper cymbals and sent the dust from the road fogging through the house. She blamed her headache on it.

Lettie and Aunt Em sat in the hallway after dinner. Lettie pretended to read while Aunt Em stitched a pillow-case, replacing a lace edge that had come loose in washing, and made desultory conversation. Ranny and Lionel were out back in the kitchen with Mama Tass, who had decided to bake bread and tea cakes sweetened with molasses while it was as cool as it could possibly be in late July. They were to have the tea cakes, when they were done, with milk that had been cooled in a bucket lowered in the well.

"I talked to Peter while I was over at Elm Grove this morning. It seems he is reconciled to having a Yankee for a father. Thomas has promised him a pony cart and a pony to pull it. It's wrong to try to buy the boy's affections, but I suppose all's fair in love and war. Who would have thought a soldier would have the means to do all he's done? Not that it signifies. There must have been a lot of men in uniform these last few years who would never have taken up the sword except to protect what they own."

"On both sides, I'm sure," Lettie said.

"Sally Anne is still cool toward him, but at least she talks to him. I'm not sure whether she's keeping him at a distance because she doesn't care for him or from sheer pigheaded pride. Things will be in a pretty mess when all's said and done if she refuses him, but he got himself into it. In the meantime, Elm Grove is protected from the tax collector or anyone else who might want to take over the place. That's a terrible way to look at it, but it's true."

"A practical way, rather."

"Yes, we have to be practical." Aunt Em knotted her thread and held up the pillowcase to look at it. "Sally Anne was upset. It seems Angelique, Marie Voisin's friend, has received what I can only describe as an indecent offer. Some man has had the nerve to ask her to go to New Orleans with him and become his mistress. If she wanted to be practical, she would accept."

"Because she is of mixed blood?" Lettie's voice was sharper than she had intended.

"What else is there for her? There's no suitable man for her among the *gens de couleur libre*, she has too much breeding and education to marry a freedman even if she would consider it, and there is no longer the huge dowry that might have persuaded a white man to accept her as a wife."

"But a mistress!"

"Such women are given a certain respect in New Orleans. They have a house of their own, horses, a carriage. The arrangement can, and often does, last for years, sometimes until the man marries, sometimes for life. Any children are educated and provided for by the father. Somewhere below a wife but much above a woman of the streets, it isn't a bad life."

"Possibly not, for the man."

"I can't help wondering who made her the offer. O'Connor was taken with her. I hope she won't trust herself to him if that's who it was. He may have heard about such arrangements, but I'll be bound he doesn't understand how they work. He's likely to keep her for a month or two, then that'll be the end of it. But I haven't heard anything about him moving to New Orleans."

Lettie made a sound that could be taken for interest. She wished the other woman would stop talking. All she wanted to do was to sit quietly and wait for the hour when she could pretend to go to bed, the hour when she must keep her appointment.

A large, pale green lunar moth came fluttering in at the door. It circled, hesitating as if testing its welcome, then flew straight toward the lamp. Lettie reached to bat it away from the lamp chimney and the scorching flame inside. The moth caught and clung to her hand, its swallowtail quivering. She sat staring at it, intrigued and repelled and oddly touched by its confidence in her. It could not know she was not to be trusted.

"Speaking of moving, they say Mrs. Reeden is going to live with relatives in Monroe. She can't bear to stay where her son was killed, or so the story goes. It's the scandal she can't bear. But there, I shouldn't say such things. We all have our burdens and carry them as best we can."

"I suppose we do." The moth, alarmed by her voice, lifted in the air and flew away. Lettie watched it circle and land on the gilded frame of a picture.

"Goodness, but you're pale, my dear. I hope you aren't sickening for something. You've been very healthy, but newcomers are often ill until they get used to the heat. Maybe I should have been giving you sassafras tea. The old folks swear by it as a blood thinner and purifier."

"I just have a little headache."

"Would you like some of Ranny's laudanum? I'll be glad to get it for you. I know how it is. I don't get a headache often, but when I do it's a dandy."

"No, no, I'll be fine." Laudanum would put her to sleep. That was the last thing she wanted. "Here is Ranny with the tea cakes. Maybe that's what I need."

The evening passed, the minutes and hours going faster and faster until finally the clock in the parlor struck eleven and it was time to go. Lettie slipped from the dark house by way of her jib window. Her stockinged feet made no sound on the veranda floor or the steps. When she reached the ground, she stopped to put on her riding boots, then went quickly through the gate and along the drive to where the colonel waited. She mounted the horse he had brought for her with the aid of a leg-up, then gathered the reins in her hands.

Even then she could have stayed behind. There was no need for her to go. Her visit to the colonel that morning was enough. He and his men could have done the rest.

She could not let them. She was compelled to see what would happen. It was her duty, she told herself. She had begun this thing and must see it through. For Henry and for all the other people who had died, she must see the Thorn captured once and for all.

But there was more to it than that. She wanted to know, needed to know, who the man was who had tricked and deceived her, used her and taught her to love. She could not stand not knowing another hour, another day. Her curiosity was like an illness festering inside her. It gave her no surcease, would allow her no peace until she learned his identity and where he lived and how.

And still that was not all. As at the death of some favored dream, she felt the need to hold a vigil. She had allowed herself to think for a time, against all odds, that there might be a man who risked his life so that others might live, who held his principles strong and untarnished, who fought against what was wrong not because he had anything to gain or lose but because he knew it wasn't right. The demise of a hero deserved a mourner or two.

But more than these things, she had to be there because she had to face him. It was necessary for her to see him as a man, only a man. She wanted him to be angry, to curse her as he was put into bonds. She wanted to see him made small so that he would resume his normal size in her mind, so that she could see him as the calculating killer she knew him to be. She wanted proof, justification, a consciousness of being right so that the nagging doubts in her mind would be resolved, so that she could sue for peace with her soul.

Finally, she wanted to be there for Henry in order to be true, at last, to his memory. She wanted to know that the man she had helped to entrap was her brother's murderer, that she had brought about what she had come so far to do. She wanted reassurance that she had kept faith with Henry so that she could leave this place and never return.

Reasons and more reasons, but in the end it was a small thing really that she required. She just wanted to see him. And she felt she owed it to him to see him alone, for the sake of past consideration.

Lettie and the colonel made good time. Thirty minutes before the hour set for the meeting, they were within a mile of it. The colonel's men had been deployed well before dark in case the Thorn should take the time to watch the place before he came in. There was no reason to suspect that he might fear a trap, still, it was best to be prepared. The colonel drew rein, and Lettie pulled up beside him.

"Are you sure you want to meet him alone?" he asked.

"I'm sure."

"I'll warn you again, it may be dangerous if he decides to shoot it out."

"I appreciate your concern."

"I want your word that at the first sign of trouble you will drop to the floor and stay there."

"I'll do that."

"My men and I will never be far away. It will be over before you know it."

"Please don't worry about me."

He swore. "How can I not? I shouldn't let you do this. I'd order you to stand back and let us take care of it if I thought it would do any good. You know that if anything happens to you, Sally Anne will never forgive me."

"That is, of course, something for me to worry about," she said with wry humor.

"Oh, the devil, you know what I mean!"

"I do know, and I promise you I'll be all right."

"See that you keep that promise."

She rode on without him, leaving him to reach the rendezvous by a more circuitous route.

The night was moonless and dusty. The wind with the breath of the Texas plains in it dried out her face so that the skin felt tight and stretched. It also made her horse skittish. Or it might have been her own edginess affecting her mount. She was not without a certain apprehension. In fact, her nerves were tied in knots. It wasn't her safety that troubled her, however, but rather this terrible need to be assured that she had done the right thing.

She thought the colonel, from the way he had looked at her, suspected her of setting this trap for revenge. He could not know all the reasons she might have for doing that. Weren't the deaths of two men, her brother and Johnny, enough?

Still, he was wrong. Or was he? She felt no need to

gloat over the Thorn, and yet remnants of her anger lingered. It was her own weakness that enraged her most. To see the man laid by the heels might assuage it, it very well might, but it was not her main object. Her motive was much more complicated than that.

Was it really?

She had told herself a great many things, marshaled reasons by the score, but in the end she thought that what she wanted most of all was to hear what the Thorn would have to say in his defense. If there was anything he could say.

The turning that led to the corncrib lay before her. The woods around it were quiet, so quiet. The colonel's men were well hidden; she saw not a sign of them. The track was narrow and overreached by the rampant new growth of the summer. The briers of vines tugged at her poplin skirts, and the tassels of some blooming grass sent out floating bits of fluff that tickled her nose as she passed.

The low corn crib was a dark shape more sagging and forlorn than when she had seen it last, and the lean-to seemed lower and more ramshackle. She unhooked her knee from the side horn and slid to the ground, then stood holding to the stirrup while she stamped the prickles of cramp from her legs.

She stared about her in the darkness. This was where the Thorn had spent the night when she had forced him at gunpoint out of the corncrib into the inclement weather. He must have huddled against the wall over there, away from the dripping rain. It was a wonder he had not crept back inside and disarmed her while she slept. She had never thought of that.

And there was no point in thinking of it now. Holding one hand before her, she felt in the darkness for a post and tied up the horse. The animal pushed at her with his head, as if wondering where his oats were, and she stood for a moment holding the bridle, rubbing her hand over his nose. She gave him a last pat and turned toward the corncrib.

The door creaked as she pulled it open. The familiar smell of cornhusks and mice and dust assailed her, bringing memories she would just as soon forget. She had a sudden impulse to slam the door and run, run and never stop running until she reached the outskirts of Boston.

It wouldn't do. She must finish what she had begun. She owed it to Johnny. It was here that she had stood talking and joking with him while they waited for the Thorn to come to take him to Texas. Here that they had first seen that caricature of an old woman, that deadly old woman.

If she concentrated on those things, she might hold those other memories at bay, the ones she had tried so hard to wipe from her mind.

It could not be done.

She should have set this meeting for somewhere, any-where, else. Inside the crib, she leaned against the wall and closed her eyes, fighting to keep her mind blank. Still, they crowded in on her, the memories. The unbelievable cataclysm of desire she had shared with a murderous stranger. The wonders of touch. The magic of joined bodies. That odd sense of recognition, not of his identity, but of something inside him that made him seem a familiar soul. These things were imprinted on her mind and heart beyond forgetting. There was only one thing that could remove them, and that was death.

The time was drawing near.

Almost, she wished he would not come. She would have done her duty but would be relieved of this terrible weight of responsibility.

Oh, but to spend the rest of her life not knowing? That, too, would be intolerable.

Hoofbeats.

They were no more than a distant drumming, fading and growing louder with the wind. A shiver ran through her. She clasped her hands together. She thought that Thomas wanted the Thorn alive for questioning, but she had not thought to ask. Why had she not asked?

Hoofbeats.

Louder, thudding with an irregular rhythm. Suppose they shot him on sight, before there was a chance to see him, to speak to him?

Hoofbeats.

He was coming fast. Was he anxious to see her, or was he angry that she had summoned him again? What was he thinking as he rode? Was he noticing the stillness, the lack of night sounds?

Hoofbeats.

A steady thunder. Could she stop this thing if she wanted to? If she ran screaming out into the night, would he turn and fly or would he ride in to discover what was wrong?

Hoofbeats.

Soon. She was such a fool to not know her own mind, to have any compunction for the capture of such a vicious man.

Hoofbeats, slowing, jogging down the track. Nearer. Nearer.

She didn't want to know. She didn't. She was afraid. There was something that nagged at her, some warning unheeded, some knowledge buried deep.

A bit jingled. Saddle leather creaked. A horse made a soft, snuffling sound and another whickered in response. The door made a scraping sound. It swung open.

His tall form was outlined against the gray darkness, broad of shoulder, easy of stance, a hat tipped at a slight angle on his head. He stood for a moment, letting his eyes adjust to the darkness. He took a step forward. When he spoke, his voice was soft, faintly curious.

"Miss Lettie?"

She came erect, and the rush of the blood in her veins was like poison with the fear that gripped her. "Ranny? What are you doing here? Go away! Now!"

The night erupted with the figures of men shouting and cursing as they ran. The door crashed against the wall as it was flung back on its hinges. Four soldiers threw themselves on Ranny while two others whirled inside, then stood back with their rifles trained on the struggling, thrashing group. There came the thud of blows, the grunts of effort.

Lettie, recovering from her frozen consternation, plunged forward. She caught a uniformed arm, pulling, clawing. "Stop it! Stop! It's the wrong man! You have the wrong man!"

She was jerked this way and that, tripping over her skirts. The blow came out of the darkness. It caught her on the shoulder. She staggered, reeling, and fell against the wall.

An order rang out. The night was full of men and the bristling barrels of rifles. A lantern flared, its light blinding, virulent in its brightness.

The fight was over.

Ranny was hatless, his arms twisted behind his back and his legs wide apart. There was a trickle of blood at the corner of his mouth and his golden-blond hair was sliding into his eyes as he stood with his head down trying to catch his breath. Slowly he squared his shoulders, lifted his head. His gaze found Lettie, resting on her as she pushed into a sitting position on the floor.

He met her eyes. Slowly he moved his head from side to side. "Oh, Miss Lettie, what have you done?"

The men were pushed aside as Thomas Ward stepped

into the crib. "Lettie," he exclaimed as he saw her on the floor. He moved toward her with long strides. "Are you all right?"

She gave him her hands and he pulled her to her feet. "Thomas, make them let him go. It's Ranny."

The colonel barely glanced at his prisoner. "I would let him go if I could, but there has to be an investigation."

"What are you talking about? This is Ranny!"

"This is the man who found the letter you left in the tree, Lettie."

She stared at him in confusion and feverish disbelief. What he said might be true, but there had to be some other explanation, there had to be. She turned to Ranny. "Tell Thomas why you came here. Tell him how you knew to come."

"I came because I found the letter," Ranny said obligingly.

"Yes, but how? How did you find it?"

"I saw you go. I followed you. We put a letter in the tree one time before."

Lettie swung around to Thomas. "You see! He was with me the first time I used the hollow tree to contact the Thorn. That's all there is to it!"

"I'm not so sure. For my part, it all fits a little too well. I'll have to take him in."

She put out her hand to clutch his arm. "Thomas, no. Please!"

He removed her hand from his sleeve. His voice was firm when he spoke. "It's a matter of duty, Lettie, however unpleasant. I have to do it."

Ransom watched Lettie. It was almost worth the drubbing he had taken to hear her plead for him. He would like to hear her do a great deal more pleading, though not to Thomas Ward and not for Ranny.

It was no use blaming her, however. He had known how

disturbed she was, known also that she was his weakness. Still, most women would have thought it necessary to demand an explanation for Johnny's death, to throw his failure to save him in his face and threaten to expose him. That was what he had expected tonight. He had given too much weight to the physical rapport between them and not enough to her conscience. But he had meant to end the farce he had been playing with her. He had come as Ranny because it seemed the best way to do it. He had actually been looking forward to dropping the mask he had worn for so many years, to revealing his true self. It seemed he must wear it a little longer, as long as it would serve.

The colonel snapped an order. Ranny was hauled around and marched out the door. The soldiers guarding him swung around smartly and followed him. Thomas, with his hand under Lettie's arm, gave her no choice except to do the same.

The horses were brought up, including Lettie's mount from the lean-to. In a short time, they were all in the saddle. Thomas walked his horse to where Lettie sat in the darkness and touched his hat brim.

"Are you sure you weren't hurt just now?"

"No." Her voice was cold.

"Good. Good. I would hate for any harm to have come to you over this."

"I'm perfectly fine."

"I don't think I need to tell you again how much the United States Army appreciates your cooperation."

"No. I know it very well."

He brought his hand down on his leg in exasperation. "Hang it all, Lettie, I'm only doing my job!"

"I realize that. It's extremely important that you not let such a desperate and dangerous man, such a ferocious killer, ride free about the countryside."

"He could be all of those things."

"A man who can't bear to stick a pin in a butterfly?"

"Be reasonable! I have to look into it."

"Certainly."

"Think about it, Lettie. He was a soldier, a daredevil, an actor in theatricals."

" 'Was' is the right word."

"Dink's Pond is near his house. The Thorn came at least once to Splendora itself; you saw him there!"

"Look at him!" she cried. "He could be taken for the angel Gabriel."

"Gabriel carries a sword."

"The Thorn doesn't, and he isn't the Thorn!"

"You should know, of course, since you've seen the man. Or is it just that having seen him now without his disguise you've changed your mind?"

"Why are you so determined that he's the Thorn? Is there a promotion for you if you catch him?"

Thomas straightened in the saddle, gathering up his reins. His tone was cutting when he answered. "I hope that by the time I talk to you in the morning you will be in a more reasonable frame of mind. In the meantime, I will detail a man to see you home."

He was leaving. With his prisoner. Lettie put out her hand in haste to touch his arm. "I'm sorry for what I said. Please remember the hospitality of Splendora that you and your men have enjoyed. Remember, and be kind."

The detail moved out. Lettie followed with her escort at a slower pace. At the Red River crossing at Grand Ecore, she had to wait for the ferry to return for her after taking the last of the detail over. By the time she reached the other side, the soldiers and their prisoner had disappeared in the direction of Natchitoches.

Her escort left her at the gate of Splendora. She opened it and moved along the path and up the steps. She paused for a long moment on the gallery, breathing the scented air. Nowhere else, she thought, smelled like Splendora.

The wind had died. There was only a singing silence. She could feel it all around her, that Southern summer night. But the house looming over her felt empty.

Think, Lettie.

She would not. Ranny had passed his test. He had been here at Splendora when he said he had a headache. There was no other time when he could have done all the things of which the Thorn was accused.

He had not been in bed. He was outside on the veranda, so he said, but he might have heard her in his room before he left and returned to confront her.

He had been injured long before there was a need for the Thorn to fight the changes brought about by Reconstruction.

But he had been in prison for a long time, and after he returned home he had been ill for months more. He might have regained his senses in time to have a reason for failing to make it known.

She had been with him for weeks, talked to him, taught him, with no sign that he might be other than a brain-injured man.

Perhaps he had been damaged for a time so that he knew the signs. Or perhaps there had been others in the Washington hospital where he had been treated so that he learned them.

He was so gentle, so loving. Surely that could not be counterfeited?

He was the right size.

So were any number of others, including Martin Eden and Thomas Ward.

His eyes were the right color.

Or were they? It was difficult to tell. Ranny's still seemed just a little bluer. Besides, the two voices were so different, and that was something not easy to disguise.

Those amateur theatricals. Perhaps there was some actor's trick?

Aunt Em was too honest, too forthright, and possibly too garrulous to keep up such a masquerade for so long, and how could so important a development as Ranny's recovery of his faculties be kept from her?

A man daring enough to begin the subterfuge could find a way.

The Thorn had made love to her. Surely there would have been some response within herself to that fact when Ranny had touched her?

That feeling of longing and depravity. Oh, God.

But if Ranny was the Thorn, then he was a killer. A man who could murder his best friend, then cry over the news when it came; a man who could throw that friend's body down a well as if it were a broken toy, then play a sweet and mournful dirge over his grave.

No.

If Ranny was the Thorn, then he was no killer.

The Thorn was a killer.

Then Ranny was not the Thorn.

Unless . . .

Unless he was not himself when he killed? Unless the injury to his brain had been such that it had caused some form of madness?

There was a terrible sense of rightness to that possibility. If Ranny did not know he was committing the crimes, then in the light of day he would seem no different. Perhaps there was something, some kind of violence or danger, that triggered the instinct to kill. There had been something about him that had disturbed her when he had interrupted the fight between Thomas and Martin and also on the night when the Knights came.

But how did that fit in with the avenging Thorn who set out at night to redress the injustices of the countryside, who spouted Latin and evaded the best efforts of the sheriff and the military? Surely any man who could do that for the better part of two years could not be mad?

It was she who was insane, or who would become so if she did not end this uncertainty.

She was so weary, the result not only of the tension and upsets of the evening but of weeks of fitful rest. She would like to go straight to her room, climb into bed, and pull the sheet over her head. She could not be so callous or so cowardly, however. There was an unpleasant duty that she must perform. What the outcome would be, she did not know, but it could not be avoided.

Her footsteps slow and heavy, she walked into the house. In the hallway sitting room, she fumbled with matches to light a lamp. When it was burning, she picked it up and went along the hall to the door of Aunt Em's bedchamber. She paused for a moment with her head bowed, then, lifting her chin with resolution, she raised her hand and knocked.

17

"Nothing worse'n a viper in the bosom, that's what I say. She-snakes are the worst of all, and as for Yankee she-snakes . . ."

It was Mama Tass who spoke, muttering as she brought a coffee tray and set it down on the table on the back veranda. There was venom in her eyes when she looked at Lettie, and her lower lip was thrust out in a manner that was belligerent as well as sullen.

"I'm sorry," Lettie said, for what seemed like at least the one hundredth time. "I didn't mean for Ranny to be caught."

"Sorry don't butter no bread. I say—"

"Please, Mama Tass!" Aunt Em said, rubbing a hand over her face.

The cook clamped her lips together. With her head high, her back stiff with anger and hurt feelings, and her wide hips rolling like the sea in a storm, she took herself back to her kitchen where shouts and the crashing of pots and pans could be heard. The calico cat came shooting out of the open door a few seconds later with its tail low and a biscuit in its mouth. A chunk of stove wood sailed after it. The shouting died away to muttering once more, and the steady sounds of something being stirred in a bowl with vigor could be heard.

It was fairly pleasant there on the back veranda, but beyond the eaves the sun was already achingly bright and hot. It was going to be another scorching day.

"Pay no attention to Mama Tass," Aunt Em said. "Ranny has always been the apple of her eye; I sometimes think more so than her own son."

Lettie, leaning her head back on her chair, looked at the other woman. "It doesn't matter; I suppose I deserve it. Are you certain it wouldn't be more comfortable for all of you if I moved into town to the hotel? I will quite understand if you prefer it."

"Nonsense. You acted according to what you thought was right. It was just bad luck that Ranny was caught. I don't suppose Colonel Ward will keep him long."

On the other side of the table that held the coffee tray sat Sally Anne. A message had been sent at daybreak to Elm Grove. Sally Anne had come at once, in time to go with Aunt Em to the Federal jail. The younger woman had brought a message that her mother and father would be with Aunt Em later. Now she spoke up. "He had better not."

"My dear, he's only doing his duty. He isn't an unreasonable man at all. You know he let me see Ranny before sunup and didn't search all the baskets and bundles of things I had brought for him very hard."

"He's an idiot if he seriously thinks Ranny could be guilty, and so I told him."

"I'm sure that helped immensely!" Aunt Em said with some asperity.

Sally Anne sent her a dark look. "It helped my feelings, as much as anything can. I have never been so incensed in my life."

"We must be patient."

"But just think of what people are going to say!"

"As if that makes a bit of difference." Aunt Em sounded seriously annoyed for the first time.

"Oh, I don't mean the silly gossip. I was thinking of the whispers and pointing fingers Ranny will have to endure.

A lot of people avoid him already. Only consider what it will be like if they think he may be dangerous."

"No one who knows him at all will believe for one minute that he's capable of these murders."

"People," Sally Anne said, with a quick glance in Lettie's direction, "will believe anything."

If Lettie had thought to gain some idea of whether Aunt Em and Sally Anne thought it possible that Ranny could have committed the crimes while in a temporary state of madness, she had soon put it aside. So partisan were the two ladies, and so delicate her own position as a stranger and a former enemy among them, that it was impossible to suggest such a thing. She had tried to dismiss the possibility during the night, or what had been left of it after talking to Aunt Em, but it would not go away. It worried around the edges of her mind, a theory so close to fitting the facts as she knew them that it could not be dismissed.

Aunt Em's forebearance was unexpected. Lettie would not have been surprised to be told to pack her bags and leave before dawn. It might have been more comfortable for her if she had. There was the feeling, largely unspoken by her hostess and Ranny's cousin out of good manners and their concern for him, that Lettie had committed a treasonous act by attempting to entrap the Thorn. They might sympathize with her in her need to see her brother's killer brought to justice, but not if it endangered a man they thought of as their champion.

"They won't hold Ranny long," Aunt Em said again, though there was a pained look in her eyes. "The real Thorn is bound to show himself, go on another of his escapades. Everyone will see how ridiculous it is, arresting Ranny like that, and that will be the end of it."

"I hope he does something soon."

So did Lettie. She longed for proof that Ranny was as she had thought him: good, gentle, and fine.

"I suppose it would be useless to put a note in the hollow tree and ask him to stage some public display?" There was a certain hopefulness in Aunt Em's voice.

Sally Anne looked at Lettie. Lettie reflected that it was a little strange that they saw her both as the Thorn's potential destroyer and the nearest thing to an authority on him. Still, she answered as honestly as she could. "I expect if he saw the commotion last night and has heard what happened, he will stay as far as possible from Dink's Pond."

That was, of course, if he was not now sitting in custody in town.

"Of course he will hear, why didn't I think of that? And I can't imagine that he will want Ranny to suffer for the things he is supposed to have done. We will be hearing in a day or two of some new stunt he has pulled."

Lettie turned her head on the chair back to look at the older woman. "You sound as if you think he lives among you."

"Well, it stands to reason, doesn't it? He must be someone who knows something about the community in order to know what to do to help. He has to live somewhere within a score or so of miles on either side of Natchitoches for him to know so much about it that he can lead the soldiers around in circles. He must have someplace to go, some hiding place somewhere in that same area; otherwise, how could he disappear the way he does? Or if he doesn't have a hiding place, he must be known to two or three people who permit him to conceal himself until the chase is over."

The observations were all too familiar to Lettie. "Knowing that, is there no one you think it might be?"

There was a tight silence. It became distressingly obvious that if there was someone, neither Aunt Em nor Sally Anne felt inclined to speak his name in Lettie's presence.

"Forget, please, that I asked that," Lettie said.

"Oh, goodness, these are such trying times. When I think of how simple and pleasant life used to be, I could cry."

"Such awful things are happening now," Sally Anne agreed.

Lettie caught a glimmer of an opening for the subject she wanted to broach. "Awful indeed. Does it strike you that there is something . . . crazed about these killings?"

"Crazed?"

"Such as the way that poor man's neck was broken and the callous manner in which Johnny's body was hidden."

"It sounds rather like the doings of a pack of animals to me," Aunt Em declared. "Animals who think no more of taking a human life than they would of swatting a fly. Now I've wrung the neck of many a chicken. The reason it's done is because it's quick, it's bloodless, and it's not so noisy as other methods. I expect it was the same with the man who was killed. Maybe someone was coming, or maybe there was a house close enough for people to hear and investigate the sound of a gunshot. As for Johnny, the carcasses of dead animals and other garbage are often thrown into abandoned wells, and there are a lot of those around since people are packing up and moving. I would imagine it was just convenient. The wonder is that anybody ever found him."

"You are saying, then, that you think the outlaws are to blame."

"Outlaws, jayhawkers, whatever name you want to give them."

"And you still think the Thorn's emblem was put on the bodies to place the blame on him?"

"There's no other explanation."

"Doesn't that strike you as too convenient?"

"Anything else strikes me as too unlikely. Why should a man who risks his life to save others suddenly turn and kill?"

"To save himself when he is recognized."

"You don't want to accept it because it would mean that you have been wrong, that your brother was wrong." The older woman's voice was stern.

"All right, then," Lettie said, her voice tight, "let's say that there is no connection between the Thorn and the outlaws Johnny knew. Let's say that someone wants to throw suspicion on the Thorn for the outlaws' activities. Why?"

"I think the reason in the beginning was to delay as long as possible the knowledge that there was outlaw activity in the area. I think the first incident when it was used may have been your brother. With the hue and cry directed toward the Thorn, there was that much more time for the outlaws, and the man who is feeding them information, to get rid of the payroll gold. It worked once, so it was used again and again."

Lettie watched the older woman with her eyes narrowed in thought. It made sense. "And this man, this messenger?"

"I've been thinking about that, too. It stands to reason that it's somebody who may have an idea who the Thorn is, somebody who can guess when he comes and goes so that nothing is done in his name when there are witnesses to say he was somewhere else entirely."

"Such as?"

Aunt Em threw up her hands. "I have no idea."

"Someone who disguises himself like the Thorn, do you think?" It was Sally Anne who asked the question.

"Probably," Aunt Em answered.

That particular possibility raised specters Lettie would just as soon not face. Suppose the man with whom she had made love was not the Thorn but the messenger?

No. Her mind slammed some deep internal door on the thought.

Was it possible that Ranny could be the messenger?

He was in a position to hear a great deal with the Union army practically encamped on his doorstep these past few weeks. In addition, he was in and out of town all the time driving Aunt Em or Sally Anne or herself. People had a tendency to speak in front of him as if he wasn't there, though she had often thought that he heard and understood much more than they expected.

Or suppose the Thorn himself was the messenger? Suppose the good deeds he had done were merely a cover for other, more lucrative crimes?

There were too many possibilities. Lettie wished that she could have Aunt Em's simple faith, wished that she could believe in the explanation she gave. There was a simplicity to it that was seductive. Good and evil were clearly and evenly balanced. The Thorn was a force for right, the outlaws were the devil's henchmen, and Ranny was an innocent victim. Few things, Lettie had discovered, were that easy.

Good and evil. Angel and devil.

She was haunted by those words, as if they had some meaning she should be able to decipher. It eluded her now as it had from the beginning.

At a gesture from Aunt Em, Sally Anne picked up the coffeepot that had been neglected until now and began to pour out cups of the hot, strong brew for them. "I suppose we will have to wait. I questioned Thomas, but he is determined to hold Ranny. I think the fact that there is another payroll due tomorrow may have something to do with it. When it comes in and is sent on to Monroe, Thomas may be more reasonable."

"He told you about the shipment?" Lettie could not suppress her surprise.

"I'm afraid I was rather persistent, and he knows he can trust me. He even told me when it will go out again: on Tuesday at four-thirty A.M., with an escort of two men."

"If someone tries to take the payroll—" Aunt Em began.

"Then Ranny will be safe."

Peter had been playing in the backyard with Lionel. Lionel had not come around the veranda but had stayed well away from Lettie. Now and then she saw the older boy looking at her from the corners of his eyes and frowning in furious concentration. She was, illogically, more hurt by his defection than anything else. She had expected him to understand, even if no one else did, how little she wanted to hurt Ranny, how much she regretted that he had been caught in her trap. More than that, she had thought that he had some small affection for her, too.

Now the younger boy came running around the end of the house and leaped up the stairs. "Look!" he cried. "Look what I found."

"Slow down before you break your neck," Sally Anne scolded, her attention on the level of the coffee cup she was filling. As Peter slowed to a quick walk and came to lean against her chair with his fist outstretched in front of her, she reached with her free hand to brush back his fine blond hair, which was falling into his face. "Your hair needs combing."

"Yes, ma'am, but look, Mama."

He opened his hand.

The coffeepot Sally Anne held crashed to the table as she cried out. Aunt Em sat forward with a sharp exclamation. Lettie froze into immobility.

Peter was so startled by their reaction that he jumped. The locust shell fell off his palm, whispered down the side of Sally Anne's skirts, and landed on the floor where it tumbled like a falling leaf. It came to a stop in the bright sunlight that edged the floor in front of them and lay there in the hot glow, gleaming like gold.

Aunt Em recovered first. "Where did you get that?"

Peter's face was pale as he looked around in bewilderment. "On the side of the magnolia tree. I didn't kill it. It was already empty. Ranny says the bugs inside leave them hanging on the trees when they are through with them."

"So they do, every year about this time," Aunt Em said. "I remember telling him the same thing when he was your age."

"Can I have it?"

"By all means, and as many more of the pesky things as you can find."

Peter picked up the locust shell and put it on his nose, then went skipping away. Sally Anne sat back in her chair with her hand on her bosom. "I thought it was a—a calling card."

"So did I," Aunt Em said. "Too bad it wasn't."

The sun slowly crept near the house wall, forcing a move to the front veranda, before the Tylers, Sally Anne's mother and father, arrived. Mrs. Tyler brought with her a layer cake iced with blackberry jelly that she had made. They had it with more coffee and sat speaking in soft, subdued voices of Ranny's escapades as a boy and young man. They did not ignore Lettie, they were not that obvious; still, they had little to say to her. She was trying to think of some graceful way to take her leave and go to her room when Martin Eden drove up.

"Aunt Em," he said as he came up the steps with his hat in his hand, "I can't tell you how sorry I am to hear about Ranny."

Aunt Em opened her arms and he came forward to give her a hug. "It was good of you to come," she said.

"I've already been to see him. I did my best to convince

Colonel Ward that he's making a mistake, but he's so determined to have a scapegoat, however unlikely a specimen, that he wouldn't listen."

"I hardly think that's a proper way to refer to Ranny!" Sally Anne told him.

"I beg your pardon, Aunt Em. I only meant that—"

"Never mind, Martin," the older woman said, "I know what you meant."

"Is there anything I can do for you, anything I can take to Ranny?"

"I appreciate the offer, but I don't think so, not today."

"I wondered if he had his harmonica? That might give him some entertainment."

"Now that you put me in mind of it, I don't think he does. I'll look for it, and you can take that."

"Good. I'll feel better doing something for him, no matter how small, since I'll be going out of town for a day or two."

"Business, Martin?" Sally Anne asked.

"Yes, unfortunately."

"Union business, but then I suppose you have to jump when your masters snap the whip?"

"That's the way it is," he agreed, his voice dry.

"Too bad."

"Why? Was there something you wanted of me?" He tilted his dark head, his manner at its most charming.

"I rather thought you might do something to free Ranny instead of just delivering his harmonica." Sally Anne's tone was petulant.

Martin smiled. "Don't tell me you don't trust your Yankee colonel to see justice done?"

"You may leave Thomas out of this. He's only obeying orders."

"Is he now?"

"What do you mean by that?" The woman sat forward in her chair.

"Nothing, nothing." Martin held up his hands in a gesture of surrender.

"Besides, he isn't my colonel!" She threw herself against her chair back.

"I'm glad to hear it. But just what miracle was it you had in mind for me to perform to get Ranny released?"

"I don't know. Something. Anything. Use your connections."

"I doubt it will help. This is a military matter now and the sheriff won't interfere. The governor is hardly likely to step in unless it's to his benefit." He gave her a sly look. "Of course, I suppose I could always try to bribe the colonel."

"That isn't funny!"

"And in any case, he's richer than I am, isn't he? So what's left?"

"The Knights?"

It seemed to Lettie that Ranny's cousin slanted a quick look at her father as she made the suggestion. The older man stared out over the railing as if his thoughts were elsewhere.

"Breaking men out of jail isn't their specialty."

"Maybe not," Sally Anne agreed, her gaze on Martin steady, "but the Thorn could do it."

There was a silence on the veranda. Every glance, in that brief instant, was on Martin. He looked taken aback. "My dear girl, I'm not your man!"

"I would hardly expect you to admit it, but if you have any feeling for Ranny—"

"No," Lettie said.

Martin was no longer the center of attention.

"What do you mean, no?" Sally Anne demanded.

Lettie gave her a level look. "It won't work. Anyone who tries to free him will just get him killed, along with themselves."

"Not necessarily." The other woman's tone was defensive.

"And even if it worked, what would become of him? He couldn't come back to Splendora. He might be able to take care of himself in Texas or farther west, but he wouldn't be happy away from everyone."

Martin Eden stared down at her. "I have no intention of doing anything foolhardy, Miss Mason, but I think it highly impertinent of you to be deciding Ranny's fate."

"That may be, but it seems to me his chances are better if he depends on the colonel to discover the truth."

"Even after he and his men search Splendora for evidence, as they will?"

"Are you implying there is something to be found?"

"Are you certain there's not? Or that the colonel won't manufacture what he doesn't find?"

What did he really believe behind that smiling, handsome façade of his face? It was impossible to tell. "I'm amazed you would suggest such a thing, amazed you can't see that Ranny is better as he is."

"There are many things about us that amaze you, aren't there, a lot of things you don't understand. Like Ranny and the Thorn. You interfered there, and look what happened. Now you want to tell us what's best for him? It may be, Miss Mason, that you would be better off if you went back North where you belong."

No one spoke. No one chided Martin for his breach of manners or protested that he was wrong. It was as if he had merely put into words what they all felt. They had silently closed ranks against her, the interloper, the traitor.

Lettie rose to her feet. "You may be right, Mr. Eden. You may be exactly right."

She walked into the house. The close, stifling stillness of her bedchamber had no appeal, and she continued along the hallway and out the back doors. She crossed the back veranda and went down the steps with her skirts trailing over the treads, then moved along the brick walk past the herb garden and the kitchen building. The tempo of her footsteps increased the farther she went from the big house. Faster she walked, faster, until by the time she reached the schoolroom she was almost running. She hurried into the small cabin and shut the door behind her. With her hand still on the knob, she leaned against the door panel and closed her eyes.

Martin was right; she should go. To stay when everyone wished her gone was like inflicting a penance upon herself. She felt it and longed to have the whole thing over and behind her, but she could not seem to bring herself to think seriously of packing and arranging for the journey. Not while Ranny's fate was undecided.

Splendora seemed so empty without him. As quiet and unassuming as he was, it was extraordinary how he had made his presence felt. Everyone and everything, to one degree or another, depended on him. He was the sun around which the household revolved. Without him, it was bleak and purposeless.

Even this schoolroom. She opened her eyes and looked around. It appeared the same, had the same dry smells of books and chalk and glue and old leather bindings. The sunlight falling through the window in a wide beam had the same brilliance and the same slowly turning dust motes caught in its shafts. Still, the room felt dull and deserted.

Lettie let her breath out in a tremulous sigh. She pushed away from the door and walked to her desk where she trailed her fingers along its surface. She put her hand on the back of her chair, then dragged it toward the window and sat down. It was here that Ranny had asked her to marry him. He had been so persuasive, so serious, so intent. She could almost hear his voice as, in his simple sentences, he had offered his love, his home, himself. If she had agreed . . .

What had she done to him? What had she done?

Aunt Em and Sally Anne and all the others seemed so certain that he was innocent. She wanted desperately for it to be so. There was a part of her that could not conceive of it any other way. But there was also the part of her that remembered and weighed and added up and stood puzzled over the sum of the man who was Ranny, Ransom Tyler.

Sometime soon, in a day or two days or a week, the Thorn would ride out on some deed of good or ill, and the questions would be answered. When that time came, she would be glad, incredibly glad. In the meantime, she prayed that Thomas Ward would see to it that no harm came to Ranny, that any interrogation was conducted along official lines without recourse to barracks tactics or brutality.

A shiver ran through her as she remembered Ranny in the hands of the soldiers, disheveled, his hair in his eyes and blood at the corner of his mouth. There were means that could be used, she had heard, to make a man confess to anything. Pain, she thought, would not daunt Ranny for a long time, but there were limits to the endurance of any human. The worst that could be used against him might be mental persuasion. He would have few defenses against it, few wiles or mental acrobatics with which to protect himself. He might be tricked into saying what he did not mean or led to believe that admitting to the crimes of the Thorn would protect someone else. It was useless to think that Thomas Ward would not do such a thing; he might do it without the least intention of entrapping an innocent man.

As she had done.

All that would not matter if the Thorn were to make another move. What would happen, however, if he did not? What would become of Ranny if the man who played the part of the righter of wrongs decided that this was a fine time to fade from sight? What would happen if Ranny was indeed the Thorn and there was no possibility of an incident occurring to gain his release?

The charges laid at Ranny's door included assault, theft, interfering with the official duties of the United States Army, and murder. The penalty for the least of these would be several years in a Federal stockade; for the worst, it would be hanging.

Hanging. Ranny.

The idea was so unthinkable that she got out of the chair and began to pace with her skirts swinging about her ankles. It couldn't happen. It couldn't.

But if it did, she would be to blame.

The thought of it was intolerable.

She stood with her hands clenched to her stomach as if that would still the ache of guilt and fear and misplaced caring that she refused to call love inside her. Nothing could. It was possible that nothing ever would.

One thing that would help for the moment was to see Ranny again. To see if he had forgiven her. She would go as soon as the others had left Splendora, as soon as the way was clear so she need not explain what she did not entirely understand herself.

Lettie pulled the buggy up in front of the big, old two-story house that had been taken over as headquarters for the occupation army. She took out her handkerchief and blotted the perspiration from her face, then flicked away the dust that had settled on her clothing. The afternoon was so hot that the sky seemed to have a brassy sheen and the leaves hung limp on the trees. The streets of the town were deserted. The proprietors of stores stood in their doorways, fanning themselves. Here and there, on the shady side of a building or under a tree, a man was lying asleep. The cats and dogs had withdrawn to the cool crawl spaces under the houses where they lay stretched out, panting, waiting for sundown.

Inside headquarters, a clerk at a desk in what had once been the hall sat with his feet up and a piece of newspaper over his face, snoring mightily. Lettie's clearing of her throat failed to rouse him. With a look of irritation, she moved to open the nearest door.

An officer looked up from a desk littered with papers. His hair looked as if he had been scratching his head and there were inkstains on his fingers. As he got to his feet, a paper clung to the underside of his forearm that was beaded with sweat above his rolled sleeve, and he snatched it free and flung it down before coming around the desk toward her.

"May I help you, ma'am," he began, then exclaimed, "Miss Lettie, what are you doing here?"

He was one of the men who had been to Splendora that summer. He was from Kentucky and had a sister named Marcy, Lettie knew, but she could not recall his name. She smiled at him with warmth, however. "I was looking for Colonel Ward."

"Sure thing. This way, Miss Lettie."

The lieutenant put on his uniform jacket before he led the way back out into the hall. As he passed the sleeping clerk, he swept the man's feet from his desk without ceremony, then moved with quick strides to open a door farther along. Thomas Ward's office had once served as a dining room, if the punkah hanging from the ceiling was any indication. The punkah was in motion, swinging back and forth as a small Negro boy sitting in a corner pulled on its rope. Two men stood near the windows at the far end of the room. One was the colonel, the other Samuel Tyler. They turned as Lettie entered.

"Miss Lettie to see you, sir," The man from Kentucky announced, then with a smile and a wink went away again.

Tyler said a few last words, only one of which Lettie caught and that was the word *money*. No doubt they were discussing some detail of the mortgage on Elm Grove.

"If I intrude," she said, "I can wait outside."

"Not at all, I was just going," Sally Anne's father said. He nodded to the colonel and Lettie before replacing his hat. "Good day, Thomas. Miss Mason."

The door closed behind him.

Thomas Ward came toward Lettie and took her hands. "To what do I owe this pleasure?"

"I won't keep you long. It's about Ranny."

"You want to see him? My dear girl, you and half the rest of the world. The other half of his well-wishers have sent him some kind of food or other comfort. I'm about worn out with looking through everything for files and keys and whatnot."

"Have they convinced you yet that you have the wrong man?" Her tone was rallying, but beneath it ran a thread of hope.

"Not entirely."

Lettie lowered her lashes to hide her disappointment. "I suppose you have questioned him?"

"I have, between visits."

"What does he say?"

"Say? Next to nothing. He sits there and smiles and looks as innocent as a choirboy at Christmastime, but having been a choirboy myself, I refuse to be taken in."

She played with the strings of her purse, which hung on her arm. "Suppose he never says anything? What then? You wouldn't—that is to say—you would not allow him to be questioned too harshly, even mistreated, would you, Thomas?"

"Is that what's worrying you? Is that what you think of me and of the United States Army?"

"You won't, I hope, try to say that it never happens."

"You and Sally Anne. The two of you must think I'm a real bas—a real brute."

Lettie supposed that the other woman had as much right to be concerned about Ranny's welfare as she did, more in fact. It was completely illogical for her to be annoyed.

She ignored his near slip of the tongue. "I think that you are a fine officer, but you are under a great deal of pressure to put an end to the Thorn's activities and to the atrocities that have been committed in his name."

"That sounds as if you think the Thorn may not be the guilty party, whether or not Ranny is our man."

"I don't know. I don't know!" she exclaimed.

He was silent for a long moment, watching her, his gaze on her flushed checkbones. "Just what is Tyler to you? Sally Anne I can understand, she's related to him, but I don't see why you're so upset."

"I hardly see that my relationships are any concern of yours."

"Strictly speaking, no, but it isn't just idle curiosity. I get the feeling that you just may be regretting what you've done and I'd like to know why."

Lettie lifted her gaze, staring at the open window and the empty, sunbaked street. "If I am, which I don't admit, it's because of Ranny, because he was caught. He—he's like no one else I've ever known. He's kind and generous, and there is a sweetness to his nature that catches at the heart. He's sensitive, with a soul that is somehow not quite as protected as the rest of us. He's funny and gallant and sometimes so tragic that I can't—"

"It sounds to me that if he were normal you would be in love with him."

She sent him a quick, startled glance, her color deepening. "I will admit that I'm fond of him. I suppose it's natural; a teacher is often fond of certain pupils."

"Fond?"

"What else, pray?" She lifted her chin to give him a challenging look.

"Nothing, if you say so," he answered, but there was a considering expression in his eyes.

"I will remind you," she said, her tone even, "that Ranny stepped in once to save you injury, that day at Splendora with Martin Eden."

"I haven't forgotten. Nor have I forgotten how he brought me to my senses at Elm Grove when I came so near to ruining my chances with Sally Anne."

"Well, then?"

"Well, then, you have my word that I will handle him with kid gloves. This may come as a surprise to you, but I never intended to do anything else."

A smile curved her lips, rising to her eyes. "And I never expected otherwise, but it's nice to hear you say so."

"Yes, well, I would have mauled him about a bit for the fun of it, and maybe battered him here and there, but he has too many friends. Though it makes me sound like a damned coward to say so, I'd rather not risk having my neck stretched some dark night— the fate Samuel Tyler was seeking to warn me of just now."

"That is, of course, your only reason."

"What else?" he said, and as he moved to open the door and then hold it for her, the lift of his brow dared her to accuse him of kindness. "Shall we visit the prisoner?"

The jail was in the raised basement under the main floor of the house, the same small room with a single barred window and door that had been used to hold dangerous or unruly slaves in years past. To reach it, they went along the hall to the back doors, then down to the ground-floor veranda. Thomas unlocked the double doors that led into this lower floor and escorted her along the hallway that bisected it to the jail room in the righthand front corner. There were a few rooms in this area that were ordinarily used for storage. The basement was dim and smelled faintly of mildew and dust, but had the advantage of being much cooler than the upper rooms.

Thomas stopped at the barred doorway of the jail room where the outline of a tiny window crossed with bars, a washstand, and a narrow cot with the figure of a man lying upon it could just be seen. The colonel rapped on the wall with his knuckles. "Someone to see you, Tyler." He turned away and went down the hall, saying over his shoulder to Lettie, "Five minutes. I'll be back."

Ranny got to his feet, a solid yet indistinct figure in the gray light of the room. He was silhouetted against the window as he turned to her, his broad shoulders nearly blocking the light, the tilt of his head inquiring. He began to move toward her with his easy, swinging stride, coming out of the dimness.

Lettie saw the shape of his body, the molding of his head and neck, the way he moved, and felt her heart turn in slow and aching pain inside her. She could not think, could not speak. The blood in her veins seemed congealed, so thickened that she felt she might never move from that spot.

Ranny came nearer. The light from the doors at the end of the hall picked up the soft gold of his hair, the bronze of his skin, the gentle curve of his mouth. His big hands closed around the bars of the door. He said softly, "Miss Lettie."

"Oh, Ranny," she whispered, her voice breaking.

"You came. I didn't think you would."

Tears rose, hurting, pooling in her eyes. She stepped forward without knowing she was going to and placed her hand on his. "Are you all right?"

"Yes, ma'am, I'm fine. But your hands are cold. You aren't sick?"

"No, no."

His lips were bruised and cut. She reached through the bars to trail her fingertips over the warm skin, which was faintly stubbled with beard, at the side of his mouth, gently soothing those injuries that had been inflicted upon him because of her. The need to press her lips to his was so strong that she felt light-headed with the effort of restraint. He turned his head, brushing her fingertips with a kiss before he captured her hand and held it to his chest.

"I'm so sorry, Ranny, so sorry."

Where the words had come from, she didn't know, but she was glad when they were spoken. She moved closer, clutching at a bar with her free hand.

"It doesn't matter."

"But it does. What am I going to do?"

"Nothing. There's nothing you can do, Miss Lettie."

"There must be something."

"Don't think of it. I'll be all right."

Was that a warning? Or was it just his concern for her feelings? She drew back, looking at him, impressing his features on her mind's eye. He looked the same, perhaps a little strained, a little tired, but the same. The difference was in herself, in the way she saw him.

"Ransom Tyler," she said, trying the name, hearing the syllables echoing in her memory along with images she would never forget.

"Miss Lettie?"

His voice was puzzled, but the grasp of his hand had tightened perceptibly. For an instant, she had an overpowering urge to demand that he drop his pretense and face her as he really was, himself and none other.

But it was too dangerous for him. There might be someone listening beyond the window or in the next room. In any case, it wasn't necessary.

"Never mind," she said quietly.

Ransom had never loved her more. She was pale, there were shadows of sleeplessness under her eyes, and the hat tipped forward on her head was so drab that it drained her face of vitality. Still, the look in her eyes made him feel that there were no such things as bars.

She knew; he sensed it. And she had betrayed him. But he had handed his life to her with a rose when they had first met and he had no right to complain if she had tossed both away. If she had asked, he would have told her what she wanted to know. She didn't, and he was glad. It indicated that she understood more than he had ever dreamed she would. Or so he wanted to believe. It could also mean that she didn't care to know, that the burden of guilt for what she had done was so intolerable that it no longer mattered. Either way, he was satisfied.

Footsteps sounded on the steps leading down from the upper floor. The colonel was returning.

His voice deep, Ransom said, "Kiss me, Miss Lettie."

She went on tiptoe, straining against the bars, feeling the cool metal against her heated face as she met his lips through them. Firm and sure, there was in the contact both wrenching pleasure and a pact sealed in silent abnegation.

Thomas was whistling as he came. The sound was sharp, a warning. Ranny released Lettie and she stepped back. Her cheekbones carried a hectic flush and her voice was unsteady when she spoke for the benefit of the colonel.

"Do you have everything you need?"

"Except you. To read to me," he answered, his eyes bright in the dimness.

She managed a smile, acknowledging that faint edge of comic longing. Then Thomas was beside her.

"Ready?"

She said her final farewell and placed her hand on the blue sleeve that covered the colonel's arm. Holding on to her composure, breathing slowly, steadily, she walked away, leaving behind her Ranny, Ransom Tyler, who was without doubt the Thorn.

18

Nothing would ever be the same. Lettie knew it would not, but she couldn't bring herself to care. That fact should have been shocking, but it wasn't. So great was her relief at being freed from her doubts that she wanted to sing, to shout, despite the weight of fear inside. She did neither. She drove sedately home to Splendora, a frown of such fierce concentration on her face that the tax collector O'Connor, pausing to tip his hat to her on a Natchitoches street, stared after her in astonishment as she bowled past him without a sign of recognition.

Lettie hoped to find Aunt Em alone. She should have known better. Not only was Sally Anne still visiting, she had been joined by Marie Voisin and Angelique. The two young women had apparently been seeking Sally Anne so that Angelique could say her good-byes. They were all gathered in Aunt Em's bedchamber, perhaps because they had interrupted the older woman's afternoon rest or possibly because some privacy was desired. It was Lionel who pointed out their location and told Lettie who was present. A few hours earlier, Lettie might have hesitated, uncertain of her welcome, but now she had no thought except to see Aunt Em and speak to her as soon as possible.

Lettie heard their voices as she lifted her hand to knock. They stopped abruptly when her tap sounded. A moment later, she was told without ceremony to come in.

Aunt Em sat in a slipper chair with Sally Anne standing on one side and Marie Voisin on the other. Angelique knelt on the floor, her tearstained face in the older woman's ample lap. She sat up, searching for a handkerchief as Lettie stepped into the room.

"Oh, it's you, Lettie," Aunt Em said. "I thought it might be Mama Tass coming for the coffee tray."

"I can take it away if you like and save her the trouble." The offer was sincere. Lettie had the distinct feeling that it would be better if she came back later.

"Mama Tass will be along directly."

Lettie closed the door and came forward. Her tone stiff, she said, "I didn't mean to intrude."

Angelique used her handkerchief, emerging from behind it after a moment. "Oh, no, I'm being s-silly. I will be c-calm in a minute."

"We were just going, anyway," Marie said.

"Is there nothing I can say," Aunt Em asked, touching Angelique's arm, "to convince you this is unnecessary?"

The girl gave a small, hopeless shrug. "You know how it is with me."

"It doesn't have to be that way. A lot of your people are going to California or to Mexico where they are accepted as—"

"As Spanish. Yes, I know, but Papa won't consider it. He will hold on to his land until the end because being a great landowner is his pride. I need something more."

"Not this. Not some half life. It won't be the same as it was before the war. Nothing is."

"It will be enough, with the man who has chosen me."

"Can you trust him? I mean, really trust him?"

"I must." The sadness of all the women in the world was in the girl's tremulous smile.

Aunt Em sighed. "I don't like it. There's no use pretending I do, but it's your choice, and I can't honestly say that if I was in your shoes I would do any different. When do you go?"

"Tomorrow night."

"Tomorrow night? But why?"

Angelique looked away. "That must be obvious."

"The man's a fool."

"He has his reputation to think of. As you said, things are not the same. It's no longer the fashion for a man to have a woman of color as his mistress."

"Fashion, my eye! What kind of life is it going to be for you if he never wants to be seen with you in public?"

"The only kind I can have. But—I could be wrong. It may have something to do with the fact that we are going to Monroe to catch the river packet."

"Monroe?" Aunt Em's frown seemed to demand an explanation.

"He has Federal business there, possibly, or it may be that he would rather not risk having to introduce me to his friends, as he might if we left from here to catch the train at Colfax."

Sally Anne leaned to put her hand on the girl's shoulder. "Angelique, please, don't go."

Angelique smiled, with a mist of tears rising once more in her liquid brown eyes. "I appreciate your concern and I will remember it, but I have no other choice."

"A man of your own race would be better than this— this insensitive idiot who is taking you away." That she did not speak the name of the tax collector was a matter of delicacy.

"My own race? But I am only a quarter Negro, just a quarter. What is my race?"

They were all silent, abashed, for the law was specific that any trace of Negro blood made a person nonwhite. It was a position that was both rational and irrational, one that the war and the laws of Reconstruction had done nothing to change.

Angelique pushed herself upright and kicked her skirts

out of the way so that she could get to her feet. She would have turned away, but Aunt Em put out her hand to catch her wrist.

"You are a fine and beautiful woman and a worthwhile human being; never forget that. If things don't work out, don't be too proud to come back home."

"I won't," Angelique said, her voice soft. "I would not have cried all over you if you had not been so understanding, but I'm glad you were. You have helped me so much. I'm grateful."

Aunt Em shook her head. "You know we wish you happiness?"

"I know. Well, I had better go if I'm to be packed in time."

Angelique looked around for her hat, which lay on a nearby table. She put it back on and secured it with the pin that was thrust through it. Marie moved to straighten the veil that fell down the back, then reached for her net purse, which lay on the bed.

They left the room in a group and moved out onto the veranda. There was a series of good-byes, then the two visitors went down the steps to their buggy. Lettie, Sally Anne, and Aunt Em stood watching and waving until they were out of sight.

Aunt Em lowered her arm. Her face grim, she said, "If O'Connor had never asked her to go to New Orleans, Angelique would have been perfectly happy where she was. I could kill that man."

"I have a better idea," Lettie said, her eyes gleaming with the inspiration that had been growing for the better part of the past half hour.

"What are you talking about?"

"What do you mean?"

The two women spoke at the same time. There was

suspicion in Aunt Em's voice. Sally Anne sounded irritated and intrigued as she turned to search Lettie's face.

Lettie told them exactly what she had in mind.

There were five of them when they set out the following evening. Sally Anne refused to allow Lettie to go alone; she couldn't bear to miss out on the excitement. Aunt Em insisted on going because it was simply too dangerous for the two young women without protection. Lionel would not stay behind because he wanted to help Mast' Ranny. And Mama Tass would not let Lionel go without her.

Lettie did not object to the company. Reinforcements were welcome, so long as they stayed out of sight. It was entirely possible that they would be needed. What she was going to do was risky at best; at worst, it could be disastrous. With the others present, the situation might be saved by turning it into some kind of monstrous practical joke.

They left before nightfall, to all appearances just the family from Splendora traveling by wagon to some gathering, with a saddle horse trotting along behind. Lettie was driving with Aunt Em up beside her. The others were in the back sitting on a bench, with their feet propped on a long, quilt-wrapped bundle. Smiling, chatting among themselves in an attempt to appear at ease, they passed through town and continued south toward Isle Brevelle.

It was dusk dark by the time they came within a half mile of the turnoff for the drive of the house that belonged to Monsieur La Cour, Angelique's father. It was Aunt Em who had chosen the place, first of all because it had a plum thicket and a grove of scrubby post oaks just beyond a tight curve, and second because just back up the road was an abandoned farmhouse.

They pulled into the farmyard and wheeled the wagon around behind the old house with its blank windows and sagging door so that it was well hidden. Lionel was dispatched to make his way to the La Cour house to watch for a short while to be certain their quarry had not already come and gone. Mama Tass unpacked a basket containing a cold supper, and they all ate standing up as they waited for Lionel.

In between bites of biscuit and cold chicken, Lettie took the long bundle from the back and unwrapped it. She laid the weapons it contained on the seat, then shook out the man's hat, coat, shirt, and trousers; the feather pillows; the large black kerchief; and a revolver, the same one she had taken from the Thorn at the corn crib. Removing her own clothing, she began to put the other things on.

By the time Lionel returned, night had fallen. Angelique was still at the house, he reported; he had seen her through the windows moving back and forth in her room.

The boy was handed biscuits and chicken, and the rest of the food was put away. Aunt Em and Sally Anne each took a rifle from the wagon seat. Mama Tass fished a wicked-looking carving knife from underneath it. Lionel, holding the biscuit he had left in his mouth, reached into his pocket and brought out a slingshot and a handful of rocks. Mama Tass was detailed to stay with the wagon, ready to send it back toward Splendora at speed if necessary. The others moved quietly after Lettie, who led the horse, as they made their way toward the road.

Lettie moved on past the plum thicket Aunt Em had marked out, drawing her mount into the cover of the grove of post oaks. The others pushed their way into the thorny concealment of the low-growing plum trees, though not without a sharp exclamation or two under their breaths and even what sounded like a few mild oaths.

In the grove, Lettie turned the horse's head toward the road. She looked up at the man's saddle with a pillow tied to the seat, then down at her own form made portly with more pillows. With her mouth set in a determined line, she put her foot in the stirrup, grasped the saddle with both hands, and pulled herself upward.

She couldn't do it. Her pillow-clad breast hit the edge of the saddle and she dropped back to the ground. She tried again. The same thing happened.

The sounds of hoofbeats. Someone was coming. She had to be ready. She reached higher, gave a mighty heave.

She was in the saddle, sitting high on the pillow that was to give her a man's stature. She quieted the dancing horse that had been disturbed by her strange appearance and her efforts. With one hand, she shifted the pads in the shoulders of her coat for the correct broad appearance, then adjusted her hat lower across her face, pulled her black kerchief higher over her nose, and looked up the road.

For a moment she thought she was seeing a ghost. It was not yet moonrise, and in the darkness all that was visible was a shifting white blur. She closed her eyes tight and opened them again. The blur was a light-colored shirt worn by a man on a dark-colored horse. Closer he came. It was an old black man slouched in the saddle of a nag so rawboned and ancient it was comical in its ugliness.

A single horseman, not a man in a buggy. He was not their quarry. Lettie sat still. The old man trotted past and faded into the night.

The minutes passed. She relaxed and lowered her kerchief, then scratched her upper lip with one careful finger. Her mustache with its spirit gum adhesive itched infernally. Heaven alone knew how Ransom had been able to stand it so often and for so long at a time. She took off her hat and fanned herself with it. Hot, it was so hot girded around with pillows as she was. It would be a good thing if it rained again soon to cool things off and to wash the dust from the trees. At least the mosquitoes weren't out tonight.

Strange, ridiculous things went through Lettie's mind. What was she going to say? "Stand and deliver!" like some highwayman on an English heath? Or would a simple "Stop!" do? Maybe she should have constructed a bulbous nose for herself? It would have been a better disguise in case there was a carriage lantern, and it might have changed the sound of her voice if it had pinched her nostrils.

What did she think she was doing? Was she crazy?

It was best not to answer such questions. She thought instead of the ease with which Mama Tass had gone about finding the things she needed for her role, as if it was not an unaccustomed task, and of Lionel's easy acceptance of his role as spy.

Ranny. He had been so innocent. She regretted his loss. The love he had offered her, so simple and pure, had been besmirched. She had not known how much she had come to depend on it until it had been taken away. That was not something she could easily forgive.

At the same time, she was devoutly thankful to know that her responses to him, which could not be characterized as either simple or pure, were not the perversion she had thought them to be. She could hold her head up again, look herself in the eye in the mirror. Her transgressions were at least understandable, and so forgivable. It was possible that she could, eventually, come to live with them.

It was such a relief to be through with doubts, to know once and for all that Ransom Tyler was the Thorn, and no killer. Where that left the matter she could not quite see. It appeared, however, that Aunt Em might be right. But at least she was free, at last, of any compulsion to discover who had murdered her brother and Johnny. That was a job for the law, and she would let them do it. There was only one last thing that had to be done by her now, tonight, and then she could go with a clear conscience and basically an easy mind. If at times she dreamed of masked men, of phantom lovers who visited in the dark, that was her penance, one she would gladly pay.

A vehicle was coming, driven fast. She replaced her hat and kerchief, gathered the reins in her hand, and sat up straight, her every sense alert. It was odd how strong was the smell of dust and oak leaf mold, crushed grass and bitter weeds from where they had turned into the overgrown drive of the farmhouse. Odd, too, how soft and velvety the air felt against her skin and how friendly the concealing darkness seemed all around her. She could feel her heart jarring against her ribs, feel the blood pulsing along her veins. Alive, she was so alive. She was going to remember this night and others when she was a very old lady.

The buggy was coming nearer. She kept her head turned, watching it through the trees as it appeared down the road. It carried no lanterns. In the gleam of starshine it was a dark, moving shadow trailing a gray plume of dust. She nudged her horse with her heel, moving closer to the edge of the trees. From the direction of the plum thicket issued a clear, sharp whistle. Lionel. She smiled a little, a smile that quickly faded as she steeled herself for what lay ahead.

The driver of the buggy wasn't going to check for the curve. Yes, now he was slowing. The horse he was driving leaned into the swing of the road, its mane tossing. The man's arms were taut, his hands full.

Now!

She kicked her horse and charged out of the trees and into the road. She pulled up hard so that the animal reared, neighing, dancing on its hind legs. The buggy horse shied violently, jerking in the shafts. The man on the seat cursed and came to his feet. He sawed on the reins, dragging the animal to a plunging, snorting standstill. Lettie brought her mount under control and drew her revolver as she straightened.

"What in hell is the meaning of this?" the man in the buggy shouted with fury. "Get out of my way!"

She had been practicing her hoarse whisper for twenty-four hours, until her throat was raw and the sound was as coarse as she could wish. She almost forgot to use it as she recognized the voice of the man in the buggy. Was this the gentleman for whom Angelique was waiting? There could be little doubt of it. No wonder the girl had been confident of her future.

There was no time to reconsider, no time to change plans. He had released one hand from the reins, reaching inside his coat.

"Don't!" she rasped. "Put your hands in the air. Now!"

He obeyed her, though slowly. "You stupid bastard," he said, his tone low and grating. "Do you know who I am?"

"I know. Get down."

"What?"

"You heard me. Get down!" She raised the gun, pointing it at his heart. At this distance, she couldn't miss.

"I'll have your balls for this!"

"Try," she said.

The amusement in her whisper seemed to enrage him. He surged to his feet, reaching once more toward his inside coat pocket. She aimed and squeezed the trigger of the weapon in her hand without conscious thought or remorse.

The gun exploded, the recoil numbing her arm. Orange fire spat from a cloud of smoke. The man whipped around, falling back on the seat and grabbing his arm. His virulent curses singed the air.

Lettie had not wanted to hurt him, not that he deserved much consideration after what he intended to do to Angelique. In any case, he had brought it on himself.

She had to hurry now. The La Cour family might board themselves up inside their house at the sound of a shot in the night or they might come running to investigate. Behind the buggy, there was a movement at the edge of the plum thicket and the gleam of starlight on a rifle barrel. An instant later there was nothing.

"I would advise you not to try that again!" she said, the words hard. "Now get down."

"Who the hell do you think you are? The Thorn?"

The gibe was thrown at her as he wrapped the reins around the whipstock and climbed down slowly, holding his arm. It shocked her, for that was the impression she wanted to convey. If she did not, what was the point? The certainty that she was not who she pretended to be rang so loudly in his voice that it sounded strange to her ears, but there was no time to consider it, nothing to do but to continue. She walked her horse a step closer and to the left, keeping the man well in sight.

"Take off your clothes."

There were more curses, but he obeyed. His jacket was thrown in the dirt. His cravat landed on it in a silken twist, followed by his shirt. His suspenders were lowered with difficulty as he favored his arm. There he stopped.

"Boots and trousers, too."

"Go to hell!"

"After you," she answered. She meant the words to be harsh and drawling, but instead they had a crisp sound.

He stared at her for a long moment. Abruptly he said, "I know your voice."

A frisson of terror and purest dislike ran through her. She repeated slowly, as if to an idiot, "Boots and trousers."

"It will come to me, and when it does . . ."

He allowed the threat to hang in the air as he bent, hopping on one foot, to tug off first one boot, then the other. He lowered his trousers and stepped out of them, leaving him dressed only in his linen drawers.

"Over against the tree." She waved the gun toward a post oak she had selected earlier. There were several lengths of grass rope around her saddle horn. She took them in her hand without removing her gaze from the pale figure of the man before her. Kicking her foot from the stirrup, she slid to the ground and ducked under her mount's head.

"Arms behind you," she snapped.

"I'm bleeding, damn you."

He was, but not seriously. She had done no more than plow a furrow across his forearm, a source of satisfaction even as the sight of the damage made her feel a little queasy. Holding the revolver steady, keeping her distance, she eased around behind the tree.

How to keep him covered and tie him up at the same time? There was no need to struggle with the question. Lionel was there, a silent shadow. As she grasped the man's wrist and pulled it back, the boy took the grass rope from her and looped it about her prisoner's hand, drawing it tight as she brought the other wrist behind the tree. In a moment it was done. To secure his feet presented no problem. As a final precaution, she took a handkerchief from her hip pocket and, stretching to her full height, bound his eyes.

The man had fallen silent as if in angry concentration. She paused, considering whether to gag him or not. It made no real difference if he was found, providing they were well away by that time. She decided against it. At her gesture, Lionel melted back into the grove of oaks, heading toward the plum thicket. She saw the thicket shake as the others began to move out.

She eased away from the tree, surveying her handiwork. It appeared that it would do. It would have to do.

She had almost forgotten. From the pocket of her coat,

she carefully removed the locust shell pierced by a thorn. She considered the man before her for long seconds. She could hang the emblem in the hair on his chest, but it might not stay. His nose was a handy place, but the handkerchief over his eyes was in the way. She allowed her gaze to settle on his drawers. There was a conspicuous spot. Before she could change her mind, she reached out and attached the locust shell.

She swung away. Striding to the buggy, she unwrapped the lines, then slapped the horse on the rump with them, sending the buggy rattling away into the night. She turned to her own mount, taking up the trailing reins. Only then did she notice the pile of clothes. Her face grim, she made a bundle of them, tying the sleeves of the coat around it. Something in one of the pockets made a dull, clanking sound.

Her prisoner began to jerk at his bonds, uttering frantic protests and curses. Lettie ignored them as she slung the bundle up and looped it on her saddle horn. Her heart was beating so strongly, there was such excitement in her veins, that this time it was as nothing to mount her horse. She turned its head in the direction of the dark farmhouse.

The others, using the covering sound of the departing buggy, had already moved the wagon into the road and some distance along it. Lettie kicked her horse into motion, catching up to them. They paused long enough for her to toss the bundle of clothing into the wagon and climb in after it. The moment her horse was secured to the tailgate and Lionel's eyes were covered, she began to strip. In a few brief moments, they were only a party of women and a small boy once more.

They proceeded sedately homeward. Behind them, struggling and cursing against the post oak, they left not the tax collector O'Connor but Martin Eden.

. . .

They toasted the success of their mission with blackberry cordial, using Aunt Em's special glasses of fragile Venetian crystal that had been a wedding gift. Even Lionel had a glass of it, though two minutes after he had drunk it, he put his head down on the kitchen table and closed his eyes.

Their spirits were treetop high with their success and the relief that the ordeal was over. The other women had little doubt that when Martin was found with the locust symbol on his drawers, it would be taken as another exploit of the Thorn, and Ranny's release would shortly follow. Aunt Em speculated endlessly about when Ranny would be home. Her best estimate would not allow her to think he would make it before dinner of the following day; still, she and Mama Tass had an enjoyable time planning the meal they would give him in celebration. Sally Anne put in a suggestion now and again. Lettie listened to them and smiled at their sallies, but she could not be quite so sanguine about the outcome of what they had done.

"Lettie, honey," the older woman said, "let me pour you a little more cordial. You are still so pale. You aren't going to turn all vaporish on us now that it's over, are you?"

She shook her head, her lips curving in a faint smile. "I just keep thinking of Martin. What if he frees himself before anyone can find him and see the locust? What if he doesn't report what happened? It will all be for nothing."

"Not report it? Of course he will!"

"Will he? When it will make him a laughingstock?"

"At least you didn't put a sign around his neck like the Thorn did O'Connor."

"No, but something about his attitude bothers me. He was so insistent on knowing who I was, as if he was certain I could not be the Thorn."

"Well, naturally he thought the Thorn was in jail. It's what everyone thought."

"I'm not so sure that's all it was. Besides, he nearly recognized my voice."

"Oh, dear. Oh, dear me."

"That was always the weak point," Sally Anne said.

Lettie agreed. "I didn't expect to have to talk so much. I don't think I would have, except that he was so suspicious, so—so unimpressed."

"You don't think he will place you?"

"I have no idea."

Aunt Em, worry in her face, said, "He's so hot-tempered."

Sally Anne turned her cordial glass in her fingers. "I couldn't believe it when I heard him speak. I was so sure it was O'Connor who was setting Angelique up in New Orleans. She never said so, of course, but I just assumed it. What's so strange is that Angelique never mentioned his name."

"I don't see that it's strange at all," Aunt Em said. "She knew he was a friend of the family, knew that he had once fancied you. It showed great delicacy on her part, but then that's how these things have always been arranged."

"It certainly makes more sense that she was so willing to go with him," Sally Anne said, her tone dry.

"Yes, indeed. Martin would know the rules. Besides, he is a gentleman and an attractive man."

"What I don't understand," Lettie said, "is why they were going to New Orleans. One would think he would make some provision for her here, closer to his home."

"Yes, there is that," Aunt Em said slowly. "It might be that she would not agree, for her family's sake, but it seems a long way to go for—well, you know what I mean. On the other hand, I can't believe Martin would simply move lock, stock, and barrel without saying goodbye."

"Unless he didn't want anyone to know he was going?"

"Because he was embarrassed? There would have been no need to tell us who his companion would be."

Sally Anne, frowning, said, "Lettie is right. Why would he leave? He was doing quite well here."

"There were people, you know, who wouldn't speak to him because of his work with the carpetbaggers. Maybe he wanted to put all that behind him and start out fresh in New Orleans. Or maybe he loves Angelique enough to go for her sake."

"Maybe," Sally Anne said.

Lettie's gaze fell on the bundle of Martin's clothing that had been flung down beside the kitchen door. "There might be an answer in there."

"Go through his pockets?" Aunt Em said with unease in her voice.

"I know it doesn't seem right."

"It might help Ranny," Sally Anne said.

Mama Tass, sitting and listening to them, rolled her eyes heavenward in silent comment on such scruples. She heaved herself to her feet, moved to fetch the bundle, and plopped it down in the middle of the table. With a few swift, capable movements, she untied it and spread out the garments.

Aunt Em sat looking at them. Sally Anne lifted a shirt-sleeve and let it fall. Lettie reached for the coat and gingerly patted its folds. Mama Tass, with a great deal of expertise, took up the trousers and turned out the pockets.

Martin's belongings were soon piled in the center of the table. There was a gold pocket watch and chain with fobs, a handkerchief, a small pearl-handled derringer, an ivory toothpick, a folded slip of paper, a few loose coins, and a long leather purse with a snap top. The purse bulged so thickly that Lettie picked it up, weighing it in her hand. On impulse, she opened the catch and poured the contents out onto the table. The gold coins gleamed, clanking musically, as they made a tall pile.

Sally Anne raised a brow. "There must be several hundred dollars there."

"At least."

"For Angelique, do you suppose?"

Aunt Em looked scandalized. "It wouldn't have been that kind of arrangement. But I suppose he had to pay for their passages on the river packet and their stay at a boardinghouse or such a place until a house could be bought."

"It does look as if he meant to go away permanently," Lettie mused. She picked up one of the coins. It appeared to be freshly minted. She began to scatter the others with a fingertip. They were, every one of them, twenty-dollar liberty-head gold pieces. New.

An idea, vague and uncertain, began to form in her mind. She picked up the folded piece of paper and spread it out. Whatever she had expected, she was disappointed. There was only a short string of letters and numbers written upon it.

"TU0430E2," she murmured.

"What was that?" Sally Anne's voice was sharp.

Lettie began to repeat the string. Halfway through it, something clicked in her mind. She looked up at Sally Anne, her eyes wide. "The payroll."

"Leaving Tuesday morning at four-thirty—in military parlance, 0430 hours—with an escort of two."

"Then Martin must be the contact."

"And if he's the contact," Aunt Em said, "then he must be the one who—"

"—who killed Johnny."

Lettie's wine-brown eyes were grim as she finished the statement. Martin was also the one who had arranged the trap for her brother that had led to his death in a fern-carpeted wood beside a spring. It was even possible that the newly minted gold pieces before them were part of the payroll for which he had been killed.

Aunt Em had been right all along. If Lettie had not been so set on the guilt of the Thorn, she might have seen it earlier. If she had, there were many things that might have been different.

"Oh, thank God," Sally Anne said, burying her face in her hands. "Thank God!"

"My goodness," Aunt Em said, reaching out to touch the woman's shoulder. "You should be happy. It means Ranny is safe."

Sally Anne gave a sniff and wiped her eyes. "It means to me that Thomas is innocent."

"Thomas!"

The woman nodded with a watery smile. "He was so wealthy, a mere soldier, and it seemed no one else had quite the same access to the information. Besides, he's a Northerner, and not—not as warm-blooded as—as other men. I've been so afraid."

"Good gracious, Sally Anne! Just because a man doesn't drag you into a corner and smother you with kisses doesn't mean he isn't warm-blooded, nor does it mean that he's a murderer."

"I know, I know, but with everything else, it seemed all too likely."

Lettie had every sympathy with Sally Anne's fears, with good cause, but there were other things on her mind at the moment. "The question is, What are we going to do about it? It appears to me that we should lay the evidence in front of Thomas at once. Otherwise, Martin may get away."

"We could go out and bring Martin in," Sally Anne said.

"Too dangerous," Aunt Em said promptly. "The reason he pitched such a fit when Lettie took his clothes wasn't just because of his gold, but because he knew what she might find. He may have heard the wagon, too, even if he didn't see the rest of us. If we return, he'll know what we're about, and there'll be no holding him. I say let the army handle it."

"If they can or will," Sally Anne said.

"You still don't trust Thomas?"

"Oh, yes, so long as the sheriff doesn't mix into it. He and Martin are friends."

"Oh, dear."

"It might almost be better if the Knights could take care of it."

"Yes," Aunt Em said slowly.

"But why should they?" Lettie asked in exasperation. She had an extreme sense of time going to waste while they sat there discussing it.

"They aren't interested in political justice alone," Sally Anne said.

"That may be, but this seems a military matter since the army payroll is involved. I say let's go see Thomas. Now."

Sally Anne nodded. "You and Aunt Em do that. I think I should speak to Papa—that is, I believe that I should go on home. He—he will be worried about me."

Lettie gave the woman a direct look. So far as she knew, Samuel Tyler was not aware of his daughter's midnight activities but rather thought she was merely spending the night with her aunt. There was no time to question or argue, however. She got to her feet. "As you like. Shall we go, Aunt Em?"

"You—you won't tell Thomas what I said?" Sally Anne asked.

Lettie smiled as she put on her hat and thrust a pin through it. "Now why should I do that?"

"No reason, of course."

"Because I'm a cold-blooded Yankee?"

"You might think that he has a right to know."

Did she really seem that prim and self-righteous? She would not think of it. In a few days it would not matter.

Gently she said, "Tell him yourself when the time is right, or don't tell him at all. It's nothing to do with me; I'm not the judge of any man or woman."

19

"*I* don't see why you can't stay until Ranny gets home. It shouldn't be more than another hour or so."

Lettie put her hairbrush into her round-topped trunk and closed the lid. "And it may be tomorrow, Aunt Em, and you know it. Thomas didn't promise; he just said he would try for today if all the proper forms were filled out."

"If only Martin had not gotten away. I'm very much afraid the colonel wants to keep Ranny until he has another prisoner to put in his place."

"It's just this Reconstruction bureaucracy. No one seems to have the ultimate authority to make decisions, so everyone is careful."

"It makes no real difference. What matters is that Ranny will be home soon, and he's going to be upset to find you gone without so much as a good-bye."

Lettie clung to her patience. "I'm sorry. As I said before, I just feel that I've imposed enough, that I've brought enough harm to all of you. My mind is satisfied, finally, about my brother and it's time I went home."

There was more to it than that, of course. It might be cowardly of her, but she did not think that she wanted to face Ransom Tyler. She had loved Ranny, had been comfortable with him. He was gone as surely as if Ransom had destroyed him. In truth, there never had been such a person. He was only the creation of a fertile mind and an actor's art. The same might be said of the Thorn. The real Ransom might not be nearly so endearing or forgiving or strong. She did not think she wanted to find out precisely what he was like. So long as she did not see him, she could keep her memories unsullied.

"I really don't see why you have to go at all," Aunt Em persisted. "You have your teaching, your school. Everything was going so well. I thought you liked it here with us."

"I do like it."

That wasn't quite true. She loved it. She had come to adore the cool, dew-washed mornings and the drowsy, hot stillness of the afternoons; the lingering bluish purple evenings and deep velvet-plush blackness of nights that throbbed with life. Oh, she would miss it, miss the warmth of the people and the soft sounds of the voices, miss the big old open house that closed no doors either to the night air or to lonely strangers. She would miss the laughter and the music and the easy acceptance of love and life and death. On cold winter days in Boston, she would think of them, and of the blinding sunlight, the abundance, and the joy.

And yet, because she had seen them and shared them, they were a part of her. She would never be quite the same, never be quite so quick to blame and accuse, never be quite so ready to turn away from a smile, a touch, a kiss. She would, in some deep innermost part of her, always be a little Southern. As Thomas had said, it seemed to affect some people that way.

"If you like it, then don't go," Aunt Em said with simple logic.

"I have to, I really do."

Lettie put on her hat and gloves and gave a nod to the young man, a nephew of Mama Tass's, who waited to take her trunk out to the buggy. She gave one last look around the bedchamber that had been hers. Already it wore a strange, indifferent air, as if she had never belonged there.

She turned her back on it and opened her arms to hug Aunt Em.

"Thank you for everything. You've been so good to me, I don't know how to tell you or to say how much I appreciate it."

"Pshaw," Aunt Em answered, giving her a fierce squeeze. "All I want to hear is when you'll be coming back."

"I don't know. Maybe someday."

"Make it soon, or I swear I'll send Ranny and Lionel after you."

Lettie smiled. There was a hard lump in her throat. Disengaging herself with a last quick kiss on the older woman's soft cheek, she turned away toward the hall. Mama Tass and Lionel were there. She had small gifts for them, a set of cameo earrings for the cook and a book on medieval knights for her grandson. She shook hands with Mama Tass but gave Lionel a brief hug, then ruffled the soft wool of his hair as he gave her a cheeky grin.

The buggy was waiting. She walked from the house toward it, letting herself out the gate and picking up her skirts to climb up into the seat. Mama Tass's nephew gave her a hand up. He would be driving her to town in order to return the buggy to Splendora. She gave him a smile as he settled on the seat beside her, then leaned around him to wave good-bye.

"Hurry back now, you hear? You hurry back! Come back to see us. Hurry back!"

The cries grew faint, fading away as the carriage rolled down the drive. Lettie strained backward in her seat, waving at the trio of figures on the veranda until they were small and indistinct with the distance, the roiling cloud of dust, and the moisture that stood in her eyes.

Hurry back.

She would never return, she knew; still, it was lovely

to be wanted. The warmth of the farewell served to ease the cold desolation inside her, though nothing would ever erase it entirely. She faced forward, straightening her hat, pressing the tips of her gloved fingers under her eyes.

Hurry back. The call still rang in Lettie's ears long after she had been dropped at the stage office and the buggy had bowled away back toward Grand Ecore, long after the great lumbering stage, swinging on its springs, had pulled out of Natchitoches on its way to the railhead at Colfax. She would always remember it, she thought, and was forced to conquer a strong tendency to weep once more at the memory. How sentimental she had become. It seemed a hazard of increased sensibility, one she must guard against if she didn't want people like her sister and brother-in-law to stare at her in amazement. Not that she cared. Let them think what they liked.

Lettie's traveling companions were a brush drummer, a short, rotund preacher with silver-gray hair, and a large white male rabbit in a crate. Of the three, the rabbit was the most interesting since the other two leaned back, put their hats over their faces, and went to sleep before the wheels had made a complete revolution. Lettie spent a few minutes scratching the rabbit behind the ears through the bars of its crate until its eyes closed also.

She turned to stare out the window, hanging onto the strap and watching the trees and the sights she had glimpsed during the past weeks go by, thinking and trying not to think. She would be glad when she was on the train. Maybe then she would begin to feel as if she were really leaving the events that had taken place behind her, that she was on her way to forgetting.

The stage jolted and bounced in and out of holes. It swung and dipped, flinging Lettie this way and that, rattled and shook as if it would fall to pieces at any moment.

Overhead, a box or trunk thumped and bumped with maddening regularity. The man on the box yelled and cursed at the horses and cracked his whip. The dust that rolled from under the horses' hooves sifted inside the stage in a fine haze that soon coated everything with a gritty powder. The wind of their passage fluttered the veil on Lettie's hat, the fur of the rabbit, and the end of the drummer's cravat that was out of his waistcoat, though it did little to temper the heat of the sun striking through the windows as the morning advanced. The only respite was the few minutes they stopped in the shady yard of a farmhouse to water the horses. The dust and heat seemed worse when they started off again. Lettie clenched her teeth and hung on with dogged endurance, and as her reward, the miles fell away one by one.

The rider came from behind them. The stage was so noisy that she did not hear the sound of his horse's hooves until he was even with the window. There was no time or need to wonder and fear. She saw the shape of the man's head and his broad back and knew at once who he was and what his purpose must be. Her heart began to beat with a sickening rhythm, and she clasped her hands so tightly together in her lap that a seam of a glove split.

She heard the man call to the driver, something about a message for one of his passengers. There were rules, she was sure, about stopping for such trifling causes. In the way of many rules in this part of the world, however, it seemed likely to give way to human consideration. The stage began to slow. Then it bucked and jolted to a halt. The drummer awoke with a snort. The preacher opened his eyes and unfolded his hands from across his waistcoat.

The door beside Lettie was wrenched open. "Lettie, honey," Ransom said, "there's a thing or two you seem to have forgotten. Won't you step down and let me tell you about them?"

"It will serve no purpose," she said, meeting his gaze squarely, hoping that he would understand without her having to go into detail under the interested gaze of the preacher and the annoyed glare of the drummer. She should have known better.

"You could be right, but I prefer to think otherwise," he said, his hazel eyes gleaming.

"This is most irregular," the preacher said in a pompous tones. "If the lady doesn't wish to speak to you, you have no recourse—"

"Sir, this doesn't concern you," Ransom said.

The preacher, his eyes starting from his head at the steely tone of the quiet rebuff, drew back in a prudent huff. Ransom turned to Lettie.

"Be reasonable. Let these good folks go on their way unmolested while you and I have a few words."

Was there a threat in his request? She rather thought that if there was, it was not directed at the men with her. "You are the most unscrupulous, unprincipled—"

"And unhanged, too, thanks to you. I can treat these gentlemen to a list of your virtues, but I don't think they would be entertained. I give you my most solemn promise that when I have spoken I will see you to Colfax in time to catch your train, if you will come with me now, and if that's what you want. Otherwise, I will not be responsible."

There was no longer any amusement in his tone. She had been offered a choice. She could go with him willingly or he would use force and take the consequences.

"Lady, for heaven's sake," the drummer began, then fell silent at a quick, hard glance from Ransom.

"Oh, very well," she exclaimed, a trace of despair in her annoyance. She had thought to avoid this confrontation. If she could not, then she would face it with some modicum of dignity.

He held out his hand. She placed her fingers in his and climbed down without looking at him. He stepped back, drawing his mount aside and waving at the driver of the stagecoach. The driver shouted and snapped his whip, and the clumsy vehicle began to move.

"My trunk!" Lettie cried.

"It will be waiting for you at Colfax stage office."

She stared after the stage until it was out of sight around a curve. When it was gone, she fixed her attention on the woods that closed in around them at that spot, on the silent forest of pine and oak, ash and hickory and sweet gum.

"Lettie, look at me."

It was the last thing she wanted to do. Her muscles were stiff with reluctance and the restraint that she held on herself as she turned to face him. She lifted her gaze to his, then went still.

He had removed his hat. It was Ranny who stood before her with the sun shining in the soft gold of his hair and his face serious, waiting. But Ranny had never been real. A spasm of pain crossed her face. She swung away from him. "Don't!"

"Don't what? This is me. This is who I am."

"No, it isn't!"

He caught her arm, turning her to him once more. "Yes, it is. What are you afraid of?"

"Nothing! Just let me go. That's all I want!"

"I can't, not like this. I love you, Lettie."

"Indeed? Which one are you?" she demanded in bitter anguish.

He stared down at her with comprehension gathering in his eyes. "So that's it."

"What did you expect? I have seen two men and loved them both in different ways, but neither one was real."

Almost, Ransom reached out to her because of the admission she had made and because she was so lovely standing there with dust on the brim of her hat, which was tilted forward on her high-piled hair, and the soft tulle of its veil softening the defiance in her eyes. But she had said loved, as if she felt that emotion no longer. As if it were past.

"Is it so impossible," he said, his voice deep and quiet, "that I am both?"

The sound of his words vibrated deep inside her, setting off waves of feelings like a rock thrown into a still pond. She wanted to believe him, wanted to fling herself against him and be held in his arms. Something prevented it. Her answer came unbidden, rising from that same hidden source.

"You can't be."

"Why?" There was an ache in his chest more grievous than any wound he had ever received. He could not reach her with words and dared not try to force her physically for fear of making her despise him, and rightly so. There seemed no way to prove what he said.

"It's beyond belief that two men so different could reside in the same person. One must be false."

"Which one?"

"That I don't know," she said, the look in her eyes clouded.

He watched her, his gaze steady. "If you could choose, if you could say this is the one that I prefer, which would it be?"

"I don't want to choose!"

"But if you could?"

She opened her mouth to speak, to say that she preferred Ranny, only to be snared by the light in his eyes. It was a light that reminded her of a gray, rain-swept night and unbidden pleasures, of a rocking ferry and a dark dream of ecstasy. It wasn't a fair question, for the answer was an impossibility. She would prefer that he was both, wished with painful fervency that he could be both.

There was a shifting movement at the edge of the trees to the left and behind Ransom. A man stepped out of the deep shade, moving into the sunlight. He was tall and wore a rough shirt and trousers and a pair of broken boots. In his hand was a gun.

Lettie drew in her breath, but before she could sound a warning, he spoke.

"I advise you to take Ranny," Martin Eden drawled. "The Thorn is too wild and full of devilment to make a comfortable husband."

Ransom, seeing the widening of Lettie's eyes as she looked past his shoulder, spun around before the words were out of Martin's mouth. His muscles jerked to stillness at the sight of the gun. He relaxed with care, easing in front of Lettie. His gaze infinitely watchful, he said, "I'm sure she's obliged to you, Martin."

"I thought she might be. Just as I am obliged to you for taking our Lettie off the stage for me. I was afraid she might make her escape, but I depended on you to prevent it, if I stuck with you long enough. Clever of me, wasn't it."

"Brilliant."

"I knew you would appreciate it. You were always so quick, Ransom. I used to wonder why you didn't suspect that I was the one using your sign, blaming you for the things I had done."

"It occurred to me, but you were my friend—mine, and Johnny's."

Martin shrugged. "You and Johnny, so trusting, both of you. It was hardly sport to fool you."

"And was it sport to kill him?"

"Hardly at all. Do you know what he did? He turned around and came back here after you had seen him into Texas. He actually came to me in the middle of the night and warned me that he was going to make a clean breast of it and that I had better prepare to take the consequences. I did that, all right. I rode out with him, and when the way was clear, I shot him. He looked so surprised. I can't think why he looked so surprised."

His voice, so light and without any emotion beyond sneering self-satisfaction, grated on Lettie's nerves. "Because he was a man of honor who could not betray a friend, who was haunted at his betrayal of strangers. You wouldn't understand that, of course."

"Honor? I had honor enough before the war. I was full of honor, in fact, honor and chivalry and pride. I had all that knocked out of me at Shiloh and Gettysburg and half a dozen other battles, as well as in a Yankee prison camp before I bribed a guard to let me escape. Honor doesn't fill your belly or stop your pain or give you back what you have lost. It isn't worth a damn."

"Without it, man is nothing more than an animal."

"All right, then I'm an animal, a rich animal."

"And a thief and murderer." Lettie stared at him, at his narrow face and shallow eyes and his lack of breadth in the shoulder, and wondered how she could ever have thought that he might be the Thorn. She must have been blind, willfully blind.

He smiled, a mirthless twist of the lips that did not affect the coldness of his eyes. "You left out scalawag. But I won't be that for much longer. I'm getting out. No more stepping off the sidewalk for puffed-up former slaves. No more licking the boots of carpetbaggers and being their errand boy. I'll have more money than I ever did and be a bigger gentleman. That's what it takes: money, not honor."

"You're wrong," Ransom said.

"Am I? We'll see when I collect on this new payroll, when I'm sitting in New Orleans with a house in the Garden District and an aristocratic Creole wife, when I stroll from coffeehouse to saloon all day and visit the opera house and my quadroon mistress on Rampart Street at night."

"It won't happen."

Martin's eyes narrowed. "Oh, it'll happen. You just won't be here to see it, you and Miss Lettie."

"You won't get away with it."

"Won't I? Being without all that honor, I've decided you will still make a fine scapegoat. As for Miss Lettie, I have a grudge to settle with her. She left me tied to a tree in my drawers with the mosquitoes feasting on my blood. More than that, she took my money and my watch and fixed it so that Angelique's papa would find me and forbid her to go with me to New Orleans. She made a fool out of me. Oh, yes, I do have a grudge."

"It seems to me that we are not yet even," Lettie said with a lift of her chin. "You had my brother killed."

"That I did not."

"Surely—surely it was you who sent the outlaws to intercept him."

"No."

Something cold and clammy and more fearful than the man who faced her with a gun touched Lettie. She had placed her faith in Aunt Em's theories, had wanted to believe them. Now the old suspicions came crowding back so that she felt sick and suddenly old. She turned her head slowly to look at Ransom Tyler.

Ransom gazed back at her, aware of what must be going through her mind, aware, too, that there was nothing he could say to combat it. He had already stated his case beside the clear, cool waters of the spring where Henry Mason had died. Either she believed him or she did not.

She swung back to Martin. Her voice laden with scorn, she said, "You must have."

He smiled, the bright smile of a man who has achieved a triumph and wants someone to know it. "No, I didn't have him killed. I killed him myself."

Pain robbed Lettie of her voice. She whispered, "You."

"It was almost an accident, almost. I knew he was carrying the gold, knew he was traveling alone. I had papers to carry to Monroe, all very open and aboveboard. I caught up with him at the spring. I'm not sure what was in my mind, except that I was tired of being poor, tired of watching other people—Yankees, strangers, fat fools like O'Connor—grab everything. We went down to the water to drink. He got down on his knees to use the gourd dipper. It was so easy, so easy. I couldn't resist."

The picture he painted was vivid; Lettie could see it all too well. She put her hands to her mouth, afraid she was going to be ill.

"That was how it began, there at the spring. Because a pair of jayhawkers, outlaws by the name of Laws and Kimbrell, saw me. They took half the gold, damn them, and told me I had better send them news they could make use of or they would spread the tale. They didn't reckon on who they were dealing with; two could play that game. I told them I'd send them word for half the profits, or else the sheriff might learn the names of the outlaws operating in the backwoods. It worked like a charm, especially as long as the supply of locusts and thorns held out."

"It's over now."

He shrugged. "So it is. I think it's time we all took a little walk down into the woods there."

Lettie stood still. "I don't see what you hope to gain by this."

"Didn't you hear me? Satisfaction, from you. You robbed me of Angelique's favors; I think the least you can do is repay me in kind. As for Ransom here, I think I'll make it look as if you killed him after he had . . . enjoyed you.

A pocket full of locusts and thorns and a copy of the note you no doubt found concerning the next payroll shipment will confuse the issue, make it look as if he was the messenger while I—well, I will play the dupe, one who was taken in by a friend and innocently let fall vital information. Of course, for it to work, you, dear Lettie, will have to die of your mistreatment at the hands of this foul fiend. A pity, so tragic."

"You're mad!"

"Am I? Possibily. These are times to make men mad. But I don't think so."

Ransom stirred, and his voice was hard and steady when he spoke. "Mad or not, you have miscalculated."

"Have I? You will naturally enlighten me as to how. Do you think the sheriff, poor, confused man, will suspect me?"

"Colonel Ward has seen the evidence."

"Oh, but I am a collaborator, and I have made it my business to have friends among the radical Republicans. I don't think he will be allowed to touch me so long as there is any doubt of my guilt. Too scrupulous an observance of the law among the scavengers would be a dangerous precedent."

It made sense in a horrible way, Lettie thought. It was possible that Martin would really get away with it, if they allowed it. But if Ransom was worried, he gave no sign of it.

"There is one more thing. It's important, I think you will agree. The proof has also been presented to the Knights of the White Camellia."

The color left Martin's face so that his mustache stood out dull and rather straggly. "The Knights," he repeated, then his face cleared. "They could not have known for long."

"A matter of some hours."

Martin gave a sour laugh. "I appreciate the warning, then. It only means that I'll have to hurry."

"They may be on your trail even now."

"In broad daylight?" Martin laughed out loud. "Don't think you can stampede me. Turn around, both of you, and start walking."

The gun was pointed unerringly at Lettie. Ransom gave Martin credit. He knew that he himself would be very careful as long as she was the target. His greatest fear, however, was that Lettie would refuse to move, would invite injury out of her unwillingness to bend to Martin's commands. He knew from experience how stubborn she could be and how wily. Now, while Martin was ready and waiting for some sudden move, was not the time.

He reached out to touch her arm, trying to convey that warning. Whether she heeded it or was still dazed by the things she had learned, he did not know, but at that pressure, she turned and began to walk into the woods beside him.

The shade and moist air under the tall trees closed in around them. The contrast with the hot and dusty road was so great that it seemed many degrees cooler. Last year's dead leaves were thick on the ground, along with the decayed tree limbs, large and small, that had fallen or blown down from above. Clumps of fern and briers and the ragged heads of sand burrs and beggar lice and sedge grass sprang up here and there, leaning together over the tunnels of rabbit runs. The air was heavy, however, with the smell of warm pine needles and dry leaf mold and spent grass blossoms.

Quiet, it was so quiet and still. As they weaved among the saplings and smaller trees of the forest understory, their footsteps and Lettie's skirts made whispering sounds. The crunching of leaves under their shoes was muted, like soft cries. Somewhere faraway a bird called, a clear, pure trill that echoed away into silence.

Lettie walked with her head down, outwardly the image of submission, but inside her anger grew and her thoughts ran at a furious pace. Martin's confidence was galling beyond words. She longed to overset it, to shock him. His point in covering her with the revolver was not lost on her, either. She realized that she was a handicap to Ransom, a hostage for his good behavior. If he was prevented from acting out of fear for her, then it must be her part to remove herself from immediate danger. But how. How?

They came to a small clearing. Martin, his voice gloating, said, "This will do."

Vanity. He was eaten alive with selfish vanity. That was why he had so carefully told them what he had been about, why the treatment to which she had subjected him had him thirsting for revenge, why Angelique's defection galled him. That was his weakness. Well, then.

Lettie moistened her lips, summoned a crooked, congratulatory smile, and turned. Her voice low in her throat, she said, "Take me with you to New Orleans."

Martin's brows snapped together. Beside her, Ransom's breath left him in a near-soundless grunt.

Lettie paid no attention to either. As the silence continued, she went on. "I admire a man who comes out on top, regardless of the odds. I was leaving here, anyway, and I've never seen New Orleans."

Martin actually looked shocked. "You would go with the man who killed your own brother?"

She tipped her head to one side. "The alternative is not too attractive. If I am to make love with you, I may as well do it with some prospect of enjoyment. I'm not one of your Southern belles, you know, all swooning and shrinking and maidenly sensibility."

"I can see that," he sneered.

There was interest in his eyes, however. She had his attention, even if it was of a sarcastic kind.

"I believe in facing facts, and the fact is that you are the victor here. And, as I'm sure you would say, to the victor goes the spoils. You wanted a woman on your arm in New Orleans? I may not be a woman of mixed blood, but I have some experience at pleasing a man. You might find you would enjoy the—shall we say—turning of the tables, the Southern victory over this particular Yankee."

"I might at that," he said slowly.

"Lettie," Ransom said, a raw sound to the word. Sweat beaded his brow and upper lip, and his hands curled slowly into fists at his sides.

She grimaced prettily at Martin. "You hear? He doesn't want to share me. He thinks that I should be faithful to him even unto death. Isn't that sweet? Unfortunately, or perhaps fortunately, I'm not that self-sacrificing. Few of us are."

"Very true."

She gave him a roguish glance under her lashes as she moved a step closer to him. "I thought you might agree. As for your earlier suggestion, you could certainly sample the . . . spoils here, but it would be much more comfortable, more invigorating when we are well away, don't you think? These things shouldn't be rushed. They should be savored, thoroughly explored to the last tingling secret place and final gasp of fulfillment."

A flush had risen to Martin's face. The gun in his hand was aimed at a point between her breasts, but he seemed to have forgotten it. "You make a great deal of sense."

"But of course. Did you think that we Northern women were cold inside simply because we like to maintain an appearance of coolness? How little you know us! But you will, oh, you will, or at least you will know one." She moved nearer, swinging her hips, holding her breath with her rib cage lifted so that her breasts stood out full and round. The promise in her eyes was as lascivious, as vivid, as a few hours spent on the gently rising and falling deck of a ferry could make it.

He licked his lips. "But then, I could have a taste of what you are offering now, to see if it's worth the packet ticket."

"Of course you could, if that's what you really want," she said, and laughed, a sound of lascivious promise she didn't know she could make. Allowing anticipation to rise in her eyes, she reached out to trail her fingers along his free arm. She encircled his wrist with her hand, drawing it toward her as if to place it around her waist and stepping nearer as she reached up to touch his slack jaw. She stood on tiptoe, her lips lifted, her eyes only half open, watching, watching. He began to lower his head. His mouth parted. She could see his tongue. She trailed her fingers lower, under his chin.

With a sudden vicious shove, she pushed the heel of her hand up under his chin. She heard his teeth snap together on his tongue, and she shoved with all her might, knocking his hand with the revolver wide.

Then Ransom lunged past her, swift and silent. He was upon Martin, grabbing him by the shirtfront. He swung a jarring left that flattened Martin's lips against his teeth. The revolver flew wide, skidding into the grass.

Martin, cursing, stabbed a right toward Ransom's heart. Ransom twisted, the blow skidding along his ribs. He spread his legs and hooked a fist into Martin's belly, putting every ounce of his disgust and sense of betrayal behind it. Martin grunted, bending to the impact. Ransom hit him again, knocking him to the ground.

Martin came up with a pine knot, a piece of pine with its crystalline and inflammable pitch hardened to steellike consistency. He rushed at Ransom with it, swinging, smashing it across his head and shoulders. Lights burst inside Ransom's brain. On the next swing, he stepped inside the blow and hit the other man with his full strength behind it.

Martin staggered back, dropping the pine knot. Ransom closed in on him in cold fury, striking, battering. Martin came up against a tree and used it to lunge forward, swinging a right to Ransom's heart. Ransom gasped on a painful breath, his mouth wide. Toe to toe they stood, slugging, beating each other. They grappled, flinging each other first one way, then the other.

Lettie circled them, watching, darting from side to side to see as she worked her way toward the revolver. The way they tore at each other until their shirts were in shreds, the thud of flesh on flesh sent chills of revulsion through her. The gasping of their breathing, the blood on their faces gave her a feeling of panic. She had to stop it. She had to.

Ransom threw Martin from his hip. As the man landed, sliding in the pine straw, Lettie ran nimbly, almost reaching the black shape of the gun in the grass to one side before Martin swayed to his feet once more, blocking her way.

Ransom planted his feet and whipped a left and then a right into Martin's face. Martin's eyes were glazed, his mouth that had spoken such terrible words to Lettie a swollen red smear. Ransom surged forward with all the hard, lean force of his body behind his shoulder as he caught Martin at the waist. Martin bent double. His arms flopped, waving, as he was flung backward. He fell in a jarring sprawl, rolling with his own momentum, landing on his belly in the high grass almost at Lettie's feet. His glazed eyes focused on her, on the revolver beside her, not three feet from him. He began to crawl, reaching out with a hand that shook, a hand with bloody, cut knuckles.

Lettie darted forward. She knelt in a billow of skirts. Her hand closed around the revolver and her finger found the trigger. She lifted the heavy barrel. Centered it between Martin's eyes. Close, so close. No need to aim, no need to reason. Impossible to miss. She tightened her grip. She took a deep breath.

"*L*ettie, no!"

It was Ransom who called, a plea and a command.

Hard on the words came another voice, one Lettie had heard before on a night she did not care to remember. It was even, yet heavy with finality.

"That's right, Miss Lettie. Don't."

Martin gave a strangled cry. Ransom made not a sound. Lettie looked over her shoulder. Her breath caught in her throat and the blood left her face. She sat back on her heels, lowering the revolver. Then she got slowly to her feet.

The men in their white sheets drifted out of the woods like spirits, or like the quiet hunters most of them had been all their lives. Menacing in their silence, they formed a circle around the three of them—Martin, Ransom and Lettie—closing them in. In the hands of the leader was a coiled rope. Worn and supple, dangling casually at his side, it was knotted at one end in a hangman's noose.

Ransom stepped to Lettie's side, placing his arm around her. She held the revolver with one hand on the grip and one under the barrel, but she made no effort to raise it or to fire. There were too many of them.

It was so quiet you could hear the soft crackling sound the sedge grass made as it raised itself from where it had been trampled. Lettie's chest was tight and her nerves were as taut as stay strings. It could not end like this; it was not fair that it should end like this. Ransom was the Thorn, but he was no criminal to be left swinging from a tree. He had meted out punishment only to those who deserved it, had done his best to right the many wrongs he saw and to readjust the scales of justice that were out of balance. As Ranny, he had defied these men, but only in defense of his property and his friend. Nothing he had done merited so shameful and ignominious a death.

She took a step forward. "You can't do this!"

"We are the only ones who can."

"But it isn't right! It isn't just!" Her voice was rising, the tears stinging her eyes.

"What is, just now?" The leader waved the rope and two of the other sheet-clad men moved forward to drag Martin to his feet. He turned back to Lettie and Ransom. "You two will oblige us by leaving. We will handle it from here."

It was a moment before his meaning penetrated. Martin realized it first and cursed, his voice rising, becoming shrill as he started to beg.

Ransom stood his ground. "We go only if Martin comes with us."

"Get out of here, son. We let you have your way with Bradley Lincoln, but not this time. Leave us to it."

"To the justice of the rope? Let me take him, turn him over to the military."

"So he can talk his way out of it? Not likely. He's scum. Blame the war or the carpetbaggers or whatever you like, but he's still scum."

"No matter what he is or what he's done, he deserves a trial."

"He's had it. We're the judge and jury."

"You'll only make matters worse for everybody this way. I can't let you do it."

It was hopeless. There were just too many of them and they were too determined, Lettie could see that. She could also see that Ransom had to try. It was the way he was made, and knowing it completely at last, she felt such a swelling of love and pride in her chest that it came close to crowding out her fear.

"It's nothing to do with you. You can't stop it," the leader said, and made a quick gesture. The men in sheets who carried rifles brought them up, covering Ransom. In a ringing voice as hard as iron, their spokesman went on. "I tell you again, get out of here before something happens that we'll all regret."

"This is wrong—"

"Please," Lettie said, and put her hand on Ransom's arm as the armed Knights began to advance. "Please, take me away."

She could feel the tension of the struggle inside him. For a moment she thought that he would refuse, that he would fight them all, not just for Martin, but for what he thought was right.

"Please, Ransom?" she whispered.

It was the use of his name that reached him, she thought, that and his concern for her. She sensed the tremor that ran through him as he conceded defeat. His fingers covered Lettie's on his arm, pressing so hard that her hand was numb.

Their movements stiff, they turned away. The circle of white-clothed figures parted as the two of them walked from the clearing. Then it closed behind them and narrowed around Martin Eden. The handsome scalawag began to plead once more.

Ransom walked faster. Lettie stumbled along with him, tripping over her skirts, ducking under tree limbs as he held them for her. She looked back only once, when Martin began to scream. She could not see him for the men in sheets that surrounded him. Shuddering, she turned forward again, nearly running from the woods.

They found the horses, Ransom's mount and Martin's, cropping grass at the edge of the road, trailing their reins. Martin would not be needing his. Ransom shortened the stirrups with quick efficiency. He took the revolver from her and shoved it into his belt, then held the horse, made nervous by Martin's hoarse cries, for her to mount.

Abruptly the screaming stopped. Lettie, catching the stirrup, put her head against the horse's shoulder for a long moment, waiting for the trembling to leave her legs. Ransom moved to her side and put his hand on her shoulder.

"There was nothing we could do. Nothing."

"I know," she whispered.

"What happened he brought on himself."

"I know that, too. It's just that . . ." She clenched her fists in a sudden spasm of angry chagrin.

"What? Tell me." She blamed him for not preventing the hanging, in spite of everything, Ransom thought. Or maybe he blamed himself.

Her throat closed so that the words came out in an anguished whisper. "Dear God, I thought it was going to be you!"

His pent-up breath left him. His grasp tightened for an instant. In ragged tones, he said, "Let's get away from here."

They rode fast, with their faces set. They looked neither to the right nor the left. The sun burned down and they hardly felt it. A trail of dust followed them, settling on the leaves of the trees and bushes along the way. They crossed a stream and let the horses drink, then rode on.

Lettie hardly noticed the roads they took, paid no attention to the direction they were heading in. If she thought about it at all, she assumed they were riding back toward town and Splendora. Until they turned down a side road and pulled up before an all-too-familiar cabin set back under pin oak trees.

Lettie looked at Ransom sharply then, but made no comment. He helped her down from the saddle and led the horses away to tend to them. She moved slowly, as if she had been beaten, to take a seat on the cabin steps. She took off her hat and thrust the pin through it, laying it aside as she smoothed her hair. Propping her elbows on her knees, she put her hands over her face and breathed deeply in and out as she waited for Ransom to return.

Rage, she felt such pure rage and grief over this final trick of bringing her here. That it was camouflage for the pain buried beneath it did not matter. It could be used as a shield.

"Are you all right?"

She had not heard him return. His ability to move soundlessly, to surprise her, was so annoying that it was all the trigger she needed. She straightened, her eyes blazing.

"Of course I'm all right; whyever should I not be? I've merely been abducted, nearly been raped, watched two men beat each other half to death, and been as near a witness to a hanging as makes no difference, but what of it? A perfectly normal morning!"

"I'm sorry that it had to be that way."

"You're sorry? A fine lot of good that does! I don't know why you took me off the stage in the first place. Nor do I know why you brought me back here! You must realize this isn't exactly the scene of fond memories."

"I wanted to talk to you. I have to talk to you, to explain—"

"I've heard all I want to hear, and I've said all I have to say. I want to go home, back to Boston. I want to go now. The only thing you can do for me is to see that I get on my train before my trunk disappears!"

"No."

The single word was calm, without heat. She stared at him, her fury growing. Her tone ominous, she said. "What do you mean, no?"

"I mean," he answered, "that I have no intention of letting you go until I have had my say."

She got to her feet. Where she was on the steps made her eyes nearly on a level with his as he stood at the bottom with his hands on his hips. "If you think you can keep me here—" she began.

"I don't just think it, I know it."

He was blocking her way, his broad shoulders a most effective barrier. But far more effective was the hard, determined light in his hazel eyes.

She met his gaze squarely. Her voice soft with menace, she said, "You will be sorry."

"No doubt." His smile was wry as he surveyed her from the flush on her cheekbones to the quick rise and fall of her breasts to her fists that were on her hips in imitation of his belligerent stance. "But first I mean to find out just why you were afraid for me."

Her wayward tongue. Why could she not have kept silent? She lifted her chin. "You are a fellow human being. It appeared to me that the Thorn was about to meet retribution, just or unjust. I didn't care to see it."

"I don't think that was it, or at least not all of it. I think you feel something for me whether or not you are willing to admit it."

"Oh, yes, if that's what you mean," she agreed with a show of carelessness that took her own breath away. "You are a most attractive man, as you must know. It seems I am easily influenced, you might even say excited, by a set of shoulders or a mustache."

"Don't say that!" For the first time there was real anger in his voice.

"Whyever not? You saw it yourself."

"I saw nothing of the kind. What are you trying to do, punish yourself for using the wiles God gave you?"

"Me? Goodness, no! Mere wiles, were they? Here I was thinking I had been playing the brazen temptress at the very least, a veritable Delilah! And you were in such agony at the sight, so embarrassed. Men turn women into creatures whose sole purpose is to attract men and then are outraged when women turn that attraction into a weapon. There's no logic in it, or fairness."

"If I was in agony, it was because I was afraid your wiles were going to work so well that I would be forced to stand and watch your rape."

"You thought I was deserting you, admit it!"

"If it was to save your life, you were welcome to do it. But I never thought any such thing. I trusted you, damn you, Lettie! I knew you, and so there was never a moment when I had the least doubt of what you were doing. If there had been, I would not have been ready."

Ready to step in when the time came, ready to help. It was true. Something deep inside her lifted, the easing of a weight so great that she realized that he had been right. She had been punishing herself, or at least accusing herself before he could accuse her. She looked away over his shoulder and took her fists from her hips, clasping her hands together in front of her.

That sign of uncertainty gave Ransom his first hope. "It was only," he said quietly, "that I could not bear to see you do my fighting for me, whatever your methods."

"I had to stand and watch you fight, too. Do you think it was easy to see Martin pound and tear at you while I did nothing?"

"You didn't just stand and watch. You were ready and waiting."

She looked at him, a blind light in her eyes. "I nearly killed him. He was so close and the gun was there, and I had no more feeling about it than if he had been a poisonous snake that I had to destroy. I wanted to kill him, I really did."

"I know."

"I never knew it could be so easy, for me, for a woman. Did you?"

"I learned it, in the war."

She lowered her head and turned from him. She picked up her skirts and walked up the last two steps to the porch. He followed her as she moved to stand with her back to one of the peeled cypress posts. She refused to look at him, staring out over the yard.

"There is nothing of the lady in me, no delicacy, no refinement."

"I have no use for ladies. I want you, as you must know."

Her lips curved in a humorless smile, though the look in her eyes was weary. "Of course I know. I'm not a fool, though I must have seemed like one. You duped me so easily, didn't you? How you must have laughed."

"Never. I swear it."

"Oh, come. All that playacting. 'Would you kiss me, Miss Lettie?' 'Is there anything else you can teach me, Miss Lettie?' When I think of it, I could—I could—"

"You could what? Scream? Hit me? Do it, then! Do it and get it over with. I can't stand to see you like this."

His voice was low and intense. He stood before her, unguarded, with pain in his eyes.

She barely looked at him. "And that night on the ferry. A forfeit for Johnny's life. You asked it and, like a mindless idiot, I paid it. So easy, it was so easy." She balled her hands into fists once more and held them to her eyes.

The leash he had been holding on his temper snapped. He reached to grip her wrists and dragged her toward him. "Stop this! Don't do it to yourself. Don't do it to us."

She jerked at her arms but could not free herself. With

her lips in a tight line, she glared at him. "I'm not doing it to me or to us, you snake. I'm doing it to you! So upright and valiant, such a crusader against evil you pretend to be, so good and pure and fine and gentlemanly. But what you did to me wasn't right, and it certainly wasn't the act of a gentleman."

"No, it wasn't," he said, his eyes steady though he was pale under the bronze of his skin. "I try to do what is right, but I've never pretended to be a saint. I've tried to apologize, tried to make amends—"

"Oh, yes," she mocked. " 'Marry me, please, Miss Lettie.' "

He gave her a shake that loosened her hair from its pins so that it uncoiled down her back. Abruptly he pulled her against him, drawing her arms around his neck, encircling her waist with an iron grasp as he thrust his fingers into the silken twist of her hair. He took her mouth, plundering its sweetness as he held her against his hard body like a man who fears some long-sought treasure will be snatched from him.

Lettie felt a rush of tenderness and vital desire. It grew, pressing, flooding in upon her. She twined her fingers in the clean silkiness of his hair and let the feeling take her, surrendering to it this one last time. It could do no harm.

He kissed the corners of her lips, her cheeks and chin and quivering eyelids. His chin against her temple, he said, "Dear God, Lettie, you drive me insane."

"You were that way already," she said, her voice thick. She tried to draw back, but he would not allow it.

"No, not until you came. From the moment I first saw you, no more than a shadow in a room that should have been empty, from the moment first I touched you, I lost control and integrity. You are my nemesis, my just punishment for all the years when I thought love tokens silly things and men who lost their heads over women, who could not keep their hands off them, spineless weaklings. My need of you is so great that there is nothing I won't do, no trick so low or ruse so debased that I won't use it, to have you."

"You make it sound as if it's my fault, what happened between us."

"No, no, mine, only mine, for falling in love with a stubborn, opinionated, headstrong Yankee woman!"

"And I'll never change, either," she said against his shirt collar. "I'll never fit into your image of gentle Southern womanhood like Sally Anne."

"Sally Anne is a fine woman, for a cousin. I prefer someone with more spirit."

She gave an involuntary chuckle, scarcely noticing as she felt another layer of resistance and suspicion dissolving. "She would show you spirit if she heard you say that. She would scratch your eyes out."

"Very likely."

"In a very ladylike way, of course. She wouldn't be— wouldn't be shameless about it."

"You have my permission, even my encouragement, to be as shameless as you like," he said, his tone rich with amusement. "As a matter of fact, I have a great interest in the exploration of tingling secret places and gasps of fulfillment."

"Don't!" she cried in distress, pushing away from him. "Don't mock me."

Silently he cursed his uncontrollable tendency to tease. It was a part of the deep vein of loving affection for her that ran through him, though she was too suspicious, too highly strung at the moment to realize it.

"I would never do that. Never. I only meant that you are free to do as you like, be as you like, without fear of censure. I take no right for myself to judge you or anyone else. I enjoy what and who you are. I don't require that you change in any way to please me. I would not want you to be any other way than you are now."

She gave him a frowning glance. "You called me head-strong."

"Aren't you? How else am I to describe a woman who goes galloping off in my clothes stuffed with bed pillows and wearing my mustache? Except, of course, to say that she is also gallant and stout of heart?"

Her forehead smoothed. The corners of her mouth twitched, lifted. She made a small sound that might have been a breath of laughter. "You are really the most—"

"What?"

"Never mind. The mustache itched."

"I know." His face was solemn, though his eyes were not.

She looked at him, studying his features one by one as if to etch them on the walls of her memory. Compelled by something inside her, she reached out with tender finger-tips to trace the new split place on his lip, the old bruise at the corner of his mouth and chin from his mishandling by the soldiers, the puffy place at the corner of his eye, the dark scar. Despite everything, he was still beautiful.

"Your poor face. Does it hurt?"

"Not now."

She sighed, letting her fingers fall. She met his gaze, her own serious, sad, but firm. "It wouldn't work, you know. We are too different. The worlds we live in, that we come from, are too different. There would always be misunderstandings, doubts, and fears, even if there wasn't this—this bad beginning between us."

"I don't call it bad."

"That's because you're as stubborn as I am, maybe more. Anyway, it isn't the normal beginning."

"We aren't normal, either of us." He would fight to the last against what he sensed was coming.

"That's why it won't work. One of us should be. I think it's best if I go. If you care for me in the least, you will help me do that. You will take me to Colfax now before we do something both of us will regret."

She moved away from him, walking with grace and steadiness toward the steps. He watched her go, admiring the turn and swing of her hips under her skirts with their small, ridiculous bustle even as his heart slowly swelled toward bursting inside him. She had reached the steps before he found the words he needed.

"I'll take you to hell itself if that's where you want to go. But don't patronize me, Lettie, not now, not ever again. And don't tell me what is best for me. I'm not Ranny. Once and for all, I am Ransom Tyler and I know what I want. I want to sleep beside you for the rest of my life, to hold you when you have my child inside you, to worry with you over the little hellions we will create, to sit with you on the veranda in the dusk of our lives, and to lie beside you in some churchyard through eternity. I want everything I own to smell and to taste of you. I want, damn you, to breathe the air you breathe, to rest where you rest, to eat what you eat. I want to drink from your glass."

There was a rending feeling inside her chest, as if the ice of eons was cracking, breaking away, dissolving. She turned to look at him with stark wonder in her eyes. Her voice hushed, shaking, she said, "You *do* love me."

"What in the name of all that's wonderful did you think I have been saying?"

"I thought it was another word for—"

He groaned, closing his eyes. "God preserve us, woman, you think too much."

In two strides he was upon her, catching her close and whirling her slowly round and round and round with his face buried in the swinging swath of her hair.

A long time later, they were sitting on the floor, Ransom

with his back to a post and Lettie lying across his lap. Her head was resting on his chest as she leaned against him in the circle of his arms. For the sake of comfort, the revolver had been removed from his belt, and it lay beside them. The sun was slanting toward the west, but it was cool under the shade of the trees and a vagrant wind drifted down the porch, lifting the golden-brown tendrils of Lettie's hair. Drowsy and content, they sat and looked at the patterns the sun made through the leaves of the trees and the bright yellow-white ribbon of the road.

At last Lettie stirred. "Was I wrong or was that your Uncle Samuel with the Knights?"

"Shh," he said, kissing the top of her head.

"But wasn't it?"

"Yes, but it will be better if we don't talk about it."

She was silent for seconds only. "They may go after Bradley again. What will you do?"

"Stop them if I can. But if I can't, Bradley will take his punishment and do what he must. It's all any of us can do."

"What about Sally Anne and the colonel? Do you think they will marry?"

"Whenever Sally Anne is ready, which will be soon."

"She thought that he . . ."

"I know. That's their business," he said firmly.

She frowned a little. "Reconstruction can't last forever. The South will be free to go about its business in another year or two, free of the carpetbaggers like O'Connor, free to recover, finally, from the war. When it does, Splendora can be made to pay again, can't it?"

"I suppose so."

"You suppose? Aren't you dying to see?"

"Not," he said, taking the curling end of a long strand

of her hair and brushing the curve of her cheek with it, "at the moment."

She moved her face slightly in enjoyment of the caress, but her mind was elsewhere, straining toward the future, their future. "What about the Thorn? It will be so dangerous to continue. I'm not sure Aunt Em will ever believe that he and her Ranny are the same, but other people will begin to put two and two together."

He sighed and dropped the curl. "I think he has made his last appearance since he's to become a wedded man."

"Do you regret it?"

When he did not answer immediately, she sent him a quick upward glance. He was engrossed in the way that the strand of hair, in falling, had made a mesh net to catch and hold the curve of her breast that was outlined under her shirtwaist. Catching her eye, he hastily shook his head. "Never."

"And Ranny?"

"What about him?"

"Will you go on pretending?"

"What would you prefer?"

She smiled a little. "I don't mind. He's rather dear to me."

"I'm jealous. But you needn't worry about being tied to him. I think he will be much more normal as a result of being hit on the head by the Federal army. They should be good for something."

"I wasn't worried! In fact, I'm going to miss him dreadfully."

He brushed his lips against her forehead. "If you want him, all you have to do is call."

"I'll remember. But I may do even better. I may make a Ranny of my own. It could take a little time, say ten or twelve years . . ."

"Witch," he said, lifting the mesh net of hair over her breast and rubbing the peak with his fingertip. "Maybe I'll help you."

"Devil," she murmured.

He lifted his hand to her chin, urging her to look at him. His eyes bright with laughter and desire, he said, "When shall we start?"

Author's Note

I am particularly indebted to Carol Wells of the Eugene P. Watson Memorial Library, Northwestern State University, Natchitoches, Louisiana, for her guidance in searching out source material and also for her help in procuring one of the last leather-bound copies of *Cane River Country*, an invaluable source of data, old maps, and photographs that she researched and edited. Among the many other books consulted that proved of special significance was *Lost Louisiana, 100 Years of Photographs* by Norman C. Ferachi. Without his photo of a hand-drawn ferry with horse, buggy, passengers, and operator, this book would not be the same. And, as always, I would like to recognize the staff of the Jackson Parish Library, Jonesboro, Louisiana, for their aid and comfort and ready answers to cries for help.

Historical romances often create their effect by blending fact and fiction. For those who enjoy separating the two, or who want to know what happened later, here are a few details.

The murder of a Union payroll officer by the West-Kimbrell outlaw gang, or clan, at the old springs near Goldonna, Louisiana, is an enduring local tradition. It is commemorated in the name of the church that was built close to the site in the late nineteenth century and is still in use today, the Yankee Springs Methodist Church. Richard Briley III, late Winn Parish historian and author of *Nightriders, Inside Story of the West-Kimbrell Clan*, gives the name and rank of the officer as Colonel Henry Butts, along with many details of the killing and its aftermath gleaned from oral accounts from old-timers in the area. Official documents supporting the stories are scant to nonexistent, however. There is a single reference to a Lieutenant Butts killed in the Natchitoches military district during the Reconstruction period, but without any indication of where, how, or why. Numerous researchers have attempted to make the connection but have failed. The legend does seem valid; there was apparently a payroll officer killed at the spring. Lacking proof of his identity, however, and having every intention of constructing a fictional background for him for *Southern Rapture,* it seemed best to give this fallen soldier a fictional name as well.

The West-Kimbrell outlaw gang operated under the confused and near-lawless conditions of the Reconstruction era much as indicated. Their depredations were ended in the spring of 1876 by a vigilante group made up of local citizens who rounded up and disposed of the leaders and known members by firing squad and hangman's noose. There was, to my knowledge, no involvement of the Knights of the White Camellia, a well-known organization of night riders of the time.

The Reconstruction period in Louisiana was more corrupt, venal, and violent than is possible to show within the scope of a single romance novel. It lasted for eleven long years, until 1876, when President Grant, fearing another civil war on top of other political disasters, finally lifted the military occupation. There was no rider of the night called the Thorn to right the wrongs and soothe the injustices that were perpetrated. In the best tradition of storytellers and their heroes from D'Artagnan to Luke Skywalker, I feel there should have been.

The way of life, attitudes, and regional characteristics depicted in *Southern Rapture* are a part of my heritage.

This, more than mythical mansions like Greek temples and fancy dress balls lighted by thousands of candles, is my South. It was, and still is, a place of hard work close to the earth, cherished family relationships, pride, and the joy of living. The view of the time period covered faithfully reflects what I have been taught over the years and what I have discovered for myself. Before you call it biased, remember that victors write the history books, and consider that among my ancestors I number not only three Confederate soldiers but also a Union sympathizer and a Yankee officer—and the lady who after being widowed during the war took that same Yankee officer as her second husband.

When Reconstruction was finally over, there appeared in the New Orleans *Daily Picayune* an exultant and prophetic editorial that ended: "The years may come and go, the woods decay and wither, but father shall hand the story down to son, how she struggled, suffered, and triumphed, poor, proud, heroic—Louisiana."

The writer failed to acknowledge that mothers could hand the tale down to daughters. It was an oversight. *Southern Rapture* is, in a sense, a remedy.

Jennifer Blake
Sweet Brier
Quitman, Louisiana
April 1986

ABOUT THE AUTHOR

Jennifer Blake was born near Goldonna, Louisiana, in her grandparents' one-hundred-twenty-year-old hand-built cottage. It was her grandmother, a local midwife, who delivered her. She grew up on an eighty-acre farm in the rolling hills of north Louisiana and married at the age of fifteen. Five years and three children later, she had become a voracious reader, consuming seven or eight books a week. Disillusioned with the books she was reading, she set out to write one of her own. It was a Gothic—*The Secret of Mirror House*—and Fawcett was the publisher. Since that time, she has written thirty books, with more than eight million copies in print, and has become one of the best-selling romance writers of our time. Her recent Fawcett books are *Royal Seduction. Surrender in Moonlight, Midnight Waltz, Fierce Eden, Royal Passion*, and *Prisoner of Desire*. Jennifer, her husband, and their four children are currently enjoying their house near Quitman, Louisiana—styled after old Southern planters' cottages.